Gray Wing was aware of a moment of grief. He knew that this place wasn't as wonderful as they had hoped when they set out from the mountains, or even when they first arrived on the moor after crossing the Thunderpath, but in the torrential rain no cat had the appetite for more journeying.

We're here . . . we have to make the best of it.

WARRIORS

OMEN OF THE STARS

Book One: *The Fourth Apprentice*

Book Two: *Fading Echoes*

Book Three: *Night Whispers*

Book Four: *Sign of the Moon*

Book Five: *The Forgotten Warrior*

Book Six: *The Last Hope*

DAWN OF THE CLANS

Book One: *The Sun Trail*

Book Two: *Thunder Rising*

Book Three: *The First Battle*

EXPLORE THE WARRIORS WORLD

Warriors Super Edition: Firestar's Quest

Warriors Super Edition: Bluestar's Prophecy

Warriors Super Edition: SkyClan's Destiny

Warriors Super Edition: Crookedstar's Promise

Warriors Super Edition: Yellowfang's Secret

Warriors Super Edition: Tallstar's Revenge

Warriors Field Guide: Secrets of the Clans

Warriors: Cats of the Clans

Warriors: Code of the Clans

Warriors: Battles of the Clans

Warriors: Enter the Clans

Warriors: The Untold Stories

Warriors: The Ultimate Guide

MANGA

The Lost Warrior

Warrior's Refuge

Warrior's Return

The Rise of Scourge

Tigerstar and Sasha #1: Into the Woods

Tigerstar and Sasha #2: Escape from the Forest

Tigerstar and Sasha #3: Return to the Clans

Ravenpaw's Path #1: Shattered Peace

Ravenpaw's Path #2: A Clan in Need

Ravenpaw's Path #3: The Heart of a Warrior

SkyClan and the Stranger #1: The Rescue

SkyClan and the Stranger #2: Beyond the Code

SkyClan and the Stranger #3: After the Flood

NOVELLAS

Hollyleaf's Story

Mistystar's Omen

Cloudstar's Journey

Tigerclaw's Fury

DAWN OF THE CLANS

WARRIORS

THE SUN TRAIL

ERIN
HUNTER

HARPER
An Imprint of HarperCollinsPublishers

Special thanks to Cherith Baldry

The Sun Trail
Copyright © 2013 by Working Partners Limited
Series created by Working Partners Limited
Map art © 2013 by Gary Chalk

Library of Congress Cataloging-in-Publication Data
Hunter, Erin.
    The sun trail / Erin Hunter. — First edition.
        pages   cm. — (Warriors. Dawn of the clans ; [1])
    Summary: "A tribe of cats leaves their mountain home in search of a
better life, and find themselves in a lush forest filled with water, prey, and
unexpected dangers"— Provided by publisher.
        ISBN 978-0-06-206348-9 (pbk.)
        [1. Cats—Fiction.   2. Fantasy.]   I. Title.
PZ7.H916625Su 2013   2013021366
[Fic]—dc23   CIP
                                                                  AC

Typography by Hilary Zarycky
14 15 16 17 18   CG/OPM   10 9 8 7 6 5 4 3 2 1
❖
First paperback edition, 2014

CATS OF THE MOUNTAINS

TRIBE-HEALER **TELLER OF THE POINTED STONES (STONETELLER)**—old white she-cat with green eyes

QUIET RAIN—speckled gray she-cat

GRAY WING—sleek, dark gray tom with golden eyes

CLEAR SKY—light gray tom with blue eyes

BRIGHT STREAM—brown-and-white tabby she-cat

SHADED MOSS—black-and-white tom with dark green eyes

TALL SHADOW—black, thick-furred she-cat with green eyes

DAPPLED PELT—delicate tortoiseshell she-cat with golden eyes

RAINSWEPT FLOWER—brown tabby she-cat with blue eyes

TURTLE TAIL—tortoiseshell she-cat with green eyes

MOON SHADOW—black tom

DEWY LEAF—tortoiseshell she-cat

TWISTED BRANCH—brown tom

SHATTERED ICE—gray-and-white tom with green eyes

CLOUD SPOTS—long-furred black tom with white ears, white chest, and two white paws

STONE SONG—dark gray tabby tom

HOLLOW TREE—brown tabby she-cat

QUICK WATER—gray-and-white she-cat

HAWK SWOOP—orange tabby she-cat

FALLING FEATHER—young white she-cat

JACKDAW'S CRY—young black tom

SHARP HAIL—dark gray tom

MISTY WATER—very old gray she-cat, with milky blue eyes

LION'S ROAR—very old golden tabby tom

SILVER FROST—old gray-and-white she-cat

SNOW HARE—old white she-cat

FLUTTERING BIRD—tiny brown she-cat

JAGGED PEAK—gray tabby tom with blue eyes

THE SUN TRAIL

CAVERN

MOUNTAINS

TWOLEGPLACE

FOREST RIVER

Thunderpath

Small Thunderpath

TANGLE OF THUNDERPATHS

TOWARD HIGHSTONES

NEW HUNTING GROUNDS

HIGHSTONES

THUNDERPATH

THE FOUR
TREES

FALLS

RIVER

PROLOGUE

❧

Cold gray light rippled over the floor of a cave so vast that its roof was lost in shadows. An endless screen of water fell across the entrance, its sound echoing from the rocks.

Near the back of the cavern crouched a frail white she-cat. Despite her age, her green eyes were clear and deep with wisdom as her gaze traveled over the skinny cats swarming the cave floor, restlessly pacing in front of the shimmering waterfall: the elders huddled together in the sleeping hollows; the kits mewling desperately, demanding food from their exhausted mothers.

"We can't go on like this," the old she-cat whispered to herself.

A few tail-lengths away, several kits squabbled over an eagle carcass. Its flesh had been stripped away the day before as soon as their mothers had caught it. A big ginger kit shouldered a smaller tabby away from the bone she was gnawing at.

"I *need* this!" he announced.

The tabby sprang up and nipped the end of the ginger kit's tail. "We *all* need it, flea-brain!" she snapped as the ginger tom let out a yowl.

A gray-and-white elder, every one of her ribs showing through her pelt, tottered up to the kits and snatched the bone away.

"Hey!" the ginger kit protested.

The elder glared at him. "I caught prey for season after season," she snarled. "Don't you think I deserve one measly bone?" She turned and stalked off, the bone clamped firmly in her jaws.

The ginger kit stared after her for a heartbeat, then scampered, wailing, to his mother, who lay on a rock beside the cave wall. Instead of comforting him, his mother snapped something, angrily flicking her tail.

The old white she-cat was too far away to hear what the mother cat said, but she sighed.

Every cat is coming to the end of what they can bear, she thought.

She watched as the gray-and-white elder padded across the cave and dropped the eagle bone in front of an even older she-cat, who was crouching in a sleeping hollow with her nose resting on her front paws. Her dull gaze was fixed on the far wall of the cave.

"Here, Misty Water." The gray-and-white elder nudged the bone closer to her with one paw. "Eat. It's not much, but it might help."

Misty Water's indifferent gaze flickered over her friend and away again. "No, thanks, Silver Frost. I have no appetite, not since Broken Feather died." Her voice throbbed with grief. "He would have lived, if there had been enough prey for him to eat." She sighed. "Now I'm just waiting to join him."

"Misty Water, you can't—"

The white she-cat was distracted from the elders' talk as a group of cats appeared at the entrance to the cave, shaking snow off their fur. Several other cats sprang up and ran to meet them.

"Did you catch anything?" one of them called out eagerly.

"Yes, where's your prey?" another demanded.

The leader of the newcomers shook his head sadly. "Sorry. There wasn't enough to bring back."

Hope melted from the cats in the cave like mist under strong sunlight. They glanced at one another, then trailed away, their heads drooping and their tails brushing the ground.

The white she-cat watched them, then turned her head as she realized that a cat was padding up to her. Though his muzzle was gray with age and his golden tabby fur thin and patchy, he walked with a confidence that showed he had once been a strong and noble cat.

"Half Moon," he greeted the white she-cat, settling down beside her and wrapping his tail over his paws.

The white she-cat let out a faint *mrrow* of amusement. "You shouldn't call me that, Lion's Roar," she protested. "I've been the Teller of the Pointed Stones for many seasons."

The golden tabby tom sniffed. "I don't care how long the others have called you Stoneteller. You'll always be Half Moon to me."

Half Moon made no response, except to reach out her tail and rest it on her old friend's shoulder.

"I was born in this cave," Lion's Roar went on. "But my

mother, Shy Fawn, told me about the time before we came here—when you lived beside a lake, sheltered beneath trees."

Half Moon sighed faintly. "I am the only cat left who remembers the lake, and the journey we made to come here. But I have lived three times as many moons here in the mountains than I did beside the lake, and the endless rushing of the waterfall now echoes in my heart." She paused, blinking, then asked, "Why are you telling me this now?"

Lion's Roar hesitated before replying. "Hunger might kill us all before the sun shines again, and there's no more room in the cave." He stretched out one paw and brushed Half Moon's shoulder fur. "Something must be done."

Half Moon's eyes stretched wide as she gazed at him. "But we can't leave the mountains!" she protested, her voice breathless with shock. "Jay's Wing promised; he made me the Teller of the Pointed Stones because this was our destined home."

Lion's Roar met her intense green gaze. "Are you sure Jay's Wing was right?" he asked. "How could he know what was going to happen in the future?"

"He had to be right," Half Moon murmured.

Her mind flew back to the ceremony, so many seasons before, when Jay's Wing had made her the Teller of the Pointed Stones. She shivered as she heard his voice again, full of love for her and grief that her destiny meant they could never be together. "Others will come after you, moon upon moon. Choose them well, train them well—trust the future of your Tribe to them."

He would never have said that if he didn't mean for us to stay here.

Half Moon let her gaze drift over the other cats: her cats, now thin and hungry. She shook her head sadly. Lion's Roar was right: Something had to be done if they were to survive.

Gradually she realized that the cold gray light in the cave was brightening to a warm gold, as if the sun were rising beyond the screen of falling water—but Half Moon knew that night was falling.

At her side Lion's Roar sat calmly washing his ears, while the other cats in the cave took no notice of the deepening golden blaze.

No cat sees it but me! What can it mean?

Bathed in the brilliant light, Half Moon remembered how, when she first became Healer, Jay's Wing had said that her ancestors would guide her in the decisions she must make— that, sometimes, she would see strange things that meant more than they first appeared. She had never been directly aware of her ancestors, but she had learned to look out for the signs.

Possible meanings rushed through Half Moon's mind, thick as snowflakes in a blizzard. *Maybe the warm weather is going to come early. But how would that help, when there are so many of us?* Then she wondered whether the sun was really shining somewhere else, where there was warmth and prey and shelter. *But how would that help us, up here in the mountains?*

The sunlight grew stronger and stronger, until Half Moon could barely stand to look into the rays. She relaxed as a new idea rose in her mind.

Maybe Lion's Roar is right, and only some of us belong here. Maybe some of us should travel toward the place where the sun rises, to make a new home in the brightest light of all. Somewhere they will be safe, and well fed, with room to nurture generations of kits.

As Half Moon basked in the warmth of sunlight on her fur, she found the certainty she needed within herself. Some of her cats would remain, a small-enough group for the mountains to sustain, and the rest of her Tribe would journey toward the rising sun, to find a new home.

But I won't leave the cave, she thought. *I will see out the twilight of my days here, a whole lifetime away from where I was born. And then maybe . . . just maybe . . . I'll find Jay's Wing again.*

CHAPTER 1

Gray Wing toiled up the snow-covered slope toward a ridge that bit into the sky like a row of snaggly teeth. He set each paw down carefully, to avoid breaking through the frozen surface and sinking into the powdery drifts underneath. Light flakes were falling, dappling his dark gray pelt. He was so cold that he couldn't feel his pads anymore, and his belly yowled with hunger.

I can't remember the last time I felt warm or full-fed.

In the last sunny season he had still been a kit, playing with his littermate, Clear Sky, around the edge of the pool outside the cave. Now that seemed like a lifetime ago. Gray Wing only had the vaguest memories of green leaves on the stubby mountain trees, and the sunshine bathing the rocks.

Pausing to taste the air for prey, he gazed across the snow-bound mountains, peak after peak stretching away into the distance. The heavy gray sky overhead promised yet more snow to come.

But the air carried no scent of his quarry, and Gray Wing plodded on. Clear Sky appeared from behind an outcrop of rock, his pale gray fur barely visible against the snow. His jaws were empty, and as he spotted Gray Wing he shook his head.

"Not a sniff of prey anywhere!" he called. "Why don't we—"

A raucous cry from above cut off his words. A shadow flashed over Gray Wing. Looking up, he saw a hawk swoop low across the slope, its talons hooked and cruel.

As the hawk passed, Clear Sky leaped high into the air, his forepaws outstretched. His claws snagged the bird's feathers and he fell back, dragging it from the sky. It let out another harsh cry as it landed on the snow in a flurry of beating wings.

Gray Wing charged up the slope, his paws throwing up a fine spray of snow. Reaching his brother, he planted both forepaws on one thrashing wing. The hawk glared at him with hatred in its yellow eyes, and Gray Wing had to duck to avoid its slashing talons.

Clear Sky thrust his head forward and sank his teeth into the hawk's neck. It jerked once and went limp, its gaze growing instantly dull as blood seeped from its wound and stained the snow.

Panting, Gray Wing looked at his brother. "That was a great catch!" he exclaimed, warm triumph flooding through him.

Clear Sky shook his head. "But look how scrawny it is. There's nothing in these mountains fit to eat, and won't be until the snow clears."

He crouched beside his prey, ready to take the first bite. Gray Wing settled next to him, his jaws flooding as he thought of sinking his teeth into the hawk.

But then he remembered the starving cats back in the cave,

squabbling over scraps. "We should take this prey back to the others," he meowed. "They need it to give them strength for their hunting."

"We need strength too," Clear Sky mumbled, tearing away a mouthful of the hawk's flesh.

"We'll be fine." Gray Wing gave him a prod in the side. "We're the best hunters in the Tribe. Nothing escapes us when we hunt together. We can catch something else easier than the others can."

Clear Sky rolled his eyes as he swallowed the prey. "Why must you always be so unselfish?" he grumbled. "Okay, let's go."

Together the two cats dragged the hawk down the slope and over the boulders at the bottom of a narrow gully until they reached the pool where the waterfall roared. Though it wasn't heavy, the bird was awkward to manage. Its flopping wings and claws caught on every hidden rock and buried thornbush.

"We wouldn't have to do this if you'd let us eat it," Clear Sky muttered as he struggled to maneuver the hawk along the path that led behind the waterfall. "I hope the others appreciate this."

Clear Sky grumbles, Gray Wing thought, *but he knows this is the right thing to do.*

Yowls of surprise greeted the brothers when they returned to the cave. Several cats ran to meet them, gathering around to gaze at the prey.

"It's *huge*!" Turtle Tail exclaimed, her green eyes shining as she bounded up to Gray Wing. "I can't believe you brought it back for us."

Gray Wing dipped his head, feeling slightly embarrassed at her enthusiasm. "It won't feed every cat," he mewed.

Shattered Ice, a gray-and-white tom, shouldered his way to the front of the crowd. "Which cats are going out to hunt?" he asked. "They should be the first ones to eat."

Murmurs came from among the assembled cats, broken by a shrill wail: "But I'm *hungry*! Why can't I have some? I could go out and hunt."

Gray Wing recognized the voice as being his younger brother, Jagged Peak's. Their mother, Quiet Rain, padded up and gently nudged her kit back toward the sleeping hollows. "You're too young to hunt," she murmured. "And if the older cats don't eat, there'll be no prey for any cat."

"Not fair!" Jagged Peak muttered as his mother guided him away.

Meanwhile the hunters, including Shattered Ice and Turtle Tail, lined up beside the body of the hawk. Each of them took one mouthful, then stepped back for the next cat to take their turn. By the time they had finished, and filed out along the path behind the waterfall, there was very little meat left.

Clear Sky, watching beside Gray Wing, let out an irritated snort. "I still wish *we* could have eaten it."

Privately Gray Wing agreed with him, but he knew there was no point in complaining. *There isn't enough food. Every cat is weak, hungry—just clinging on until the sun comes back.*

The pattering of paws sounded behind him; he glanced

around to see Bright Stream trotting over to Clear Sky. "Is it true that you caught that huge hawk all by yourself?"

Clear Sky hesitated, basking in the pretty tabby she-cat's admiration. Gray Wing gave a meaningful purr.

"No," Clear Sky admitted. "Gray Wing helped."

Bright Stream gave Gray Wing a nod, but her gaze immediately returned to Clear Sky. Gray Wing took a couple of paces back and left them alone.

"They look good together." A voice spoke at his shoulder; Gray Wing turned to see the elder Silver Frost standing beside him. "There'll be kits come the warmest moon."

Gray Wing nodded. Any cat with half an eye could see how friendly his brother and Bright Stream had become as they stood with their heads together murmuring to each other.

"More than one litter, maybe," Silver Frost went on, giving Gray Wing a nudge. "That Turtle Tail is certainly a beautiful cat."

Hot embarrassment flooded through Gray Wing from ears to tail-tip. He had no idea what to say, and was grateful when he saw Stoneteller approaching them. She took a winding path among her cats, pausing to talk to each one. Though Stoneteller's paws were unsteady because of her great age, Gray Wing could see the depth of experience in her green gaze and the care she felt for every one of her Tribe.

"There's still a bit of the hawk left," Gray Wing heard her murmur to Snow Hare, who was stretched out in one of the sleeping hollows, washing her belly. "You should eat something."

Snow Hare paused in her tongue-strokes. "I'm leaving the food for the young ones," she replied. "They need their strength for hunting."

Stoneteller bent her head and touched the elder's ear with her nose. "You have earned your food many times over."

"Perhaps the mountains have fed us for long enough." It was Lion's Roar who had spoken from where he sat, a tail-length away.

Stoneteller gave him a swift glance, full of meaning.

What's that all about? Gray Wing asked himself.

His thoughts were interrupted by Quiet Rain, who came to sit beside him. "Have you eaten anything?" she asked.

All we ever talk about is food. Or the lack of it. Trying to curb his impatience, Gray Wing replied, "I'll have something before I go out again."

To his relief, his mother didn't insist. "You did very well to catch that hawk," she meowed.

"It wasn't only me," Gray Wing told her. "Clear Sky made this amazing leap to bring it down."

"You *both* did well," Quiet Rain purred. She turned to look at her young kits, who were scuffling together close by. "I hope that Jagged Peak and Fluttering Bird will be just as skillful when they're old enough to hunt."

At that moment, Jagged Peak swiped his sister's paws out from underneath her. Fluttering Bird let out a wail as she fell over, hitting her head on a rock. Instead of getting up again, she lay still, whimpering.

"You're such a silly kit!" Jagged Peak exclaimed.

As Quiet Rain padded over to give her daughter a comforting lick, Gray Wing noticed how small and fragile Fluttering Bird looked. Her head seemed too big for her body, and when she scrambled to her paws again her legs wobbled. Jagged Peak, on the other hand, was strong and well muscled, his gray tabby fur thick and healthy.

While Quiet Rain took care of his sister, Jagged Peak scampered to Gray Wing. "Tell me about the hawk," he demanded. "How did you catch it? I bet I could catch one if I was allowed out of this stupid cave!"

Gray Wing purred excitedly. "You should have seen Clear Sky's leap—"

A loud yowl cut off Gray Wing's story. "Let all cats be silent! Stoneteller will speak!"

The cat who had made the announcement was Shaded Moss, a black-and-white tom who was one of the strongest and most respected cats of the Tribe. He stood on a boulder at the far end of the cavern, with Stoneteller beside him. The old cat looked even more fragile next to his powerful figure.

As he wriggled his way toward the front of the crowd gathered around the boulder, Gray Wing heard murmurs of curiosity from the others.

"Maybe Stoneteller is going to appoint Shaded Moss as her replacement," Silver Frost suggested.

"It's time she appointed some cat," Snow Hare agreed. "It's what we've all been expecting for moons."

Gray Wing found himself a place to sit next to Clear Sky and Bright Stream, and looked up at Stoneteller and Shaded

Moss. Stoneteller rose to her paws and let her gaze travel over her Tribe until the murmuring died away into silence.

"I am grateful to all of you for working so hard to survive here," she began, her voice so faint that it could scarcely be heard above the sound of the waterfall. "I am proud to be your Healer, but I have to accept that there are things even I cannot put right. Lack of space and lack of food are beyond my control."

"It's not your fault!" Silver Frost called out. "Don't give up!"

Stoneteller dipped her head in acknowledgment of the elder's support. "Our home cannot support us all," she continued. "But there is another place for some of us, full of sunlight and warmth and prey for all seasons. I have seen it . . . in my dreams."

Utter silence greeted her announcement. Gray Wing couldn't make sense of what the Healer had just said. *Dreams? What's the point of that? I dreamed I killed a huge eagle and ate it all myself, but I was still hungry when I woke up!*

He noticed that Lion's Roar sat bolt upright as Stoneteller spoke, and was staring at her, his eyes wide with astonishment.

"I believe in my heart that the other place is waiting for those of you who are brave enough to make the journey," Stoneteller went on. "Shaded Moss will lead you there, with my blessing."

The old white cat glanced once more around her Tribe, her gaze full of sadness and pain. Then she slid down from the top of the boulder and vanished into the tunnel at the back of the cave, which led to her own den.

A flood of shocked speculation passed through the rest of the cats. After a couple of heartbeats, Shaded Moss stepped forward and raised his tail for silence.

"This has been my home all my life," he began when he could make himself heard. His voice was solemn. "I always expected to die here. But if Stoneteller believes that some of us must leave to find the place of her dream, then I will go, and do my best to keep you safe."

Dappled Pelt sprang to her paws, her golden eyes shining. "I'll go!"

"So will I!" Tall Shadow added, her sleek black figure tense with excitement.

"Are you flea-brained?" Twisted Branch, a scraggy brown tom, stared incredulously at the two she-cats. "Wandering off with no idea where you're heading?"

Gray Wing remained silent, but he couldn't help agreeing with Twisted Branch. The mountains were his home: He knew every rock, every bush, every trickling stream. *It would tear my heart in two if I had to leave just because Stoneteller had a dream.*

Turning to Clear Sky, he was amazed to see excitement gleaming in his brother's eyes. "You're not seriously considering this?" he asked.

"Why not?" Clear Sky demanded in return. "This could be the answer to all our problems. What's the point of struggling to feed every mouth if there's an alternative?" His whiskers quivered eagerly. "It will be an adventure!" He called out to Shaded Moss: "I'll go!" Glancing at Bright Stream, he added, "You'll come too, won't you?"

Bright Stream leaned closer to Clear Sky. "I don't know . . . would you really go without me?"

Before Clear Sky could reply, little Jagged Peak wormed his way forward between his two older brothers, followed by Fluttering Bird. "I want to go!" he announced loudly.

Fluttering Bird nodded enthusiastically. "Me too!" she squeaked.

Quiet Rain followed them, and drew both kits closer to her with a sweep of her tail. "Certainly not!" she meowed. "You two are staying right here."

"You could come with us," Jagged Peak suggested.

His mother shook her head. "This is my home," she said. "We've survived before. When the warm season returns, we'll have enough to eat."

Gray Wing dipped his head in agreement. *How can they forget what Quiet Rain told me when I was a kit? This place was promised to us by a cat who led us here from a faraway lake. How can we think of leaving?*

Shaded Moss's powerful voice rose up again over the clamor. "No cat needs to decide yet," he announced. "Give some thought to what you want to do. The half-moon is just past; I will leave at the next full-moon along with any—"

He broke off, his gaze fixed on the far end of the cave. Turning his head, Gray Wing saw the hunting party making their way inside. Their pelts were clotted with snow and their heads drooped.

Not one was carrying prey.

"We're sorry," Shattered Ice called out. "The snow is heavier than ever, and there wasn't a single—"

"We're leaving!" some cat yowled from the crowd around Shaded Moss.

The hunting party stood still for a moment, glancing at one another in confusion and dismay. Then they pelted down the length of the cavern to listen as their Tribemates explained what Stoneteller had told them, and what Shaded Moss intended to do.

Turtle Tail made her way to where Gray Wing was sitting and plopped down beside him, beginning to clean the melting snow from her pelt. "Isn't this great?" she asked between licks. "A warm place, where there's plenty of prey, just waiting for us? Are you going, Gray Wing?"

"I am," Clear Sky responded, before Gray Wing could answer. "And so is Bright Stream." The young she-cat gave him an uncertain look, but Clear Sky didn't notice. "It'll be a hard journey, but I think it'll be worth it."

"It'll be *wonderful*!" Turtle Tail blinked happily. "Come on, Gray Wing! How about it?"

Gray Wing couldn't give her the answer she wanted. As he looked around the cave at the cats he had known all his life, he couldn't imagine abandoning them for a place that might only exist in Stoneteller's dreams.

CHAPTER 2

Growling in his belly woke Gray Wing. The pangs of hunger had seemed even sharper since Stoneteller's announcement a few sunrises ago. And the cavern hadn't stopped buzzing with discussions about whether it was a good idea to leave, and what the new place might be like.

Still curled up in his sleeping hollow, Gray Wing could hear excited chatter from cats nearby.

"What do you think we'll get to hunt?" Gray Wing recognized Dappled Pelt's voice. "Maybe different kinds of birds—or those . . . squirrels that the elders put in their stories."

"We'll have to be careful." That was Cloud Spots, sounding thoughtful as usual. "If we eat too much we'll get too fat to hunt, and then where will we be?"

Gray Wing heard a snort of laughter from Snow Hare. "That's a problem I'd *like* to have!"

He lifted his head to see the three cats sitting close together, along with Tall Shadow, who extended her black-furred limbs gracefully as she rose to her paws. "I wonder what new hunting techniques we'll need to learn. It's bound to be different in the new place."

"Well, you've always been good at creeping around," Snow Hare mewed teasingly. "You'll be able to sneak up on your prey while it's asleep."

Tall Shadow gave her chest fur a complacent lick. "I just might do that."

Scrambling out of the sleeping hollow, Gray Wing shook scraps of moss and feather from his pelt and arched his back in a good long stretch. He decided to go and hunt. *There's no point in wondering about prey somewhere else when we need to eat now.*

Sunlight came slanting into the cave, turning the screen of water into a dazzling sparkle. As Gray Wing emerged from the path behind the fall, he saw that the sky was clear blue. Gray Wing's pads tingled at the beauty of the peaks outlined against it. He took great gulps of the cold, crisp air, relishing the way it felt like water against his fur.

How could I leave all this?

Continuing along the snow-packed ledge, hardened by the paw steps of many cats, Gray Wing heard voices coming from somewhere above.

"Bright Stream, you *have* to come with me."

Looking up, he spotted Clear Sky and Bright Stream at the top of the cliff where the water poured over the lip of the rocks.

"It'll be great," Clear Sky went on, "exploring new places together."

Bright Stream turned her head away. "I don't know. . . . This is my home, and we've survived so far."

"Don't you want more than just surviving?" Clear Sky asked, curling his tail persuasively around Bright Stream's shoulders. "I want to go, but it wouldn't be the same without you."

Bright Stream's eyes shone, but she shook her head. "I've still got a few days to decide," she mewed.

Leaving Clear Sky gazing after her, she bounded lightly down the rocks. Despite himself, Gray Wing's heart quickened as he saw her approaching. *She's lovely . . . but she'll be Clear Sky's mate one day. He's a lucky tom, that's for sure.*

"Can I hunt with you?" Bright Stream asked as she leaped off the last rock to stand at Gray Wing's side. "Just don't be like Clear Sky and pester me about leaving the mountains with Shaded Moss!"

"I won't," Gray Wing promised. "I haven't made up my own mind yet."

"For once I wish you poor hunting!" Clear Sky called down from the top of the rocks. "Then you'll realize that we have to leave."

Gray Wing gave him a good-humored wave of his tail, and headed for the ridge. Bright Stream scrambled after him. As they drew closer to the summit, icy wind blasted their fur and scoured the snow from the rocks, leaving them bare and gray. Dark, yellowish clouds massed on the horizon, promising more snow to come.

With his back to the gale, Gray Wing gazed around and spotted three more cats farther down the valley—tiny black shapes, too far away for him to distinguish who they were, pursuing a hawk that flew low over the slopes and gradually drew out of sight.

Bright Stream's voice broke the vast silence of the mountains. "Gray Wing—what do you think about Stoneteller's dream?"

Gray Wing hesitated before replying. "I don't know," he confessed at last. "Can Stoneteller *really* have discovered a new place for us to live, without knowing exactly where it is? Why haven't any other cats had the same dream?"

"Maybe it's something only Stoneteller can do," Bright Stream suggested. She paused, blinking thoughtfully; Gray Wing could see anxiety in her beautiful green eyes. "I love living in the mountains," she went on. "In spite of the cold and hunger. I always imagined I'd raise my kits here . . . but then, I always imagined their father would be Clear Sky."

As she finished speaking she turned her head away, giving her shoulder a couple of embarrassed licks. Gray Wing was surprised that she had confessed so much to him; she was always perfectly confident and self-contained. He felt a stab of envy that she had the courage to put aside her own hopes and dreams to travel into the unknown with Clear Sky—and that her bond with his brother was so strong.

Before he could decide what to say, Bright Stream gave her pelt a shake. "You should probably forget I said all that!" she meowed. "And don't you dare tell Clear Sky! I don't want him to think I've made a decision yet."

"I won't say a word," Gray Wing promised.

I'm being torn in two, he thought. *Clear Sky and I have always done everything together. Now I have to choose between going with him or staying here with the rest of my kin, in this place I've always called home.*

A flicker of movement distracted him from his problems. *Snow hare!* Spinning around, he raced across the slope after his prey. Its thick white pelt hid it against the snow, but it stood out clearly when scampering over the rocks of the windblown ridge.

Bright Stream joined the chase, but Gray Wing outpaced her, relishing the feeling of the wind in his whiskers as he sped over the rocks.

With a final mighty leap he flung himself onto his prey; the hare's squeal of panic was cut off as Gray Wing's jaws met in its throat.

"Great catch!" Bright Stream panted. "You're so fast!"

"It's not bad," Gray Wing mewed, prodding his prey with one paw. For once there seemed to be some flesh on its bones. "We can eat and still take some back to the cave."

He and Bright Stream settled down side by side to enjoy the catch. As they feasted, he took in the magnificent peaks and valleys that stretched in front of them.

"You're going to stay, aren't you?" Bright Stream asked, fixing him with her clear green gaze.

Gray Wing took a deep breath. "Yes, I am."

When they had eaten their fill, the two cats picked up the remains of the hare and headed back toward the cave. Triumph flooded through Gray Wing at the thought of feeding his Tribemates.

When the waterfall came in sight, he spotted a group of

cats toiling up the slope toward them. Shaded Moss was in the lead, with Clear Sky padding along at his shoulder. Tall Shadow, Dappled Pelt, and Rainswept Flower followed close behind. Turtle Tail brought up the rear.

"Hi," Clear Sky meowed as the group came up. "Hey, you caught a hare!"

Gray Wing gave a nod of satisfaction. "Yes, we're just taking it back."

"We're climbing up to the ridge," Clear Sky explained, sweeping his tail around to include his companions. "We want to look for the best way to get out of the mountains toward the sunrise."

"Aren't you joining us?" Turtle Tail asked, bounding up to Gray Wing's side.

Gray Wing hesitated. He was sure now about his decision to stay, but he didn't want to share it with the other cats just yet. "We're tired from hunting," he replied. "Maybe later."

Entering the cave, Gray Wing could feel how restless his Tribemates were. Some were gathered in little groups around the edges of the cavern, talking together in hushed voices. Others paced to and fro as if they were too anxious to settle. There was no sign of Stoneteller.

"Do you think they're really going to leave?" Stone Song muttered as he and his mate Hollow Tree padded past.

"I guess so," Hollow Tree responded. "Are they flea-brained? They have no idea what's out there, or whether the place they're looking for even exists."

Gray Wing knew that they spoke for many of the Tribe.

He wished that Stoneteller had never had her vision, or that she had never spoken of it. *Doesn't she know how it's tearing the Tribe apart?*

"But *why* can't I go?" Jagged Peak was heading for the cave entrance, only to be intercepted by Quiet Rain.

"For the last time," his mother meowed, her tail-tip twitching impatiently, "you are too little to be out of the cave."

"It's not fair!" Jagged Peak's shoulder fur bristled as he glared at his mother.

"Come on, Jagged Peak." Snow Hare padded up, dipping her head to Quiet Rain as she approached. "I'll show you a new game. Let's see if you can catch this stone." She swiped her paw and sent a flat pebble skimming across the floor of the cave.

Jagged Peak pelted after it with an excited squeal.

"Thanks, Stone Hare," Quiet Rain murmured. "I can't let him go out while there's deep snow on the ground."

"You're welcome," the elder responded.

Gray Wing carried the remains of the hare over to his mother and dropped it at her paws. "Here, do you want some?" he asked.

Quiet Rain purred her gratitude. "That's a fine catch," she told him. "I'll take some of it to Fluttering Bird." Her voice quivered as she added, "She couldn't get out of the nest this morning. But she'll be much better after she's had something to eat."

Gray Wing followed his mother as she carried the hare across the cave to the sleeping hollow where Fluttering Bird was curled up.

"Are you going with Shaded Moss?" Quiet Rain asked him as she set the prey down at the edge of the hollow. "I know Clear Sky will go. . . ." She was clearly trying to speak lightly, but her words ended with a sorrowful sigh.

"I'm staying," Gray Wing told her, touching her ear with his nose. "This is my home. I want to catch enough prey so that the rest of us can survive. Many moons ago, our ancestors left the lake and came *here*. I can't believe that was for no reason."

Quiet Rain rested her muzzle on the top of his head. "I'm so proud of you," she murmured. For a few heartbeats Gray Wing felt the same sense of comfort and security as when he was a small kit, suckling at his mother's belly.

Stooping over the sleeping hollow, Quiet Rain licked Fluttering Bird's shoulder. "Wake up, little one," she mewed. "I've got some food for you."

A sharp pang of anxiety stabbed through Gray Wing as he looked at Fluttering Bird; she hardly seemed to be breathing.

"Fluttering Bird!" Quiet Rain prodded her with one forepaw, but the kit still didn't wake. "Gray Wing, fetch Stoneteller," his mother said, panic in her voice.

Gray Wing sped off across the cave and plunged down the tunnel that led into the Cavern of the Pointed Stones. He had only been there once before, and he slowed as he reached the entrance, overcome by awe in spite of his urgency.

Creeping into the cave, he saw narrow beams of sunlight slanting through the hole in the roof, lighting the columns of stone that stretched upward for many tail-lengths. Pools on the ground reflected the sunlight, and the huge hollow space was filled with the sound of steadily dripping water.

At first Gray Wing couldn't see Stoneteller. Then he spotted her sitting in the shadows, her tail wrapped around her paws and her eyes closed.

Is she asleep? he wondered as he approached.

But as he drew closer, Stoneteller opened her eyes. "Gray Wing—is something wrong?" she mewed.

"It's Fluttering Bird," Gray Wing explained, his heart beating fast. "She won't wake up."

At once Stoneteller rose to her paws. Turning to a crack in the rock, she took out a few shriveled leaves. Gray Wing caught a glimpse of her pitifully small store, and knew there would be no more healing herbs until the snow melted and warmer weather brought new growth.

He followed Stoneteller to where Fluttering Bird lay. Quiet Rain stood beside her, flexing her claws impatiently. Looking into her eyes, Gray Wing saw how desperate she was, already sick with grief for her daughter.

Stoneteller bent over the tiny kit and rested one paw on her chest to feel her breathing and her heartbeat. Chewing up one of the leaves, Stoneteller pried open the kit's jaws and pushed the pulp onto her tongue. "Come along, little one," she murmured. "Swallow this. It will make you feel better."

But Fluttering Bird stayed still. She didn't even open her eyes.

Looking up at Quiet Rain, Stoneteller whispered, "She is far, far away from us. The hunger inside her is too great. You must prepare yourself, Quiet Rain."

Gray Wing's mother crouched down, her claws scraping on the stone floor of the cave. "This is my fault," she mewed. "I should have given her all my food. What was I thinking, having kits in the cold season?"

His heart swelling with grief, Gray Wing padded over to Quiet Rain and pressed himself close to her. "It isn't your fault," he mewed.

"I should have—"

Stoneteller interrupted Quiet Rain with a raised paw. "Hush, Quiet Rain. Fluttering Bird might be able to hear you. Don't let her go into the dark knowing that you're scared and angry."

Gray Wing could see the massive effort his mother made to calm herself. She slid into the sleeping hollow and curled herself around Fluttering Bird, giving her comforting licks. "I'm so proud of you, my only daughter," she murmured. "You mean so much to all of us. We will never forget you."

Misery swept over Gray Wing as he watched. His sister's flank rose once more, and then was still. "Good-bye, Fluttering Bird," he whispered.

Stoneteller dipped her head to Quiet Rain and padded away toward her tunnel.

Gray Wing turned back to his mother. "Do you want me to help you take Fluttering Bird outside and bury her?" he asked.

Quiet Rain curled herself more closely around her daughter's body. "Not while her fur is still warm," she replied. "Please, go and fetch Jagged Peak for me."

Gray Wing glanced around and spotted Jagged Peak at the

far side of the cave, playing with some of the other kits. He raced over and beckoned his brother with a flick of his tail.

"What is it?" Jagged Peak asked, looking up from where he was wrestling with a tabby she-cat.

"Our mother wants you," Gray Wing replied.

Jagged Peak scrambled to his paws and trotted across the cavern to the sleeping hollow. Quiet Rain spoke quietly to Jagged Peak; he stared at her, then opened his jaws in a shrill wail.

Quiet Rain stretched out her tail and pulled Jagged Peak to her. Pain stabbed through Gray Wing like a spike of icy rock as he watched her holding both her kits close, one dead and one alive, her nose buried in their fur.

He wondered if she would ever let Jagged Peak go again.

Gray Wing turned toward the cave entrance at the sound of voices, and saw Shaded Moss returning with Clear Sky and the others who had gone to look for a route away from the mountains.

"It was great!" Clear Sky shook himself, scattering melting snow everywhere. "We've found the path we should take."

"It runs along the side of the valley," Shaded Moss meowed, sounding more cautious. "It leads to a gap that should take us clear of the mountains. There's a frozen stream at one point that we'll have to cross, and we'll need to be careful."

"But it's still the quickest route!" Turtle Tail interrupted with an enthusiastic wave of her tail.

"It looks like it," Shaded Moss agreed, "and with any luck we'll avoid the drifts farther down."

While the other cats crowded around to question Shaded Moss, Gray Wing padded up and touched Clear Sky on his shoulder with his tail-tip. Clear Sky glanced around, spotting Quiet Rain in her sleeping hollow with the two kits. His eyes widened.

"What happened?" he asked.

"Fluttering Bird is dead," Gray Wing told him.

Clear Sky paused for a heartbeat with a sharp indrawn breath, then bounded across the cave to his mother's side. Gray Wing padded after him more slowly.

"I'm so sorry!" Clear Sky exclaimed, bending his head to touch his nose to his sister's ear. "Fluttering Bird, we'll miss you so much!" Straightening up, he looked down at his mother and added, "This will never happen when we reach our new home. If you join us, I'll protect you and hunt for you for the rest of my life. Please come."

Quiet Rain shook her head. "I will never leave my daughter here alone."

Rising from the sleeping hollow, she allowed Gray Wing and Clear Sky to pick up Fluttering Bird's tiny, twiglike body and carry her out of the cave. The other cats fell back and formed a respectful line on either side as they headed for the entrance and along the ledge that led behind the waterfall.

Quiet Rain and Jagged Peak followed as they maneuvered Fluttering Bird's body along the narrow path. Drops of water landed on her fur. Gray Wing winced when he realized that she would never be able to lick them off.

Climbing carefully over the icy rocks, they made their way

to the plateau above the cave and set Fluttering Bird down beside the river. Gray Wing and Clear Sky scraped away small stones and frozen soil to make a shallow hole, and Quiet Rain laid the tiny kit inside. She touched her nose to her daughter's fur one last time, then stepped back while her sons covered the body with earth and larger stones. For a moment all four cats stood beside the grave, their heads bowed.

Jagged Peak was the first to move, turning around to stare in amazement at the vista of mountains that stretched away on all sides. His eyes were huge and his fur bushed out; he looked tiny against the boulders.

"Have you been to all those peaks?" he asked in a hushed voice.

"Not all of them." Clear Sky moved to stand beside him, pointing with his tail. "There's the gap in the mountains we'll be aiming for when we leave."

Jagged Peak's eyes grew even wider. "I wish I was coming too," he meowed.

"Don't talk nonsense, little one." Quiet Rain padded up and laid her tail across the kit's back. "You've been out long enough for your first time. Back to the cave with you."

"But I don't *want* to go back inside!" Jagged Peak protested. "There's too much to see."

Clear Sky gave his younger brother a friendly nudge. "You can see it another day. The mountains don't move. Now show us how well you can climb down the rocks."

Still grumbling, Jagged Peak followed his brother.

Gray Wing stood for a moment at the cliff's edge, gazing

out at the cold sweep of the mountains. Rage was slowly building inside him like a storm cloud. How could such a beautiful place be so cruel? But the sharpest edge of his anger was directed at himself.

I should have caught more prey. I shouldn't have let Fluttering Bird starve.

He became aware that Quiet Rain had come to stand beside him. "This is a cruel place," she sighed, echoing his thoughts, "but it's my home, for better or worse."

"I won't let this happen again," Gray Wing meowed, his voice rough with grief and fury. "There must be better ways of hunting. We—"

"You have to leave," Quiet Rain interrupted. "Jagged Peak is too small for such a journey, but *you* must go with Clear Sky to find a better place to live. I don't want to have to watch your kits die, too."

Gray Wing stared at her, astounded. "But I thought you wanted me to stay!" he exclaimed.

Quiet Rain gazed back at him steadily, her eyes full of sorrow. "I love you too much for that," she mewed. "For my sake, go."

CHAPTER 3

Dawn light had begun to filter through the screen of falling water, though shadows still lay deep at the sides of the cave. Gray Wing hauled himself out of his sleeping hollow and spotted Shaded Moss huddled with Clear Sky and the other cats who wanted to leave. The group was larger than before.

Their heads turned toward Gray Wing as he padded over to join them; there was surprise in their eyes.

"You've changed your mind?" Clear Sky asked, blinking hopefully.

Gray Wing dipped his head. "I'm thinking about it," he responded reluctantly.

Turtle Tail came to sit by his side. "I'm so pleased you're coming with us," she purred, her eyes shining.

"It's not long now before we leave," Shaded Moss meowed, his gaze traveling over each cat in turn. "All of you should rest up and eat as much as you can."

"Lying around while others hunt for us?" Dappled Pelt objected. "I don't like the sound of that."

Shaded Moss flicked his tail impatiently. "It's only for a day or two," he pointed out. "And once we leave, the others will have enough prey to go around. But if we don't have our full strength before we set out—"

A screech from the other side of the cave interrupted him. Gray Wing looked around to see Dewy Leaf charging toward them across the cavern. The tortoiseshell queen halted in front of Moon Shadow, her legs stiff with fury and her neck fur bristling.

"What are you doing, skulking around over here?" she demanded. "I'm going to have your kits! You promised that you'd stay with me!"

"Uh-oh . . . trouble," Turtle Tail breathed into Gray Wing's ear.

Moon Shadow flinched backward. "There isn't enough food," he explained awkwardly. "Our kits will be better off if there are fewer mouths to feed."

Dewy Leaf bared her teeth in a snarl. "And who's going to catch prey while I'm still nursing them?"

Hearing her complaints, other cats hurried over to find out what was going on.

"She has a point," Twisted Branch meowed, glaring at Moon Shadow. "Cats with responsibilities should stay here."

"Are you saying we're irresponsible to leave?" Tall Shadow snapped back at him.

"Yeah." Shattered Ice sprang to his paws to stand beside the black she-cat, his green eyes narrowed. "We're going off into the unknown, into *danger*, to make a better home for you and the other cats who stay here. You don't have to do anything!"

Sharp Hail thrust himself forward, his tail lashing. "No—just sit here and starve!"

In the midst of the commotion, Gray Wing noticed Bright Stream hanging back, not part of either group and not joining in the argument.

Has she really made up her mind to leave with Clear Sky? he asked himself. *She doesn't look as if she knows what she wants.* His heart ached for her, and for Fluttering Bird, and for all his Tribemates who seemed ready to fight with claws and teeth over the future.

"Enough!" The voice came from the back of the cave, not loud, but with such authority that it cut through all the wrangling. The cats fell silent, parting as Stoneteller limped into the center of the group. "I can't bear to see you squabbling like this," she continued. "My vision promised something better for those cats willing to go in search of it. But I could be wrong." She shook her head, clearly wracked with uncertainty. "Perhaps we should forget about finding somewhere else to live. . . ."

As she was speaking, Lion's Roar came up behind her and stood close to her side. Bending his head, he spoke into her ear; though his voice was low, Gray Wing managed to make out the words.

"Don't lose faith in what you saw." Addressing all the cats, he went on, "My mother told me that before she and the others left the lake, they held a vote to decide their shared future. Why don't we vote again now?" he suggested. "If most cats want us to stay here and take a chance with the rest of the cold season, then Shaded Moss won't leave. What do you think, Stoneteller?"

The old white she-cat blinked thoughtfully, then turned to Shaded Moss. "Would you accept the result of a vote?" she asked.

Shaded Moss nodded. "I don't want to go without enough cats to stand a chance of surviving the journey."

Stoneteller glanced around at the other cats. Gray Wing could see that their anger was dying down. "Gray Wing, Bright Stream," the Healer mewed, "please collect as many stones as there are cats."

"Even me?" Jagged Peak squeaked, with an excited bounce.

Quiet Rain stretched out her tail to caress her son's ear. "No, not the kits—" she began.

"Even the kits," Stoneteller interrupted gently. "Every cat will have a chance to be heard. We are still one community, friends and kin over seasons upon seasons. We must all have a part in deciding our future."

Dipping his head to Stoneteller, Gray Wing headed out of the cave with Bright Stream. They found a scatter of small stones not far from the waterfall, under an overhang, and began to roll them together into a heap.

"Quiet Rain wants me to leave," he told Bright Stream after a moment.

Bright Stream's eyes widened and her ears flicked up in surprise. "I'd have thought she would want you and Clear Sky to stay now."

Gray Wing shook his head. "She believes we stand a better

chance of survival in the place that Stoneteller has seen."

Bright Stream added another stone to the pile before she responded. "Are you going to go?" she asked hesitantly.

"I don't know." Gray Wing found himself giving voice to his inward struggle. "The way Fluttering Bird died showed me how vulnerable we are here in the mountains. But . . . is it cowardly to run away?"

"No cat could think that you're a coward, Gray Wing," Bright Stream told him.

When they had collected enough stones, they carried them back into the cave, a few at a time. Shaded Moss and Tall Shadow gathered the pebbles into a pile at Stoneteller's paws, their gaze solemn with the importance of their task.

"Now," Stoneteller meowed, "every cat must take a stone. Place it on the waterfall side of the cave if you think Shaded Moss and all the cats who want to go should leave the mountains, and on the inner cave wall if you think they should stay. Shaded Moss, you go first."

Shaded Moss stepped forward and dipped his head to Stoneteller with deep respect. "I trust you with my life," he told her. "If you have seen a better place for some of us to live, I promise I will find it."

Taking a stone in his jaws, he carried it to the waterfall side of the cave and laid it down so close to the cascade that drops of sparkling water splashed over it.

Meanwhile the rest of the Tribe lined up for their turn to vote. Jagged Peak scraped his claws along the cave floor as if he was too excited to wait.

Lion's Roar was the next cat to pick up a pebble, and he laid it down near the waterfall. "My old bones won't carry me on the journey," he rasped. "But if I were young enough, I'd leave."

Snow Hare and Misty Water followed, both voting for the cats to stay. Clear Sky came next, in a little group with Dappled Pelt and Turtle Tail, all of them taking their stones to the waterfall side. Then Jagged Peak bounced up to the pile of stones and took one, carefully carrying it over to set it down beside his brother's.

Quiet Rain shook her head. "My beloved son, I can't allow you to leave. But the *older* cats should have the chance to go." She took her stone and laid it by the waterfall beside her kits'.

Jagged Peak's eyes sparkled rebelliously as he stomped toward the sleeping hollows, his tail high in the air.

Bright Stream was the next cat to take a stone. Without hesitation she placed it with the others beside the waterfall.

Clear Sky's fur fluffed out with surprise as he watched her, a look of warm affection creeping into his eyes. "Thank you," he whispered as she joined him, standing so close that their pelts were brushing.

"I did it for all our future kits," she responded.

Gray Wing realized that his turn to vote had come. He felt a hard jolt in his belly, as if a falling rock had struck him. *I can't put off my decision any longer.*

Looking around, he noticed afresh the jutting bones of his companions, their dull eyes, their air of exhaustion. At last he met his mother's gaze, and saw her eyes full of pleading. He knew that she believed his future safety lay in leaving the cave.

But what about her *safety? And Jagged Peak's? And all the cats who want to stay here? They need strong hunters.*

When Gray Wing took up a stone, he felt as though he were trying to move the whole mountain. But his paw steps were steady as he carried it to the inner wall and set it down.

Without looking at his mother again, Gray Wing padded back to rejoin the other cats around Stoneteller. He was in time to see Moon Shadow pick up a stone and march determinedly over to the waterfall.

Dewy Leaf padded alongside him. "Your kits will never know their father's name!" she hissed.

Moon Shadow didn't reply. After a heartbeat, Dewy Leaf whisked around, picked up her own stone, and carried it to the inner wall.

The rest of the cats voted in silence. When the last stone had been set in place, Stoneteller examined the piles. Without looking closely, Gray Wing thought that they seemed about the same size.

What will we do, if the votes are equal for staying and leaving?

At last Stoneteller limped back to the center of the cave. "There are more stones in the leaving pile," she announced.

A murmur passed through the cats who surrounded her, like wind blowing over rock. They looked at each other with apprehension in their eyes, as if they had suddenly realized the magnitude of the decision they had helped to make.

"Good luck to those who wish to leave," Stoneteller continued. "We will always remember you."

The mood in the cave remained somber. Gray Wing couldn't sense any feeling of triumph, or even relief, that a firm decision had been made.

"Come on," Shaded Moss meowed at last. "We'll go and scout the route again. We need to know exactly what we're doing before we finally set out."

He led the way to the cave entrance, and the cats who planned to go with him followed.

Gray Wing stayed behind, feeling awkward as he watched Clear Sky and the others disappearing into the dazzle of light from the falling water. After a moment he realized that Quiet Rain had padded up to him.

"I told you to leave," she murmured. "You need to consider your future."

Gray Wing stretched out his neck to touch noses with her. "My future is here," he told her. With a brief nod, he headed out of the cave and toward the ridge, his ears pricked and his jaws parted for the faintest hint of prey.

As he climbed, Gray Wing spotted Shaded Moss and his followers on top of the ridge. Shaded Moss seemed to be explaining something with waves of his tail, while his companions offered comments and suggestions. *They're making their plans to leave*, Gray Wing thought, with a pang of loss at his heart.

He didn't want to meet them. Turning, he bounded in the opposite direction, down into the valley, hoping he might come across another hare. From the corner of his eye he glimpsed a flicker of movement and veered toward it, his paws skidding in a flurry of snow.

It was a small creature—a mouse or vole—scampering rapidly over the icy surface. Gray Wing put on an extra burst of speed, but just before he caught up, it slipped through a narrow gap between two boulders and was gone. Gray Wing tried to squeeze through after it, but the space was too small.

He halted, letting out a growl of frustration. His tail drooped dejectedly, and for a few heartbeats he lost all hope. *Why is it so hard to go on living here? Why must so many cats leave?*

A faint sound from behind made him whirl, his claws extended. Then he froze with astonishment. Stoneteller stood in front of him, her white pelt barely visible against the snow. Gray Wing couldn't remember the last time she had left the cave.

"Are—are you all right?" he stammered.

"I'm fine," Stoneteller responded. Padding past him, she clambered awkwardly to the flat top of a nearby rock. "I just wanted some fresh air," she continued. "It's been a long time. . . ."

Gray Wing leaped up to sit beside her. "Stoneteller," he blurted out, "are you *sure* there's a better place beyond the sunrise?"

Stoneteller turned her green gaze on him. "I felt more certain during my dream than ever before in my life," she assured him. "I'm sad to watch so many cats leave, but I truly believe it will give all of us the best chance of survival."

"Then why did you leave the lake?" Gray Wing asked. He was awestruck to be questioning Stoneteller about an event that had happened so long ago. *She was there . . . she remembers all of it.* "Was it worth it, to come and live here?"

"It was," Stoneteller replied, a wistful note in her voice. "We left for the best of reasons, and for a long time now these mountains have sheltered us well. And I had the honor of leading the Tribe in our new territory."

Gray Wing felt a pang of pity for the old she-cat. *Stoneteller gave up her whole life in our service. She never had the chance to have a mate and kits of her own.*

"Things could have been different for you," he suggested awkwardly. "Did you ever want another kind of life?"

Stoneteller shook her head, seeming to understand what he meant. "All the cats in the Tribe are my kits, even the elders. And as for finding a mate . . . I knew love once, and once was enough. We can never be sure of our future, Gray Wing," she added quietly. "All we can do is trust that what we believe is right."

"Well, *I* believe that it's the right thing for me to stay here," Gray Wing meowed.

Stoneteller did not reply in words, but the nod she gave him silenced his doubts.

CHAPTER 4
♣

Gray Wing stood on top of the rocks in the pale dawn light, his fur buffeted by the wind. All the cats, even the kits, were gathered around Stoneteller, who stood on a boulder near the waterfall. Those leaving with Shaded Moss stood close together. Gray Wing watched them flexing their paws impatiently, exchanging excited, apprehensive glances.

As they waited for Stoneteller to speak, Clear Sky broke from Shaded Moss's group to pad over to where Gray Wing stood beside their mother and brother.

"Good-bye," he murmured, brushing his muzzle against Quiet Rain's shoulder and then Gray Wing's, before stooping to touch Jagged Peak's ear with his nose. "I hope everything will go well for you now. And who knows?" he added, clearly trying to sound cheerful. "One day I might come back and visit."

Gray Wing exchanged a glance with Quiet Rain, seeing that she knew perfectly well that would never happen.

But neither of them spoke their thought aloud.

"Travel safely, my son," Quiet Rain mewed.

"Why can't I come with you?" Jagged Peak broke in loudly. Quiet Rain silenced him with a glance; the young kit scrabbled sulkily at the loose pebbles beside the river. Quiet Rain's glance drifted beyond him, to the small pile of stones that covered Fluttering Bird.

"Are you sure you won't come?" Clear Sky meowed to Gray Wing. "It won't be the same without you."

Gray Wing touched his muzzle to Clear Sky's, and the two brothers twined tails. "I'm sorry you have to do this without me," Gray Wing responded, loss piercing his heart like an eagle's talon. "But my place is here, with Quiet Rain and Jagged Peak."

"I'm glad they have you to care for them," Clear Sky told him.

He dipped his head one last time and padded back to stand beside Bright Stream. She held her head high, but Gray Wing could see the uncertainty in her eyes.

At last Stoneteller flicked her tail toward Shaded Moss. "Tonight the moon will be full," she mewed. "It is time for you to leave us. Shaded Moss, do you wish to speak?"

The sturdy black-and-white tom leaped up onto the boulder beside her and glanced around at the assembled cats. "We trust the Teller of the Pointed Stones to know where our future lies," he began. "We will follow the path to the rising sun, but we will always carry the mountains, and all of you, in our hearts."

"That won't stop us missing you," Misty Water muttered.

Shaded Moss bowed his head in respect to the elder before continuing. "I hope that, with fewer cats to feed, the hunting will become easier."

As Shaded Moss finished speaking, Stoneteller touched his shoulder with her tail-tip and took a step forward. "I thank you, Shaded Moss, and all departing cats, for your selfless courage. This is the greatest gift that you could give us. We will never forget you." She took a breath, and focused her bright green gaze on the cats with Shaded Moss. "You'll meet strange creatures on your journey," she continued. "Hairless creatures called Twolegs, because they walk on their hind legs. And shiny roaring beasts that seem like monsters, racing along hard black tracks we called Thunderpaths."

Turtle Tail's eyes stretched wide and she let out a gasp of dismay. "You mean those are real?" she asked. "I thought they were just elders' tales."

Stoneteller shook her head. "They're real, but they can be avoided. The monsters seem unable to leave the Thunder-paths, but you'll still need to use all your cunning." Her voice sounded more anxious now. "Don't forget that there'll be new enemies too—not just birds, but foxes and badgers. And did I tell you that there might even be trouble from other cats?"

Shaded Moss dipped his head. "We discussed all this, Stoneteller."

"Don't forget," Cloud Spots put in, "Dappled Pelt and I know a lot about herbs and healing. If things go wrong, we'll be able to help."

The old white cat's whiskers twitched and her shoulder fur began to rise. Gray Wing's pads tingled with apprehension as he realized that she wasn't as certain as she had always seemed.

"Trust *nothing*," Stoneteller meowed urgently, "but your own instincts."

Shaded Moss laid his tail reassuringly over Stoneteller's back. "We will learn as we travel," he responded gently. "We have trusted you to send us toward the sun; now trust *us* to travel safely and to find this new place to live."

Stoneteller let out a long sigh. She slid from the rock and padded over to those who were leaving with Shaded Moss, touching her nose to each cat's shoulder as she spoke. "Find somewhere that suits all of you," she mewed. "Tall Shadow, your gift for stalking and guile; Clear Sky, your gift for bringing down birds from the air; Turtle Tail, your speed and sharp eyes; Rainswept Flower, your ability to track far-off prey by scent alone. All of your talents must find the right place to blossom." She gazed at the cats, her green eyes full of love and grief. "Good luck," she added at last.

Shaded Moss waved his tail and led his group down the rocks toward the pool below the waterfall.

"Good-bye!" Gray Wing called, his gaze fixed on his brother. "Stay safe!"

"Good *riddance* is what I say!" Dewy Leaf snarled. "Cowards! They're just leaving us all to starve."

"Right," Twisted Branch agreed. "Well, we don't need them."

Gray Wing stood beside Quiet Rain and watched the departing cats as they wound their way down the mountainside until they were out of sight.

The remaining cats stood for a moment in silence, looking at one another. The Tribe seemed so small now, with so few cats left. Gray Wing realized elders and kits now outnumbered the stronger cats. His paws tingled with apprehension, but he crushed it down.

"We can't stand here all day," he meowed at last. "Stone Song, Twisted Branch, Dewy Leaf, we should hunt while it's still light."

"What?" Dewy Leaf lashed her tail. "Have you forgotten I'm expecting kits?"

You don't let us forget it, Gray Wing thought, though he stopped himself from speaking the words aloud. "We're the strongest cats left behind," he went on quietly. "We must try to catch enough food for every cat."

Twisted Branch nodded, a look of determination in his amber eyes.

"You're not Stoneteller. You don't get to order me around," Dewy Leaf muttered. She paused for a heartbeat, then shrugged. "Okay, I'll hunt."

As Stoneteller began to lead the rest of her Tribe down toward the cave, Sharp Hail and Silver Frost stayed behind. "We'll hunt too," Silver Frost announced. "We might not be as young as you, but our claws are still sharp."

"Right," Sharp Hail agreed. "We owe it to the cats who have gone not to give up now. We need to find a new way to survive."

"Thank you," Gray Wing responded, grateful for the older tom's wisdom.

Leaving the other cats behind, Gray Wing trekked along the cliff edge, moving away from the river. The mountains seemed even quieter than usual. He paused from time to time, straining his ears for any sign of the traveling cats farther along the valley, and gazed around him in the hope of catching one last glimpse of them. But they had vanished against the snow and rocks.

I'll never see them again.

A dark shadow passed over Gray Wing's head and he looked up to see a young hawk skimming the surface of the snow as if it too was searching for prey. As it mounted into the air again Gray Wing flung himself upward, remembering Clear Sky's favorite move.

His claws snagged one wing; he and the hawk fell to the ground together and rolled over in the snow. Gray Wing felt talons rake through his pelt. With a yowl of mingled pain and fury he sank his claws into the hawk's breast and brought his teeth together in its throat with a swift snap.

The hawk went limp. Puffing, Gray Wing scrambled to his paws and shook the snow off his pelt. Then he picked up the hawk by the neck and began plodding back to the cave, his prey's strong, barred wings trailing in the snow.

By the time he reached the path behind the waterfall the other hunting cats were also returning. Stone Song and Silver Frost had each caught a mouse, and Twisted Branch and Dewy Leaf were dragging a snow hare between them.

"We caught it together," Twisted Branch mumbled through a mouthful of fur. "I chased it, and it doubled back—right into Dewy Leaf's claws. It was great!"

The other cats gathered around as the hunters dropped their prey on the floor of the cave. Even so, Gray Wing thought that the cavern seemed quiet and empty, with so few cats remaining. Their voices seemed to echo strangely as they shared the prey, taking a mouthful and then exchanging with one another.

"I will hunt tomorrow," Quiet Rain promised.

"So will I," Hollow Tree agreed, brushing her tail along the flank of her mate, Stone Song.

"Why don't we take turns?" Stone Song suggested. "So every cat keeps their hunting skills sharp, and no cat has to go out every day."

Stoneteller gave the dark gray tabby tom an approving nod. "A very good idea. Stone Song, would you like to arrange it?"

Stone Song's eyes gleamed at his Healer's praise. "I'd be glad to."

Gray Wing glanced at his Tribemates, and caught the same look of determination on all their faces. He felt reassured that the sacrifice of the cats who had left would not be wasted.

We can make this work.

A paw prodding him in the side woke Gray Wing the next morning. He blinked blearily in the light that slanted through the waterfall, and made out Stone Song standing over him.

"Are you okay to hunt?" the tabby tom asked. "I'm arranging the new plan, starting today. Quiet Rain and Hollow Tree are going out, and I'll go myself. I want to find out if four cats hunting every day are enough."

"Sure."

The light from the cave entrance was brighter than Gray Wing had seen it for many days, as if the sun was shining outside. *Maybe that's a good sign*, he thought. *Better than trying to hunt in a blizzard, anyway.*

As he loped toward the entrance he heard the swift pattering of paws behind him, and Jagged Peak's voice rose shrilly. "Gray Wing! Wait for me!"

Gray Wing turned as Jagged Peak skidded to a halt beside him. "I want to hunt with you," the kit announced.

Gray Wing suppressed a sigh. "You're too young," he replied. "Go and play with the other kits."

"They only want to do *dumb* stuff," Jagged Peak muttered. "Pouncing on a pebble and pretending it's an eagle! I want to pounce on *real* eagles."

"An eagle would just make a mouthful of you," Gray Wing meowed.

"Would *not*!" Jagged Peak protested. "I'm *big*! I'm the oldest kit—I should be allowed to hunt."

Reluctantly, Gray Wing admitted to himself that his brother had a point. *Maybe it is time he started to train. We could certainly use another hunter.*

"What's the matter?" Quiet Rain asked, padding up to them. "Jagged Peak, are you making a nuisance of yourself?"

"He wants to learn how to hunt," Gray Wing explained, before Jagged Peak could reply.

He caught a swift flash of fear in his mother's eyes, as if she was thinking of all the dangers outside the cave for a cat as small as Jagged Peak. "He's so young. . . ."

Jagged Peak's fur bristled. "I'm the oldest—"

Gray Wing slapped his tail over the kit's mouth, earning himself an indignant glare.

"He is nearly old enough," he told Quiet Rain. When his mother still looked doubtful, he added, "Better he comes with me than tries to sneak out on his own."

Quiet Rain hesitated for a moment longer, then gave a reluctant nod. "All right." Turning to Jagged Peak, she added, "Stay with Gray Wing, and do *exactly* what he tells you."

Jagged Peak nodded vigorously. His eyes were bright and he began pacing with excitement. "Let's go!"

Gray Wing held Jagged Peak back with his tail as the kit tried to scamper up the path that led behind the waterfall. "The first thing you have to learn," he said, "is not to go dashing off. Follow me, and keep quiet."

Though Jagged Peak's eyes still sparkled, he settled down and padded after Gray Wing. Quiet Rain brought up the rear. Stone Song and Hollow Tree had already left; when he emerged into the open, Gray Wing spotted them together, climbing the opposite slope.

Quiet Rain caught up to Jagged Peak, hesitated, then mewed, "Good hunting," before she headed up the rocks toward the top of the cliff.

Gray Wing guessed that she would rather have stayed with her kit, but she knew she had to concentrate on her own hunting.

"Okay," he began, "the most important thing to remember is that, out here, *you* can be prey too. Some of these birds are strong enough to fly away with a full-grown cat in their talons. *Always* be aware of what's going on above your head. Got that?"

Jagged Peak's eyes stretched wide. "Got it."

Gray Wing was relieved that his brother seemed to be

taking the warning seriously.

"The next thing," he went on, "is searching for prey. Charging around is pointless—you'll just scare the animals back into their holes. Use your eyes and nose, and taste the air for scent. Try it now, and see if you can pick up anything."

Jagged Peak stood still, his ears pricked and his jaws parted. His gaze swiveled around, taking in the snow-covered slopes; Gray Wing was glad to see that he kept casting glances upward as well.

"Can you spot anything?" he asked after a moment.

Jagged Peak dipped his head, looking disappointed. "No."

"Don't worry, neither can I," Gray Wing told him. "Prey doesn't usually come this close to our cave. We'll go and look somewhere else in a moment, but first I want to show you how to stalk. You have to learn to get as close as you can to your prey without it knowing you're there. How do you think you might do that?"

Jagged Peak crouched down into the snow. "Keep as small as I can?" he suggested.

"Right. But when there's snow on the ground, don't drop so low that it clogs your fur and slows you down. Move like this. . . ."

Gray Wing lowered himself into position so that his belly fur was just brushing the surface of the snow. Then he crept forward slowly and carefully. Jagged Peak stayed by his side, copying.

"That's good," Gray Wing told him, impressed by how quickly his brother was learning. "And what about scent?

How can you stop your prey from scenting you before you're close enough to pounce?"

Jagged Peak thought for a moment, his whiskers quivering, then grumbled, "I don't know."

"Think about wind," Gray Wing prompted.

"Wind . . ." Jagged Peak sank into deep thought again. "I know!" he exclaimed at last. "The wind carries scent, so I've got to make sure that it's blowing from my prey to me, and not the other way."

Gray Wing let out a satisfied purr. "You'll be a hunter in no time. Now let's go and see what we can find. Don't forget to keep looking at the sky."

He led the way up the slope toward the ridge. "This is a good place for finding snow hares," he told Jagged Peak. "Remember that their fur turns white in the cold season, so it's hard to spot them unless they're against the bare rocks. And they're very fast, so you need to get as close as you can before they know you're there. If you end up chasing one, you'll likely lose it."

As he spoke, Gray Wing realized that Jagged Peak was distracted, constantly staring into the distance. "Hey—concentrate!" he meowed.

"Sorry." But after a few more paw steps, Jagged Peak was gazing around again.

Gray Wing stopped, irritated, but before he could speak he spotted movement among the rocks above. The white-furred body of a hare was just visible between two boulders.

Nudging Jagged Peak, he flicked his ears in the direction

of the hare. "Want to see if you can catch it?" he whispered.

Jagged Peak's eyes widened in excitement. Crouching down carefully, he crept closer to his prey.

He's forgotten the wind, Gray Wing realized, though he said nothing.

Jagged Peak had covered about half the distance when the hare suddenly sat up, its long ears erect and its nose twitching. Then it burst from the shelter of the boulders and fled across the slope, snow spraying from under its paws.

Letting out a yowl of frustration, Jagged Peak hurtled in pursuit. As he was so small and light, his paws skimmed easily across the surface of the snow. Gray Wing raced after him.

At first Jagged Peak seemed to be gaining ground, but the hare was bigger and stronger, and soon started to outpace him. *We're going to lose it*, Gray Wing thought, forcing his muscles to bunch and stretch in an effort to catch up.

A heartbeat later, a harsh cry rang out. A hawk plummeted from the sky, talons outstretched. The hare let out a squeal of terror and swerved away, heading back toward Jagged Peak.

The young cat sprang and collided with the creature in a small storm of flying snow. Gray Wing saw a thrashing knot of legs and Jagged Peak's wildly waving tail.

But the hawk hadn't given up. It dived again. Gray Wing realized that if it couldn't catch the hare, it would settle for Jagged Peak.

With a wild screech, Gray Wing leaped for the hawk as it bore down. He felt his claws scrape the underside of the hawk's wing. With another harsh cry the bird mounted into the air, higher and higher until it was only a black dot in the sky.

Once he was sure it wasn't a threat anymore, Gray Wing spun around toward his brother. He saw Jagged Peak standing shakily on all four paws, the body of the hare stretched motionless in the snow in front of him.

"I got it!" he exclaimed. "I'm a hunter now!"

"Terrific!" Gray Wing praised him. "You did really well. But don't forget," he added, "you still have a lot to learn."

The hare was bigger than Jagged Peak, and he needed Gray Wing's help to drag it back to the cave. The rest of the Tribe gathered around, exclaiming in wonder when Gray Wing told them how Jagged Peak had made his catch.

"Prey had better watch out!" Lion's Roar gave the young cat a friendly prod with his tail.

"It's your prey," Gray Wing pointed out to his brother. "So you can eat first."

Jagged Peak's eyes gleamed as he tore into the hare. Watching him gulp down mouthful after mouthful, Gray Wing reflected on how hungry the kit had been for so long. *This could be the first good meal he's ever had.*

There was still plenty left when Jagged Peak drew back. "I'm stuffed!" he declared.

The rest of the Tribe was just beginning to eat when Quiet Rain came back, a hawk dangling from her jaws.

"You had good hunting," she remarked, dropping her prey beside the remains of the hare.

"Jagged Peak caught it," Gray Wing replied, while Jagged

Peak puffed out his chest with pride.

Quiet Rain's eyes glowed as she gazed at her young son. "Wonderful!" she exclaimed. "Gray Wing, thank you for teaching him so well."

As Gray Wing settled down to eat his share of the prey he wondered once again what their departed Tribemates were doing. It still felt strange that there were so few cats left in the cave. *I hope they're all safe, and that they've found enough to eat.*

"Can we go out again?" Jagged Peak mewed when Gray Wing had finished eating. "Hunting's really exciting!"

Gray Wing glanced toward the cave entrance and saw that the short day was already coming to an end, dusk gathering beyond the waterfall.

"Not now," Quiet Rain responded, before he could speak. "It's time for you to go to your nest. You can hunt again tomorrow."

"But I'm not tired!" Jagged Peak protested. "I can—" His words were interrupted by an enormous yawn.

"No more arguing," Quiet Rain mewed briskly.

She nudged Jagged Peak across the cavern to their sleeping hollows, and Gray Wing followed. As he settled down, he realized once again how empty the nest now felt. He desperately missed the feeling of his brother's fur against his.

I wonder where the traveling cats are now. . . .

Gray Wing woke abruptly to see pale dawn light filtering through the waterfall. Quiet Rain was pacing nervously beside him, and he realized that her growls had awoken him.

"What's the matter?" he asked, springing out of his hollow.

"Jagged Peak's nest is empty," his mother replied. "He must have gone out by himself—and he *knows* that he's not supposed to do that."

Gray Wing let his tail-tip rest on his mother's back comfortingly. "He couldn't have gone far," he meowed. "I'll bring him back."

He scanned the slopes as he emerged from behind the waterfall. Nothing moved in all the snowy landscape.

"Jagged Peak! Jagged Peak!" he yowled.

Silence.

Stupid kit, he thought, scrambling up the rocks that led to the plateau. Wind buffeted his fur as he reached the top and looked around carefully. There was no sign of his brother, and no reply when he called out again.

Beginning to feel troubled, Gray Wing returned to the cave to find his mother waiting anxiously beside the waterfall, a few of the other cats gathered around her. "I'm sorry," he mewed. "I can't find him. He's not beside the pool or on the plateau."

Quiet Rain began pacing again. "A hawk must have taken him!" she wailed. "Or he's been smothered in a snowdrift."

Silver Frost brushed her tail along Quiet Rain's side. "Jagged Peak is a strong young cat," she said. "And he's not stupid. He knows to keep himself out of danger."

"That's right," Lion's Roar agreed. "He'll probably turn up soon, with a piece of prey twice his own size!"

"I wish I could believe you," Quiet Rain murmured.

Gray Wing was worried too. "I'll go out and take another look," he promised. "Misty Water," he added, turning to the elder, "will you come with me?"

"What?" Snow Hare pushed herself between Misty Water and Gray Wing. "She's too old, and her eyesight is failing," she hissed into Gray Wing's ear. "She'll be no help!"

"That's not true." Gray Wing gently nudged Snow Hare aside. "Misty Water," he mewed, "Broken Feather told me many times that you were the best scent tracker he had ever known. If any cat has a chance of tracking Jagged Peak, it's you."

Misty Water blinked up at him with milky blue eyes. "I'll come," she responded.

Gray Wing led the way out of the cave, and Misty Water followed, her paw steps stiff and shaky. As soon as she came to the end of the path, she grew more alert, her nose to the ledge, her jaws open to draw in scent. "He went this way," she announced, beginning to haul herself awkwardly over the rocks that led to the plateau. "I'll *claw* that pesky kit when I catch him," she panted. "My old bones aren't fit for this."

Gray Wing scrambled up beside her. "This can't be right," he protested, struggling with disappointment. "Jagged Peak was up here two days ago, with the rest of us, when we said farewell to the others."

Misty Water halted and glared at him. "You think I can't tell a two-day-old scent from a fresh one?" she demanded. "This scent is laid *on top of* the older one. You young cats think you know everything."

Gray Wing kept quiet and followed the elder as she dragged herself over the lip of the plateau, then padded to the little heap of stones that covered Fluttering Bird.

"Did Jagged Peak come over here two days ago?" she asked.

Gray Wing thought back, picturing the scene in his mind. "No," he replied at last.

"Well, he came here *today*," Misty Water mewed. "His scent has pooled, so it shows he spent some time here. . . ." She paused, scenting all around the heap of stones, before clambering down beside the waterfall again. "Then he went this way."

The old cat branched off over a clump of boulders.

Gray Wing stared at her in amazement. "Are you sure?"

Misty Water glanced back, her eyes narrowed in an icy glare. "Are you saying I'm too old to recognize a scent trail?"

"No, but . . . that's the way the traveling cats went."

As Gray Wing spoke the sun finally pierced through the dark clouds that were massing on the horizon, casting a yellow beam over the side of the mountain. Realization hit him like a blow from a falling rock. "Jagged Peak left to find the traveling cats!" he exclaimed. "He's following the trail of the sun."

Misty Water gave the boulders a last sniff, then returned to Gray Wing's side. "Stupid kit," she muttered. "He'll be back when his belly starts rumbling."

Gray Wing wished he could share her confidence. *Jagged Peak is so stone-headed. And since he caught that hare, he probably thinks he can catch anything he wants.*

He helped Misty Water down the rocks, then ran ahead

back to the cave, where he found Quiet Rain anxiously telling Stoneteller what had happened. She whipped around as Gray Wing raced over to her. "Did you find him?" she asked.

Gray Wing shook his head. "Misty Water picked up Jagged Peak's scent," he explained. "It looks as if he went to say good-bye to Fluttering Bird at the pile of stones, and then followed the other cats heading out of the mountains."

Quiet Rain gasped in horror, her eyes wide with dismay. "Oh, *no* . . ." Her voice quivered with anguish. "He'll be killed!"

Gray Wing pressed his muzzle against his mother's shoulder. "Jagged Peak can look after himself—"

"He *can't* look after himself!" Quiet Rain's voice rose to a wail. "He's too young." Straightening up, she took a deep breath, obviously fighting for self-control. "Gray Wing," she meowed, "you wouldn't leave when I told you to before. But now you *must*. You have to find your brother and make sure he reaches this new place safely."

Gray Wing glanced at Stoneteller. The old white she-cat didn't speak, but he saw encouragement in her green eyes. Glancing around the cave, he saw Twisted Branch and Dewy Leaf on their way out to hunt. The Tribe would not lack for hunting with those two around.

Then he remembered the golden path of sunlight that he had seen stretching across the valley, tugging him away from his home in the cave.

He turned back to meet his mother's pleading gaze. "All right," he agreed. "I will go after Jagged Peak."

CHAPTER 5

❧

Gray Wing headed for the cave entrance, but halted when he saw Dewy Leaf and Twisted Branch returning, only heartbeats after they had left. Both were covered in snow, and stopped to shake their pelts.

"There's a blizzard out there," Twisted Branch announced. "We won't be able to catch anything until it's over."

Dewy Leaf gave a snort of disgust. "The wind nearly blew me off the mountain."

Quiet Rain padded to Gray Wing's side. "You can't leave in weather like this," she mewed, her voice sharp with anxiety.

Gray Wing understood how worried she must be about Jagged Peak, especially now that the snow had set in. "I can try—"

"No!" Quiet Rain interrupted. "Do you think I want *all* my kits to freeze to death?"

"She's right." Stoneteller approached and touched Quiet Rain's ear with her nose. "Jagged Peak will find shelter, and so will Shaded Moss and his cats. You won't fall any further behind by waiting until the storm is over."

Gray Wing's paws itched with impatience as the day

continued, snowflakes outside whirling like white feathers out of a gray sky. By the time the storm blew itself out, the sun was setting behind the mountains in a dull red glow. Sharp Hail and Hollow Tree went out to hunt, but Gray Wing knew that it was too late for him to start his journey.

Grief and apprehension had settled over the cave like a low cloud. Every cat feared the worst for Jagged Peak. Gray Wing could only hope that Stoneteller was right, and his little brother had been able to find shelter.

His mother bore the waiting with quiet dignity, though her eyes were dark pools of pain. Gray Wing padded to where she crouched near the cave entrance.

"It doesn't seem fair that you should lose all your kits," he murmured, sitting beside her.

"I have no choice," Quiet Rain sighed. "And I still have Fluttering Bird near me, beneath her pelt of stones."

Gray Wing leaned closer to his mother so that his fur brushed hers, and sat with her as the light from the gray screen of falling water faded to darkness. His heart felt like it might burst with grief.

The sound of paw steps roused him and he saw Hollow Tree and Sharp Hail returning, their legs and belly fur plastered with snow. Hollow Tree was carrying a small, scrawny bird.

"Gray Wing, you should have this," she meowed, dropping it in front of him. "It will give you the strength to follow Jagged Peak."

"I can't," Gray Wing protested, with a glance toward his

Tribemates deeper inside the cave. "No cat has eaten today."

Sharp Hail pushed the bird closer to Gray Wing with one paw. "And this miserable thing won't fill one cat, let alone the whole Tribe."

"You need it," Stoneteller agreed, appearing from the shadows. "None of us would begrudge you a mouthful."

"Thank you," Gray Wing mewed.

He gulped down the bird in a few bites, then went to his sleeping hollow. Even though he knew he needed to rest for his journey, it took a long time for him to sleep. Curled up with the noise of the waterfall in his ears, he wondered drowsily if this was the last time he would ever hear it.

Toward dawn he sank into deeper sleep, and woke to the sound of a cat padding past him. Turning his head, he spotted Stoneteller heading toward the cave entrance, where she sat and stared into the thunderous water. Gray Wing went to join her.

As he sat down at her side, Stoneteller glanced at him. "I don't know if I did the right thing by sending so many cats away," she admitted. "But the vision of the sun trail seemed to offer a way out of the agony of seeing my Tribe starve to death in the long cold season. . . ."

Her voice was quiet, almost as if she was talking to herself. Gray Wing hardly knew what to say. "None of us knows what the future holds," he mewed at last. "We can only trust our instincts."

Stoneteller dipped her head in acknowledgment. "We'll miss you, Gray Wing."

"I didn't want to leave," Gray Wing confessed. "But now I know there's something I must do. I promise that I'll find Jagged Peak and take him to join the others in their new home."

Light began filtering through the waterfall, and Gray Wing heard the sounds of his Tribemates stirring. One by one they gathered around him and Stoneteller.

"Remember to be careful where you're putting your paws," Lion's Roar advised. "This fresh snow could be hiding all sorts of dangers."

I'm not a kit, Gray Wing thought, though he didn't speak the words aloud. He realized that the elders only wanted to make sure he traveled safely.

"I wouldn't want to set off all on my own," Stone Song confessed, giving Gray Wing a friendly nudge. "You're a brave cat."

Hollow Tree nodded. "We'll be thinking of you."

Gray Wing didn't feel brave. Now that it was time to leave, his belly churned with apprehension. But he had no choice: Jagged Peak needed him.

Among the gathered cats, he spotted Dewy Leaf. "Do you want to come?" he asked her. "It's your last chance to be with Moon Shadow again."

Dewy Leaf hesitated, glancing at her rounded belly, then shook her head. "My kits belong in the mountains," she replied, her tone not bitter, but resigned. "And I think things will be better here now. But when you see Moon Shadow, tell him I hope he's happy in his new home."

"I will," Gray Wing promised.

Misty Water nudged her way to the front of the crowd. "Don't forget the route I showed you," she meowed. "Over those boulders and around the side of the mountain."

"I know." Gray Wing dipped his head respectfully. "We wouldn't know where Jagged Peak went, if it wasn't for you."

Misty Water gave a satisfied snort.

Quiet Rain was the last cat to step forward. "I'll come with you a little way," she murmured, giving Gray Wing's ear a lick.

With a final farewell to the other cats, Gray Wing led the way out into the open. Quiet Rain padded softly behind him. On the mountainside the dawn light was still gray and dim, the sky covered with clouds, though a gathering brightness on the horizon showed where the sun would rise. A stiff breeze blew loose snow into their faces.

Together Gray Wing and Quiet Rain climbed the rocks toward the plateau, halting beside the boulders where Jagged Peak had veered aside. "Wait here a moment," Gray Wing murmured, before scrambling up the rest of the way and heading across to the heap of stones that showed where Fluttering Bird was buried.

"I don't know if you can still hear or see me," Gray Wing whispered, bowing his head, "but I promise I will never forget you."

After a couple of heartbeats he turned away and clambered back to his mother. Side by side they skirted the boulders and made their way along the ledge where they had last seen Shaded Moss and his companions.

Gray Wing had been afraid that the fresh snow would have

blotted out the trail, but here and there, in crevices where little snow could reach, he picked up traces of the traveling cats, and Jagged Peak's fresh scent lying on top.

"He did come this way," Quiet Rain mewed, sounding a little encouraged.

Jagged Peak's faint scent led them around the flank of the mountain; a shiver ran through Gray Wing from ears to tail-tip as he glanced back, taking one last look at the waterfall. For a little while, their surroundings were still familiar from hunting expeditions, but well before sunhigh they were padding into new territory, where every paw step felt strange.

The trail began to lead into a valley, and he heard the sound of a river. He halted on the bank with Quiet Rain at his side and looked out across a fierce, tumbling torrent, pouring steeply down the side of the mountain. A cobweb-thin casing of ice stretched from bank to bank, with dark water gurgling along underneath.

"The ice will only take one cat across," Quiet Rain mewed. "This is where my journey ends."

Though her voice was calm, grief welled up in her eyes, and Gray Wing knew how hard it must be for her to bid good-bye to her last kit. He pressed against her side, twining his tail with hers and parting his jaws to draw in her scent.

"I'll find Jagged Peak," he promised. "And I'll never let him and Clear Sky forget our home."

Quiet Rain let out a long sigh, then nudged him away. "Go quickly," she told him. "Before the sun rises higher and melts the ice."

With a final good-bye, Gray Wing stepped out onto the ice, uncomfortably aware of how fragile it was. If it gave way, the turbulent water would sweep him down the mountain to a certain death on the rocks below. He placed one paw after another cautiously, not daring to stop or look back; he just kept his gaze fixed on the safety of the rocks at the other side.

Then there was an ominous creaking underpaw.

Quiet Rain screeched, "Run!"

Gray Wing sprang forward, hurling himself at the opposite bank. Behind him he heard the ice give way and fall into the river; spray boiled up from the thunderous water, blotting out the firm ground ahead. His forepaws landed on rock just as the ice finally shattered and he felt freezing water surge around his hindquarters. Scrabbling frantically, he dragged himself to safety and whirled, peering through the spray for Quiet Rain on the opposite bank. But the mist had risen between them and he couldn't see her.

"I'm alive!" he yowled as loudly as he could.

For a few heartbeats he ran up and down the bank, trying to get a clear view of his mother, but the water was too fierce, the spray too thick, and every moment he risked losing his balance on the slippery rocks and plunging into the torrent.

"Good-bye!" he yowled again, hoping that Quiet Rain could hear him. He could hardly bear the thought that she might believe he was dead too. "I won't forget you, or the mountains!"

Turning away from the river, Gray Wing tried to work out where he should go next. The sun was only a pale disc behind the clouds, hardly enough to guide him. *I'll just have to hope that Jagged Peak came this way too*, he thought.

By sunhigh, Gray Wing needed to rest. His paws ached. "I've never traveled so far in my life," he muttered as he looked for a sheltered spot. *And maybe that's the problem*, he thought. *We've always hunted close to home. We might have found more prey if we'd spread our search a bit wider. Not that I've seen much prey out here . . .*

The breeze stiffened and became an icy wind, swirling up loose snow. Gray Wing dived thankfully into shelter under a split rock. Familiar scents wrapped around him as he flopped down.

The other cats were here!

But he couldn't detect Jagged Peak's scent among the others. *It should be stronger and fresher than the rest, but I can't pick it up at all.*

He cast his mind back to the iced-over river. *Jagged Peak had no experience of walking on ice. Maybe he was too afraid to try.*

Gray Wing wondered if Jagged Peak had headed into the valley instead, trying to find a safer place to cross.

Determination to find his brother flooded through him. He forced his way into the wind again. There was no fresh snow falling, only sharp flakes tossed up by the gale.

His fur flattened to his sides, Gray Wing blinked as he peered down into the valley, then up the trail where the other cats had gone. He knew they might be close. . . .

I can't go on up the trail without looking for Jagged Peak first.

Gray Wing plunged down the slope as fast as he could, bounding from boulder to boulder. In his haste he landed clumsily and slipped, letting out a hiss of pain as skin scraped off one of his pads. Agony shot up his leg, but after a few limping paw steps the cold numbed his injury.

To his relief, the wind dropped as he reached the valley. A broad stretch of ground lay in front of him, riddled with deep-set streams and scattered with boulders. A few stunted trees and bushes poked up through the snow. Feeling hunger gnawing at his belly, Gray Wing stayed alert for signs of prey, as well as traces of Jagged Peak's scent. But he found nothing of either. All he could see was the body of an old snow hare lying under a bush.

Disgusting! His nose wrinkled as he sniffed at it. *A cat eats fresh prey, not buzzardfood.* But with nothing else to quiet his growling belly, he forced himself to bite into the frozen flesh.

When he could force down no more, his belly feeling chilled and uncomfortable, Gray Wing studied the valley. Looking back in the direction he had come, he could see the river crashing down the mountainside, and wondered if Jagged Peak could be behind him now. His little brother might have taken a long time to work his way down among the rocks at the river's edge.

Gray Wing began to head up the valley, but it was slow going because he had to wind around so many boulders. Limping and frustrated, he glanced around to find the biggest one and scrambled on top of it.

From his vantage point he could scan the valley in both directions. There was no sign of Jagged Peak between him and the river, but his brother was small enough to be hidden amongst the boulders.

Turning to look along the valley in the direction the traveling cats would have headed, Gray Wing saw that it was empty too, except for a flicker of movement above as an eagle swooped from a crag. His gaze tracked its flight closely, trying to spot where its prey was hiding. *If it misses, I might be able to catch the prey later*, he thought.

The eagle flung itself down and Gray Wing heard its screech of fury as it came up again empty-clawed. Beneath the screech, Gray Wing thought he could make out a faint yowl.

His heart slammed into his throat. *Jagged Peak?*

Gray Wing leaped from the boulder, ignoring his injured pad as the wound broke open, and raced toward the eagle, which had begun another dive. As he drew closer he saw that the bird was young, with soft feathers around its face and legs.

Good! That means it'll be easier to deal with.

As he scrambled desperately among the rocks, Gray Wing could hear the panic-stricken caterwauling more clearly.

"Leave me alone! Help!"

"I'm coming!" Gray Wing yowled in reply. "Hold on!"

The eagle had alighted on a rock, and was reaching down with one claw, trying to grab Jagged Peak from a narrow crevice below. Gray Wing could just make out the tips of his brother's ears, and realized that he was trapped in the tiny space.

I'll have to distract the eagle so that Jagged Peak can escape.

Gray Wing sprang forward and crouched in front of the

bird, his lips drawn back. The eagle flapped awkwardly around to fix its beady yellow eyes on him. It lunged, squawking. Gray Wing tried to dodge aside, but his injured paw made him stumble. With a stab of panic he felt the bird's talons fasten in the loose fur at his neck. He thrashed to free himself and fell back among the rocks, but before he could struggle to his paws the eagle beat its mighty wings and grabbed hold of him again.

"Gray Wing! I'm coming!"

Gray Wing heard his brother's shriek and caught a glimpse of Jagged Peak scrambling out of the crack, fearlessly launching himself at the eagle.

The bird flapped madly against the weight of two cats, and Gray Wing felt himself lifted from the ground. The pain in his neck was shooting through all his body and a red mist covered his eyes. He struggled to stay conscious. Then he felt the eagle let go with one talon to grab at Jagged Peak.

Hah! he thought. *Mistake, greedy-belly!*

He managed to twist around and batter at the eagle's underbelly with his hind legs. With a screech the bird released him and he plunged downward to hit the rocks with a bone-jarring crash.

Looking up, Gray Wing saw Jagged Peak hanging on to the eagle's wing with his claws. "Jagged Peak! Let go!" he yowled.

Jagged Peak glanced at the ground, then unhooked his claws and fell back onto the stones. The eagle swooped toward them again with another furious screech; with a heartbeat to spare, Gray Wing shoved Jagged Peak into the space between two rocks. They cowered there in the tiny gap while the eagle shrieked overhead.

Jagged Peak was trembling from pain and fear, looking like nothing more than a kit. Gray Wing curled his body around him and soothed him with long, slow licks.

"It's okay," he murmured. "You're safe now. I've found you."

CHAPTER 6

At last the screeching died away and Gray Wing dared to stick his head out of the crack. The sky was clear; the eagle was nowhere to be seen. "Okay, we can leave," he mewed to Jagged Peak.

Jagged Peak looked up at him with worried eyes. "What if the eagle's waiting for us?"

"It's not. It's gone."

Gray Wing squeezed into the open and after a moment's hesitation Jagged Peak followed. He stood quietly, still shaking a little, while his brother checked him over, nosing carefully down one side and then the other.

"You have a few scratches," Gray Wing announced at last, with a quiver of relief that it was no worse. "But you'll be fine." Anger surged up to replace his anxiety. "What were you thinking, leaving the cave like that, you little fuzz-brain?"

Recovering rapidly from his fear, Jagged Peak faced him defiantly. "I wanted to go with the others! Quiet Rain had no right to stop me!"

"She's your mother," Gray Wing meowed. "She knows what's best for you."

His eyes narrowing, Jagged Peak retreated a pace. "You

haven't come to take me back, have you?" he asked. "Because I'm not going. I'll fight you if I have to!"

Gray Wing had to suppress an amused *mrrow* at the sight of his little brother, tail lashing and claws out. "Calm down," he sighed. "I won't make you go home. We're going to find the others."

Jagged Peak's eyes widened in surprise. "But you wanted to stay!" he objected.

"You need me more than they do."

Jagged Peak's shoulder fur fluffed up with renewed indignation. "I'm fine on my own!" he declared.

"You nearly got carried off by an eagle," Gray Wing pointed out.

Jagged Peak waved his tail dismissively. "Well, I found the way down into the valley without falling."

Gray Wing realized that there was no point in arguing. "We still have a long way to go before we're clear of the mountains," he continued. "Things could get even more dangerous."

"We'll be okay," Jagged Peak asserted. "We have each other now! And did you see how I fought off that eagle? You'd have been chickfeed if it wasn't for me!"

The little cat set off again, bounding over the boulders. Gray Wing followed more slowly; the pain from his neck and torn paw pad stabbing him like sharp thorns. The sun had vanished behind the mountains, and dusk was gathering around them.

"We need to look for somewhere to shelter!" he called to Jagged Peak.

His brother halted and turned to look back at him. "I want to keep going," he mewed obstinately. "The others will be so far ahead by now!"

"It's too dangerous to travel in the dark," Gray Wing insisted. "There are still places to fall, even though we're in the bottom of the valley. Tomorrow we'll follow the ledge up there," he added, pointing with his ears.

Jagged Peak looked as if he was about to argue, then gave in and dipped his head. Gray Wing led the way to a sheltered spot in a hollow between the roots of a scrubby tree. As he was scraping out some of the gritty earth to make the den bigger, he heard Jagged Peak's belly growl.

"Are you hungry? Do you want to hunt?" he asked.

Jagged Peak shook his head. "I'll be fine until morning," he mewed bravely.

Gray Wing had given up expecting Jagged Peak to apologize for running away, but as they settled down in the hollow the young cat nestled into his fur. "I'm glad you're here," Jagged Peak murmured drowsily.

I guess that's good enough, Gray Wing thought.

Gray Wing woke to a cold, gray morning. Through the branches above his head he could see the sky was heavy with clouds, threatening more snow. Jagged Peak was curled into a tight ball with his tail wrapped over his nose, deeply asleep. The journey must be even more exhausting for such a small cat. Listening to his brother's snuffling breath, Gray Wing had to admit how brave Jagged Peak had been to leave the cave on his own, and to attack the eagle.

If he's this determined to find our new home, then I'll make sure he gets there.

Soon Jagged Peak stirred and lifted his head, blinking sleepily. "Where's Mother?" he asked with a yawn. "Has she gone out hunting?"

"You're not in the cave anymore," Gray Wing reminded him. "You stay here and wake up properly, while I go and see if I can find some prey."

Clambering out of the hollow he padded up the valley. Soon he spotted a mouse scuffling around in the debris under a thornbush. *At last, some good luck*, he thought, springing to kill it.

When he returned to their makeshift sleeping hollow, he found Jagged Peak sitting on a tree root, grooming himself. The little cat's eyes brightened as he saw the limp body dangling from his brother's jaws.

"You got something!" he exclaimed.

"Yes, and it's all for you," Gray Wing meowed, ignoring his own grumbling belly as he dropped the prey in front of his brother. "You need to keep your strength up."

Jagged Peak didn't need to be told twice. "Thanks!" he mumbled, gulping the prey down in famished bites. His blue eyes sparkled as he swallowed the last mouthful and swiped his tongue around his jaws. "Today's going to be great!" he exclaimed. "The others will be so surprised when we catch them!"

Gray Wing murmured agreement as he studied their

surroundings, looking for the best route up to the rocky shelf. The clouds seemed thicker than ever, and the air smelled of snow. *We need to get up as high as we can, and quickly*, he thought. *It's going to snow again, and we might get stuck in drifts*.

There was no obvious track. Gray Wing decided it was best to make straight for the ledge. "This way," he meowed, waving his tail for Jagged Peak to follow him.

Once they set out, he found the ground wasn't as clear as he had hoped. They had to climb over boulders, and once they came to a wide stream chattering over stones. The edges were frozen, but there was a clear channel in the middle. Gray Wing leaped over it, and turned to face Jagged Peak.

"Jump as far as you can," he advised. "I'm here, ready to grab you."

With a determined expression on his face, Jagged Peak backed away several paw steps, then bounded up to the bank of the stream and launched himself, letting out a squeal as he soared upward with his paws splayed out. He landed on the ice at the far side; Gray Wing heard it start to crack, and grabbed Jagged Peak by the scruff just before he fell into the swiftly running water.

"Thanks!" Jagged Peak gasped as he straightened up. "Hey," he added, "that was a good leap, wasn't it?"

"It was fantastic," Gray Wing assured him.

A little farther on, the ground began to rise steeply. Eventually they came to a halt in front of a sheer wall of rock that stretched as far as they could see in both directions.

Jagged Peak gazed upward in dismay. "Now what do we do?"

Gray Wing studied the rock face carefully, realizing that it wasn't as sheer as he had first thought. There were ledges, even if they were only as wide as a claw-scratch, and crevices where clumps of grass had rooted themselves.

"I think we can climb it," he mewed.

Jagged Peak's eyes widened. "Are you fuzz-brained? I'm not climbing *that*!"

Gray Wing shrugged. "Okay, we go home."

Jagged Peak hesitated for a moment; then, without another word, leaped onto the rock face, and started clawing his way upward. Gray Wing watched, ready to break his fall. Grit and scraps of grass showered down on Gray Wing's head, but at last Jagged Peak reached the top.

Gray Wing began to climb, digging his claws into the cracks and scrabbling strongly with his hind paws. He winced as sharp pain stabbed up his leg from his injured paw. There was one heart-stopping moment when he slipped, but he forced himself upward with all the strength in his legs until he stood beside Jagged Peak on the slope above the cliff.

From here, Gray Wing could see a clear track zigzagging in the direction of the ledge they were making for. "Come on," he meowed as he headed off, setting a brisk pace.

He assumed that Jagged Peak was following him until he heard a plaintive, "Hey, Gray Wing!" from some way behind. He looked back to see his brother plodding to catch up.

"We haven't got all day for you to dawdle," he commented.

"I'm *not* dawdling!" Jagged Peak protested indignantly. "My legs are shorter than yours."

Gray Wing realized that his brother was right: Not only

did Jagged Peak have shorter legs, but his muscles were soft from living in the cave all his life. "Okay, I'll slow down," he sighed, picturing the other cats drawing farther and farther ahead.

Trying to match his brother's pace, Gray Wing felt impatience rising inside him. When they reached a large rock blocking the track, he grabbed Jagged Peak unceremoniously by the scruff and hauled him over the obstacle.

Jagged Peak twitched his whiskers as Gray Wing set him down. "I *could* have gotten over that by myself!"

We wouldn't have to do this at all if it wasn't for you! Gray Wing bit back the words he wanted to say.

Jagged Peak stalked up the track, his tail high in the air. As he followed, Gray Wing noticed that the first flakes of snow were beginning to fall. He quickened his pace until he was padding beside Jagged Peak again.

"We must find shelter," he meowed. "Let's try that boulder up there."

The place he pointed out was only a few tail-lengths away, but by the time he and Jagged Peak reached it the snow was already falling heavily, and the wind was blustering around the rocks, making Gray Wing afraid that his lighter brother would be blown off his paws.

He shoved Jagged Peak into the narrow gap between the boulder and the mountainside, and scrambled in after him tail-first. Gazing out of the cleft, he saw that everything had been blotted out by a screen of driving snow.

"We're never going to find the others," Jagged Peak

muttered fearfully, peering out over his brother's shoulder. "We might even freeze to death!"

"We won't," Gray Wing assured him, his irritation vanishing. "And the others won't get too far ahead in this weather."

He hoped he was right.

Jagged Peak curled up and closed his eyes; shortly afterward, his light snores told Gray Wing that he was asleep. Gray Wing finally dozed off, dreaming he was pursuing the other cats over endless mountain peaks, sometimes picking up a scent-trace but never managing to catch them. He jerked awake when Jagged Peak prodded him in the side.

"Look!" his brother exclaimed. "The snow has stopped!"

Gray Wing blinked in the dazzling light. The sky had cleared and the sun shone down on the fresh, untouched expanse of white. His eyes widened in dismay as he realized that the blizzard had completely transformed the landscape. The track they had been following was covered, and so was the ledge they had been headed for.

While he was still trying to work out their route, Jagged Peak pushed past him and bounded enthusiastically into the snow. The surface gave way beneath him and he was floundering in a drift, letting out squeaks of alarm.

Gray Wing approached him cautiously, managing to find firm ground under the white covering, and stretched out his neck to grab Jagged Peak by the scruff.

"Next time, don't go dashing off," he warned, as he set his brother down beside him. The kit shook himself vigorously so that melting snow spattered over Gray Wing, who shivered.

"Listen, Jagged Peak, you need to watch where you're putting your paws. If you look carefully, you can see the shapes of rocks under the snow—that's how you'll know it's safe to walk there. And if you can't *see* any rocks, then test the snow as deep as you can with one paw before you put your weight on it."

"I understand," Jagged Peak meowed.

The next stage of their climb was slow and exhausting. Gray Wing thought he could remember where the ledge should be, and led the way toward it, testing each paw step and struggling to find a safe route around boulders that lay in their way.

Eventually the boulders thinned out and a flat stretch of snow lay in front of the two cats. He tested the first few paw steps and discovered hard earth a little way down. *At last*, Gray Wing thought, *somewhere easy to run across!*

He launched himself onto the white expanse, relishing the chance to stretch his muscles and the feeling of the wind rushing through his pelt. "Come on, keep up!" he called behind to Jagged Peak.

Without warning the snowy surface gave way beneath Gray Wing's paws. He let out a screech as he plunged into icy water. Paddling furiously, managing to keep his head clear, he tried to climb out, but the snow around him was deep and slushy, and broke away when he tried to put his weight on it.

Gray Wing had fallen into a stream, which was carrying him slowly down the mountainside. Fighting to stay afloat, he looked around for Jagged Peak. The little cat was running along the bank, his eyes wide with panic.

"What can I do?" he wailed.

Gray Wing looked around, trying to stay calm as his legs weakened. Bitter claws of cold gripped him. A little farther down the mountain he spotted a branch sticking out of the snow, and guessed it had been carried there when the stream was in flood.

"See that branch?" he called. "Push one end of it toward me."

Jagged Peak bounded ahead and began struggling to drag the branch out of the snow. Gray Wing waited as he was carried down toward it. He was so cold now that he couldn't feel his legs, and his soaked pelt dragged at him.

If this doesn't work, I'm buzzardfood.

"That's right," he meowed as Jagged Peak freed the branch. "Now push it across the stream. Keep it anchored, though."

Slowly Jagged Peak dragged the branch until it stuck out across the stream. He crouched down on the other end, using all his weight to hold it still, his claws dug firmly into it.

Gray Wing felt a stab of terror as the current surge carried him to the branch, and almost dragged him past it. Forcing his aching limbs to move, he stretched to grab the end with his teeth.

Jagged Peak backed away from the edge of the stream, tugging determinedly at the branch. In the midst of his fear Gray Wing felt a flash of admiration for his brother's sturdy strength and courage. The little cat went on struggling, pulling Gray Wing out of the slush; Gray Wing paddled desperately with his legs until he felt firm ground underneath him.

Once he was sure he was safe, Gray Wing collapsed, drenched and freezing. For a moment he couldn't move. Then through a fog of fatigue he realized that Jagged Peak was licking him with strong tongue-strokes, just as Quiet Rain had done when they were kits. He felt his brother stretching to curl himself around his body. With a long sigh Gray Wing relaxed, feeling Jagged Peak's rough, comforting tongue until his fur dried and warmth crept through his body.

At last Gray Wing felt revived enough to sit up.

"I thought you were going to die," Jagged Peak mewed, his eyes wide and scared.

"I'm fine," Gray Wing responded. "Thanks to you."

Embarrassment crawled through his pelt at the thought that he had to be rescued. *I can't believe I ran across that open space, after all I said to Jagged Peak!*

Not wanting to go near the snowbound stream again, Gray Wing headed directly upward, testing the snow cautiously with every paw step to make sure that they stayed on the bank.

"Look!"

Jagged Peak's scared voice came from just behind. Turning, Gray Wing saw that another eagle was hovering lazily overhead. And there was nowhere to hide. The snow-covered slope was smooth, without even a boulder poking above its surface.

Gray Wing glanced upward again. The eagle didn't seem to have spotted them yet, but it wouldn't be long before its piercing gaze picked them out.

"I know!" he gasped, shivering with relief as an idea came to him. "We'll dig scoops in the snow and bury ourselves."

The eagle had flown higher up the mountain, skimming

the surface as it cast about for prey with its beady gaze. Knowing they only had heartbeats to hide themselves, Gray Wing dug furiously at the snow and shoved Jagged Peak inside.

"I'll suffocate!" Jagged Peak protested as Gray Wing scooped snow on top of him.

"You *won't*. Now shut up and keep still."

With no time to dig another hole for himself, Gray Wing crouched down and burrowed into the drift until he felt as if he was fully covered. Claws of cold pierced his pelt; he had to clench his teeth to stop them from chattering in case the eagle heard. His ears were muffled with snow, but he could see the shadow of the bird swoop over them.

Nothing for you here, he thought, holding his breath. *Just keep going....*

The shadow slid away over the white surface until Gray Wing couldn't see it anymore. He waited for as long as he could bear before bursting out of his hole. His bones felt like sticks of ice as he scanned the sky, letting out a sigh of relief when he saw it was clear.

Still checking for movement above his head, Gray Wing turned to where he had buried his brother and began scraping snow away.

Jagged Peak scrambled out, shaking clots of snow from his pelt. "Is it gone?"

"For now. Come on—we should run to warm ourselves, and find a better place in case the eagle comes back."

On numb, stumbling legs the two cats staggered up the slope. At first, all Gray Wing could think about was finding somewhere to hide, and when at last he paused to look around, he realized that they had climbed much higher than the ledge they had been headed toward. The jagged rocks of the ridge were only a few tail-lengths away.

"I'm sorry," he panted to Jagged Peak. "We've come too far."

Jagged Peak looked up at the ridge, his eyes bright with excitement. "We might as well keep going to the top," he mewed. "I've never been so high!"

Gray Wing let out a faint purr, understanding the little cat's excitement. "Okay, let's do it," he agreed.

Wind buffeting their fur, the two cats hauled themselves up sheer rock and onto a tiny pinnacle, with barely enough space for them to stand side by side.

"Wow!" Jagged Peak breathed out. He gazed round-eyed at summit after summit rolling away on all sides. "I never knew there were so many mountains! I didn't know the *world* was as big as this!" Stretching up, he added, "Can we see the waterfall from here?"

"No," Gray Wing replied. "We've come too far. I think it must be hidden behind that crag over there." He pointed with one paw.

Turning in the other direction, toward the sunrise, Gray Wing felt a tingle of excitement in his fur. *Somewhere out there is our new home, just like Stoneteller promised. And we're going to find it!*

Jagged Peak let out a sudden squeal, startling Gray Wing so much that he almost lost his balance on the pinnacle. "What?" he demanded. "Another eagle?"

"No! I can see the others!"

Gray Wing squinted at where Jagged Peak was pointing, and made out a line of tiny shapes on the side of the valley, a long way ahead.

"Come on!" Jagged Peak was bouncing up and down precariously. "Let's go!"

"Calm down, before you fall," Gray Wing told him. "We have to plan our route carefully. It's too windy and exposed up here, so we'll need to head down, but forward as well, so we can catch up to them."

Side by side the two cats studied the terrain. To Gray Wing's relief there was more cover in the direction they needed to go.

"Why not head for that fallen tree?" Jagged Peak suggested, pointing with his tail at a tangle of dead branches poking up out of the snow.

"Okay," Gray Wing agreed, impressed that the young cat had such a good idea of the best route, with cover from dangerous birds. "But let me take the lead."

"Just as long as you don't fall in any hidden streams," Jagged Peak meowed, his eyes sparkling.

This time they made better progress, hopping over boulders and treading carefully where the snow concealed slopes of loose scree.

Before they had gone very far, Jagged Peak halted. "I smell prey!" he announced.

Gray Wing glanced at him in surprise, sure at first that his brother must be wrong. He couldn't see anything but, after a moment, he picked up a very faint scent trail. "Wow, you're good at this," he told Jagged Peak. "You'd better track it."

He admired how his brother instinctively dropped into the correct crouch, and his light steps as he followed the scent trail. Gray Wing watched as the younger cat crept closer to a small pile of stones. A small mountain shrew shot out of the heap; Jagged Peak pounced, piercing it with his sharp claws.

"I got it!" he exclaimed in astonishment, as if he couldn't believe his success. He bent down to take one bite and then pushed the rest of it over to Gray Wing.

"You caught it," Gray Wing protested. "You should eat it."

Jagged Peak shook his head firmly. "We share," he mewed. "That's the *proper* way to behave."

Gray Wing dug in, then swiped his tongue around his jaws to catch the last juices. "Thanks," he purred. "I feel so much better now."

The next stretch of their journey meant slithering down a tricky stretch of boulders, where small stones skidded from beneath their paws. Gray Wing was thankful to come to a halt on a narrow ledge that led in the direction they wanted to go.

Then as he drew in a breath he realized that a familiar scent was bathing his muzzle. Jagged Peak picked it up at the same moment. "This is the path the others took!" he exclaimed, sounding as thrilled as if they had caught up with their friends already.

"Don't get too excited," Gray Wing warned, though his own paws were tingling. "There's still a good way to go."

The sun was behind them, casting long shadows ahead as it sank behind the mountaintops.

"We need to stop and find shelter for the night," Gray Wing meowed.

"No," Jagged Peak objected. "I want to keep going. We might not be able to see, but I can follow the scent trail!" He closed his eyes tightly and padded along the ledge with his nose to the surface of the snow. Gray Wing darted to one side, ready to catch him in case he came too close to the edge, but the kit walked confidently, his tail held high.

"See?" Jagged Peak mewed at last, halting and opening his eyes again.

Gray Wing gave in to his desire to find the other cats. "Okay. But we have to stop if it starts feeling too risky."

Jagged Peak nodded eagerly, then set off in the lead.

The night was cloudy, and although the moon was still close to full it only shone fitfully. There were times when Gray Wing couldn't see his own whiskers. Jagged Peak headed along the ledge, slowly and carefully, seeming certain of where the scent trail was leading him. Gray Wing followed a paw step behind, until suddenly he bumped into his brother. "What's the matter?" he asked.

"I'm not sure," Jagged Peak responded.

In the dim light Gray Wing could just make out that Jagged Peak was casting around as if he had lost the scent. At last he straightened up. "The trail veers off here," he announced.

Gray Wing paused before replying, wondering if this was the point when they should stop and wait for daylight. But he knew Jagged Peak would argue. "Let's follow it, then," he mewed at last. "But be very careful."

Jagged Peak led the way a short distance up the mountain,

then began doubling back toward the ledge.

"What's going on?" Gray Wing asked, with a hiss of annoy-ance as he set his injured paw down on a sharp stone. "Why not just go straight along the ledge? It would be a lot easier."

"I don't know," said Jagged Peak as the stones gave way beneath his paws. He slid down, ending up on the ledge again. "But this is the way the other cats went."

Gray Wing could detect the scents too, although not with Jagged Peak's precision. Reaching his brother's side, he looked back, puzzled. At that moment a ray of moonlight pierced the cloud cover, revealing a yawning gap behind them where the path had completely slipped away.

"Look at that!" he exclaimed, feeling his legs shake at the thought of what might have happened. "If it wasn't for your tracking skills, we would have fallen!"

Jagged Peak's eyes shone with pride, and he headed along the trail even more confidently.

Soon the young cat's paw steps began to falter. Gray Wing's own legs ached, and his sore pad was troubling him again. Jagged Peak must have been exhausted.

"We've done enough," Gray Wing meowed. "We need to rest now. I'm sure we'll catch up with the others tomorrow."

Jagged Peak opened his jaws to argue, then sighed. "I *am* pretty tired," he confessed.

Together the two cats curled up at the side of the path beneath an overhanging rock. Jagged Peak fell asleep almost at once, his whiskers twitching as if he was still following the scent trail in his dreams.

Gray Wing dreamed that he was back in the cave, with

sheltering walls around him and the roof lost in shadows. The murmuring voices of other cats were all around him.

"It's time we were moving off again," Shaded Moss meowed.

"First, we should hunt," Clear Sky objected. "My belly thinks my throat's clawed out."

"Whatever, just wake up Moon Shadow first," Turtle Tail added.

More voices joined the debate. Gray Wing wondered vaguely why all the cats he could hear were the ones who had left the cave to follow the sun trail.

He opened his eyes to see the sun beginning to rise above the mountaintops, with wisps of cloud scattered across a pale blue sky. His jaws parted in a huge yawn and he stretched his stiff limbs, daunted by the thought of another day plodding through the snow.

Then he realized that he could still hear the voices from his dream. The mewing of several cats reached his ears—and then Clear Sky's voice, raised clearly: "Well, Shaded Moss, we're seeing the sun at last. It should be easier traveling today."

"Jagged Peak! Jagged Peak!" Gray Wing leaped to his paws, weariness forgotten, and prodded his little brother in the ribs. "The others are here!"

Jagged Peak stared at him for a moment, his blue eyes still confused by sleep, then bounced up to stand beside him. "What are we waiting for?"

With Gray Wing in the lead they raced along the ledge and around a corner, their paws skidding on the hard snow.

"I've found their scent!" Jagged Peak announced excitedly.

At the same moment Gray Wing spotted the traveling

cats a short way down the slope, milling around a hollow tree trunk. The first rays of the sun were just reaching them. More cats were emerging from inside the trunk, arching their backs for a good long stretch.

Then Bright Stream looked up and let out a yowl. "Look! It's Gray Wing and Jagged Peak!"

The rest of the cats followed her gaze, then bounded toward the newcomers.

"Gray Wing!" Turtle Tail was one of the first to reach them. "It's really you!"

"I can't believe this!" Clear Sky exclaimed, joy in his eyes, as all the cats crowded around the two newcomers. "I thought I'd never see you again."

"You did well coming all this way by yourselves," Tall Shadow added.

"But what are you doing here?" Shaded Moss asked.

The first astonished mews of welcome died away and Gray Wing saw some of the cats exchange flickering glances of anxiety.

"Is all well in the cave?" Bright Stream asked.

"Is Quiet Rain okay?" Clear Sky added.

"Every cat is fine," Gray Wing reassured them.

Jagged Peak stepped forward, puffing his chest out proudly. "I came to find you!" he announced. "I voted to leave, remember? Then Gray Wing came after me."

"Oh, so you just set off on your own?" Clear Sky meowed, giving his little brother a friendly shove. "Why am I not surprised? You took a huge risk, and you're very lucky that Gray Wing found you."

"I know," Jagged Peak admitted with a glance of gratitude. Then he let out a gleeful *mrrow* and added, "I had to rescue him, too!"

"That's true," Gray Wing mewed. He turned to Clear Sky. "And how are all of you?"

"We're fine," his brother replied. "The blizzard slowed us down, but we're pretty sure we're heading in the right direction."

"We climbed right up to the top," Gray Wing reported, gesturing with his tail. "From up there, we could see land beyond the mountains. It's still a long way off, but you'll see it once you've crossed this next ridge."

"That's great!" Clear Sky exclaimed, his eyes gleaming.

"We need to get moving as soon as we can," Shaded Moss meowed, glancing around and gathering the rest of the cats around him with a wave of his tail.

"Just as soon as we've eaten," Moon Shadow put in.

As he spoke, Gray Wing spotted Quick Water and Jackdaw's Cry toiling up the slope, dragging a snow hare between them.

"Great catch." Shaded Moss praised them as they reached the group and let their prey drop, blinking in surprise when they spotted Gray Wing and Jagged Peak.

All the cats gathered around to share the prey. Turtle Tail sat beside Gray Wing, pressing herself close to him. "I'm so glad you changed your mind," she murmured.

Gray Wing looked around at the other cats, sensing their excitement. "I'm glad too," he mewed.

CHAPTER 7

As the cats were finishing their meal and beginning to groom them-selves, Shaded Moss came to stand beside Gray Wing and Jagged Peak. "How is Stoneteller?" Blinking with a trace of anxiety in his eyes, he added, "It seems as if we've been away from the cave for moons already."

"She's okay," Gray Wing replied. "But she's desperately worried about all you cats who have left; she's afraid she made the wrong decision."

"*We* were the ones who decided," Shaded Moss pointed out. "Each cat who came on the journey. Stoneteller just pointed out the opportunity."

Try telling Stoneteller that, Gray Wing thought wryly.

The cats gathered for the day's traveling. Shaded Moss was clearly in command, though Gray Wing noticed that Clear Sky didn't hesitate to offer his opinions.

"Why don't we head for that tree?" he suggested, flicking his tail. "Then we could cross the stream to avoid that stretch of rock."

Shaded Moss nodded. "Good idea."

The cats set out; Shaded Moss took the lead, with Clear

Sky and Bright Stream close behind him. Jagged Peak trotted hard on Clear Sky's paws, clearly proud of the adventures that had led him here. The youngest cats, apart from Jagged Peak, were Hawk Swoop, Falling Feather, and her brother Jackdaw's Cry. Because they weren't fully grown they had trouble scrambling over the larger boulders. Shaded Moss's daughter, Rainswept Flower, and Shattered Ice walked beside them, offering help where they needed it.

Farther back in the line, Quick Water and Cloud Spots padded along together, reserved but alert. Just behind them, Dappled Pelt and Moon Shadow walked side by side. "Did you see how I frightened off that eagle yesterday?" Moon Shadow asked boastfully. "It would have carried off Jackdaw's Cry if I hadn't been there."

Dappled Pelt rolled her eyes. "Yeah, you and the rest of us," she muttered, only just loudly enough for Gray Wing to hear.

Leaving the cave hasn't changed Moon Shadow, Gray Wing thought. *He's still annoying.*

Moon Shadow's sister Tall Shadow, loping along in his paw steps, made no comment about his boasting. Gray Wing remembered that even back in the cave she hardly ever spoke; but when she did, she was always worth listening to.

How could one litter produce one intelligent cat and one fuzz-brain?

As the cats followed Shaded Moss they gradually fell into a line, two by two. Gray Wing glanced aside to see that Turtle Tail had caught up with him.

"May I walk with you?" she mewed gently.

"Sure," Gray Wing responded.

"I like being in the rear," Turtle Tail confided as they padded on. "I like seeing that my denmates are all safe in front of me."

Gray Wing purred understandingly. His heart lifted as they climbed along the side of the valley, the sun warming their fur.

"It's definitely hotter than it was a moon ago," Turtle Tail remarked. "The cold season is really coming to an end."

Soon, the cats came to a pool where a stream spread out before plunging farther down the mountain. The ice that covered the surface had begun to melt in the strong sunlight. There was enough space for every cat to gather around the edge, to drink and bathe their sore pads.

Gray Wing settled beside Dappled Pelt, stretched out his neck and lapped at the icy water. It tasted of stone and mountain air. "I'm so glad we found you," he remarked. "I was worried about Jagged Peak."

"Yes, he's really too small for this," the tortoiseshell cat responded. "But he's doing very well. And when—"

Dappled Pelt broke off, swiftly dipping one paw into the water and flicking a plump silver fish onto the rock beside her. It flapped and wriggled in the air until she killed it with a swipe of her claw.

"Where did you learn to do that?" Gray Wing asked, as the other cats clustered around with exclamations of surprise.

Dappled Pelt shrugged. "I used to catch fish sometimes in the pool below the waterfall, before the cold season came," she explained, bending her head to take one bite from the fish before pushing it toward her companions. "Here, try it."

One by one the rest of the cats came up to take a bite. Gray Wing wasn't sure that he liked it, preferring the earthy taste of hare, but Falling Feather gulped down her mouthful with relish.

"Will you teach me how to do that?" she asked Dappled Pelt.

The she-cat's golden eyes gleamed as she gazed at Falling Feather. "Of course. When we get where we're going."

"I'm not sure about this." Jackdaw's Cry licked his lips as if he didn't like the taste. "No offense, Dappled Pelt, but I think I'll stick to hares and eagles."

"Hey, it's food!" Moon Shadow mewed cheerfully, eyeing the remains of the fish as if he hoped he would get a second bite.

"I think it's great!" Bright Stream purred, and Rainswept Flower nodded agreement.

"I guess you'll want to eat more fish when we find our new home," Bright Stream continued, her tone gently teasing as Clear Sky ate his share.

"Hmm . . ." Clear Sky looked doubtful, then brushed his mate's pelt with his tail. "Maybe I'll have to give in if our kits have a taste for it." He and Bright Stream exchanged a glowing glance.

Gray Wing gave his brother a prod. "Is Bright Stream expecting kits?" he whispered.

Clear Sky nodded, blinking happily. "She thinks so. I know the timing's not ideal, right at the beginning of our journey, but . . . I can't wait to be a father."

"Bright Stream will be a wonderful mother," Gray Wing mewed, ignoring the stab of envy he felt.

When all the cats had eaten their share, they gave in to the temptation to lie on the rocks around the pool, enjoying the warm sunlight.

"Hey, Turtle Tail!" Quick Water pointed to a turtle basking in a sunbeam at the opposite side of the pool. "You've found your natural home here!"

Good-humoredly Turtle Tail flicked the gray-and-white she-cat with her paw. "So is your home anywhere it's *raining*, Quick Water?"

Meanwhile, Clear Sky was watching the small birds that circled overhead. "Do you want me to see if I can catch any of those?" he asked Shaded Moss.

Shaded Moss glanced along the trail in the direction they needed to go, then shook his head. "We haven't traveled far enough yet."

"What's the rush?" Moon Shadow complained. "This new home, wherever it is, won't disappear, will it?"

"That's right," Jackdaw's Cry agreed. "We've been walking for ages!"

Other cats murmured in agreement.

"You lazy bunch!" Turtle Tail exclaimed. "We've only been traveling for four sunrises. We haven't even left the mountains yet." Her neck fur fluffed up with indignation. "No cat said it would be easy."

Before any cat could argue, Tall Shadow rose to her paws

and pointed with her tail to a distant clump of pine trees on the side of the mountain. "Let's aim for those by tonight," she suggested.

"Good idea," Dappled Pelt agreed.

To Gray Wing's relief, the threatened discord vanished like frost in sunlight as the cats rose to their paws, ready to set out again. As they moved off, he fell in beside Bright Stream. "Clear Sky tells me you're having kits," he mewed. "That's great!"

Bright Stream glanced at her paws in embarrassment. "I don't want any cat to know yet," she murmured. "I don't want the others to think I'm going to slow them down."

"No cat will think that," Gray Wing reassured her. "And your kits will be a great start for our new home, wherever we end up."

Sunhigh had just passed when Shaded Moss drew to a halt; the other cats bunched up behind him. Gray Wing saw that the ledge they had been following had petered out. A wide slope of slippery scree lay in front of them, leading to a sheer drop into a valley far below.

"I don't like the look of that," Hawk Swoop muttered.

"Me neither," Jackdaw's Cry added. "Do we have to go this way?"

"Yes, we do," Shaded Moss stated firmly, before any cat could start arguing. "We'll take it slowly, in pairs. The younger, less experienced cats can walk on the inside."

"Can I go with you, Clear Sky?" Jagged Peak asked, wriggling forward until he stood at the edge of the scree.

Gray Wing admired his little brother's courage. Guessing where he could be of most help, he padded over to Jackdaw's Cry. "You can come with me if you like," he mewed.

Jackdaw's Cry gave him a grateful glance. "Thanks." His whiskers twitched nervously, but his voice was steady as he added, "I keep worrying about the drop into the valley. It's a long way down."

"Then don't look down," Gray Wing advised. "Stay close to me, and make sure there's something solid under your paws before you put your weight on them."

Jackdaw's Cry listened seriously to what Gray Wing told him. "What about using my tail for balance?" he asked.

"Good idea. Keep your gaze fixed on the far side, and whatever you do, don't panic," Gray Wing added.

Jackdaw's Cry nodded. "I'm ready now."

Shaded Moss had already started off across the scree, heading slowly and steadily for the mountainside beyond, where boulders and scrubby thorns broke up the slope. Clear Sky set out after him, with Jagged Peak at his side.

Bright Stream and Falling Feather followed, with Bright Stream taking the outer position, nearer the cliff edge. Glancing back, Clear Sky looked uncertain for a moment, as if he wanted to go back and help his mate.

"I'll be fine!" Bright Stream called out to him. "Watch where you're putting your own paws."

Gray Wing exchanged a glance with Jackdaw's Cry, and ventured out onto the scree with the young black tom at his side. Even though he didn't look, he was aware of the sheer drop into the valley, only a couple of tail-lengths away. His paws slipped as he dislodged some of the smooth, flat stones and sent them skittering over the edge. For a heartbeat he thought he was going to follow them, but he managed to regain his balance.

"Are you okay?" Jackdaw's Cry asked, his eyes wide and his ears flattened.

"Fine," Gray Wing replied tersely. "Just keep going."

Glancing over to the far side, he saw that Shaded Moss had already reached safety, and Clear Sky was nudging Jagged Peak up onto a flat, snow-covered stone before clambering off the scree and sitting down beside him.

"Come on!" Jagged Peak called encouragingly in his shrill voice. "It's not too hard!"

Bright Stream and Falling Feather reached them a few heartbeats later. Gray Wing began to relax a little, seeing the solid ground was only a few paw steps away. He risked a glance over his shoulder and saw the long line of cats behind him, moving steadily.

I think we'll be okay.

A sudden screech split the quiet air. "Eagles! Eagles!"

Jagged Peak was leaping up and down on the flat rock, his tail waving at the sky. Gray Wing looked up to see two huge birds swooping down toward the cats exposed on the scree.

Yowls of panic rose up and the cats began to run, loose stone sliding beneath their paws as the well-organized line broke up. A horrible vision flashed through Gray Wing's mind of cats plummeting helplessly into the valley, or shrieking as they were carried away in the eagles' talons.

Jackdaw's Cry had frozen in terror a tail-length from safety. Gray Wing grabbed him by the scruff and hurled him off the scree toward Clear Sky and Shaded Moss. Then he whipped around and headed back toward his Tribemates.

His paws slipping as he tried to hurry, Gray Wing noticed that Dappled Pelt had lost her footing completely and was sliding helplessly down the slope. She let out a panic-stricken yowl as she struggled to find a firm paw hold.

"I'm coming!" Gray Wing called.

He ran between Dappled Pelt and the line of his Tribemates, dodging the rain of loose stones that pattered around him, dislodged by the other cats' paws. Reaching a place above the she-cat where the stones weren't moving, he cut back down toward her, aiming for a spot just below her where he could halt her fall.

Dappled Pelt stared at him, her eyes stretched wide with fear and her tail waving as she scrabbled vainly at the scree.

Reaching the spot, Gray Wing dug his paws firmly between the stones to find a firm purchase, and braced himself to take Dappled Pelt's weight. When she slithered into him he panicked for a moment as he felt the ground shift under his paws, but he managed to hold her.

Still frantic, Dappled Pelt tried to claw back up the way she had come, but there was nothing solid for her to grip.

"Keep still!" Gray Wing gasped. His belly lurched with fear as he saw the eagles swooping lower, their claws extended and their wing tips brushing the heads of the cats. Most of the others had reached safety, but Hawk Swoop and Rainswept Flower had fallen behind, and Gray Wing couldn't make any progress with Dappled Pelt.

We're chickfeed, for sure!

As Dappled Pelt kept on struggling, Moon Shadow came bounding down the slope just ahead of them. "Come on . . . this way," he meowed to Dappled Pelt, bracing his shoulder against her.

Dappled Pelt stumbled forward, heading paw step by paw step toward the end of the scree, with Moon Shadow taking part of her weight. Gray Wing followed, scrabbling to keep his paw hold.

When they reached solid ground, Moon Shadow boosted Dappled Pelt ahead of him, then clambered up beside her. Gray Wing raced after them as they dived underneath an overhanging rock where the rest of the cats were hiding. Rainswept Flower and Hawk Swoop joined them a heartbeat later, just managing to dodge an eagle's outstretched claws.

"Is every cat okay?" Shaded Moss asked, gazing around at the group as they cowered under the rock.

"We're fine," Clear Sky replied.

"Just scared out of our fur," Turtle Tail added.

Dappled Pelt was crouching with her head down and fur still fluffed out. She was shaking. "I'm so sorry," she murmured. "I panicked back there, and I could have got you both killed."

"Don't worry about it." Moon Shadow puffed out his chest. "You'll know better next time."

Turtle Tail leaned over to whisper into Gray Wing's ear. "I'm quite impressed by how Moon Shadow saved Dappled Pelt. But I'd never tell him so!"

Gray Wing nodded, grateful for her humor. "He's brave, but he's still an annoying furball," he whispered back.

Quick Water, who had been keeping watch at the edge of the overhang, glanced over her shoulder. "Those eagles are out there," she reported. "They know we're here, and they seem prepared to wait all day."

Gray Wing remembered how helpless he had felt when the eagle was trying to lift him off his paws. "If it's the only way to stay safe, we'll have to put up with staying under this rock," he pointed out.

"For how long?" Hawk Swoop demanded. "I don't know about any other cat, but I need some prey!"

Indignant murmurs showed that some of the others agreed with her.

"We have to protect ourselves," Shaded Moss decided, with a nod to Gray Wing. "It's just a matter of waiting."

With a few more grumbles the cats settled down, licking pads sore from crossing the scree, or curling up to sleep. At first they seemed glad to rest, but as the day dragged on their anxiety began rising again.

Cloud Spots stuck his head out into the open, then jerked back into cover. "There are two more eagles out there," he reported, his eyes wide with dismay. "They're sitting on the top of this rock."

More screeches split the air and Gray Wing shivered. It

was as if the eagles were challenging the hidden cats. *They know exactly where we are.*

As daylight faded, the eagles showed no signs of leaving. Even worse, one of them hopped down and stretched its neck under the rocky overhang. His heart pounding with fear, Gray Wing shoved Turtle Tail behind him to keep her away from the snapping yellow beak. All the cats shrank back, pressing themselves against the rock wall in a shuddering heap of fur. The eagle watched them for a few heartbeats with malignant yellow eyes, then flapped out of sight, but every cat knew that all four eagles were still there.

"We're not mice!" Clear Sky announced when the eagle had withdrawn. "We will not be treated like prey! We need to show these eagles that *cats* are the hunters around here."

"And how are we going to do that?" Rainswept Flower demanded.

Clear Sky's glance raked the cowering group. "By catching one of the eagles ourselves," he meowed.

Gray Wing couldn't stifle a gasp of shock. Looking around, he saw the others exchanging scared glances.

"That's impossible," Shaded Moss stated, in a tone that didn't invite contradiction. "There are four eagles out there!"

Clear Sky was undaunted. "And there are more of us in here," he retorted.

Admiration for his brother's courage rose inside Gray Wing, bringing a trickle of hope like the first thawing of an icicle. "Let's at least hear what Clear Sky has to say," he urged the others.

Shaded Moss hesitated, then gave a curt nod.

"I believe that four cats could bring down one eagle," Clear Sky explained. "Me, Tall Shadow, Quick Water, and Jackdaw's Cry." Glancing at the cats he had named, he added, "We can all jump high, and together we have the strength to pull down a bird."

Gray Wing took a pace forward. "I want to help," he meowed.

"You will," Clear Sky responded. "You're the fastest among us. I want you to draw the other birds away. Take three cats with you."

Shaded Moss shouldered his way forward until he stood beside Clear Sky. There was quiet authority in his voice. "Tell me exactly what you think we should do."

Clear Sky scraped a few pebbles together with one paw and began to lay them out as he spoke. "Here are the four eagles. Gray Wing and his cats will get three eagles to follow them. My group will isolate the fourth and surround it."

The other cats had gathered around him, watching closely. Gray Wing tried to picture the plan in his head, and eventually nodded. "It could work," he agreed.

"Or we could just wait until dark and sneak away," Turtle Tail suggested.

Clear Sky turned on her in outrage. "And let the birds follow us tomorrow, and the next day, and the next? We have to take them on *now*, so that they leave us in peace."

"Clear Sky is right," Tall Shadow declared.

No other cat looked so certain, but they all gradually let out murmurs of agreement.

"Okay," Clear Sky mewed briskly. "We must move fast, because it'll be dark soon."

"Turtle Tail, Cloud Spots, and Bright Stream will go with Gray Wing to lure three of the birds away." Shaded Moss gave his orders calmly. "Leave the fourth eagle as close to the rock as you can, so that Clear Sky and his cats can spring out and catch it."

Clear Sky's whiskers twitched in alarm as his mate's name was mentioned. "I'm not sure Bright Stream is fast enough," he objected.

Shaded Moss flicked his ears in surprise. "She's almost as fast as Gray Wing."

Gazing at his brother, Gray Wing knew exactly why Clear Sky was reluctant for his mate to play such an important part in their plan. *He's worried about their kits.*

"I'll be fine," Bright Stream insisted, her tone full of hidden meaning. "Gray Wing will take care of me," she added, flicking Clear Sky playfully over the ear with her tail-tip.

"And what about the rest of us?" Jagged Peak asked, his tail twitching irritably. "I've attacked an eagle before, you know. I've got experience!"

"The rest of you will stay here under the overhang, ready to rush out and help wherever you're needed," Shaded Moss meowed. Solemnly he added to Jagged Peak, "You must be ready to pounce at any moment."

Jagged Peak nodded eagerly and crouched down at the edge of the overhang, ready to spring.

Gray Wing motioned to Turtle Tail, Bright Stream, and Cloud Spots with a flick of his ears, and they ventured out from beneath the overhang. The gathering darkness helped to conceal them as they crouched low among the rocks until they were some distance away.

"Now!" Gray Wing mewed.

Together they sprang into the open, caterwauling loudly to attract the attention of the eagles. All four birds were perched on the crags above them. A shudder went through Gray Wing from his ears to his pads as four heads swiveled toward him and his denmates.

Two of the eagles took off with cumbersome wing-beats to gain height—then they swooped.

"Cloud Spots! Turtle Tail!" Gray Wing yowled. "Run to the next boulder! Lure the birds toward you!"

The two cats took off, racing across the snow-covered slope, and the pair of eagles flapped after them. Gray Wing and Bright Stream huddled into the shelter of a boulder as the birds passed over their heads.

"I'll attract the others," Bright Stream whispered.

Before Gray Wing could respond, she slipped out into the open, and began trotting in circles, pretending to limp. As the other two eagles took off and flew toward her, she darted back under the rock where Gray Wing was waiting.

"That was risky," he muttered.

"It worked, didn't it?"

The two eagles settled, one on top of the rock and one on the ground, peering underneath. Gray Wing spotted Clear Sky and the others creeping out from under the overhang, preparing to surround the bird on the rock.

We have to lure the one on the ground farther away, Gray Wing thought.

Hoping Bright Stream would understand, he gestured with his tail toward a nearby bush. Bright Stream nodded. "I'm ready."

Together Gray Wing and Bright Stream sprang into the open, right in front of the eagle on the ground. Gray Wing heard it screech as it took off after them. Glancing over his shoulder he saw Clear Sky powering upward, leaping so high that he grabbed the neck of the eagle on the rock. It tried to take off, but Clear Sky's weight was too much for it. The other three cats crowded after him and dragged the bird down to the top of the rock.

Transfixed by the sight, Gray Wing didn't look where he was going. His flying paw struck something and he stumbled. *Haredung!* he hissed, spotting a gnarled tree root almost concealed by snow.

His pace faltered as a sharp pain sliced through his leg. He could sense the pursuing eagle swooping down on him and struggled to move faster. A heartbeat later Bright Stream's pale tabby-and-white pelt reappeared in the dim light and he realized that she had swerved around to help him. Boosting him with her shoulder, she shoved him toward the bush, into a narrow gap beneath the thorny branches.

His vision blurred by terror, Gray Wing scrabbled to pull himself farther in and give Bright Stream space to follow. But when he turned, he saw her sliding backward, her claws digging uselessly into the ground.

What . . . ? Pain made Gray Wing slow to realize what was happening. Then he saw that the eagle had caught hold of Bright Stream, its cruel talons sunk into her haunches. She shrieked as the bird lifted her off the ground.

"Gray Wing! Help me!"

CHAPTER 8

Ignoring the pain in his leg, Gray Wing scrambled out from under the bush and launched himself upward. But his outstretched claws only brushed Bright Stream's tail as the eagle flapped out of reach, screeching in triumph.

"Fight back!" Gray Wing yowled to Bright Stream as he raced along the ground below. "Get free somehow!"

He spotted the two eagles who had chased Turtle Tail and Cloud Spots circling back to join their companion. Out of the corner of his eye he glimpsed Clear Sky and the cats with him finishing off the fourth eagle with bites to its neck.

The other three eagles soared higher. Bright Stream's cries faded as she was carried into the sky. Horror gave speed to Gray Wing's paws as he followed, leaping from boulder to boulder, skidding on loose stones, flaying the skin off his pads.

"Gray Wing! Stop!" Dimly he heard Turtle Tail's voice screeching after him.

Cloud Spots and Turtle Tail raced up to him, pacing him on either side. "You can't help her now," Cloud Spots panted.

With a shriek of loss and frustration Gray Wing skidded to a halt and found himself on the very edge of the cliff. A few more paw steps and he would have toppled down into the valley below.

"Bright Stream!" he gasped out, his flanks heaving as guilt and grief flooded through him. "It was my fault!"

Cloud Spots pressed himself against Gray Wing's side. Turtle Tail's voice shook as she tried to comfort him. "You did everything you could."

Gray Wing hovered at the cliff edge, imagining himself crashing down below, his body shattered on the rocks. For a moment he swayed, his head spinning; then he felt Cloud Spots's claws drag him back from the edge.

"Come on," the black-and-white tom meowed. "We have to go back to the others."

As Gray Wing turned away from the precipice, Clear Sky and Tall Shadow came running to meet them.

"We did it!" Clear Sky exclaimed triumphantly. "We killed the eagle!"

Even Tall Shadow, usually so reserved, was excited, her green eyes gleaming.

Jackdaw's Cry came racing up behind them. He had a torn ear, but otherwise looked uninjured. "Those birds won't trouble us again," he declared with satisfaction.

Clear Sky halted, and gazed around, puzzled. "Where's Bright Stream?" he asked.

Gray Wing opened his jaws to reply, but found no words, grief crashing over him again.

"I'm so sorry," Turtle Tail mewed gently. "One of the eagles took her."

Clear Sky stared at her, as still as a cat made of ice. "Impossible!" he rasped. "Bright Stream is too fast to be caught like that! Gray Wing," he went on, turning on his brother, "why didn't you help her?"

"I . . . hurt my leg," Gray Wing stammered. "She was helping me escape, under a bush."

Horror welled up in Clear Sky's eyes. "You left her *outside*?"

Gray Wing shook his head helplessly. "It wasn't like that . . ." he began to protest, then let his voice die away, because there was nothing he could say that would convince any cat, least of all himself, that he wasn't responsible for Bright Stream's death.

"Don't," Cloud Spots murmured, brushing one paw along Gray Wing's flank. "It wasn't any cat's fault."

"Right." Clear Sky straightened and swung around, scanning the landscape. "Which way did the eagle go?"

While the rest of the cats stared at him, Gray Wing saw Shaded Moss approaching from the overhanging rock where they had sheltered. Tall Shadow ran back toward him, mewing urgently as she told him what had happened.

Approaching the group, Shaded Moss laid his tail on Clear Sky's back. "We won't be able to find Bright Stream now," he meowed.

"We *must*!" Clear Sky protested, his voice full of love and pain. "She's going to have my kits!"

Gasps of horror came from the assembled cats. Gray Wing felt more wretched than ever, remembering the tiny lives that had been destroyed with their mother.

Shaded Moss shook his head. "So much loss . . ." he murmured.

Keeping his tail across Clear Sky's back, he coaxed him toward the overhang where the other cats were waiting. Turtle Tail ran ahead to break the news, while Cloud Spots padded alongside Gray Wing.

A grief-stricken silence greeted the cats as they slipped under the overhang again. Even Moon Shadow was too stunned for his usual chatter.

They gathered around Clear Sky, offering hushed words of comfort, but Gray Wing knew there was nothing any cat could say that would ease his brother's pain. They couldn't even reassure him that Bright Stream had died quickly and painlessly.

Gray Wing crept into a corner and lay down, resting his head on his paws. A moment later Turtle Tail settled down beside him, so close that her pelt brushed his.

"It wasn't your fault," she whispered.

But it was, Gray Wing thought in anguish. *It absolutely was.*

No cat got much sleep that night. As a gray, chilly dawn began to break, they crept out into the open. When Gray Wing emerged, Shaded Moss was dragging the body of the dead eagle across the snow toward them.

"We need to eat," he announced, dropping the prey in the midst of the group. "We have to keep our strength up."

Clear Sky was the last cat to appear, his eyes dark with grief. At first he turned away from the bird, but Tall Shadow nudged him closer, and eventually he crouched and choked down a few mouthfuls.

"Clear Sky," Shaded Moss began when he had finished eating, "do you want to return to the cave?" The usually confident leader sounded uncertain. "Because Bright Stream died here, in the mountains, you might want to stay."

Clear Sky hesitated, then shook his head. "I promised Bright Stream that there was a better place for us to live. I will keep my promise by finding it—for her sake, and our kits'."

A fresh pang of grief and guilt clawed at Gray Wing's heart at his brother's courage.

"Bright Stream gave her life so that we could escape from the eagles," Shaded Moss meowed. "Honor her by carrying her in your heart, always."

Clear Sky bowed his head, but did not respond.

"Right," Shaded Moss continued, clearly finding it hard to sound as brisk and efficient as usual. "We'll carry on toward the clump of pine trees. We should get there by sunhigh."

Sadness clung around the cats like fog as they set off again. Gray Wing noticed that all the cats seemed uneasy around Clear Sky. He braced himself to go over and walk at his side. *I'd deserve it if he clawed my ears off, but I can't ignore him.*

But at that moment Moon Shadow stepped forward. "Come," he murmured to Clear Sky. "I'll walk with you today."

As they headed for the pines, Cloud Spots fell in beside Gray Wing. He didn't offer words of sympathy. They just padded along in comfortable silence.

As Shaded Moss had predicted, it was almost sunhigh when

they reached the wind-blasted copse of pines. Tall Shadow sprang up the trunk of the tallest and balanced precariously on a thin, prickly branch that swayed under her weight.

"I can see the way out of the mountains!" she called.

"Wow! We're almost there!" Turtle Tail exclaimed.

"What's it like?" Quick Water asked.

But the excited comments died quickly to silence. Gray Wing knew that every cat was remembering Bright Stream, grief-stricken that she didn't make it this far.

"Which way now?" Shaded Moss asked, looking up at Tall Shadow in the tree.

"Down this slope," Tall Shadow replied, gesturing with her tail. She dug her claws into the bark, beginning to edge her way down. "Around the shoulder of this peak there's a narrow valley that leads to the end of the ridge. It's *flat* down there!" she finished triumphantly as she leaped down the last couple of tail-lengths.

As the cats continued, the sun shone into their eyes and wind buffeted their fur. Gray Wing felt uneasy as they crossed an open expanse of stone—a pair of eagles circled high above. But they came no closer.

"They've learned their lesson about messing with cats," Jackdaw's Cry declared.

Gray Wing wondered silently if he was right. *Or does it just mean that the birds fed well yesterday?*

He wished that he could go to Clear Sky, admit his guilt and tell him how sorry he was that he had let Bright Stream die. But he knew that he could never find the words. Instead, he padded along a few paw steps behind his brother, biting pain in his heart.

Soon, the ground became less stony; expanses of short, wiry turf appeared through a much thinner covering of snow. The mountains had changed, too; the rocky pinnacles giving way to softer, rounded shapes.

Continuing around the flank of the mountain, the cats began a steep descent into a narrow valley. Lower down were taller trees. Used to the wind-blasted pines around the waterfall, Gray Wing gazed in wonder at their wide-spreading branches.

As they climbed farther down, Gray Wing spotted movement against the trunk of one of the trees. A small russet creature was swarming upward. *A squirrel!* he thought. *Just like in the elders' tales!*

He launched himself toward it, but Quick Water was faster, flashing past him in a blur of gray and white. She clawed her way up the tree after the squirrel as it tried to escape along a branch. She grabbed it and killed it with a quick bite to the neck.

"This is great!" she exclaimed as she dropped her prey to the ground and jumped down triumphantly after it. "We haven't left the mountains yet, and already there's prey!"

All the cats crowded around and took a bite from the squirrel, except for Clear Sky, who turned away. "I'm not hungry," he muttered.

Gray Wing forced himself to eat his share, but it tasted like dust in his mouth. He glanced after Clear Sky, wishing that he knew what words would ease his brother's grief.

At the bottom of the valley a shallow river gurgled over stones. On its far side, a grassy path led to a wide stretch of flat land.

"We've really done it!" Rainswept Flower exclaimed. "We're leaving the mountains!"

"Almost." Shaded Moss touched his daughter's shoulder with his nose. "First, we have to find a way to cross this river."

The cats spread out, padding up and down the bank in search of a place where they could safely cross. Though the river was shallow near the banks, there was a deeper channel in the middle, and the current looked strong enough to carry a cat off its paws.

"Over here!" Hawk Swoop called out from farther upstream. "Look," she continued as the rest of the group crowded together to see what she had found. "We might be able to cross by these rocks."

Gray Wing saw that here the current was broken by rocks poking out of the water, though some of them were spaced very far apart, and one or two had water lapping over them.

"I'm not sure I like the look of that," Jackdaw's Cry muttered; Gray Wing could see that some of the others agreed with him.

"Well, I doubt we'll find anything better," Shaded Moss declared. "Well spotted, Hawk Swoop. I'll go first."

Gray Wing watched as their leader's sturdy figure leaped from rock to rock, making the crossing seem easy. Clear Sky followed, so quickly and carelessly that Gray Wing wondered whether his brother was even thinking about staying safe.

At first Gray Wing hung back as some of the others crossed, but when Jagged Peak launched himself onto the first rock, he followed close behind, ready to help if the kit got into trouble. But Jagged Peak leaped across strongly, squealing in excitement. He reached the far bank with hardly a splash, and padded about importantly with his tail in the air.

Gray Wing turned to watch the final cats crossing. Quick Water was taking a long time, bracing herself for each leap and flinching if the least drop of water splashed up onto her fur. Halfway across, she halted on a flat rock. "I don't like water lapping over my paws," she complained.

"Then don't stand there!" Moon Shadow yowled back unsympathetically.

Quick Water hissed back angrily, jumping for the next rock without sizing up the leap. Gray Wing winced as she landed badly, her paws scrabbling against the slick, wet stone. A heartbeat later she let out a terrified screech and fell into the water, thrashing frantically.

Remembering his previous struggle, Gray Wing looked around for a branch to help her out, but there was nothing in sight.

Before any other cat could react, Falling Feather leaped from the bank and paddled over to Quick Water. Gray Wing found it hard to breathe as he watched. There was no grace in her swimming, but she was confident and fast, catching up with Quick Water as she began sinking.

Holding her head high out of the water, Falling Feather

grabbed Quick Water by the scruff of the neck. Even though Quick Water was much bigger than she was, Falling Feather managed to flounder toward the opposite bank, pushing the gray-and-white she-cat in front of her.

Gray Wing and Shaded Moss crouched on the bank as they approached, reaching down to haul Quick Water to safety. Falling Feather clambered out behind her, and shook water droplets from her fur.

"That was great!" Jagged Peak exclaimed, staring at Falling Feather with admiring blue eyes. "You were so brave."

"I only did what any cat would have done," Falling Feather mewed.

"Most cats don't jump *into* rivers," Hawk Swoop pointed out.

Quick Water was lying on the bank, shivering and coughing up water. "I'm so sorry!" she gasped. "I was stupid, and I put Falling Feather in danger."

"Well, everything's okay now." Turtle Tail comforted Quick Water, bending to dry her fur with long, strong licks.

Gray Wing and Cloud Spots joined Turtle Tail to get Quick Water's fur dry faster. Meanwhile Falling Feather gave her own pelt a couple of swipes with her tongue. "It's dry, it's fine," she mewed when Dappled Pelt offered to help her. "Come on. We don't want to stay here all day."

By this time, sunlight was fading. Shadows gathered around the cats as they trudged along the path beside the river, growing more tired and chilled with every paw step.

"My fur is so cold," Quick Water grumbled. "No cat should have to get that wet."

Jagged Peak, padding alongside Gray Wing, let out a faint snort of amusement. "I think Quick Water should change her name to No Water!"

Eventually Shaded Moss halted beside a thicket of bushes and raised his tail to signal that they should stop. "We'll spend the night here," he announced. "Do any of you feel like hunting?"

"It's too dark," Hawk Swoop objected.

"But I can scent prey," Moon Shadow meowed, licking his jaws in anticipation. "I'll see what I can track."

"Me too!" Jagged Peak added enthusiastically.

"It's great that you want to try," Dappled Pelt remarked. "But I seriously doubt you'll catch anything."

As the two hunters set off, the rest of the cats started to find spots for makeshift nests among the bushes. Gray Wing took a step toward his brother, hoping they might share a nest as they had in the cave, but Clear Sky turned away and curled up underneath a low branch. Gray Wing sighed and went to find his own spot. He was flattening a clump of longer grass when Shaded Moss padded up to him.

"You shouldn't blame yourself for Bright Stream's death," the black-and-white tom began. "Every cat knew the dangers when they chose to come on the journey."

"But it *was* my fault," Gray Wing insisted bleakly. "She was trying to help me instead of taking care of herself."

Shaded Moss fixed Gray Wing with a gaze full of sympathy and understanding. "You would have done exactly the same thing in her position. If she were still alive, she wouldn't blame you."

Gray Wing turned his head away, unable to meet that penetrating look. "If she were still alive, she wouldn't *need* to blame me," he rasped.

Shaded Moss said no more, and Gray Wing heard him padding away. He curled up in his grassy nest and closed his eyes. After a moment he felt another cat curling up beside him. Turtle Tail's scent washed over him.

He was slipping into sleep when he heard bounding paw steps and Jagged Peak's triumphant voice. "Look what we caught!"

Gray Wing scrambled to his paws along with Turtle Tail and the rest of the cats, who crowded around Jagged Peak and Moon Shadow. On the ground in front of them lay a small brown bird and a plump rat almost the size of a kit.

"Who said we couldn't hunt at night?" Jagged Peak meowed.

After the days of near starvation in the mountains the prey seemed like a feast, and the cats' spirits rose. Even Clear Sky ate a few mouthfuls.

"We should remember Stoneteller at times like these," Shaded Moss announced when the prey had been eaten. "We should thank her for directing us out of the mountains to a place where there's enough food, even in the cold season."

I do thank you, Stoneteller, Gray Wing thought, raising his eyes to the stars. *I just wish I could tell you that we've made it this far.*

Gray Wing awoke at dawn and scrambled to his paws. Around him the other cats were emerging from their nests in the thicket. The sun was just beginning to rise ahead of them, its golden beams pouring down to illuminate the valley. The narrow cleft where they had slept opened out into a soft green landscape that stretched flat and welcoming all the way to the distant blurry horizon.

"Wow!" Dappled Pelt whispered. "It's the sun trail, just like Stoneteller said."

A breeze was blowing toward them from the valley, carrying harsh, unfamiliar sounds. Gray Wing pricked his ears, trying to make sense of the distant buzzing, but it was like nothing he had ever heard before.

Turtle Tail came to stand beside him. "Why do I feel that our journey is only just starting to get difficult?" she asked.

Gray Wing nodded. "I know what you mean."

Clear Sky appeared, climbing the bank from the river and shaking water droplets from his whiskers. Gray Wing noticed that he was moving more resolutely, with new determination in his eyes as he strode up to Shaded Moss. "This is it," Clear Sky meowed. "We leave the mountains today. For Bright Stream's sake, I'll help you find our new home."

"Good." Shaded Moss touched the younger cat on the shoulder with his tail.

Gray Wing squared his shoulders. If Clear Sky, after all he had lost, could focus on their journey, then he could, too. He still felt full from his share of the prey the night before, and he guessed that the others were, too; they were all ready to set out after a drink from the river.

Quick Water padded along briskly; she had found time to

groom herself, and looked recovered from her fall into the river.

Gray Wing quickened his pace to walk alongside her. "Are you okay?" he asked.

"I'm fine." Quick Water gave her chest fur a couple of embarrassed licks. "But I still feel really stupid for falling off that rock."

"Don't worry about it," Gray Wing purred. "At least we found out that Falling Feather doesn't mind swimming. That could be useful at some point."

As the cats continued, the mountains fell away on either side. The last vestiges of snow vanished from the landscape. Emerging from the mouth of the valley, every cat halted to stare in silent astonishment.

The river flowed away through flat stretches of green grass, dotted with huge spreading trees. The closest stretch of grass was enclosed by shiny mesh and lines of thick bushes growing close together. Inside were strange animals that looked like clouds, though they had hard black paws and black faces that bent to nibble the grass.

Warily the cats approached to peer through the bushes. The nearest animal turned to look at them and let out a weird bleating cry. Gray Wing jumped and flinched back a pace, then felt embarrassed until he realized that all his companions had done the same.

"I'm pretty sure those are sheep," Shaded Moss meowed. "I remember the elders telling tales about them. They're not dangerous."

"Just *huge*." Jackdaw's Cry gulped.

Jagged Peak crept up to the line of bushes again. "I wonder what they taste like."

Gray Wing gave him a gentle flick over the ear with his tail. "You will *not* start hunting sheep!"

Turning away from the creatures, the cats padded on beside the river. Gray Wing was nervous about venturing into the vast open stretch of grass, and guessed that his companions felt the same.

"This is a bit scary," Turtle Tail confessed, coming to walk at his side.

"I know," Gray Wing agreed. "There's nowhere to hide!" *But I could run so fast here*, he thought with a twinge of longing. *I could stretch my legs farther than ever before.*

Gazing across the landscape he spotted a flicker of movement: something small and brown hopping through the grass. *Rabbit!* Without pausing to think, Gray Wing took off, racing over the ground until the land and the sky vanished into a blur. The rabbit hurtled away from him, but he kept his gaze fixed on it.

Everything seemed to slow down. Gray Wing felt his muscles bunching and stretching under his fur, his paws pushing off from the soft grass, propelling him forward. Suddenly the rabbit was in front of him; he leaped on top of it, killing it with a swift bite.

Slightly dazed, Gray Wing stood up. On the far side of the grass, his companions were watching him, openmouthed. A bleat from one of the sheep startled him, making him realize how close the strange creatures were. Stumbling a little with the rabbit hanging from his jaws, he trotted back to the riverbank.

"That was . . . *fast*," Cloud Spots mewed.

"Amazing!" Jagged Peak added.

Gray Wing wasn't sure what had taken hold of him. He set the rabbit down and stepped back. "Come on, eat," he invited with a wave of his tail.

Dappled Pelt shook her head. "Thanks, but I'm not hungry," she murmured.

"Neither am I," Tall Shadow agreed. "I mean . . . great catch, Gray Wing, but we all ate well last night."

"Even so, we should all eat whenever we have the chance." Shaded Moss crouched down beside the rabbit. "Who knows when we'll find more prey?"

The rest of the cats watched him dig in, then moved forward to take their share. Gray Wing was the last to eat, and when he was full there was still some of the rabbit left. He took another mouthful, but it was hard to choke it down.

"I can't manage any more," he meowed, feeling shocked at the sight of leftover prey. "If no cat wants it, we'll have to leave it."

Shattered Ice looked just as shocked. "What kind of place is this," he asked, "where there is *too much* food?"

CHAPTER 9

The sun rose higher as the cats made their way beside the bank of the river. Huge stretches of green grass lay along their route, enclosed by bushes or the weird shiny meshes. Sheep watched them curiously as they passed. Gray Wing was unnerved by their stares, and could see that his companions felt the same.

Shaded Moss took the lead as before, with Clear Sky and Tall Shadow beside him. Soon, he paused under a large tree and gathered the other cats around him.

"Now that we're not high up," Shaded Moss began, "it's impossible to see much of the route ahead. But we'll head straight for the point where the sun rises." He gestured with his tail: "That will lead us to those pointed stones."

Gray Wing looked at the place his leader indicated. The ground ahead still led gently downward, and just visible on the horizon were dark peaks outlined against the bright sky. *That's an awfully long way off*, he thought, with a prickle of apprehension.

"We'll never get that far!" Jagged Peak gulped. He glanced up at Gray Wing, his blue eyes full of misgivings. "Our paws will be worn away to nothing!"

"It's just one step at a time," Shaded Moss said encouragingly.

As they continued they still clung to the riverbank. Gray Wing wondered if he was the only one comforted by the sound of running water. Though it was much softer than the waterfall, it was almost the only familiar thing in this strange land.

Cloud Spots and Dappled Pelt sniffed at the lush clumps of herbs hanging over the water. Dappled Pelt's whiskers quivered with excitement as she spotted each new patch of growth.

In several places the lines of thick bushes stretched down to the water's edge, and the cats had to push their way through, their pelts catching on thorns and sharp twigs. Small birds flew up in twittering flocks, startled by the cats' presence.

The first time they saw the birds, Moon Shadow and Hawk Swoop sprang forward—only to halt, confused, when Shaded Moss called them back.

"We're not hungry yet," he told them. "There's no need to waste prey."

Moon Shadow and Hawk Swoop exchanged bewildered glances. "It just seems so *wrong*, letting prey escape," Moon Shadow mewed.

Gray Wing remembered the rabbit they had been unable to finish. For once, he thought the black tom spoke for all of them.

Jackdaw's Cry walked beside Gray Wing, staring around, wide-eyed. "The grass is so *soft*!" he said. "And there are so many creatures . . . not just the sheep, but the birds too." The excitement faded from his voice. "Who knows what else might be hiding in the bushes and watching us?" he finished, shivering.

Gray Wing understood what the young tom meant. "Don't forget we're faster than most animals," he murmured. "We can run away for safety."

But all the cats were walking closer together now, flinching at sudden noises, and Gray Wing wondered how long they could continue under this kind of stress. Being able to run away didn't seem as reassuring as it should have.

His ears flicked forward when he heard a rumbling sound that grew louder with every paw step. It came from the other side of a dense, bristly line of bushes. Tasting the air, he picked up a strong, acrid scent.

"What's that yucky smell?" Jagged Peak asked, passing his tongue over his jaws as if he'd tasted buzzardfood.

"I don't know." Shaded Moss drew the cats together with a gesture of his tail. "Keep together until we find out what we're facing."

The fur on Gray Wing's shoulders rose. Looking around at his denmates, he saw that they were bristling too, their eyes wide.

"I'll go through first and see what's on the other side," Clear Sky offered.

Gray Wing's belly lurched with fear. He couldn't let his brother face this unknown danger alone. "I'll go with you," he declared, stepping forward to stand beside his brother.

Clear Sky glanced at him, then looked away. "Come on, then," he mewed tersely.

Gray Wing's head drooped sadly. *He blames me for Bright Stream's death . . . and he's right.*

"Thank you both." Shaded Moss gave an approving nod. "Come straight back once you've assessed any dangers."

Gray Wing followed his brother as they thrust their way through the dense, prickly branches, hissing in annoyance as sharp twigs scraped his shoulder, snagging a tuft of fur.

"I don't get this," Clear Sky muttered as he halted to lift one paw and pull a thorn from his pad. "Why are all these bushes in a straight line? It doesn't make sense."

"I guess it's just how things are here," Gray Wing responded.

Slimmer than his brother, he found it easier to slip through the bushes, and was the first to emerge on the other side. Terror froze his paws to the ground. Huge, roaring creatures flashed to and fro a tail-length in front of him, dazzling him with their glittering, unnatural colors. A foul stench poured over him and he struggled to breathe.

I'm going to die!

Before he could warn his brother, Clear Sky slipped out of the bushes beside him. "Stupid prickles!" he hissed. "I've left half my fur—"

He broke off with a gulp of astonishment.

Gray Wing braced himself against the gusts of wind and raised his voice to a yowl. "This must be the Thunderpath Stoneteller told us about!"

Clear Sky nodded. "It certainly *sounds* like thunder. And those must be the monsters. She warned us to stay away from them."

There was a moment's peace, with no monsters hurtling past them. Gray Wing set his front paws on the path. It was made of black stone, and felt smooth beneath his pads. On the far side, thick undergrowth grew up to the edge of the stone, with bigger trees beyond, which would offer good cover from the monsters if only they could reach it.

"We'll be able to cross here," he meowed. "Unless monsters attack."

Before he had finished speaking, the roaring began again, growing rapidly louder. "Watch out!" Clear Sky screeched.

He fastened his claws in Gray Wing's shoulder, dragging him back without a heartbeat to spare as another monster growled past.

"Thanks!" Gray Wing gasped. "It must have been waiting out of sight, ready to pounce."

Another gap followed the last monster, and Gray Wing heard Shaded Moss's voice calling through the bushes. "What can you see? Are you okay?"

"Hang on!" Clear Sky replied, and added to Gray Wing, "Keep watch. Tell me if there are any more monsters lying in wait."

Gray Wing held his breath as Clear Sky padded all the way to the center of the Thunderpath. It was marked by a straight white line.

"Is that snow?" Gray Wing asked, wondering why it would be lying there and nowhere else.

Clear Sky bent his head to sniff the line. "No," he replied. "I don't know what it is."

As he spoke Gray Wing heard another faint rumble that swiftly grew into a roar. "Monster!" he yowled.

Clear Sky leaped back to safety as a shining scarlet creature roared past on round black paws.

"We'll never get across if they're waiting for us," Gray Wing meowed.

"They obviously can't see that well," Clear Sky responded thoughtfully. "It rushed straight past us. And I had enough time to get all the way across before it spotted me. I think we'll be able to cross if we're careful."

Gray Wing couldn't share his brother's confidence. "What if that last monster was old and slow?" he asked. "Faster, younger monsters might catch us before we even reach the white line!"

Clear Sky gave him a somber glance. "This journey was never going to be easy," he mewed. "We can't give up now."

Gray Wing murmured agreement. "We'd better report back."

Pushing their way back through the bushes, they described what they had seen to Shaded Moss and the others.

"What are we going to do?" Jackdaw's Cry asked, his eyes wide with dismay. "Those things will eat us!"

Tall Shadow let out a snort. "What good are we if we can't outwit them? They may be huge and stinking, but it sounds like they're pretty stupid."

"Stoneteller told us that they don't seem able to leave the Thunderpath," Rainswept Flower meowed thoughtfully. "It looks as if she's right—we haven't seen any of them on the grass beside the river. As long as we can cross the black stone, we should be safe."

"Good thinking." Shaded Moss gave his daughter an approving nod. "We'll cross in twos. Clear Sky and Gray Wing, you've seen what these creatures are like, so you can supervise."

"I'll go first," Dappled Pelt volunteered instantly. "I want to get it over with."

"I'll come with you," Rainswept Flower mewed.

Shaded Moss dipped his head. "Good luck."

Gray Wing and Clear Sky led the two she-cats to the line of bushes. When they arrived by the side of the Thunderpath, everything was quiet.

Dappled Pelt worked her claws impatiently in the grass. "What are we waiting for?"

Gray Wing held up his tail for silence and crouched beside the black stone, his ears pricked. A distant rumble swelled in his ears, from both directions.

Monsters were coming.

All four cats flinched back into the bushes as the noise and stench rolled over them.

"They're huge!" Rainswept Flower exclaimed.

More nervously this time, she and Dappled Pelt approached the edge again. "We have to do this," Dappled Pelt muttered determinedly.

"I'll come with you and keep watch from the other side," Clear Sky announced.

Standing side by side, the three cats waited, their ears alert and their eyes watchful. A monster growled past more slowly, the sun dazzling off its shiny pelt.

"Is it looking for us?" Rainswept Flower asked, crouching down in the long, tickly grass.

The others flattened themselves beside her, and the monster went by without stopping.

"It missed us." Dappled Pelt puffed out her breath in a massive sigh. "Come on, Rainswept Flower!"

The two she-cats dashed out onto the black stone. Clear Sky bounded after them. Gray Wing yowled a warning as he heard the roars of approaching monsters, but his friends were safely on the other side before two more of the huge creatures flashed past.

"So it *can* be done," he murmured, trembling with relief. "They're fine!" he called out to the others on the far side of the bushes. "Send the next pair through."

Cloud Spots and Quick Water appeared and stood by the side of the black stone. Everything was quiet.

"Is your side clear?" Gray Wing called out to Clear Sky.

Clear Sky waved his tail. "Fine! Come on!"

Cloud Spots and Quick Water raced across safely. Everything was still quiet, and Gray Wing began to wonder if the monsters had given up hunting and gone back to their dens.

But as Jackdaw's Cry and Falling Feather appeared from the bushes, yet another monster roared past, and Gray Wing realized they weren't out of danger yet. *At least with that reek they leave behind, they won't be able to scent us.*

As silence fell again he glanced both ways along the

Thunderpath, then called out to Clear Sky, who waved his tail again to signal that it was safe to cross. Jackdaw's Cry and Falling Feather crossed without trouble. Shattered Ice and Hawk Swoop took their places at the edge of the black stone.

When Gray Wing and Clear Sky had checked, they began bounding across; but, as they reached the middle white line, Clear Sky suddenly screeched, "Monster!"

Shattered Ice and Hawk Swoop ducked back toward Gray Wing, but he spotted a monster too, approaching faster than the one on Clear Sky's side.

Now they're hunting us in pairs!

"No! Keep going!" he yowled.

Hawk Swoop froze in panic, scrabbling at the black stone as if she was trying to bury herself. Shattered Ice leaped toward her and grabbed her by the scruff of the neck. Gray Wing lost sight of them as the fierce monster roared past.

Then the dust cleared. Gray Wing felt limp with relief as he saw both cats collapse, panting—but uninjured—on the far side.

"The monsters seem to know we're here."

Gray Wing started at the sound of Shaded Moss's voice and turned to see the black-and-white tom standing behind him. "The rest of us will cross together," he added.

Shaded Moss called the other cats through the bushes and lined them up beside the Thunderpath, hidden in the long grass. Gray Wing made sure to stand next to Jagged Peak, where he could keep an eye on the young cat. "Do *not* move until we tell you!" he warned.

Turtle Tail sneezed as a grass stem brushed her nose.

"Quiet! You'll bring all the monsters running!" Moon Shadow hissed.

But there was still silence from the black stone. "I think it's okay," Gray Wing meowed. "Clear Sky?"

Clear Sky waved his tail from the opposite side. "Fine! Do it!"

The remaining cats bounded forward. Gray Wing felt his paws scorched on the hot, smooth surface of the Thunderpath. Then he plunged into the undergrowth on the far side, thankful to be surrounded by the scents of the others.

Working together with Clear Sky had felt good, but when he turned to his brother he saw that Clear Sky's gaze was cold again, fixed on the trees ahead.

"Is every cat okay?" Shaded Moss asked.

"I'm a bit worried about Hawk Swoop," Dappled Pelt replied. "She had a nasty shock back there."

"It was my own fault," Hawk Swoop replied, giving her chest fur an embarrassed lick. "I'm fine now."

"It's great to be under the trees," Turtle Tail remarked as they set out again. "The monsters can't see us here."

"And with all this thick stuff, we don't have to hear them," Jackdaw's Cry agreed.

But Gray Wing felt uneasy as he made his way through the undergrowth. Plants seemed to be grabbing at his paws, as if trying to trip him. And there were noises all around him: birds calling, branches creaking, prey scuffling in the undergrowth. He longed for the silence and clear air of the mountains.

"How much farther?" Shattered Ice complained, proving that Gray Wing wasn't the only cat having problems. "I've got so many thorns in my paws I think I'm turning into a gorse bush!"

"Yes, and how can we hunt birds when we can't see the sky?" Quick Water added.

"Stop behaving like kits!" Moon Shadow barged his way through the ferns. "Just smell the prey! We could eat just by keeping our mouths open and letting it fall in."

"I want to go farther before we stop for the night," Shaded Moss called back. "There's no time to hunt yet."

Moon Shadow let out an annoyed hiss.

"I think we should see how far these trees go," Clear Sky said. "I'll climb one." Without waiting for a reply, he bounded to the nearest tree and leaped almost halfway up the trunk before digging his claws into the bark.

"Wow!" Turtle Tail stared after him. "I always knew he could jump, but that's amazing!"

Only a few moments passed before Clear Sky scrambled back down again. "I couldn't get high enough to see," he meowed. "I need a taller tree."

Padding onward, every cat examined the trees on either side until Shaded Moss halted in front of a huge one with gnarled roots and dense branches. "Try this one," he suggested to Clear Sky. "I think it must be an oak . . . my mother used to tell me about the trees where the Tribe lived before."

Clear Sky sprang into the tree with another mighty leap, and Tall Shadow followed, though she had to start climbing farther down the trunk.

"I want to go too!" Jagged Peak squealed excitedly. "I can climb!"

"Stay on the ground," Shaded Moss ordered.

Jagged Peak's tail-tip twitched irritably, but he didn't argue.

Gray Wing tipped back his head to watch Clear Sky and Tall Shadow until they vanished among the dense, leafless branches. A moment later, a triumphant yowl sounded from high up in the tree.

"Clear Sky has reached the top," Jagged Peak mewed, an envious look in his eyes.

Twigs tumbled to the ground as Clear Sky and Tall Shadow reappeared, jumping down and catching their breath.

"The trees end not far from here," Clear Sky panted.

"Great!" Turtle Tail exclaimed, with a satisfied swish of her tail. "I want to see the sky again."

"And what did you see beyond the trees?" Shaded Moss asked.

"Oh . . ." Clear Sky looked disconcerted. "I'm not sure. It looked a bit misty."

Gray Wing saw his brother exchange a meaningful glance with Tall Shadow, and wondered what the two cats were keeping back. But he knew very well that there would be no point in pressing Clear Sky with more questions; their old ease and closeness was gone.

With Shaded Moss and Clear Sky in the lead, the cats padded on through the trees toward the brightening light that heralded the edge of the woods. But before they emerged into the open, Shaded Moss halted. Gray Wing pushed forward with the other cats to see what was going on.

A flat path wound through the trees, clear of undergrowth. Gray Wing tasted the air, and sniffed along the grass at the edge, but found no familiar smells.

His friends were looking just as bewildered. The scents didn't seem to be prey; Gray Wing felt no prickle of instinct telling him to hunt. Instead, his neck fur bristled and his paws tingled as if he wanted to run.

"Which way should we—"

Hawk Swoop's question was cut off by a loud volley of harsh noises from farther down the path, drowning out the sounds of the woods.

"A dog!" Shattered Ice exclaimed.

"What's a dog?" Jagged Peak asked, gazing down the path in the direction of the noise.

"An animal you don't want to meet," Shaded Moss replied, drawing the group closer together with a wave of his tail. "We used to see them in the valleys sometimes in the warm season, but we always stayed out of their way."

As he finished speaking, a huge brown animal bounded around a curve in the path and halted, its lips drawn back in a snarl.

Shaded Moss yowled, "Scatter!"

The cats fled, diving into clumps of fern or scrambling up trees. Gray Wing pushed Jagged Peak into a bramble thicket and followed him in, clawing desperately at the thorns to make a space where they could hide.

No! he thought a moment later. *We should have kept running, but now we're trapped.*

He tugged helplessly at the tendrils that curled around

him. A tail-length away, the dog snuffled along the edge of the thicket. Gray Wing knew it would find them at any moment.

Then he heard another sound: high-pitched, clear, and crisp, with a note of anger. The dog whined in response. Gray Wing peered out of the brambles and saw a tall, thin creature walking on its hind legs, with a loose, multicolored pelt and a strange, pink, hairless face.

Jagged Peak popped up his head behind Gray Wing. "Oh, wow!" he exclaimed. "Is that a Twoleg? It's so weird!"

The Twoleg didn't seem to notice the scent of the cats. It padded up to the dog, seeming to have no problem balancing on its two hind paws, then fastened a soft tendril to the dog's neck and dragged it away.

The dog whined again. It didn't want to leave, straining toward the clumps of fern where the other cats were crouching.

No cat moved for a moment after the Twoleg and the dog had vanished down the path. Then gradually they began to emerge from their hiding places.

"I've never seen anything so awful in my entire life!" Falling Feather was shaking so much she could hardly stand. "Did you see its teeth?"

"It's okay." Jackdaw's Cry comforted her, giving her ear a gentle lick. "It's gone now."

Gray Wing could see that even Shaded Moss was struggling to stay calm. "We were bound to come across Twolegs and dogs sooner or later," he meowed. "And we survived, so let's keep going."

All the cats were happy to plunge back into the deep woods, leaving behind the trail with its dog-stench. But they were tired of the struggle through the thick undergrowth, and the thorns that seemed to lie in wait to attack their paws and muzzles.

"I thought we'd never get here!" Gray Wing exclaimed, finally emerging at the edge of the trees.

But he realized that while they were in the woods a persistent cold drizzle had started to fall, soon soaking their fur as they stood under the outlying trees.

"This is even worse than snow!" Quick Water complained.

Gray Wing stared ahead, his heart beginning to pound as he gazed at what lay ahead. *This is what Clear Sky saw from the top of the tree!* A collection of square, hard-edged blocks of stone lay in front of them, some taller than trees, with shiny square holes in the sides. A wave of unfamiliar scents washed over him. Some were warm and tantalizing, making his belly growl, while others made him curl his lip in disgust. He recognized the scent of Twolegs that had clung around the earthen path behind them.

"These must be Twoleg dens," Shaded Moss suggested.

"And this is a Twolegplace!" Shattered Ice added. "Misty Water told me about them, but I thought she was making it up."

Gray Wing thought they must be right; he could see a few Twolegs, heads ducked against the rain, running between the blocks of stone.

"Now what do we do?" Cloud Spots asked. "I don't want to go any nearer."

"Neither do I," Falling Feather agreed. "There might be more dogs!"

Shaded Moss pointed with his tail, beyond the dens, to where the sharp peaks they were heading for were barely visible through the low clouds and rain. "That's where we're heading," he meowed. "To the place where the sun rises. But it'll be dark soon. We should find shelter for the night among the dens, where it's dry."

CHAPTER 10

❧

Hunched against the rain, the cats crossed a grassy space and reached a broad path of dark stone leading toward the Twoleg dens.

"This is a Thunderpath," Tall Shadow meowed, halting at the edge. "There'll be more monsters."

But everything was quiet. Shaded Moss led the way along the Thunderpath, keeping to the edge, and the rest of the cats followed, their fur bristling.

Suddenly a throaty growl sprang up and a monster headed toward them, slowly at first and then with gathering speed.

"It's spotted us!" Rainswept Flower screeched.

"This way!" Gray Wing saw a much narrower path leading between two high walls of red stone, and raced toward it. "Follow me! The monster won't be able to reach us down here!"

The cats streamed after him, just in time as the monster bore down on them. It passed by with a roar of frustration, its eyes glowing with a harsh yellow light.

"It missed us!" Turtle Tail mewed with relief. "Gray Wing, you were brilliant."

"We still need to find somewhere safe and dry to spend the

night," Gray Wing pointed out. Bright lights like tiny suns were appearing in the dens, casting yellow squares onto the path. The shadows seemed much darker by contrast.

Taking the lead, Gray Wing walked down the narrow path, feeling trapped and suffocated between the high walls. It opened out into a square stone clearing surrounded by smaller dens. Glancing around, Gray Wing saw that one was gaping open, and padded cautiously up to it. Inside it was dark, and the reek of monsters was so strong he could hardly breathe.

"This must be a monster's den," Jagged Peak suggested, creeping up beside Gray Wing and staring wide-eyed into the darkness.

"The smell is stale and old, though," Gray Wing mewed. "Maybe the monster doesn't use it anymore."

Rainswept Flower bounded past him into the den and looked around. "We'll stay here tonight," she announced briskly. "At least it's out of the rain, and we can take turns keeping watch."

Shaded Moss nodded as he came to stand beside his daughter. Gray Wing saw how his tail drooped, and his eyes were full of weariness. *It can't be easy for Shaded Moss*, he thought. *Leading us and being responsible for everything.*

"You look tired," Rainswept Flower murmured, pushing her nose into her father's shoulder fur. "Get some sleep. I'll take the first watch."

"I'll join you," Gray Wing offered at once.

"But I'm hungry," Quick Water protested as she padded into the den. "Aren't we going to hunt before we sleep?"

"It's too dangerous here," Clear Sky pointed out. "And we haven't smelled any prey since we left the woods."

"We should have hunted earlier, when I wanted to," Moon Shadow snapped.

"He's right," Hawk Swoop added. "It was a stupid decision to come into this Twolegplace."

"No, it was our best chance of shelter," Tall Shadow pointed out, her tail lashing irritably. "Away from dogs and all the things that were watching us from among the trees."

Gray Wing agreed silently. *We may be safer than we would be out in the open, but this is still a ghastly place. Dawn can't come soon enough for me.*

He sat at the opening of the den beside Rainswept Flower, looking out into the clearing. Gray Wing's ears rang with the growl of distant monsters, shrieks of Twolegs, dogs barking—and then a yowl that made his fur stand on end.

Cats!

Rainswept Flower leaned over to whisper into his ear. "I never thought about what would happen if we met other cats! Do you think they're . . . *kittypets*?"

Gray Wing remembered the elders' tales of cats who chose to live with Twolegs, eating their food and sleeping inside their dens. Back in the cave, Gray Wing had thought the stories were just thistlefluff from the elders' brains. But here, where everything seemed so crowded and dangerous, he could imagine they were true.

"What do you think kittypets are like?" he asked Rainswept Flower. "Will they understand us?"

"Surely they'd envy us?" Rainswept Flower responded. "We've seen more than they ever will."

Gray Wing listened to his rumbling belly and looked down at his filthy pelt. *Are we* really *enviable right now?*

The yowls came no closer, and eventually Gray Wing felt sleep drifting over him. The louder roaring of a monster roused him and he saw it enter the clearing, its yellow eyes raking the walls.

Rainswept Flower and Gray Wing shrank back into the mouth of the den.

"Has it spotted us?" Gray Wing asked, struggling to control panic. "Are we in *its* den?"

"Distract it!" Rainswept Flower ordered, springing to her paws. "I'll get the others."

Gray Wing's belly trembled with terror. *Distract it? How?*

But before he could make a move, the entrance to another den gaped open and the monster crawled inside. The den mouth glided shut behind it with a clang and the growling stopped.

"That was close!" Gray Wing exclaimed. "It must have gone to sleep."

Rainswept Flower met his gaze with horror-filled eyes. "Then all these other dens could have sleeping monsters inside!" she whispered.

Gray Wing nodded. "Why do the Twolegs have their dens so close to the monsters? Aren't they scared?"

Rainswept Flower shrugged, not replying, and settled down to watch once more. Gray Wing, still quivering from shock, thought he would never close his eyes again; but the next thing he knew, Rainswept Flower was prodding him in the side.

"It's time you changed places with another cat," she told him. "Get some proper rest."

Gray Wing stumbled to the back of the den and woke Hawk Swoop by tripping over her. "It's your turn to go on watch," he told her.

"Okay, fine," she mewed drowsily, and got up to join Rainswept Flower, who rose in her turn and fetched Jackdaw's Cry before curling up to sleep.

Gray Wing lay down where Hawk Swoop had been, feeling her warmth on the dusty floor, and closed his eyes.

A heavy paw landing on his tail woke him, and he looked up to see Moon Shadow in the pale gray light filtering into the den.

"Sorry," Moon Shadow mewed. "I'm going hunting."

Gray Wing nodded, wondering if he ought to go as well, but too weary to make his legs move. "Good luck," he said, watching Moon Shadow leave the den with a murmured good-bye to Turtle Tail and Shattered Ice, who were standing guard.

When he had gone, Gray Wing drifted into sleep again. He dreamed that he stood on the cliff top with Quiet Rain, gazing out over a vista of sunlit mountain peaks.

But the vision was shattered by a dreadful yowling.

Gray Wing sprang to his paws as Shattered Ice and Turtle Tail began scrambling out of the den. "Moon Shadow is being attacked!" Shattered Ice meowed urgently.

Gray Wing raced out of the den with the others. He could hear Moon Shadow on the other side of a wall at the far side of the clearing, screeching in fury. The voices of two other cats mingled with his shrieks, as if all three were battling.

Gray Wing, Tall Shadow, and Clear Sky raced across the clearing, outpacing their denmates, and leaped on top of the wall. Fur bristling, Gray Wing looked down and saw Moon Shadow rolling over and over on a wide stretch of grass, lashing out with teeth and claws as two cats raked at his fur.

Those are kittypets? Gray Wing thought, appalled, as he took in their plump bodies and the tendrils around their necks. *None of the elders ever said kittypets were fierce!*

Gray Wing plunged down and landed on top of the nearest kittypet, a huge, fluffy black-and-white tom. Clear Sky and Tall Shadow hurled themselves at the other, a ginger she-cat.

The black-and-white kittypet flipped over, slamming Gray Wing onto the ground, and slashing at his ears. Infuriated by the stinging pain, Gray Wing reared up and snapped at the kittypet's throat, closing his teeth instead on a mouthful of fur. Choking, he felt forepaws battering at his shoulders. *This kittypet isn't as soft as he looks!*

Spitting out the fur, Gray Wing brought up his hind paws and struck out at the kittypet's belly, glad of his sharp claws and the wiry strength of his muscles.

The kittypet squirmed away, lashing out at him with clumsy blows that hardly connected. Gray Wing struggled to his paws as Moon Shadow barreled past him, butting the kittypet in the side with his head. Faced with two enemies, the black-and-white kittypet turned tail and ran. Panting, Gray Wing glanced around to see Clear Sky and Tall Shadow chasing off the ginger she-cat.

Both kittypets swarmed up a thin wall of wood on the far side of the grass. It wobbled under their weight, but they kept their balance as they turned and hissed.

"Rogues aren't welcome here!" the ginger she-cat warned. "If you're not gone by tonight, you'll be in big trouble."

With a final snarl, both kittypets disappeared down the other side of the fence.

"Good riddance!" Moon Shadow yowled after them.

"What were you doing," Tall Shadow mewed, "going off on your own like that? Are you flea-brained?"

"'Rogues'?" Clear Sky interrupted. "What did those kittypets mean—'rogues'? Is that their name for cats who don't live with Twolegs?"

Gray Wing was just as confused, though glad that they could understand what the kittypets were saying. His muscles ached from the fight, and the ear the big tom had slashed was dripping blood. *Are we going to have to fight cats all the way to our new home?* he wondered. It was a daunting thought. *In the mountains there were no cats to fight. It was just us.*

He and his friends clambered back over the wall. The other cats were huddled together in the mouth of the den.

"Who knew kittypets would fight?" Jackdaw's Cry mewed. "In the elders' tales, they're all scaredy-sparrows!"

"Maybe you should have talked to them," Rainswept

Flower suggested. "You could have explained that we're just passing through."

Clear Sky rolled his eyes. "Oh, yeah? While they were clawing our throats out? They weren't in the mood for conversation!"

Shaded Moss listened to the exchange, his paws shifting uneasily. "We have to get out of this place as soon as we can," he announced. "We can't afford more fighting."

He set off at once and the others followed, the younger cats stumbling with tiredness. Gray Wing brought up the rear with Turtle Tail, both of them tense and watchful.

Shaded Moss led the way along narrow stone paths between the Twoleg dens, crossed quiet Thunderpaths and raced through enclosed stretches of grass. Gray Wing realized that Shaded Moss was determined to travel in a straight line, toward the peaks they had seen.

While they were crossing one stretch of grass beside a Twoleg den, the air was split by an outburst of shrill barking. Every cat froze in horror. Then, as he looked around, Gray Wing spotted the dog: a little white creature trapped behind a clear shiny sheet that blocked the entrance to the den.

"Look at that!" Moon Shadow meowed, taking a pace toward it. "Hey, flea-pelt! Wouldn't you like to get at us?"

"Flea-brain!" Cloud Spots shoved Moon Shadow roughly after the others, who were already moving on. "What if the Twoleg lets it out?"

As he followed his denmates, Gray Wing kept a lookout for kittypets. He didn't see any, but their scents were everywhere.

It was a relief to reach the edge of the Twolegs' dens and gaze out again across open landscape. The rugged peaks were in plain view now.

"They're not as big as the mountains," Quick Water mewed, sounding disappointed.

"Stoneteller wouldn't have sent us to live somewhere just the *same*, would she?" Dappled Pelt observed. "Our new home will be completely different."

"I miss the mountains," Falling Feather whispered.

Gray Wing rubbed his paws over the hard black stone at the edge of the Thunderpath. He sympathized with the young white she-cat. Picturing the cats they had left behind, he wondered how they were. *If only there were a way to let them know that we're safe!*

"Come on!" Jagged Peak suddenly began marching ahead. "We're not going to get anywhere if we stand around all day."

Gray Wing suppressed a small *mrrow* of amusement at the young cat's confidence as he and the others followed. Clouds covered the sky, so there was no sun to guide them, but the outline of the peaks was clear enough.

After the noise and reek of the Twolegplace, it was soothing to be back in the open, surrounded by soft grass and animal scents and sounds. Soon they reached another line of bushes; Moon Shadow swerved off and plunged into the branches. He emerged a moment later with a small brown bird in his jaws.

Dropping the bird on the ground, Moon Shadow took a mouthful then pushed the remains toward Shaded Moss.

Shaded Moss raised a paw to stop him. "Thanks, but let's

all hunt for ourselves," he meowed. "There's enough prey here."

A shiver of excitement ran through the cats as they split up. Gray Wing headed into the open grass, searching for signs of movement. He spotted Clear Sky leaping into the air after a bird, and Jagged Peak with his nose down on a scent trail.

Tasting the air for prey, Gray Wing scrambled backward as a huge black-and-white animal loomed over him. His heart pounded as he gazed up at it and saw that more were following it, lumbering through a gap in the line of bushes.

They're even bigger than sheep! he thought, casting his mind back to the elders' stories. *Maybe they're cows?* One of them let out a deep-throated *moooo*, and Gray Wing remembered how Misty Water loved to imitate that noise, scaring the kits who were listening to her tales.

He crouched in the long grass, too scared to move in case the cows saw him and gave chase. But the vast creatures bumbled past him without taking any notice, so he crept forward, skirting them at a safe distance.

Beyond the cows, Gray Wing spotted a rabbit startled out of hiding, and set off after it. He relished the feeling of wind in his fur, though the long grass tangled his paws and slowed him down.

The rabbit reached the bushes and darted into a hole among the roots. *Haredung!* Gray Wing thought, staring in frustration at the narrow opening.

"Hey!"

Gray Wing turned to see Turtle Tail with a small bird

under her paws. "I got one!" she announced. "Do you want to share?"

Gray Wing left the burrow, still wondering whether he would be able to hunt underground. The rest of the cats were gathering in the shelter of the bushes. They had caught plenty of prey, so those like Gray Wing who had been unlucky wouldn't go hungry.

"I got two crows!" Clear Sky boasted, flicking his tail toward two heaps of untidy black feathers.

Before they began to eat, Shaded Moss stood gazing back toward the mountains they had left, now no more than a blur on the horizon. "Thank you, Stoneteller," he meowed, "for sending us to this place."

When every cat was stuffed full, there was still prey left over.

"It seems so *wrong* to leave it," Rainswept Flower murmured regretfully.

As the cats headed away, Gray Wing glanced back to see a thin, red-furred creature slink out of the grass. At first he stiffened, thinking it was a dog, but its snout was sharper and it had a stronger, rank scent. It snatched some of the remains of the prey and stood gulping it down, its gaze darting to and fro.

Gray Wing nudged Shattered Ice, who was walking next to him. "What's that, do you think?" he asked.

"I have no idea," Shattered Ice replied.

"It looks mean," said Gray Wing. He quickened his pace, but decided not to alarm the others.

By the time the light started to fade, the cats had crossed

several narrow Thunderpaths and skirted a cluster of red stone Twoleg dens where a number of dogs lurked, barking. Beyond the dens, the ground sloped down into a marshy hollow, covered by tussocky grass with clumps of reeds here and there.

"We can't go this way," Quick Water protested, staring down into the dip with a look of disgust on her face. "We'll get our paws wet."

Shaded Moss glanced in both directions; following his gaze, Gray Wing realized that the boggy area stretched out of sight on each side. "We *have* to," Shaded Moss decided. When Quick Water opened her jaws to argue, he added, "Wet paws won't kill any cat."

But when they reached the bottom of the slope, Gray Wing and the others realized that they would be lucky to escape with nothing worse than wet paws. The ground shivered as they padded across; as they moved farther into the marsh, they began to sink until every cat was wading through mud up to their bellies. The stench of it rose around them and clouds of midges billowed into the air.

"This is awful!" Hawk Swoop exclaimed. "I'll never get my fur clean."

Quick Water was muttering under her breath as she floundered from tussock to tussock, and even Falling Feather looked uncomfortable.

Jagged Peak, the lightest of the cats, was having an easier time than the rest—until he slipped sideways from a clump of grass and started to sink, his forepaws splashing vainly at the mud.

"Help!" he wailed.

Rainswept Flower hauled herself onto the clump of grass and bent over, grabbing Jagged Peak by the scruff of the neck. She dragged him out and set him on his paws again, his pelt plastered with mud.

"Thanks!" he gasped.

Every cat was cold, soaked, and filthy by the time they reached the other side of the marsh. All they could think of was finding some kind of shelter.

Not far away, they spotted a huge cave made out of wood. *It must be a different kind of Twoleg den*, Gray Wing thought.

Shaded Moss took the lead again as they trudged toward it, pausing cautiously when they reached the entrance. Gray Wing peered over his shoulder. The den contained huge stacks of pressed, dried grass, and he felt even more exhausted as he thought about the warm and comfortable nests they could make in it. There were several raised pools of water in stone hollows; Gray Wing passed his tongue over his lips, realizing how thirsty he was after taking several mouthfuls of the foul marsh water. Even better, the scent of mice wafted out to meet them, and Gray Wing could hear myriad squeaks and scufflings coming from the dried grass.

"What are we waiting for?" Moon Shadow asked, shouldering his way past Shaded Moss. "This place is teeming with prey!"

Shaded Moss nodded. "It seems safe enough. There are no Twolegs here."

With his go-ahead, the cats dived into the den, eager to hunt. *We've eaten once today*, Gray Wing thought, as his claws closed on a mouse, *but I can definitely manage more. We can't waste all this prey!*

The cats settled in the warm grass to share their catch, taking one bite and then exchanging as they did in their mountain home. Gray Wing could feel his pelt tighten as his belly swelled, full of delicious food.

"I've been thinking," Rainswept Flower announced while they were still eating. "Everything we want is here. What else could we possibly be looking for? What if we've *found* our new home?"

CHAPTER 11

❧

For a moment every cat was silent with shock. Moon Shadow was the first to speak. "Suits me," he meowed, swiping his tongue around his jaws.

"Yes, it's warm and dry in here," Quick Water agreed.

"And there's no smell of dogs," Shattered Ice added. His nose twitched. "There's a different sort of scent, but I don't recognize it. Still, if it's not dogs or eagles, it can't be dangerous."

Shaded Moss was looking thoughtful. "It could work," he said at last. "And we're close enough to the mountains to go back and visit the others now and then."

Excited murmurs rose from the group of cats, and they glanced at one another with shining eyes.

"We can make nests in this dried grass," Falling Feather mewed. "It would be a great place for bringing up kits."

Gray Wing didn't join in the plans. He couldn't help feeling a bit disappointed. *There's nothing* wrong *with this place*, he thought. *But I imagined finding our new home would feel more* right.

He looked around, trying to picture himself and his Tribemates living here. His legs felt restless at the thought of being trapped within the wooden walls. They were not as *natural* as the walls of a cave. Besides, he would have liked to know what the strange scent was.

But if it's right for the others, shouldn't I be happy to stay? he asked himself guiltily.

"What do you think?" he asked Turtle Tail, who was sitting beside him. "Is this the place we've been looking for?"

The tortoiseshell she-cat looked surprised. "I'm pretty sure it is," she replied. "Aren't you?"

Gray Wing shook his head.

"Everything beyond the mountains is going to feel strange," Turtle Tail pointed out. "It's just a case of getting used to a different way of living."

Gray Wing suppressed a sigh. "I suppose you're right," he admitted, curling up next to her to sleep.

Before he closed his eyes, Gray Wing spotted Clear Sky sitting on the hard earth floor, staring into the shadows. His brother was illuminated by a shaft of moonlight that shone through a gap in the wall, turning his light gray pelt to silver. He looked so alone that Gray Wing's heart ached for him.

If only Bright Stream were still here.

The cats burrowed into the warm, dry grass to make nests, and fell into a deep, sound sleep. They felt so safe that no cat suggested setting a watch.

An unfamiliar noise aroused Gray Wing. His eyes blinked open and he saw gray dawn light seeping through the gaps in the shelter wall. Outside he could hear a trampling noise, and knew that was what had awoken him.

Springing to his paws, Gray Wing turned to face the shelter entrance. Outside in the dimness he could see a pale, moving mass converging on the shelter. The trampling grew louder.

"Wake up!" he screeched, hurling himself at one cat after another and swiping his paws across their ears to make them wake. "Run!"

Glancing back at the entrance he realized that the pale mass had drawn closer; now he could see that it was made up of sheep—more sheep than he had ever seen before, and all of them heading for the shelter. Their trampling and bleating seemed to fill the whole world and their scent—the strange scent they had picked up before—flooded over him.

"We can't get out!" Falling Feather yowled. "They'll crush us!"

Already the first sheep were trotting into the shelter, pushing one another to get through the entrance. There was no way past them that could avoid their sharp, cruel paws.

"Over here!" Rainswept Flower gasped.

Darting after her across the tumbled heaps of grass, Gray Wing saw a tiny gap at the bottom of the shelter's wooden wall. One by one the cats squeezed through, as the shelter filled with the noisy, restless sheep.

Waiting for his turn, Gray Wing heard a shriek of pain and saw Hawk Swoop fall to the ground while a sheep trampled over her. He leaped forward but Clear Sky was faster, grabbing her by the scruff and dragging her toward the gap. He shoved her through and followed; Gray Wing was right behind him, with Shaded Moss at his tail.

"Are we all here?" Shaded Moss asked, after they had all struggled out into the open.

Gray Wing checked, and saw to his relief that no cat had been left behind. They all seemed uninjured, too, except for Hawk Swoop, who was standing with one of her forelegs at a very strange angle.

"Can you walk?" Shaded Moss asked her.

"I'll try," Hawk Swoop replied, her breath hissing through her teeth. She limped a few paces, clearly in a lot of pain.

"I don't think you can," Gray Wing meowed. He spotted a clump of long grass and nettles beside the wooden wall, and let Hawk Swoop lean on his shoulder until she could collapse there out of the chill dawn wind.

Gray Wing beckoned Dappled Pelt with his tail. "You know the most about herbs," he meowed. "What should we do for her?"

Dappled Pelt looked confused. "Daisy leaves, or elder," she replied at last. "But I don't know if they grow around here. Jackdaw's Cry, Falling Feather, can you go and look for some?"

As the two young cats bounded off, Cloud Spots padded up to Hawk Swoop and examined her carefully; she drew in her breath with a gasp of pain as he prodded her injured leg.

"I've seen injuries like this before," Cloud Spots mewed. "Her leg has come out of joint at the shoulder."

"Then she'll be stuck like that?" Quick Water sounded horrified.

"No, not at all," Cloud Spots responded. "I once watched Quiet Rain treat one of the elders for this after they slipped off a rock. Herbs will only help the *pain*, not the injury."

Hawk Swoop gasped in agony as Cloud Spots set his paws on her neck and shoulder. "This will hurt," Cloud Spots told her, "but it will soon be over." Flicking his ears at Gray Wing, he added, "Come here and hold her. Put your paws there . . . and there . . . and keep her absolutely still when I give the order."

Gray Wing placed his paws where Cloud Spots had indicated. "I'm ready."

"Good. *Now!*"

Cloud Spots yanked hard at Hawk Swoop's leg; Gray Wing was nearly rocked off his paws by the force of it. Hawk Swoop let out a shriek. Then Cloud Spots stepped back and Gray Wing saw that the she-cat's leg was back in position. She lay trembling, her breath coming in shallow gasps.

"Can you move your leg? Does it still hurt?" Cloud Spots asked.

Hawk Swoop flexed her leg. "It only aches a bit," she meowed. "Oh, thank you, Cloud Spots!"

"Well done." Shaded Moss touched Cloud Spots's shoulder with his tail.

Cloud Spots shrugged. "It's just lucky I saw what Quiet Rain did."

At that moment Jackdaw's Cry and Falling Feather returned, their mouths full of herbs. "Are these the right ones?" Falling Feather asked, dropping her bundle in front of Dappled Pelt.

Dappled Pelt sorted through the leaves. "Do you think

these are okay?" she asked Cloud Spots.

Cloud Spots carefully picked out a couple of leaves with his claws. "These look like the ones we have in the mountains," he mewed, giving them to Hawk Swoop. "Chew them well and swallow them to help the pain," he told her.

While Hawk Swoop was eating the herbs Shaded Moss padded up to her. "You need to rest. We'll stay here for the day."

Gray Wing heard a few murmurs of discontent from his Tribemates.

"I'm freezing!" Quick Water complained. "We're all getting soaked out here."

She was right; the chilly breeze carried a sharp, stinging rain. But there wasn't anything they could do about it, and Shaded Moss gave Quick Water a stern look. "You can go back into the shelter with the sheep if you like," he mewed.

Quick Water scuffled her forepaws on the ground, looking embarrassed. "I suppose out here isn't so bad."

"We could hunt," Clear Sky suggested, though he didn't sound enthusiastic.

"Our bellies are still full," Tall Shadow pointed out. "There's no sense in catching prey we can't eat."

Moon Shadow nodded, letting out a groan. "I don't think I'll be able to face another mouse!"

In the end, all the cats settled down among the long grass and nettles and fell into a doze. When Gray Wing awoke, the sky was still covered in clouds, and a thin drizzle was falling, though the wind had dropped. He guessed it was just after sunhigh.

As he rose to his paws and stretched, Gray Wing noticed that Clear Sky was walking away from the den.

"Are you going somewhere?" Gray Wing asked, running to catch up. "Is everything okay?"

Clear Sky gave him a long look. "I just wanted to stretch my legs," he replied. "I'm fine on my own, thanks."

Gray Wing watched Clear Sky pad away, feeling as if he had been struck in the belly. *I'd rather he raged at me for letting Bright Stream die*, he thought. The cold politeness was far worse to bear, because it made him feel like a stranger to his own brother.

His tail drooping, Gray Wing padded back to the long grass.

Turtle Tail was waiting for him. "Let him grieve," she whispered, brushing her tail along Gray Wing's flank. "Everything will be all right in the end."

Gray Wing wished he could believe her.

In the days that followed, Gray Wing began to believe that their encounter with the sheep had been a sign that the next stage of their journey was going to be even more difficult. The rain never stopped, and their only guide was a few glimpses of the sharp stones now and then through the mist.

How can we find our new home if we can't see the sun trail? Gray Wing wondered.

Prey grew scarcer, the small animals and birds sheltering from the rain. Hawk Swoop quickly recovered, but as the cats crossed a barrier between two stretches of grass, Tall Shadow scratched one of her pads on a sharp, shiny tendril hidden among the stems.

"I'm fine," she muttered, even though she was limping badly.

Dappled Pelt and Cloud Spots foraged for herbs, but Dappled Pelt looked doubtfully at everything they found. "I don't want to give any cat something that will make them sick," she meowed. "I've never seen most of these leaves before."

As the days went by, even Jagged Peak lost his liveliness. Gray Wing could understand: He was the youngest and smallest, with the shortest legs, and yet he had to keep up with the others.

"I'm fed up with this rain," he complained as he trudged through wet grass that soaked his pelt. "And I'm *hungry*!"

"We'll find prey when we get where we're going." Falling Feather comforted him.

"We don't *know* where we're going," Jagged Peak whined.

"Then maybe you should have stayed at home where you belonged," Clear Sky snapped brusquely.

Jagged Peak flinched at his brother's rebuke, looking so miserable that Gray Wing had to sympathize. "Every cat is grumpy," he whispered to Jagged Peak, brushing against his side reassuringly.

A stretch of woodland loomed up in front of the cats, and as they entered it Jagged Peak went on muttering. As he walked with Gray Wing at the back of the group, he began twitching his ears or his tail and stopping to glance around.

"Why are you fidgeting?" Gray Wing asked irritably.

"I think we're being watched," Jagged Peak replied.

Gray Wing suppressed a sharp response. "It's probably a piece of prey that doesn't want to be caught," he suggested.

Jagged Peak flicked his tail, but said nothing. A few paw steps later he stopped dead. "What was that?" he asked, his ears quivering.

"A falling twig!" Gray Wing answered, flicking his tail in exasperation. "Now come on! We're lagging behind the others."

Jagged Peak stayed as still as if his paws were rooted to the ground. His eyes narrowed and his face screwed up in a mutinous expression. "We're being followed," he meowed.

"No, we're not!" Gray Wing looked around, determined to prove that his brother was wrong. "Oh . . ." he added, feeling stupid, as a long-legged brown-and-gray tabby stepped out of the clump of bracken they had just passed.

"See?" Jagged Peak snapped.

Gray Wing and the stranger stared at each other for a moment.

"You're not from these parts, are you?" the stranger asked eventually.

"No," Jagged Peak piped up, stepping forward to examine the stranger, round-eyed. "We come from far away! From the mountains!"

The stranger looked surprised. "You mean Highstones?" He nodded in the direction of the sharp peaks the cats were heading for, though they weren't visible through the trees.

"No," Gray Wing replied. "We—"

He broke off as the other cats reappeared, with Clear Sky in the lead. "What's going on?" Clear Sky asked.

"Wow, there are a lot of you," the stranger mewed, though he didn't seem daunted by their numbers.

"We're just travelers, passing through," Shaded Moss told him.

"Oh," the stranger responded, "I thought you were the cats who live on the other side of Highstones."

"That's those pointed stones up ahead," Gray Wing explained.

"Are there cats who live there already?" Cloud Spots asked, shouldering his way forward.

"That's what I've heard," the stranger replied, "though I've never been that far myself. I've heard tales about how fierce they are."

"Are they . . . 'rogues'?" Gray Wing asked, remembering what the kittypet in the Twolegplace had said.

The stranger gave a snort of amusement. "'Rogues' are what kittypets call us, the soft saps." His gaze traveled curiously over the group of cats, and he added, "What are you all doing here? That kit there said you've come a long way."

"We needed a new home," Shaded Moss said shortly, casting a distrustful gaze at the stranger.

The tabby tom dipped his head and didn't ask more questions. "Well, best of luck to you," he meowed, and slid away into the bracken.

"So there's another group of cats living near those pointed stones!" Jackdaw's Cry mewed excitedly.

"Highstones," Jagged Peak corrected.

Falling Feather sniffed. "They're not *that* high."

"I think it's a good sign if there are other cats living near here." Rainswept Flower blinked thoughtfully. "Cats like us, I mean. Not kittypets."

"Yes, it means there's space and prey," Dappled Pelt agreed. "We won't be disturbed by Twolegs, or monsters or dogs."

"Maybe." Clear Sky looked less certain. "But we want to find a place of our own, where there's all the prey we need."

Shaded Moss nodded. "Suppose the other cats are hostile?"

"The cat we just met didn't seem hostile," Turtle Tail pointed out.

Clear Sky snorted. "He was heavily outnumbered!"

Turtle Tail only shrugged.

In spite of Shaded Moss's and Clear Sky's suspicions, the cats' mood was lighter as they padded on through the woods. Though the rain persisted, the branches held off the worst of it.

Gray Wing spotted movement at the corner of his eye and turned to see a squirrel halfway up the trunk of a nearby tree. Clear Sky was closer to it, and pushed off into a spectacular leap, crashing down again with the squirrel in his claws.

"That was awesome!" Jackdaw's Cry exclaimed.

Since they had stopped, Shaded Moss suggested that they take some time to rest and hunt. Moon Shadow and Shattered Ice vanished immediately into the trees.

"Don't go too far!" Shaded Moss called after them. "Stay out of trouble!"

Gray Wing opened his jaws to taste the air, and picked up the scent of mouse. He tried to follow it, finding it hard when there were so many cross trails of competing scents, and finally lost it altogether in a clump of ferns.

How can I catch prey I can't see?

Meanwhile, Dappled Pelt had padded on a few paw steps, with her head tilted to listen. Then she meowed, "Look what I've found!"

Gray Wing trotted up to her and saw water gurgling from between two mossy stones, then falling in a tiny waterfall into a pool. A shallow stream led away from it into the trees.

Dappled Pelt crouched at the water's edge, swiping her tongue around her jaws. "Fish!"

Falling Feather watched as Dappled Pelt flashed one paw into the stream and flicked a tiny fish onto the bank. A few heartbeats later she did it again, catching a bigger fish this time.

Falling Feather let out an admiring purr. "You said you'd teach me how to do it. Can I try now?"

"Sure," Dappled Pelt replied. "Come and sit here. Make sure your shadow doesn't fall on the water, because that frightens the fish. Then, when you see one, you have to be quick."

"Okay, let me try." Falling Feather gazed intently into the water, but when she dipped her paw all she brought up was flying droplets. "Haredung!" she muttered. "It looks so easy when you do it!"

Rainswept Flower had also ambled up to watch. "Okay," she mused after a moment. "So I was wrong about the wooden

den, but do you think *this* might be a place where we could live?"

Still annoyed about losing the mouse, Gray Wing hoped that she was wrong again. Among the trees, he felt trapped—as if the air was too thick to breathe properly. He longed for the open spaces they had left behind.

"No," Shaded Moss replied to his daughter. "We must climb to the top of Highstones. Those peaks are the end of the sun trail Stoneteller promised us. We have to go there before we make any decisions about where to stay."

Rainswept Flower nodded, accepting what her father said, while Gray Wing heaved a huge sigh of relief.

Moon Shadow and Shattered Ice returned with prey. After he had eaten his fill, Gray Wing lay on a rock and watched Dappled Pelt giving Falling Feather another fishing lesson. The two she-cats were obviously having fun. Even when Falling Feather leaned over too far and toppled into the stream with a massive splash, she came up quivering with amusement.

"It's easier to *be* a fish than to catch one," she spluttered as she emerged and gave her pelt a shake, scattering shining droplets into the air.

"Watch it!" Quick Water snapped, leaping out of the way. "Some of us don't want to be fish, thanks very much!"

As he gazed at the she-cats, Gray Wing began to feel the earth trembling under his paws. At the same moment the air filled with the sound of barking.

"Dogs!" he yowled.

Shaded Moss jumped to his paws. "This way!" he ordered.

Three dogs crashed through the undergrowth. They were different sizes and colors. Frozen, Gray Wing could smell their stinking breath, and feel the heat from their fur.

"Come on!" Turtle Tail barreled into him, jolting him forward. "Move!"

Terrified, the cats floundered through the undergrowth. Bursting out of the trees, they raced across an open stretch of grass. Gray Wing glanced over his shoulder and saw the dogs following, covering the ground with long, loping strides.

They're catching up!

Ahead of the cats was a sharp, shiny barrier covered in thorns.

"Don't go that way!" Shaded Moss shrieked, swerving across the dogs' path and hurtling toward the shelter of a line of bushes.

Faster and faster the cats ran. Wind plastered Gray Wing's pelt to his body, and grass scraped his belly fur. Falling Feather was dropping behind, and he doubled back to give her a shove, half carrying her toward the bushes. He risked a glance aside, and saw that Clear Sky was helping Jagged Peak.

The bushes loomed ahead, bristly and dark and solid-looking. Gray Wing couldn't see any way through, but there was no time to hesitate. With Falling Feather beside him, he hurled himself in, battling against the densely packed branches, his fur tearing as thorns caught at it. He closed his eyes to protect them from the spines.

As he forced his way out the other side the roar of a monster assaulted his ears, and he was blasted in the face by spray kicked up from its round, black paws. Blinking, he tried to see where he was. Other cats were lurching out of the bushes close by.

"Wait!" Gray Wing shrieked.

But his warning came too late. Shaded Moss plunged out of the bushes, across the narrow strip of grass that edged the Thunderpath, and straight into the path of a roaring monster. Gray Wing heard a sickening thud as Shaded Moss's body was flung into the air.

The monster growled on, leaving nothing behind but a terrible, deafening silence.

CHAPTER 12

Horror almost overwhelmed Gray Wing, but he threw himself forward to stop any of the other cats from running straight onto the Thunderpath. "Shaded Moss is hurt!" he yowled, blocking Tall Shadow as she appeared. Then he rushed to intercept Jackdaw's Cry, who was shouldering his way out of the thorns.

Glancing swiftly in both directions, Tall Shadow darted onto the Thunderpath and grabbed Shaded Moss by the scruff, dragging him into long grass. Gray Wing stopped each cat on their way out of the bushes, and shoved them toward where their leader's body lay. Monsters roared past behind him, blurring his vision and filling his ears until they ached.

Clear Sky was the last cat to emerge, thrusting Jagged Peak in front of him. His eyes widened when he saw Shaded Moss's body, while Jagged Peak let out a wail. They followed Gray Wing to the broken cat.

Cloud Spots was bending over him, prodding him gently with one paw. After a few heartbeats he looked up. "He's dead," he announced.

"No!" Rainswept Flower threw herself down beside her father, pushing her muzzle into his fur.

Gasps of horror and disbelief came from the other cats. Gray Wing stepped forward and rested his muzzle on Shaded Moss's head. He still felt warm, his fur dusty and ruffled. A thin trickle of blood ran from his nose and mouth, but otherwise he might have been sleeping.

Pure grief stabbed through Gray Wing, sharper than thorns. *Shaded Moss brought us so far. How can he leave us now?*

Clear Sky padded quietly up to Rainswept Flower and gave her a gentle nudge. "Come on," he murmured. "We can't stay here. It's not safe."

Rainswept Flower gazed up at him, her blue eyes blazing with anger and grief. "I'm not leaving him to the monsters!" she shrieked.

"There's nothing you can—" Clear Sky began.

Shattered Ice interrupted him. "Rainswept Flower is right. This is no place to abandon Shaded Moss. We can carry him across the Thunderpath."

Gray Wing cast a glance at the bushes they had come through. He could still smell the dogs. There was no going back that way.

Shattered Ice, Dappled Pelt, and Moon Shadow stepped up to carry Shaded Moss's body. Gray Wing helped them, while Clear Sky kept watch for monsters. At last there was a gap in the continual roaring, and they were able to set out across the hard, black stone, all the cats crowding anxiously around their leader's body. Gray Wing saw Shaded Moss's tail dragging limply on the ground, and grief surged over him.

My poor Tribemate . . .

Together Gray Wing and the others carried Shaded Moss into a stretch of deep grass, under the shelter of a line of bushes.

"There are no stones here." Rainswept Flower's voice shook. "We can't bury him like we would in the mountains."

Dappled Pelt touched Rainswept Flower's ear gently with her nose. "We can use sticks from these bushes, and soft grass. It will be a good enough pelt for him now."

Rainswept Flower hesitated for a heartbeat, then gave a tiny nod. She and Dappled Pelt stayed close beside her father, while the rest of the cats set off to forage.

Gray Wing noticed Clear Sky walking rigidly, alone, his eyes staring at nothing. *He's thinking about Bright Stream*, Gray Wing guessed. *She had no stones or sticks to cover her body—wherever she ended up.* He wished desperately that he could apologize to his brother, but once again the words stuck in his throat like a tough piece of prey.

Gathering some twigs and large leaves torn from a bush, Gray Wing carried them back to Shaded Moss's body. But as he began to lay them on the dead cat, Rainswept Flower reached out her tail to block him.

"Wait," she mewed. "Please can I stay with him a while longer?"

As the cats returned, they set down their bundles of sticks and leaves and sat around Shaded Moss's body.

"Good-bye," Rainswept Flower whispered. "You were the best father any cat could have. I'll never forget you."

"And no cat could have led us better," Tall Shadow added,

ducking her head awkwardly toward Rainswept Flower. "You brought us out of the mountains."

When she had finished speaking, other cats began to add their memories.

"You taught me how to stalk prey."

"You kept going when any other cat would have given up."

"You believed in this journey, and made the rest of us believe, too."

Gray Wing stretched out his neck until he could touch Shaded Moss's head with his nose. "Thank you for your courage," he mewed. "We will carry on our journey in your memory."

"And in Bright Stream's," Clear Sky put in, his blue eyes filled with sorrow.

Turtle Tail nodded. "We miss her, too," she murmured. "She was strong and confident, but so gentle."

"She would have been a wonderful mother to your kits," Dappled Pelt added.

Jagged Peak said nothing, but pressed himself against Clear Sky's side.

Night fell, but the cats stayed clustered around Shaded Moss. Pale dawn light began chasing away the stars, as Rainswept Flower laid the first twig on her father's body. The rest of the cats followed, covering him in silence, then padded away toward where the sky was brightening, with Rainswept Flower in the lead.

Though grief had brought the cats together, they were each locked in their own private misery. Even Jagged Peak had stopped complaining. Tall Shadow still limped on her injured paw, though she gave no sign of the pain she must have felt.

The sun trail took them across several grassy spaces and through a cluster of Twoleg dens. The shrill barking of a dog startled them, but their grief was stronger than fear—all they could manage was a halfhearted scamper to the next wooden wall, scrambling over it to a stretch of open ground on the other side.

Looking around, Gray Wing realized that they had come to the end of the Twolegplace. Ahead, Highstones was outlined against the sky; anticipation tingled through his paws as he saw how close the peaks were.

The cats trekked on over tough moorland grass until they reached a copse of pine trees.

"This might be a good place to hunt," Moon Shadow suggested without much enthusiasm.

Dappled Pelt shook her head. "I'm not hungry."

The others murmured agreement, and flopped down to rest in the shelter of the trees.

"Is there any point in continuing without Shaded Moss?" Turtle Tail asked Gray Wing as she settled beside him. "Should we just give up and go home?"

Gray Wing was startled by the strength of feeling that rushed through him. "No!" he protested. "We've come too far! How would it be fair to Bright Stream and Shaded Moss if this journey was all for nothing?"

Hawk Swoop, crouching nearby, turned her head and

mewed sharply, "You didn't want to come in the first place, remember?"

Gray Wing forced himself to respond calmly. "Maybe not. But I've come this far, just like the rest of you. This will be my new home too."

The setting sun covered the ground in scarlet light and cast long shadows from the pine trees. The cats settled in the copse for the night, curling up among the soft pine needles at the base of the trunks.

Gray Wing dreamed that he was snug in his old sleeping hollow in the cave, but gradually a wail of grief pierced through the thunder of the waterfall.

"Shaded Moss! Shaded Moss!"

Gray Wing jerked awake. A couple of tail-lengths away, Rainswept Flower was thrashing around, calling out for her father in her sleep.

Compassion surged through Gray Wing. Rising to his paws, he padded over to Rainswept Flower and sat beside her, stroking his tail gently over her flank. Her cries sank to a quiet whimper, and then to silence. He stayed at her side, his heart as heavy as a cloud weighed down with rain. Through the branches of the pine trees, he could see the moon, already swelling to full again.

We've been traveling for nearly an entire turn of the moon. Will our journey ever end?

During the night the wind picked up, rattling the brittle branches overhead. The noise and chill roused one cat after another. "The moon and stars give us enough light to see," Tall

Shadow mewed, stifling a yawn. "Why don't we get going?"

With every cat in agreement, they padded through the pine trees and out onto rough, bristly grass, flattened by the strong wind. The ground sloped more steeply upward to where Highstones was a faint dark outline against the night sky.

Gray Wing paused and took in deep breaths of the cold air. Hope crept into his heart. *This feels like home.* Glancing over his shoulder, he looked across the landscape that unfolded behind them in the first faint light of dawn. A dark, uneven smudge lay against the horizon.

That's the mountains! Wow, we've come so far!

"I can't believe this!" Beside him, Jackdaw's Cry echoed his thoughts. "I never imagined the world was this big!"

The ground grew steeper still, with boulders poking through the tough grass, but the cats leaped confidently from rock to rock.

"This is harder than it used to be!" Cloud Spots puffed. "All the good eating has made me heavier."

The cats spread out as the grass gradually thinned and they found themselves padding along on stone. A sense of achievement tingled through Gray Wing as he scrambled up the last few tail-lengths and stood at the top of the pointed stones.

"We made it!" Turtle Tail announced as she joined him.

The peaks were lower and narrower than their mountain home, but Gray Wing rejoiced in their familiarity. He could see that the others, even Rainswept Flower, were regaining a little of their optimism.

As they stood looking out across the land beyond, the sun

broke above the far horizon, flooding the landscape below them with golden light and stretching its warm rays right up to their paws.

We have reached the end of the sun trail!

He looked down into the pool of sunlight and saw empty expanses of grass, broken by patches of dense woodland that would offer shelter. A winding river reflected the sunlight.

"Is that where the other 'rogues' live?" he wondered aloud. "Those all look like places where cats could settle."

"I think this could be our new home," Dappled Pelt murmured.

"Yes!" Falling Feather gave her a nudge. "There's a river for you to catch fish, and for me to fall into!"

"And trees," Clear Sky added. "There'll be plenty of prey."

Gray Wing hoped his brother didn't expect to be living under the trees. *I'd much rather stay in the open spaces, where I can breathe.*

But in spite of the cats' optimism, a mist of sadness still hung above them. *I wish Bright Stream and Shaded Moss had made it this far*, Gray Wing thought.

Tall Shadow meowed, "Come on, let's go explore," hopping down from the topmost crag, still limping on her injured paw.

"When we get there, I'm going to find some herbs that will heal that paw," Dappled Pelt declared.

Tall Shadow took the lead as they headed down the slope. "Jagged Peak!" she snapped as the kit scurried ahead of her. "Get your tail back here! You don't know what danger might be waiting for us."

Jagged Peak waited for the rest to catch up, and padded alongside Gray Wing, his ears flat and a chastened look on his face.

Their path wound between huge boulders that cut off the view of the land below. As they emerged again onto a more open slope, Jackdaw's Cry let out a startled *mrrow*. "Look over there!" he exclaimed.

Turning, Gray Wing saw a massive hole in the mountainside, gaping open like a mouth rimmed with jagged teeth.

Jackdaw's Cry ran lightly up to it and peered inside, meowing loudly and listening to the echo. "Wow, it's really deep!"

Tall Shadow padded after him to the entrance and took a brief look inside. "We're not rabbits," she sniffed. "We don't live underground. Come on."

Dappled Pelt caught up to pad beside Tall Shadow as they moved off again. "You really shouldn't walk much farther on that injured paw," she murmured.

Tall Shadow nodded. "Okay. But let's get to that stretch of moorland at the edge of the forest."

The stony surface gave way to rough grass and then to softer enclosed stretches dotted with sheep. They were so familiar now that the cats ignored them, though they still kept to the bushes that edged the spaces, all their senses alert for dogs or monsters.

"Another Twolegplace," Cloud Spots pointed out, as a cluster of red stone dens came into sight.

"I can smell dog," Moon Shadow announced, wrinkling his nose in disgust.

"Then we won't go near it," Tall Shadow responded, leading

them around in a wide circle.

Gray Wing looked at the moorland sloping up ahead of them. His legs suddenly felt heavy and his paws ached as he thought of taking a long rest. *I'm tired of traveling. Even if this isn't our new home, we should be able to stay here for a few sunrises, long enough to heal our wounds and fill our bellies.*

The moorland seemed just beyond their whiskers when a familiar roar assailed Gray Wing's ears.

"Oh, no!" Quick Water exclaimed. "Another Thunderpath!"

Moving cautiously, the cats picked their way through a thin line of bushes and, at a command from Tall Shadow, halted beside the Thunderpath. Gray Wing stared at it in horror. Monsters raced up and down in both directions, growling and letting out long hooting sounds like owls, but louder than any owl he had ever heard. *This is the biggest one yet! How are we supposed to get across?*

Glancing at his friends, he saw that many of them were trembling, the memory of Shaded Moss's death fresh in their minds.

"I don't want to cross," Falling Feather whimpered, crouching down with her nose on her paws.

"Can't we stay on this side?" Hawk Swoop asked. "Back on Highstones? There was plenty of space up there."

"Yes, but no prey," Clear Sky pointed out. "We need trees, bushes, and long grass to feed us all."

"Well, you can cross without me," Falling Feather mewed stubbornly.

Shattered Ice padded up to her and rested his tail on her

back. "We've come this far together," he told her gently. "We're not leaving any cat behind now. I'll look after you, I promise."

Falling Feather rose shakily to her paws.

Gray Wing noticed that Turtle Tail was also looking terrified, and he brushed his pelt against hers. "You'll be okay," he murmured.

Turtle Tail flattened her ears. "It's too soon after Shaded Moss."

Gray Wing nodded. "I know. But the sun trail has led us here. It's just one more obstacle, that's all."

Quivering, the cats gathered at the edge of the Thunderpath. The black stone extended in front of them, the far side looking a long way away. Gray Wing watched his brother, admiring Clear Sky's courage as he ventured close to the path and scanned it in both directions, leaping back just in time as monsters roared past.

"Okay," Shattered Ice meowed. "Let's split up. Clear Sky, you lead the first group, and then keep watch for the rest of us at the other side. Quick Water, Tall Shadow, Cloud Spots, and Jackdaw's Cry, go with him." As the cats he had named gathered together, he went on: "Rainswept Flower, Dappled Pelt, Turtle Tail, and Falling Feather, come with me. And Gray Wing, you lead the last group, with Jagged Peak, Hawk Swoop, and Moon Shadow."

Gray Wing nodded in response, and braced himself for the crossing.

Every cat seemed to feel better now that Shattered Ice had come up with a plan. Clear Sky led his group to the edge of the

Thunderpath and waited for a glittering blue monster to pass. The sound of its roaring died away into silence.

"Now!" Clear Sky yowled.

His group sprang forward and raced across the Thunderpath, their paws barely skimming the surface. Clear Sky ran alongside Tall Shadow, making sure that she didn't lag behind. They reached the other side with heartbeats to spare before the next monster appeared. Gray Wing lost sight of them in the long grass.

"Well, that wasn't so bad," Shattered Ice declared, as he flicked his tail to wave his own group up to the edge.

He and his cats had to wait a long time before the next gap in the continuous lines of monsters. Clear Sky reappeared at the other side and signaled to them with his tail.

"Okay! Now!" he yowled.

The cats were leaping forward onto the Thunderpath when Clear Sky let out another shriek. "No! Go back!"

With screeches of alarm the cats retreated. Shattered Ice grabbed Falling Feather by the scruff and hauled her out of danger as a bright red monster appeared out of nowhere, flashing past with a snarl.

"Dungeater!" Turtle Tail yowled after it. She seemed to have forgotten how nervous she had been.

Shattered Ice and his group approached the edge of the Thunderpath again, more cautious than ever after their narrow escape. But this time the path cleared quickly, and no monsters threatened them as they raced across.

Gray Wing gestured with his tail to gather his own group

together. Trying to force his paws to stop shaking, he lined up Jagged Peak, Moon Shadow, and Hawk Swoop at the edge of the Thunderpath. Stooping, he pressed his ear to the stone surface, but he couldn't sense any vibrations.

"Okay . . . *now!*"

With his group hard on his paws, he bounded onto the Thunderpath. But as they reached the halfway point, he heard the roar of an approaching monster, growing rapidly louder until the sound filled the whole world.

"Faster!" Gray Wing screeched.

He had almost reached the edge when Clear Sky leaped out from the grass, barged past him and headed for the middle of the Thunderpath. Horrified, Gray Wing skidded to a halt and turned to see Jagged Peak crouching in the path of the monster, frozen with terror. Clear Sky scooped him up by his scruff and leaped back in two mighty strides, just as the gigantic monster thundered past.

"You stupid, *stupid* kit!" Clear Sky snarled, dropping Jagged Peak and glaring at him. "Don't you *know* by now not to stop in the middle like that?"

Jagged Peak cowered down into the grass as if trying to hide from his brother's fury. "I—I'm sorry," he stammered.

"It's my fault too," Gray Wing meowed. "I should have realized he wasn't with me."

Before his littermate could respond, Quick Water pushed her way forward. "Clear Sky, calm down," she snapped. "It was a scary moment for all of us." Bending over Jagged Peak, she gave his head fur a couple of quick licks. "Come on," she murmured. "You can walk with me for a bit."

Jagged Peak struggled to his paws, giving Quick Water a grateful glance.

Every cat was shaky, their fur ruffled and dirty. They stumbled up the grassy slope in front of them, their excitement gone, their courage almost spent.

CHAPTER 13

❧

The slope led onto open moorland covered in tough, springy grass and clumps of gorse. Gray Wing relaxed, reveling in the open sky and the breeze that carried the scent of rabbits.

I could live my whole life here.

Toward nightfall, they came across a shallow hollow lined with gorse bushes and small rocks that offered shelter. A pool of peaty brown water lay at the bottom.

"We'll stay here for now," Tall Shadow said. "We can rest and explore, and decide whether *this* is the place Stoneteller meant for us to find."

After a couple of days spent drowsing in the hollow, venturing out only to hunt rabbits, Clear Sky was the first to lead out a group to explore, taking Dappled Pelt, Falling Feather, and Moon Shadow with him.

"We went as far as the river," Clear Sky reported when they came back. "There's a massive waterfall, thundering down into a gorge."

"No cave behind it, though," Falling Feather mewed regretfully.

On the following day, Gray Wing set out with Cloud

Spots, Rainswept Flower, Jagged Peak, and Turtle Tail. The sun shone brightly in a blue sky, clear except for a few wisps of white cloud. A breeze was blowing from the forest in front of them, bringing with it the scent of fresh, growing vegetation.

"This feels so good!" Turtle Tail sighed, pausing to arch her back in a long stretch.

"No rain, no Thunderpaths, and plenty of prey," Rainswept Flower agreed. "What else could we want?"

"We need to learn more about the place first," Gray Wing warned her. "There might be dangers we know nothing about."

Trekking on across the moor, they came to a steep slope leading downward. Ahead of them Gray Wing spotted a clump of fresh green leaves rustling in the wind. At first he wasn't sure what it was, until he realized that he was looking at the tops of several trees.

"Let's go look!" Jagged Peak meowed eagerly, springing forward.

Gray Wing hauled him back by hooking his tail around the young cat's neck. "Yes, we'll go look," he replied sternly. "But you *will* stay with the rest of us and not dash around like a demented snow hare!"

Jagged Peak nodded, but flexed his claws impatiently as he followed Gray Wing.

The moorland grass gave way to lush fern and undergrowth. Pushing through at the head of his group, Gray Wing halted, letting out a gasp of amazement.

In front of him the ground fell away into a vast, circular hollow. The sides were lined with ferns and bushes, and at the bottom, four magnificent oak trees stretched their branches to the sky.

"Wow!" Cloud Spots breathed out at Gray Wing's shoulder.

Jagged Peak's voice rose in an excited squeak: "Why don't we live here?"

Gray Wing gave him a quelling look, but didn't reply. As he led the way down the slope, ears alert for possible danger, he began to feel once again the familiar sensation of being trapped under the trees. The branches arched overhead, interlacing so that he could only see patches of open sky.

In the middle of the four oaks, a huge jagged rock stretched many tail-lengths into the air. Jagged Peak bunched his muscles and tried to leap onto the top, but it was too high for him. He dropped back, his claws scrabbling at the rock face.

"Clear Sky would be able to leap up there!" he mewed, with an annoyed flick of his tail.

"Yes, but why would he want to?" Gray Wing pointed out. Avoiding an argument with Jagged Peak, he added, "We should stop for a while and hunt. There's bound to be prey among all this undergrowth."

Jagged Peak headed off at once.

"Stay in the hollow!" Gray Wing called after him.

The rest of the group split up. As Gray Wing had hoped, the prey was plentiful, and before long they gathered at the base of the rock to eat. As he swallowed bites of mouse, he heard rustling in the bushes on the side of the hollow. Tasting the air, he picked up the scent of cat.

"It's a rogue," Turtle Tail whispered.

Watching the movement of the branches, Gray Wing caught glimpses of a ginger pelt; the strange cat was moving toward the top of the hollow. More movement appeared farther up, and a black-and-white face popped out for a moment between the fronds of a clump of fern.

"There are more of them!" Jagged Peak sprang to his paws, his claws extended. "We should fight them off."

Cloud Spots moved to block the young cat before he could go charging off the slope. "Are you flea-brained?" he hissed. "Why should we fight them? They're not doing us any harm."

"But they—" Jagged Peak began to protest.

"Cloud Spots is right," Gray Wing meowed, remembering the claws of the kittypet he had fought in the Twolegplace. "We're not fit for fighting yet, and we need to have a much clearer idea of this place before we risk meeting hostile cats."

"For all we know, they might be friendly," Rainswept Flower added.

Jagged Peak gave a snort of disbelief, but didn't say any more. Gray Wing cast a wary eye back toward the cat peering out from the ferns. He did not know if these cats would cause them trouble or not—but he would keep his eyes and ears open, just in case.

Two sunrises later, Gray Wing was hunting alone on the moor. The warm, bright weather had given way to a raw chill, with clouds covering the sky and a smattering of rain on the wind.

Gray Wing scanned the moorland for the least sign of movement. His pads tingled with excitement as he spotted a rabbit racing across the top of the slope. He sprang forward. The rabbit veered aside with a shrill squeal of fear and Gray Wing altered course, stretching out his paws and pushing off from the tough grass to force out every last bit of speed.

He was reaching for the rabbit when something slammed into him from the side. His paws skidded out from under him and he crashed to the ground, rolling over with legs and tail waving.

Half stunned, Gray Wing scrambled up to see a wiry brown she-cat glaring at him with yellow eyes. Just beyond her, a thin gray tom was rising to his paws and shaking scraps of grass from his pelt. The rapidly fading scent told Gray Wing that the rabbit had escaped.

He lashed his tail angrily. "You made me lose my rabbit!"

"*Your* rabbit?" The gray tom stepped forward to stand beside the she-cat. "Wind, why do you think this crow-food eater thinks that was his rabbit?"

"I have no idea, Gorse," the she-cat, Wind, replied, her neck fur bristling. "We've seen you, you know," she hissed at Gray Wing. "Strolling in here, stealing our prey!"

"Yes, where did you come from?" Gorse asked aggressively. "I hope you don't mean to stay long, because—"

"We'll stay as long as we like," Gray Wing retorted. "The prey belongs to the cats who can catch it, and there's plenty here for all of us."

Wind slid out her claws. "That's not for you to say."

Gray Wing braced himself for an attack, but before Wind or Gorse could spring, a cool voice spoke from somewhere behind him. "Having trouble, Gray Wing?"

Glancing over his shoulder, Gray Wing saw Tall Shadow appearing from behind a lichen-covered boulder. Her paw had healed, and she looked formidable, her green eyes narrowing as she faced the hostile cats. Hawk Swoop was padding at her shoulder, her teeth bared in the beginning of a snarl.

"These cats knocked me over when I was chasing a rabbit," Gray Wing explained.

"*We* knocked *you* over?" Wind let out a snort of disgust. "You ran straight into us. You're as blind as a mole in daylight!"

"We're not going to argue," Tall Shadow mewed, flexing her claws. "I'd leave, if I were you. Or do you want us to make you?"

Gorse took a step back, and after a heartbeat Wind followed. "Don't think you're getting away with this," she snapped as she retreated. "You're not welcome here!"

Tall Shadow stood watching until a fold in the moor hid the two rogues, then led the way back to the hollow on the moors. Before they reached it, a thin rain began to fall, soaking the cats' pelts. Water welled up from the grass when they set down their paws.

Gray Wing felt thoroughly dejected. He was glad that Tall Shadow and Hawk Swoop had turned up before a fight started, but . . . *I shouldn't have been so quick to argue. I could have talked to Gorse and Wind . . . do we really want to fight to stay here?*

When they arrived at the hollow, Hawk Swoop told the story to the rest of the cats. "Tall Shadow made them go away," she finished triumphantly. "She was great!"

But not every cat was pleased to hear what had happened. "Will it be like that every time we go hunting?" Turtle Tail asked. "I don't want to have to fight for the right to catch prey."

"Neither do I," Rainswept Flower agreed. "Maybe this isn't where we're supposed to live, after all."

Cloud Spots nodded. "Suppose Tall Shadow and Hawk Swoop hadn't turned up when they did. Gray Wing could have been seriously hurt."

Jackdaw's Cry and Dappled Pelt exchanged glances. "If worse comes to worst, we could always go back to the mountains," Jackdaw's Cry pointed out. "Prey was scarce, but at least we didn't have to fight for it."

For the next few days the rain continued almost without a break. Exploring didn't seem exciting anymore, especially with the threat of meeting more hostile cats. Gray Wing and the others huddled under the gorse bushes for shelter, except when hunger drove them out to catch rabbits.

Four sunrises after his encounter with Wind and Gorse, Gray Wing awoke from an uncomfortable doze to see Moon Shadow crashing down the slope among the bushes, dragging something heavy behind him.

"Look what I caught!" the black tom exclaimed proudly, dropping two squirrels beside the rock where Tall Shadow was sheltering.

"Where did you get those?" Tall Shadow mewed.

"In the woodland," Moon Shadow boasted, gazing around as other cats came up to examine his prey. "It was easy."

"It was *flea-brained*," Tall Shadow snapped. "You shouldn't have gone there alone. From now on, we hunt in groups."

"Who died and put you in charge?" Moon Shadow demanded, his tail-tip twitching in annoyance.

"Shaded Moss, actually," Tall Shadow replied. "And it's not a position I ever asked for."

Did Shaded Moss make her his successor? Gray Wing wondered. *They talked together a lot. And I don't think Tall Shadow would lie.*

Though tension was rising among the cats, none of the others challenged Tall Shadow. Gray Wing was aware of a moment of grief. *We're all wondering how different things would be if Shaded Moss were still here.*

He knew that this place wasn't as wonderful as they had hoped when they set out from the mountains, or even when they first arrived on the moor after crossing the Thunderpath, but in the torrential rain no cat had the appetite for more journeying.

We're here . . . we have to make the best of it.

CHAPTER 14

❖

As the cats shared Moon Shadow's prey, Gray Wing thought that
Clear Sky seemed sad and angry. He hadn't spoken, except for
a brief word of thanks to Moon Shadow, and he only took a
couple of mouthfuls.

"You need to talk to your brother about Bright Stream,"
Turtle Tail murmured into Gray Wing's ear. "You can't avoid
him forever."

"I'll think about it," Gray Wing responded, though he
shrank from the idea of Clear Sky's fury turned against him.

Later that day the rain stopped and the sky cleared as wind
sent the clouds scudding away. Gray Wing spotted his brother
climbing the slope of the hollow alone. Briefly he hesitated.
You'll never have a better chance than this, he told himself, setting
out to follow.

Clear Sky raced across the moor in a direction Gray Wing
hadn't yet walked. *Where is he going?*

After a while, he realized that his brother was heading
toward the river. Gray Wing had never seen it up close, and
curiosity tingled through his pads as he heard the sound of
thundering water.

Clear Sky reached the riverbank at the point where a waterfall crashed down over rocks, throwing up fountains of spray. Beyond the falls, the river ran through sheer walls of stone. The recent rain had left it noisy and foaming. The sound and sight of the tumbling water reminded Gray Wing of his home in the mountains.

Watching the river, Gray Wing briefly lost sight of Clear Sky before realizing his brother was climbing down one of the narrow paths that led to the water's edge. Gray Wing followed, setting his paws carefully and hugging the rock face, away from the sheer drop into the river.

Clear Sky was in no hurry, and Gray Wing soon began to catch up. "Did you come here because it reminds you of our waterfall?" he asked him.

Startled, Clear Sky spun around. His paws skidded on the slick surface of the path, and he let out a squeal of alarm as he slid over the edge.

Gray Wing bounded forward, caution forgotten, and managed to grab his brother's scruff before Clear Sky could plunge into the gorge. For a few heartbeats Clear Sky dangled above the turbulent water, his paws flailing helplessly, Gray Wing's grip the only thing that kept him from falling. His terrified blue eyes gazed up into Gray Wing's.

An image flashed into Gray Wing's mind of how he had tried to cling to Bright Stream as the eagle dragged her away. "I won't let you die too," he hissed through clenched teeth.

Confusion battled with the fear in Clear Sky's eyes. "What . . . ?"

With a mighty effort, Gray Wing hauled his brother upward until he could set his paws firmly on the path again. Clear Sky shook himself; his blue gaze was furious as he glared at Gray Wing. "You flea-brained idiot!" he snarled, his neck fur bristling. "Did you have to creep up on me like that?"

Gray Wing was still shaking from the thought of what could have happened. "I'm sorry," he murmured.

Clear Sky glared at him for a moment longer, then let his fur lie flat again. "What did you mean, you won't let me die too?" he asked.

Gray Wing took a deep breath. Then the words he had wanted to say for almost a moon tumbled out of him. "I can't bear what happened to Bright Stream! I know it was my fault she died. I've wished over and over we could have switched places. I'm more sorry than I can ever tell you."

Clear Sky's eyes widened and he stared at Gray Wing in astonishment. "It wasn't your fault she died!" he choked out. "The whole plan was *my* idea. I should never have let her go out to fight the eagles, not when she was carrying our kits. *I* killed her!"

Gray Wing stared at Clear Sky in disbelief, then took a pace forward so that he could push his muzzle into his brother's shoulder fur. "Perhaps it was no cat's fault," he murmured, his voice rough with grief. "Just a terrible accident. We can't both live our lives feeling guilty. Bright Stream wouldn't want that. She loved you too much to want you to be unhappy."

Gray Wing wasn't sure that he was choosing the right words. He had been sunk so deeply in his own guilt for so long. But knowing that Clear Sky blamed himself, too, made him feel as if a great weight had been lifted from his shoulders.

We'll still mourn Bright Stream, we'll never forget her, but our lives will go on. Letting out a gusty sigh, Gray Wing gave his pelt a shake. "Why don't we explore a bit farther downriver?" he suggested.

Clear Sky nodded. "Let's do that."

This time Gray Wing took the lead, down the narrow path and then alongside the tumbling torrent. Bright Stream's death still pained them both, but Gray Wing was comforted to feel that they had recovered some of their old closeness.

They headed downriver. At first there was a clear path at the water's edge, but undergrowth gradually encroached on it until the cats had to battle their way through. Gray Wing muttered curses under his breath as twigs and bramble tendrils snagged in his fur.

Eventually the undergrowth thinned out and they saw a tall outcrop of rocks jutting out from the river, which swept around it in two surging channels. Gray Wing spotted stepping-stones just above the surface of the water.

"Let's explore!" Clear Sky exclaimed. Without waiting for Gray Wing's response, he jumped neatly from stone to stone until he reached the outcrop. "Come on, it's easy!" he called back to Gray Wing.

Gray Wing didn't see the point of crossing to the outcrop, but he heard the hint of challenge in his brother's voice. More hesitantly than Clear Sky, he leaped over the stepping-stones. Their surfaces were uneven and slick with water, and Gray Wing had a vision of slipping and being carried away by the swift, choppy current.

"You took your time," Clear Sky meowed as Gray Wing reached his side. He gave him a friendly butt with his head. "Let's climb to the top."

He set off with a powerful leap, and Gray Wing toiled after him. Finally they reached the summit of the outcrop, made up of several flat rocks at different levels, with deep cracks between.

Gray Wing glanced warily in all directions. "There's a lot of cat scent around here."

"I'm not surprised," Clear Sky responded. "These rocks must be great for sunning yourself. And there'll be plenty of prey in all these cracks."

"Quite right," a cold voice hissed from behind them.

Gray Wing and Clear Sky both jumped around, startled, to see a strange she-cat standing on the top of a flat rock a couple of tail-lengths away. She was completely black, except for one white paw and a white spot on one shoulder; her green eyes were narrowed, glaring at them with hostility.

"Hello," Gray Wing meowed, trying to sound friendly.

The black she-cat wasn't impressed. "Get off my rocks," she snarled, sliding out her claws.

Clear Sky's neck fur began to rise. "Who says they're *your* rocks?"

The she-cat took a threatening pace forward. "I've heard about trespassers on the moor. You're not welcome here!" She spun around and, to Gray Wing's astonishment, jumped neatly into the river. Her sleek dark head reappeared a heartbeat later as she swam strongly for the opposite bank.

"A swimming cat!" Clear Sky exclaimed.

Relieved that the encounter had been no worse, Gray Wing let out a *mrrow* of amusement. "She should meet Falling Feather," he mewed.

Together the two cats leaped over the stepping-stones again and bounded back into the trees. A squirrel darted out in front of them and fled for safety up a tree, but Clear Sky brought it down with another massive leap.

He and Gray Wing settled down side by side to share the prey.

"You know," Clear Sky murmured, glancing around him, "I could live somewhere like this."

Gray Wing swallowed the mouthful he was eating. "I prefer open sky," he responded.

Clear Sky flicked an ear at him. "Well, you have the speed to catch rabbits!"

When they had finished the prey, the two brothers headed back through the trees. Gray Wing could hear rustling, as if other cats were vanishing into the bushes.

"I think we're being watched," he hissed.

Clear Sky gave an airy wave of his tail. "So what? They're not showing themselves, so they must be scared of us. And that's fine by me. I don't want to be challenged for every mouthful of prey."

Gray Wing couldn't share his brother's confidence. "If we stay here, we need to live peacefully with these other cats," he pointed out.

The strangeness of this place washed over him again like water surging over a rock. *I feel like I don't know anything about living here.*

Clear Sky led the way back to the moor, veering away from the river to pass through the huge hollow where the four oak trees stood.

"This is a fantastic place!" he exclaimed, turning around as if he was trying to see all of it at once. Then he leaped up one of the oaks, clawing his way up the bark until he could stand where a branch forked from the main trunk.

"Come down!" Gray Wing called, not even trying to imitate his brother's jump. "You're not a squirrel!"

"There's no reason cats can't live in trees," Clear Sky responded, waving his tail playfully.

Gray Wing rolled his eyes. Before he could reply, he felt once again the sensation of being watched. Scanning the slope, he spotted a plump tortoiseshell cat scrutinizing them from the shelter of a clump of fern, her dappled pelt almost invisible in its shadow.

"We've got company," he told Clear Sky.

His brother looked where he was pointing, then climbed back to the ground, jumping the last few tail-lengths.

Before he landed, the tortoiseshell cat turned and bounded off up the slope. Gray Wing watched her go, frustrated that he hadn't had the chance to speak to her.

"She seemed really well fed," he commented to Clear Sky.

"You're right," said Clear Sky. "She was no wild cat. Do you think kittypets come into these woods?"

Gray Wing wasn't sure. He knew that some of the others

had spotted Twoleg dens through the trees, and the narrow paths carried the scents of Twolegs and dogs, but the moor and the forest were mostly left to wild creatures.

That's how it should be. I can't understand why any cat would want to live with Twolegs, he thought curiously.

Gray Wing and Clear Sky reached the hollow to hear Moon Shadow's voice raised argumentatively.

"I've told you over and over again that I'm sick of eating rabbits and getting wet! Why don't we go and live among the trees?"

He stood facing his sister, his neck fur fluffed up and his tail lashing.

"It's not as easy as that," Tall Shadow responded, her voice cold.

As Gray Wing and Clear Sky picked their way down the slope, Turtle Tail padded up to meet them. "Those two are at it again," she muttered, rolling her eyes.

"All you ever do is order us around," Moon Shadow was saying.

"And all *you* ever do is argue," Hawk Swoop interrupted, stepping between Moon Shadow and Tall Shadow. "The rest of us are tired of listening to it. Look, it's not raining now, so why don't we try hunting some birds, like we used to?"

Glancing around, Hawk Swoop pointed with her tail toward a hawk circling over some rough grass below the hollow. "Come on," she urged. "We know how to catch that kind of prey!"

Jackdaw's Cry sprang to his paws at once, followed a

heartbeat later by Dappled Pelt and Rainswept Flower. Though Gray Wing's legs were tired, he stepped forward too.

Clear Sky padded across to Tall Shadow. "Are you okay with this?" he asked.

Tall Shadow shrugged. "You can hunt whatever you like— so long as you stay out of the trees where the other cats are."

Moon Shadow looked as if he was going to start arguing again, then turned and stomped off to his nest.

"Are you coming?" Gray Wing asked Turtle Tail.

"No," said the young tortoiseshell. "I've already eaten once today. I don't need to hunt again."

With Hawk Swoop in the lead, the mountain cats climbed out of the hollow and ran down the slope toward the hawk, keeping low so as not to alert it.

"It's a bit small, isn't it?" Dappled Pelt murmured. "It looks like a sparrow, compared to the eagles back home."

"This is our home now," Hawk Swoop meowed instantly.

A heavy silence greeted her words. *Is it really our home?* Gray Wing wondered. But racing along with the wind in his fur and the sun warming his back, he began to feel content.

This could be a good place to live.

The cats surrounded the hawk, instinctively remembering their mountain hunting patterns as they closed in on it from different directions. Hawk Swoop nodded to Jackdaw's Cry; he could jump the highest, so he was a good choice to make the first leap.

The hawk was distracted by focusing on its tiny prey in the grass. At the last moment it became aware of the hunting cats, and beat its wings in an attempt to gain height.

But it was too late. Jackdaw's Cry hurled himself into the air and brought the hawk down with a yowl of triumph. The other cats rushed in to help hold it down, but Jackdaw's Cry had already killed it with a bite to its neck.

That was almost too easy, Gray Wing thought.

"Great catch," Rainswept Flower mewed admiringly. "You can keep it for yourself."

Jackdaw's Cry ducked his head, proud and embarrassed.

While they were talking, Dappled Pelt had pounced into the grass. When she straightened up, the mouse the hawk had been hunting was dangling from her jaws.

"Two catches in one go!" she mumbled through the mouthful of prey.

"That would never have happened in the mountains," Rainswept Flower commented.

Every cat looked pleased, though Gray Wing felt that their cheerfulness was slightly forced.

We're all trying too hard to pretend this is perfect.

CHAPTER 15

Gray Wing padded through the trees, following Clear Sky's lead. Jackdaw's Cry, Falling Feather, and Turtle Tail hunted with them. As always when he left the moor for the forest, Gray Wing felt uncomfortable. He couldn't hunt down his prey by running when every few paw steps a bramble tendril would trip him, and when the air was laden with so many scents it was hard to follow the one he wanted.

Falling Feather had just caught a mouse, when a loud screech echoed through the trees. It was followed by crashing in the undergrowth, and the furiously yowling voices of more than one cat.

Clear Sky froze, his ears flicking forward. "That's Moon Shadow!" he exclaimed.

He sprang forward in the direction of the sounds, and the others followed. As Gray Wing wound his way among the ferns he heard Turtle Tail meow behind him. "Wouldn't you just know that *he'd* be the one to get into trouble?"

Gray Wing remembered the Twolegplace and the fight with the kittypets. *Moon Shadow shouldn't go off by himself. But we still have to help him.*

The brothers burst into a clearing, the other cats hard on their paws. At the far side, Gray Wing spotted Moon Shadow locked in a caterwauling bundle of fur with three other cats. The struggle heaved back and forth at the edge of a bramble thicket; a tail-length or so away was the body of a squirrel.

With an ear-splitting shriek, Clear Sky hurtled across the clearing. He grabbed one cat by the shoulder and hauled him away from Moon Shadow. Gray Wing leaped on top of another and cuffed the cat around the ears until she let go of his friend.

He wasn't prepared for the cat to turn on him, or for the ferocity of the attack. Before he could think about defending himself claws were raking down his side. He tried to bring up his hind paws to thrust the cat off, but the cat wrapped her forepaws around his neck and clung tightly. Gray Wing jerked his head away to avoid teeth aimed for his throat.

He was dimly aware of more yowling and skirmishing around him. The taste of blood was in his mouth. *This cat wants to kill me*, he thought, his senses fogged with pain.

Then a heavy weight landed on top of him and his opponent. Gray Wing almost despaired, until he heard a familiar voice raised in an enraged yowl. "Get off him!"

Turtle Tail!

The other cat rolled away and Gray Wing staggered to his paws. He saw that all three strange cats had broken off the fight and stood glaring and hissing at the mountain cats. Gray Wing got a good look at them for the first time. One was the black she-cat with the white paw that he and Clear Sky had met on the rocks a few days before. The others were a small yellow tabby she-cat and a black-and-white tom. Fierce satisfaction surged through him when he saw that they all bore the marks of claws.

Moon Shadow lay panting at the edge of the thicket, a clump of fur torn away from his shoulder. Turtle Tail padded over and helped him to his paws; she had a scratched muzzle, and her fur was ruffled.

"They attacked me!" Moon Shadow exclaimed indignantly.

Turtle Tail was unsympathetic. "What did you think would happen when you wandered off on your own, flea-brain?"

"I told you before," the black she-cat snapped, glaring at Clear Sky and Gray Wing. "You're not welcome here. Why don't you go back where you came from?"

"Yes, and stop stealing our prey," the black-and-white tom added.

"*Your* prey?" Moon Shadow was outraged. "I caught that squirrel! That makes it *my* prey!"

The yellow tabby slid out her claws, her muscles tensed as if she was about to leap at Moon Shadow. Gray Wing braced himself in case the fight erupted again.

"You fight like half-dead rabbits," the black-and-white tom snarled. "You only won this time because there are more of you. But just watch your tails if you come back."

"Yeah," the yellow tabby added. "We'll be waiting."

The black she-cat waved her tail and all three forest cats headed off into the undergrowth. At the last moment the yellow tabby darted over to the squirrel, grabbed it, and dragged it away with her.

"Hey!" Moon Shadow protested, starting after her.

Clear Sky barreled into him, knocking him to the ground. "Have you learned *nothing*?" he demanded. "This isn't the time to start another fight."

Huffing indignantly, Moon Shadow got up and followed Clear Sky as he led the way back to the moor. Gray Wing found it hard going; the scratches on his side grew more painful with every step. Jackdaw's Cry was limping from a torn claw, Falling Feather had lost a pawful of fur, and blood was trickling from Clear Sky's shoulder.

This is winning? What happens if we lose? Gray Wing wondered.

"You've been told time and time again . . ." Tall Shadow faced Moon Shadow, her voice taut with fury and her tail lashing, ". . . and still you don't listen!"

The hunting party had returned to the hollow on the moor, where Clear Sky had reported the clash with the forest cats.

"Because it's a flea-brained order!" Moon Shadow retorted. "This is a smaller space than we had in the mountains. Why do you want us to sit here trembling like hunted rabbits?"

Gray Wing had to admit that Moon Shadow had a point. The hollow wasn't comfortable enough for a permanent home, and the prey-rich forest was too tantalizing for every cat to ignore.

Tall Shadow's fury ebbed and she twitched her whiskers thoughtfully. "Okay, maybe we should hunt more regularly in the forest. We can't let those cats think they've frightened us off." She fixed her brother with a fierce green glare. "But you *don't* go off on your own again, is that clear?"

Moon Shadow shrugged. "I wouldn't have to if you'd let us hunt there properly."

Cloud Spots padded up with a mouthful of herbs and set them down. "I managed to find chervil," he meowed. "Let me put some on your scratches."

He dabbed juice onto Turtle Tail's injured muzzle, then turned to Gray Wing, who lay down so that Cloud Spots could treat the scratches on his side.

"You know," Cloud Spots murmured as he patted the chewed-up leaves into place, "I'm not happy with the idea that we always have to fight these other cats. Maybe we should think about finding a way to live peacefully near them."

"I'm not sure," Gray Wing responded. "I wish we could do that, but maybe we're just too different from them."

On the following day, the sun had just cleared the horizon when Moon Shadow announced he was going hunting.

Tall Shadow turned to look at him, her tail-tip twitching. Before she could speak, Clear Sky stepped up beside Moon Shadow. "I'll come with you," he offered.

Jagged Peak, Quick Water, and Shattered Ice jumped up to join them, and after a moment's hesitation Tall Shadow gave a *mrrow* of agreement. "Okay. Good luck."

"What about you?" Clear Sky asked Gray Wing.

"Not this time," Gray Wing replied. His scratches from the fight were still sore and he didn't think he would be much use at tracking prey under the trees. He tried to convince himself that he wasn't afraid of meeting the other cats again.

Once the hunters had gone, Turtle Tail padded over to Gray Wing. "Why don't we go for a walk?" she suggested. "No catching prey, no getting into fights."

"That sounds good," Gray Wing agreed.

When they left the hollow they could still see Clear Sky and the other hunters heading across the moor toward the forest. "Are you following them?" Gray Wing asked, surprised.

"No, I just want to go to the giant oaks again," Turtle Tail explained. "I like it there!"

The vast hollow was quiet except for the gentle rustling of the oak trees. Sunlight slanted through their branches, dappling the forest floor. Turtle Tail raced down the slope and over to the huge boulder between the four oaks, clawing her way up it until she stood on top.

"Come on!" she called, waving her tail at Gray Wing. "It's great up here!"

Gray Wing followed her more slowly, and clambered up the rock, digging his claws into tiny cracks, until he stood beside her. The sun-warmed surface felt good under his pads, and he lay down on one side to let the sunlight play over his fur.

Turtle Tail sat beside him, her tail wrapped neatly over her forepaws, and sighed with contentment. "I'd like to stay here forever."

Drowsing, Gray Wing lost track of time until a voice from the bottom of the rock roused him.

"Hey, you up there!"

Side by side, Gray Wing and Turtle Tail peered over the edge. To his surprise, Gray Wing saw the plump tortoiseshell who had been watching him and Clear Sky when they came to the hollow, looking up with a cheerful gleam in her yellow eyes.

"I'm Bumble," she announced confidently. "I'm a house-cat—though I guess you'd call me a kittypet. Can I come up?"

"Sure," Turtle Tail invited with a wave of her tail.

To Gray Wing's eyes, the plump tortoiseshell didn't look as if she would be able to climb, but within a couple of heartbeats she had heaved herself to the top of the boulder beside them.

"Hello," Turtle Tail greeted her. "I'm Turtle Tail, and this is Gray Wing."

"Wow, aren't you skinny?" Bumble meowed, examining the two mountain cats with a frank gaze. "Haven't you managed to catch anything to eat?"

"We've come a long way," Turtle Tail responded; Gray Wing was amused to see she looked slightly ruffled. "There wasn't always time to hunt."

Bumble blinked curiously. "A long way? How long? From the other side of the moor?"

"Farther than that," Gray Wing replied.

"You know those jagged rocks on the horizon? Highstones?" said Turtle Tail.

The kittypet's eyes stretched wide with astonishment. "You came from there?"

Turtle Tail shook her head. "No, from the other side of Highstones. We traveled for many, many sunrises."

"Why?" Bumble sounded completely flummoxed.

"There wasn't enough prey to feed all of us where we came

from," Gray Wing explained. "And in the cold season, we would often get stuck in the really deep snow."

"And sometimes cats got carried off by birds." There was a gleam in Turtle Tail's eye, as if she was enjoying shocking this kittypet. "*Huge* birds—far bigger than the ones around here."

"That sounds so hard!" Bumble exclaimed. "You must have been cold and hungry and scared all the time. No wonder you came to live here." She looked around her with a happy flick of her tail. "It's nice."

"But you don't live here, do you?" Turtle Tail asked. "You live with Twolegs. That's . . . weird."

"Weird?" Bumble's whiskers twitched. "It's great! My housefolk's den is so cozy, and there's always plenty of food, and nothing to be scared of."

"But what do you do all day?" Turtle Tail asked.

"Sleep, mostly," the kittypet said. "Or play with my house-folk's kits. And if I get tired of that, I come here."

"The wild cats don't bother you?" Gray Wing asked.

"No. They know I'm no threat to their hunting."

For a while all three cats lazed in the sun. Gray Wing enjoyed the warmth on his fur, but after a while his growling belly reminded him that he hadn't eaten since the day before.

Turtle Tail gave him a prod. "We should hunt," she mewed.

"I'm glad I don't have to do that!" Bumble gave them a friendly nod and scrambled down the rock. "See you later!"

"What a boring way to live," Turtle Tail commented, jumping to the forest floor.

Gray Wing hesitated before following her; the rock

underneath his paws had been a pleasant reminder of the mountains.

Together the two cats headed back toward the open moor.

"I can't get used to hunting under trees," Turtle Tail confided to Gray Wing. "They're too noisy, and I'm afraid of crashing into them."

"True," Gray Wing agreed. "It's impossible to concentrate on prey."

Turtle Tail padded on in silence for a while, then murmured, "I wonder if we'll ever see Bumble again."

"I doubt it," Gray Wing responded. "She won't want to talk to ferocious wild cats like us. We might eat her!"

Turtle Tail let out a *mrrow* of amusement. A heartbeat later she stiffened. "Rabbit!" she whispered.

By now they had left the trees behind and were climbing up the swell of moorland toward their hollow. The rabbit was hopping about not far from the crest, nibbling the grass.

Both cats sprang forward. But the scratches on Gray Wing's flank slowed him down, and Turtle Tail surged ahead. The rabbit bolted, vanishing over the crest of the hill, with Turtle Tail racing after it.

When Gray Wing reached the top he looked down to see Turtle Tail standing over the body of the rabbit. "Great catch!" he meowed as he bounded down to join her.

After they had eaten their prey, Gray Wing and Turtle Tail headed back to the hollow. Clear Sky and the rest of the hunting cats caught up as they arrived. Clear Sky was dragging a squirrel, Moon Shadow had a thrush, and the others were carrying mice.

"You should have seen Clear Sky chase that squirrel!" Jagged Peak mumbled around his mouthful of prey. "He went right to the top of the tree!"

Clear Sky's eyes gleamed with pride. To Gray Wing, his brother looked more like his old self. *Maybe the cloud of Bright Stream's death is starting to lift at last.*

Tall Shadow dipped her head to the hunting cats as they carried their prey to the bottom of the hollow and set it down. "Congratulations. You've done very well." As the other cats gathered around, she added, "Thank you, Stoneteller, for sending us to this place where we can find prey."

While the cats were eating, the sun began to sink behind Highstones, flooding the sky with scarlet. Gray Wing relaxed, glad that, for once, the cats were at peace with one another. Gazing at the landscape, which was starting to feel more familiar, he began to let himself believe that they might have reached the place that Stoneteller promised.

Gray Wing paused at the edge of the moor and looked down at the tops of the four great oak trees. Already they were lusher than when he had first seen them. The sun was shining, the air was full of fresh scents, and he could see new plants springing up all around.

I can't believe how rich the growth is! It was never like this in the mountains.

Stretching his muscles, Gray Wing ran just for the joy of it, circling the edge of the moor, then heading toward the edge of the gorge. He had avoided the river ever since he had startled Clear Sky into falling, but he remembered the excitement of the thundering water and the rocks that brought the mountains so vividly into his mind.

Gray Wing hadn't gone far when he heard the squeal of a terrified rabbit and, farther away, the yowl of a hunting cat. He halted as he saw the rabbit come tearing over the crest of the moorland, with the two cats he had met before—Gorse and Wind—close behind. Gray Wing's instincts told him to join the pursuit, but he wanted to avoid hostility, and dug his claws firmly into the soil.

The rabbit flashed past him, followed by Wind with Gorse a couple of tail-lengths behind. Suddenly the rabbit dived between two stones and vanished into a barely visible hole in the ground. Gray Wing let out a gasp of astonishment as Wind, without breaking stride, dived down the hole after it.

Gorse skidded to a halt. "That's not fair!" he panted. "You shouldn't keep going underground just because you're skinny!"

Gray Wing padded over to the gray tabby tom, who turned to him with a wary look in his eyes. "It's okay," Gray Wing meowed. "I'm not looking for a fight. What did you mean, going underground?"

"You saw what she did," Gorse replied, angling his ears toward the rabbit hole. "She's so scrawny she can fit down there."

At that moment Wind reappeared, puffing as she heaved herself out of the hole with the rabbit in her jaws.

Gray Wing watched her, fascinated. "Could I go down there?" he asked.

Wind looked at him, surprised. "If you want," she replied,

dropping the rabbit at Gorse's paws. "It's not my home, it's the rabbit's."

Gray Wing padded over to the burrow's entrance, passing his tongue over his jaws at the strong scent of rabbit. But the hole looked very small, and he wasn't sure if he wanted to try squeezing into it.

Behind him, Wind heaved a huge sigh. "I'll show you how. You're skinny enough to get anywhere I can."

Pushing past Gray Wing, she led the way in. Gray Wing had to follow—otherwise, he would look like a coward in front of these strange cats. He plunged into the hole, his pelt brushing the walls on either side. The burrow was dark and stuffy, and Gray Wing found it harder and harder to put one paw in front of another.

He was wrestling with panic when he felt Wind struggle to turn in front of him and give him a strong shove down a side tunnel. "That way!" she hissed, following him in the new direction.

At once, clearer air stirred Gray Wing's whiskers and he forced himself forward, with the occasional prod from Wind, until he emerged from another hole among the roots of a gorse bush. He staggered into the open and stood with his chest heaving.

"Mouse-brain!" Wind said, though her voice wasn't entirely unfriendly. "Don't do that again. If you panic down there you'll get lost before you know it."

Gray Wing was growing calmer now that he was in the fresh air again, with the huge sky above him and the breeze in his whiskers. "Maybe that wasn't such a good idea," he mewed.

But he was still fascinated by the knowledge that there was a network of tunnels underneath the moor. A claw-scratch of memory took him back to the elders' tales of tunnels in their old home by the lake.

They set some sort of challenge to young cats, who had to find their way out. Gray Wing shivered. *I'm glad we don't do that anymore. I'm not sure my Tribemates would ever see me again.*

Gray Wing dipped his head toward Gorse and Wind. "Thanks for showing me," he meowed. "Maybe I'll see you again sometime."

The two cats bade him a rather wary farewell. Gray Wing was just relieved that this encounter with them hadn't been hostile.

CHAPTER 16

Changing his mind about visiting the river, Gray Wing headed back to the hollow. As he approached it, he met Dappled Pelt and Cloud Spots.

"We're going to look for herbs," said Dappled Pelt. "Do you want to come with us?"

"I wish you would," Cloud Spots added. "Tall Shadow says she doesn't like cats going off the moor in groups smaller than three."

Dappled Pelt let out an irritable snort. "She's just making a fuss."

"Maybe," Cloud Spots responded, "but it'll be useful to have an extra mouth to carry whatever we can forage."

Gray Wing was happy to turn back and join them as they headed down the slope toward the river. "I met those two cats again—Gorse and Wind," he mewed. "Wind actually hunts rabbits underground!"

Dappled Pelt blinked in surprise. "I'd like to see that!"

Cloud Spots led the way to where the river emerged from the gorge. Sunlight shimmered on its surface. After several dry days, the water was calmer. Gray Wing waited, enjoying the warmth, while Cloud Spots and Dappled Pelt foraged among the lush vegetation at the water's edge.

"Look!" Cloud Spots exclaimed. "There are huge clumps of comfrey here."

"And yarrow!" Dappled Pelt's waving tail was all that was visible of her above the thickly growing plants. A moment later she emerged with a bunch of herbs in her jaws and set them down beside Gray Wing. "It's good to know that what we need is close by, and so early in the warm season," she meowed.

"Back in the mountains, we could spend a whole day searching in the bottom of the valley," Cloud Spots agreed. "And even then, we'd never find as much as this."

Together he and Dappled Pelt began to make a pile of useful leaves and roots at the edge of the river. Gray Wing kept watch in case any of the forest cats appeared, but everything was quiet.

When they had almost as much as they could carry, Dappled Pelt halted, tasting the air and gazing across the river to the far bank. "I can smell tansy over there," she announced. "Jackdaw's Cry wrenched his leg practicing his leaps, and tansy is really good for that."

"There are stepping-stones farther downstream," Gray Wing told her.

Dappled Pelt studied the river for a moment. "It doesn't look too deep," she mewed. Before Gray Wing realized what she meant to do, she began to wade out into the water. "If Falling Feather can do it, so can I!"

Gray Wing and Cloud Spots exchanged alarmed glances, then watched Dappled Pelt as she splashed forward, gasping as the cold water reached her belly fur. A heartbeat later she vanished without warning, the river swirling over her head.

"Haredung!" Cloud Spots exclaimed, bounding to the water's edge. "I'd better go in and save her."

But before he could plunge into the current, Dappled Pelt's head broke the surface. She was splashing frantically, somehow managing to propel herself toward the far bank.

"Hey, I'm swimming!" she called, surprise and triumph in her tone.

"It's not natural," Cloud Spots grunted. "You look like a furry fish."

Dappled Pelt scrambled out of the water, shook herself, and plunged into the undergrowth. Moments later she reappeared with a bunch of leaves in her jaws. Wading into the river she swam back, her head held awkwardly high to keep the leaves out of the water.

"See!" she gasped as she clambered up the bank. "It was easy—but oh, that water is cold!"

"I think you're mousebrained," Cloud Spots muttered, shaking his head. "Let's get back to the hollow."

"Why not stay and catch fish?" Dappled Pelt suggested.

Cloud Spots rolled his eyes. "Don't even think about it. You're going straight back to the hollow to dry out, before you get sick."

Dappled Pelt gave in with an exasperated snort, and the three cats headed back toward the moor. Gray Wing, a pace or two behind the others, heard voices from the other side of a clump of ferns. His fur bristled with suspicion.

Have Wind and Gorse doubled back to spy on us?

But when he crept through the ferns he found Turtle Tail and Bumble crouching side by side, sharing a plump vole.

Bumble was the first to spot him. "Hello, Gray Wing," she greeted him, sounding pleased to see him.

Turtle Tail sprang to her paws. "Oh . . . hi," she meowed. "Bumble saw me catch this vole, and she wanted to know what it tasted like."

Gray Wing wondered why Turtle Tail sounded so defensive. He was wary of strange cats, but he couldn't see anything threatening about this kittypet.

"She obviously likes it," he responded, setting down his bundle of herbs as Bumble tucked in again. "Bumble, why don't you come live in the forest all the time?"

Bumble looked up, choking on a mouthful of vole. "No way! My housefolk are kind and I never go hungry. The den is nice, too," she added. "You should come see it!"

"No, thanks," Gray Wing told her. "We don't belong with Twolegs."

"What about you, Turtle Tail?" Bumble asked.

Turtle Tail's whiskers twitched with curiosity. "It might be interesting to see it . . . but not right now."

Swallowing the last mouthful of prey, Bumble meowed, "Thanks, Turtle Tail. Let's meet up again soon."

"Okay," Turtle Tail agreed. "I'll keep a lookout for you in the hollow with the oak trees."

Bumble padded off through the ferns, her tail held high, casting a final glance over her shoulder before she disappeared.

"You know," Gray Wing mewed thoughtfully, "it's not a

good idea to get too friendly with kittypets."

Turtle Tail's neck fur fluffed up. "Why not?"

Gray Wing couldn't give her a clear answer. "It bothers me, that's all," he replied.

It's like I said. We don't belong with Twolegs.

Gray Wing lay in his nest under a gorse bush at the bottom of the hollow. The half-moon shed enough light for him to see the top of the slope and beyond it a clear sky glittering with stars. He was warm and full-fed.

This is a good place, he thought. *We can live here.*

Suddenly a dark shape came between him and the stars. Gray Wing narrowed his eyes and made out a sharp snout outlined against the sky. A rank scent drifted to his nose, and he remembered the thin, red-furred creature he had seen soon after they left the Twolegplace. He had smelled the scent in the forest, too, though he'd never seen the animal that left it.

The dark shape moved, slipping down into the hollow. It was followed by another, and then a third. A terrible awareness of danger swept over Gray Wing. He sprang to his paws.

"Attack!" he screeched.

The dreadful squeal of a cat in pain drowned out his warning. In the next heartbeat the hollow erupted into yowling and thrashing. Gray Wing stared around in panic, his paws frozen to the ground. He caught a glimpse of one of the creatures with his fangs sunk deep in Shattered Ice's shoulder, shaking the silver-furred tom as if he was a piece of prey.

We are prey, Gray Wing realized with a thrill of horror. *We'll all be killed!*

CHAPTER 17

Gray Wing's first instinct was to throw himself into the battle. But he knew how that would end; he would be torn to pieces. *I can't just leave the others! There must be some way I can help.*

Turtle Tail appeared at his side. "Foxes!" she gasped.

"What?"

"Foxes—that's what these things are. Bumble warned me about them. What are we going to do?"

At that moment Clear Sky tore past, claws out and teeth bared. Swiftly Gray Wing moved to block him.

"Let me get at them!" Clear Sky snarled.

"Wait!" Gray Wing meowed urgently. "We need a plan!"

As the sounds of wailing and growling rose up around him, louder with every heartbeat, Gray Wing knew that he had to think fast. A picture rose in his mind of how they had hunted eagles in the mountains, when one cat would pull the bird down and the others pile in to make the kill.

"The three of us together." He glanced from Clear Sky to Turtle Tail and back again, willing them to cooperate. "We attack one fox, and kill it if we can. Then go for the next."

Turtle Tail nodded eagerly. "That makes sense."

"But what about the others?" Clear Sky asked. "They could be dying while we attack one fox."

"If we split up, we can't do anything," Turtle Tail responded.

"We'll just have to be quick," Gray Wing continued. "Clear Sky, when we find a fox, you attack it from one side. Turtle Tail, from the other. Confuse it."

"What about you?" Clear Sky asked.

"I'll be there, don't worry," Gray Wing replied grimly.

He took the lead as the three cats prowled around the edge of the hollow, trying to make sense of the chaos below. At last Gray Wing spotted a fox at the edge of the fighting, standing over Hawk Swoop, who was twitching feebly.

"Now!" Gray Wing screeched.

Clear Sky leaped and began clawing at the fox's flank. As it turned on him with a snarl, Turtle Tail attacked from the other side. The fox turned its head this way and that, snapping its jaws but unable to reach Clear Sky or Turtle Tail, as they darted in to claw it and leaped back out of range.

It's working! Gray Wing launched himself into the air and landed on the fox's back. Digging his hind claws into its shoulders, he leaned over its face and tore at its eyes and muzzle. The fox let out a shriek. It reared up, trying to shake Gray Wing off, but he clung tight.

Still harried from both sides by Clear Sky and Turtle Tail, the fox headed for the edge of the hollow. Once it was out on the moorland, Gray Wing leaped clear of it, and watched it flee yelping into the darkness.

"Another!" Clear Sky yowled triumphantly. "And this

time I get to leap onto it."

Spinning around, he led the way back to the bottom of the hollow. Tall Shadow and Jackdaw's Cry were battling a second fox, but Jackdaw's Cry was staggering with exhaustion, and blood dripped into Tall Shadow's eyes from a scratch on her forehead.

Turtle Tail and Gray Wing hurled themselves into the battle, attacking the fox from both sides. With a fearsome screech, Clear Sky leaped onto its back, slashing at its ears as it weaved from side to side in an attempt to escape.

Within heartbeats it too gave up and fled. The third fox turned from worrying at Cloud Spots, who was feebly swiping at it with his hind paws, and realized that it was alone. With a yelp of fear it scrambled up the slope after the others and was gone.

Clear Sky bounded after it and halted at the rim of the hollow. "Good riddance!" he yowled. "Don't come back!"

Gray Wing glanced around. Jackdaw's Cry had sunk to the ground, panting, but he didn't seem to be badly injured. Moon Shadow was limping, and Rainswept Flower had had clumps of fur torn from her pelt. Jagged Peak was bleeding from scratches on his side. The others bore their own signs of the foxes' savagery, but at least they were all moving. Gray Wing had been afraid that Hawk Swoop had been killed, but even she had managed to stagger to her paws.

Cloud Spots turned to examine Tall Shadow's scratch. Dappled Pelt twitched her whiskers approvingly, then padded over. Working together, they began to move from one cat to another, examining their wounds.

Turtle Tail and Clear Sky trotted up to Gray Wing.

"We won!" Turtle Tail exclaimed. "Gray Wing, you were awesome!"

Clear Sky gave his brother an approving nod. "Fighting together worked well," he meowed. "Maybe we should practice, in case there's more trouble."

Gray Wing gave him a somber glance. "You're right," he agreed. "Because there *will* be more trouble." *And it won't be long in coming.*

A cold dawn light showed Gray Wing the devastation in the hollow. All the nests had been scattered and trampled in the fight, the turf scored by claws, and branches broken from the gorse bushes. The injured cats huddled in whatever shelter they could find.

We're lucky to be alive, Gray Wing thought. *But what's going to happen to us now?*

He sat licking the wound on his shoulder as the dawn light gradually strengthened. After a while he saw Clear Sky get up and speak briefly to Moon Shadow; then both cats padded across the hollow until they reached Tall Shadow. Curious, Gray Wing rose to his paws and followed.

"There's something we want to say," Clear Sky began.

Tall Shadow looked up; she and Rainswept Flower were helping each other pick thorns out of their pads. "Go on, then," she meowed.

It was Moon Shadow who continued. "We think we should

go and live among the trees. The hunting is easier there, and we'd be better hidden."

"We're too exposed here," Clear Sky added, waving his tail to indicate the wreckage around them. "There's no defense against foxes, or anything else that feels like attacking us."

Tall Shadow glanced sharply from Clear Sky to Moon Shadow and then back again. "But we've always lived in high places," she objected.

"And my father wouldn't have wanted us to split up," Rainswept Flower added.

"Your father isn't here anymore." Rainswept Flower winced at Clear Sky's blunt words.

By now more of the cats had realized something important was going on, and gathered around, listening with wide, troubled eyes. Gray Wing's belly churned with tension at the thought of leaving the open spaces he loved.

"I can't imagine wanting to live among trees," Jackdaw's Cry put in. "And what about the other cats who are already there?"

"We'll deal with them," Moon Shadow replied with a confident flick of his ears. "We don't want to fight for every mouthful of prey, but there's enough for all of us."

"It's not that easy," Hawk Swoop protested. "I think it could be good to live in the forest, but I don't think we should split up."

Tall Shadow thought for a moment. "Okay," she mewed eventually. "We'll do what we did in the cave—cast stones to decide whether we move to the forest or not."

A murmur of agreement rose from the listening cats. Jackdaw's Cry and Falling Feather got up immediately and went to forage for pebbles among the torn-up grass. All the others gathered around as they carried the stones back and piled them up beside Tall Shadow.

"All right," the black she-cat meowed. "If you want to stay here on the moor, put your stone on that bare patch of grass over there." She pointed with her tail. "If you want to leave, put your stone beside that gorse bush."

She was the first to vote, putting her stone on the bare patch. Rainswept Flower did the same. Tension settled over the cats as they all moved forward in turn to pick up a stone. Gray Wing placed his on the bare patch, and as the voting continued he was relieved to see that most of the others also wanted to stay. Only Moon Shadow, Clear Sky, Quick Water, and Falling Feather chose to move to the trees.

Jagged Peak was the last to pick up his pebble. Shooting an apologetic glance at Gray Wing, he placed it under the gorse bush.

Tall Shadow looked at both piles of stones. There was no need to count them; the result was clear. "It's settled, then," she announced. "We're staying here."

"Wait!" Clear Sky sprang to his paws. "That's not fair. Those of us who want to live in the trees should be allowed to."

"Yeah," Moon Shadow added. "When we voted in the cave, the cats who wanted to stay, stayed. And the ones who wanted to leave, left. Why should it be different now?"

There was a gasp from all the cats. Gray Wing felt as though he had been struck by a falling rock. *Can we really separate, after coming so far together?*

Tall Shadow took a deep breath. "Then leave." There was no anger in her tone, only sadness. "And go with our blessing. Come back whenever you want."

The cats who had voted to leave rose and gathered together. Shock tingled through Gray Wing. *Is this truly what's right for us?*

CHAPTER 18

The cats were all glancing at one another, confusion and sadness in their eyes.

"We won't be far away," Quick Water meowed; Gray Wing could tell she was trying to sound cheerful. "Our paths will cross all the time!"

Jackdaw's Cry gave Falling Feather a friendly nudge. "You'll be back when you miss the taste of rabbit, or the feeling of wind in your fur!"

"Wait till it rains!" There was real amusement now in Quick Water's voice. "Then you'll be sheltering under the trees with us."

As the cats who were leaving began to climb the slope out of the hollow, Clear Sky hung back and faced Gray Wing. "Good luck," he murmured. "I'll see you soon."

Gray Wing dipped his head, thankful that he and Clear Sky were close once again.

"Are you sure you won't come with us?" Clear Sky asked.

Gray Wing shook his head. "My heart lies in the open, in the high places," he explained. "But I'll walk with you a little way."

Together he and Clear Sky bounded up the slope to catch up with the others. Tall Shadow and Rainswept Flower came too, padding in a tight group across the moor until they reached the edge of the trees.

"Good-bye," Tall Shadow meowed, dipping her head to Clear Sky and the others. "May you find good prey and shelter. There will always be a place for you with us."

"Thank you," Clear Sky responded. "And you will always be welcome to visit us."

Even though he knew he would see his brothers again, it was wrenching for Gray Wing to turn away and leave them. His pace was slow as he headed back to the hollow, and he felt a deeper ache in his wounds. After a few paw steps he glanced back over his shoulder, but Clear Sky and the others had already vanished into the trees.

The hollow felt empty and quiet when Gray Wing and the others returned. Dappled Pelt was still busy treating wounds, while Turtle Tail was gathering grass, trying to repair the damaged nests.

Cloud Spots padded over to Gray Wing and touched him on the shoulder with his tail. "How about hunting?" he suggested. "We'd all feel better for some prey."

Gray Wing felt his spirits reviving. "Let's do that," he agreed.

Together they headed out onto the moor. A stiff breeze was blowing away the clouds, and patches of blue appeared here and there. Gray Wing caught a powerful whiff of rabbit, and spotted the creature nibbling the grass at the bottom of a rocky bank. Angling his ears toward it, he drew Cloud Spots's attention.

Cloud Spots circled the rabbit to come at it from the other direction. Remembering how they used to hunt hares in the mountains, Gray Wing braced himself, crouching in a clump of longer grass. A couple of heartbeats later the rabbit flicked up its ears, saw Cloud Spots and fled, heading straight for Gray Wing. Leaping out of the grass, Gray Wing knocked it over with a blow from his paw. Its squeal of terror was cut off as he killed it with a bite to the neck.

"Great job," Cloud Spots commented as he padded up. "It's a good plump one, too. It'll fill a few hungry bellies. You know," he added as Gray Wing began dragging the rabbit back to the hollow, "the others' leaving won't make much difference. It's just as if our home has gotten bigger."

Gray Wing muttered agreement through his mouthful of fur, but inwardly he wasn't so sure. *I hope Cloud Spots is right. But I just feel things are changing beyond any cat's control.*

Gray Wing paused near the edge of the trees, jaws parted to taste the air, half hoping that Clear Sky or one of the others would appear. A few sunrises had passed since the cats had left the moor, and Gray Wing still felt as though half of him had been torn away.

He was turning back, disappointed, when he spotted movement under the outlying trees. A cat emerged from a clump of ferns, glancing furtively from side to side before heading up the slope toward him. But it wasn't Clear Sky or any of his group; it was Turtle Tail.

Was she visiting Clear Sky? Gray Wing wondered. *But then, why would she look as if she doesn't want any cat to see her?*

He drew back into the shelter of a rock until Turtle Tail walked past him. "Hello," he meowed, stepping out in front of her.

Turtle Tail jumped. "You frightened me out of my fur!"

"Where have you been?" Gray Wing asked her. There was a weird scent on her pelt, one that he couldn't place, and his suspicions deepened. "And don't tell me you've been visiting Clear Sky, because I know you haven't."

Turtle Tail took a step back, her neck fur fluffing at his challenging tone. "Okay, I won't," she retorted. "I was visiting Bumble in the Twolegplace."

"What?" Even though Gray Wing had been suspicious, he had never imagined that. "Are you completely flea-brained?"

"I don't know what you're so angry about. It was fine! I went right into a Twoleg den." Turtle Tail's annoyance faded and she began to bubble over with pride in her achievement. "I was really scared, but Bumble was so nice, and she showed me everything. The Twolegs have soft rocks with colored pelts in there. They're so comfortable!"

Gray Wing struggled to find words to express how shocked he was. "You have to stay away from the Twolegplace," he told her. "It's dangerous!"

Turtle Tail flicked her tail dismissively. "Stop fussing. Bumble looked after me. You should come and visit too!"

Gray Wing felt as if his whole life was coming apart. His brothers and his friends had left the group to live in the trees, and now Turtle Tail seemed to have forgotten that she was a wild cat. "You're being ridiculous!" he snapped.

"And you know so much about it, I suppose?" Turtle Tail's neck fur bristled up again as she glared at him.

"Whatever." Gray Wing was suddenly tired of arguing. "Do what you want."

Leaving Turtle Tail to find her own way home, he stalked off into the woods. Instantly he felt swallowed up in the dense green world, the air heavy with lush growth. He found a familiar trail and headed along it, steering clear of strange cat scents.

Without warning two cat shapes dropped from the trees on either side of him and landed in the undergrowth. Gray Wing braced himself for an attack, then in the next heartbeat recognized Jagged Peak and Clear Sky.

"Surprise!" Jagged Peak yowled triumphantly.

Gray Wing let out a welcoming *mrrow* and touched noses with each of them. "You scared my tail off!" he mewed.

"We've been hunting in the trees," Jagged Peak boasted. "It's awesome!"

"Why don't you join us?" Clear Sky suggested.

Gray Wing glanced up at the nearest tree. *It looks awfully tall!* "Okay," he agreed, not wanting his brothers to know that he was scared, and looking forward to spending some time with them again.

He scrambled up the trunk after Clear Sky and Jagged

Peak, and balanced on the lowest branch. Digging his claws in nervously, he glanced around, trying to enjoy the different scents and the rustling of leaves around him.

Clear Sky took off in pursuit of a squirrel leaping from branch to branch. Jagged Peak followed, and Gray Wing clambered after them, envying their confidence and speed.

The squirrel leaped from the end of one springy branch into a nearby tree. Gray Wing paused, assuming they'd lost it, but Clear Sky didn't stop. He jumped after it, almost flying as he hurtled into the next tree, right on the squirrel's tail. Gray Wing was even more surprised when Jagged Peak followed him.

"I have to do this," he muttered, struggling to keep his balance as he edged his way along the branch. Bunching his muscles, he pushed off, reaching out his forepaws to grab the nearest branch of the other tree.

Gray Wing's claws scraped along the bark and he let out a screech as he felt himself falling. At the last moment he managed to get a grip, but he was left swinging helplessly, with nowhere to rest his hind paws. Fighting off dizziness, he managed to shift bit by bit along the branch until it grew wider near the trunk. He pulled himself up and sat shaking, wondering how he was going to get down again.

His pounding heart had quieted by the time that Clear Sky and Jagged Peak came back. Clear Sky was carrying the squirrel in his jaws.

"That was a great chase!" Jagged Peak exclaimed, his eyes gleaming with enthusiasm. "Are you okay, Gray Wing?"

"Er . . . I think I'm stuck here," Gray Wing confessed.

"That's okay. I'll help you down," Jagged Peak mewed confidently. "You go tailfirst. Put your paws there . . . and there."

Gray Wing heaved a sigh of relief when he once again stood with all four paws firmly on the ground. "You're really good at this," he told Jagged Peak admiringly.

Jagged Peak ducked his head in embarrassment. "Clear Sky has been giving me a few tips."

Clear Sky leaped down the last few tail-lengths. "It helps to practice new techniques for hunting among the trees," he explained with a modest look.

"Good luck with that!" Gray Wing meowed fervently. "Give me rabbits on the ground any day!"

Gray Wing followed his brothers along forest trails until they reached a sheltered hollow with a shallow pool at the center and deep banks of fern and bramble all around.

"Welcome to our new home!" Clear Sky announced.

Quick Water and Falling Feather poked their heads out from the fern. "Hello, Gray Wing," Falling Feather mewed as they emerged into the open. "It's great to see you."

"I'm glad you came to visit," Quick Water told him. "We're settling in well, we've made nests of twigs and lined them with moss, and we've already scared off a couple of nosy cats. No way am I letting them use my nest!"

"They looked okay," Falling Feather put in. "If they're really interested in us, we might invite them to move in." Looking faintly embarrassed, she added, "They might become our friends."

Hmm . . . what has made Falling Feather so keen to have more cats join them? Gray Wing wondered, though he said nothing out loud. "I'm glad it all turned out so well for you," he told Clear Sky.

"Yes," Clear Sky mewed with a satisfied look around him. "I really feel this is the place where I was meant to be. Are you happy on the moor?" he added.

"Yes." Gray Wing dipped his head. "I am."

Gray Wing headed back through the trees, pleased to have seen his brothers and their new home. His thoughts full of them, he wasn't paying as much attention as usual to his surroundings. When a cat leaped out of the bushes ahead of him, he halted, so startled that he almost fell over his own paws, brushing against a jagged tree stump.

Gray Wing found himself confronted by a silver tabby she-cat, her green eyes narrowed in a glare.

"I've seen you before," the cat hissed. "You're one of those newcomers making trouble. We were here first, so stop stealing our prey!"

Gray Wing didn't feel like fighting. "There's enough prey for every cat," he replied mildly instead. "My name's Gray Wing. What's yours?"

The she-cat didn't answer his question. "Just so you know," she meowed grudgingly, "there's a wasps' nest in that stump you nearly fell over."

Looking more closely, Gray Wing spotted a swollen gray lump in the tree beside him, and two or three tiny black-and-yellow creatures hovering over it. He could hear a muted buzzing.

"What are they?" he asked.

The she-cat rolled her eyes. "Wasps! Don't you know anything? They sting if you disturb them. Stick your paw in there if you don't believe me."

Gray Wing backed off a pace or two from the stump. "Thanks," he mewed. "That's really useful to know."

"I'm not doing it to help you," the she-cat growled. "I just don't want your screeching to scare off all the prey." Whirling around, she spat out, "Leave us in peace!" before scampering off into the undergrowth.

As Gray Wing emerged from the trees and raced across the moor, he found the silver-furred she-cat stuck obstinately in his mind.

As he climbed the final slope toward the hollow, Gray Wing felt a twinge of guilt about his earlier quarrel with Turtle Tail. *Maybe she won't want to go to the Twolegplace if I show her how great it is here.*

Padding into the scoop, he spotted Turtle Tail under a bush, washing her ears. "Hi," he greeted her. "Do you want to hunt?"

Turtle Tail sprang to her paws, her eyes shining. "Sure!"

"I was out with Cloud Spots the other day," Gray Wing explained as he and Turtle Tail headed onto the moor. "We caught a rabbit like we used to hunt hares in the mountains, one cat driving the prey into the other cat's claws. Let's try that today."

Though dark clouds were massing on the horizon, the sky above the moor was clear blue, and the sun shone strongly.

Tiny brown butterflies fluttered among the wild thyme.

"Okay, let's find a rabbit," Turtle Tail agreed.

Before long they spotted one, hopping peacefully here and there, stopping every few moments to nibble at the grass.

"Wait here," Gray Wing murmured. "I'll send it over to you."

Turtle Tail nodded, crouching. Gray Wing crept around in a wide circle until he could see the rabbit between him and Turtle Tail, whose ears just poked up above the grass clump where she was hiding.

Letting out a yowl, he hurtled toward the rabbit. With a squeal of terror the rabbit raced off, heading straight for Turtle Tail. But Turtle Tail leaped out of hiding just a heartbeat too soon, and the rabbit veered off. Though Turtle Tail dashed after it, and Gray Wing forced an extra burst of speed, the rabbit dived down a nearby hole before either of them could catch it.

"Haredung!" Gray Wing spat as he halted, panting. "You weren't concentrating."

Turtle Tail's eyes widened with shock and hurt. "Have you never missed a catch?" she challenged him.

"Not an easy one like that."

"Well, good for you!" Turtle Tail snapped. "I'm going off to find some cat who doesn't expect me to fly like a bird and run like a rabbit."

I suppose she means Bumble, Gray Wing thought, watching as she stalked off across the moor.

Clouds gradually covered the sky, and by nightfall heavy

rain had set in. Turtle Tail still hadn't returned. Gray Wing settled into his nest under a gorse bush, but sleep was hard to come by. *Was I too hard on her?* he asked himself.

At last he fell into a troubled sleep, and awoke as the sky was growing pale with dawn. Rising, Gray Wing padded across the hollow and checked Turtle Tail's nest. It was cold and empty, and her scent was stale.

Anxiety gripped Gray Wing like a fox's fangs. *Where is she? Why hasn't she come home?*

CHAPTER 19
❧

The roar of monsters deafened Gray Wing. He could taste their reek as he crept along the hard stone paths of the Twolegplace. Rain was beating down, plastering his pelt to his sides. He felt as if Twoleg filth was soaking into him.

I've got to find Turtle Tail!

But Gray Wing had no idea where to find Bumble's Twoleg nest among all the others that looked and smelled exactly alike. He had picked up Turtle Tail's scent as he had approached the Twolegplace, but had quickly lost it among all the competing scents of dogs and Twolegs and monsters.

He was padding alongside a Thunderpath when a monster came roaring around a corner and flashed past him. A wave of filthy water surged from its paws, soaking Gray Wing before he could jump out of range.

Haredung!

Even wetter than before, Gray Wing shook his pelt and looked around. The Thunderpath stretched ahead of him, lined by dens of red stone on either side. He had no idea where to start looking for Turtle Tail; he wasn't even sure how to get back to the forest.

I'm lost!

"You again!" The voice spoke from behind Gray Wing. "What are you doing here?"

Gray Wing spun around. Facing him was the silver tabby she-cat he had met in the forest. Hot embarrassment scorched through him. She was the last cat he would have wanted to see him bedraggled and reeking and lost.

"Hello, um . . . you never told me your name," he mewed, knowing that he sounded completely flea-brained.

The she-cat rolled her eyes. "Like you need to know it."

"I told you mine," Gray Wing retorted, injured.

"So you did . . . Gray Whatsit." The silver tabby heaved an exaggerated sigh. "Okay, it's Storm. Happy now? And you still haven't told me what you're doing here. Are you lost?"

"Well . . . sort of," Gray Wing confessed.

Storm let out a snort. "Honestly, you're worse than a kit! You couldn't find your own tail if you used all four paws. Where do you want to go?"

"I think my friend is here," Gray Wing explained. "She's probably with a cat called Bumble. Bumble's a tortoiseshell . . . quite plump, with a white chest and white paws."

"Oh, I know her," Storm replied. "I'll show you her housefolk's den if you like."

"That would be great." Gray Wing was relieved that he didn't have to wander around on his own in this dreadful place anymore, but he wished it hadn't been Storm who had helped him. *She'll think I'm a complete mouse-brain.*

Storm waved her tail for him to follow her, rounding the

next corner and slipping down a narrow path between two Twoleg dens.

"I didn't expect to see you here," Gray Wing meowed, trying to sound friendly. "You don't look like a kittypet."

Storm halted and glared at him. "I am *not* a kittypet!" she snarled.

Gray Wing kept quiet after that. *If I open my mouth again I'll only say the wrong thing!*

At last Storm halted beside a section of Twoleg fence. "Through there," she told Gray Wing, gesturing with her tail. Then she tapped him on the nose with one paw, fortunately with her claws sheathed. "Sure you'll be okay now?"

"I'll be fine, thanks," Gray Wing replied.

As the silver tabby turned away, she glanced back, her green eyes glittering with humor. "I'll see you the next time you need rescuing."

Gray Wing watched her until she was out of sight, then squeezed through a hole in the Twoleg fence. A narrow path led up to the den, with grass on either side, surrounded by bushy plants with brightly colored flowers. When he tasted the air, he could pick up Turtle Tail's scent, and another that he recognized as Bumble's.

"Turtle Tail!" he yowled.

No cat appeared. Gray Wing waited so long that he was afraid the two cats had left the den. *Maybe Turtle Tail is on her way home, and I've come all this way for nothing!*

Then at last a small flap in the side of the den opened, and Turtle Tail and Bumble came bundling out. "Gray Wing!"

Turtle Tail bounded up to him, excitement in her eyes. "You've come to visit at last. I'm so glad!"

"No, I'm here to take you home," Gray Wing replied.

Turtle Tail's excitement faded, to be replaced by fury. "I don't need rescuing!" she snapped. "I only stayed overnight because it was raining! Bumble's housefolk were really kind," she added. "They even gave me food."

"They're *Twolegs*, not 'housefolk,'" Gray Wing hissed, shocked. "Have you forgotten you're a wild cat?"

"No," Turtle Tail retorted. "Have you forgotten your manners?"

Gray Wing remembered that Bumble was standing a couple of tail-lengths away, looking embarrassed.

"Bumble, I'm sorry about Gray Wing," Turtle Tail meowed. "He's not usually such a pain in the tail."

Gray Wing let out a hiss of anger. *She doesn't need to apologize for me!*

Bumble ducked her head. "It's okay."

"I'll come back with you," Turtle Tail told Gray Wing, her tail-tip twitching irritably. "But only to stop you from making a scene. Good-bye, Bumble. I'll see you by the big oaks tomorrow."

She stalked off, squeezing through the Twoleg fence. Gray Wing gave Bumble an awkward nod and followed her.

"I'm sorry I annoyed you," Gray Wing meowed after they had been walking for a while. "I was worried."

Turtle Tail glanced at him, her face softening. "Well, I'm sorry for staying out so long. But I didn't want to walk all the way back when the rain was so heavy. And it was great staying in Bumble's den! Her food looks a bit like rabbit droppings, but it tastes good. And I slept on one of the soft rocks I told you about."

Her voice trailed off and there was a shadow of disappointment in her eyes. Gray Wing felt a bit guilty that he couldn't be more interested in Bumble's den. *But we don't belong with Twolegs, and that's all there is to it.*

Gray Wing padded through the trees, alert for prey, wondering whether to pay a visit to Clear Sky and Jagged Peak. Two sunrises had passed since the heavy rain, and the sun was shining, though the ground was still wet underpaw.

Sounds from deeper in the forest made Gray Wing's ears prick, but he realized at once that they weren't made by prey. Instead he heard a vicious snarling, and a voice that exclaimed, "Filthy prey-stealer!"

Terrified that one of his Tribemates was being attacked, Gray Wing raced through the trees toward the sound. Bursting out of an elder thicket, he spotted two of the forest cats: a white tom and the small yellow she-cat he had seen before. They had trapped a third cat among the gnarled roots of an oak tree. Gray Wing's heart beat faster as he realized the third cat was Storm.

"Strangers aren't welcome here," the white tom growled. "So clear off!"

"But I'm not a stranger!" Storm protested. "I've lived here all my life."

Instead of arguing further, the small she-cat slashed her

claws at Storm, who pressed herself back against the roots.

"Leave her alone!" Gray Wing yowled, leaping forward and throwing himself on top of the white tom.

The tom turned on him with a snarl, his claws flashing. Gray Wing battered him with his hind paws, and they rolled over and over among the debris on the forest floor. He was dimly aware that Storm and the yellow she-cat were grappling together with furious hisses.

Gray Wing winced as the white tom caught him with a stinging blow on the shoulder. He lunged forward, trying to fasten his teeth in the cat's white furry throat, but the tom jerked his head away. Gray Wing's teeth met in his ear instead.

The white tom let out a screech and tore himself away. Blood trickled from his ear as he scrambled to his paws and fled. The yellow she-cat followed him, pausing to look back and snarl, "This isn't over!"

Panting, Gray Wing and Storm stood side by side, watching as the two rogues vanished into the undergrowth.

"You didn't have to interfere," Storm snapped with a single lash of her tail. "It was nothing I couldn't handle."

"I guess it was my turn to rescue you," Gray Wing retorted. Inwardly he admired the silver tabby's courage and her refusal to admit that she needed any cat. *But it would be nice to be thanked.*

"Now that you're here," Storm began, "why don't you show me where you and your friends have been living? I've heard all about you, you know."

Warm pleasure flooded over Gray Wing. "Follow me," he purred.

He led the way through the trees and climbed up until they

were close to the hollow where the cats were living.

"It's not very sheltered," Storm mewed doubtfully.

"Oh, it's dry and warm under the gorse bushes," Gray Wing assured her. "And we like the open spaces. They remind us of where we used to live."

"Where was that?" Storm asked.

"You see those peaks over there?" Gray Wing pointed toward Highstones with his tail. "Well, the place we came from is a bit like that, though the mountains are even higher. And they're so far away that you can't even see them from here."

Storm's green eyes widened; Gray Wing was pleased that for once he'd been able to impress her. "Wow!" she exclaimed. "I'm surprised you have any paws left, walking all that way!"

As Gray Wing was about to reply, he spotted Turtle Tail emerging from the gorse bushes that surrounded the hollow. She headed in their direction.

"Turtle Tail!" Gray Wing called. "Come and meet Storm."

Turtle Tail padded up and dipped her head to the silver tabby she-cat. "I'm Turtle Tail," she meowed politely. "It's nice to meet you."

"Where are you off to?" Gray Wing asked her.

Immediately Turtle Tail's neck fur began to fluff up. "Not the Twolegplace, if that's what you think!" she snapped.

Storm's ears flicked up and she flashed a surprised glance at Gray Wing.

Gray Wing sighed. "It's too complicated to explain," he told her.

Leaving Turtle Tail to go her own way, Gray Wing and Storm headed back toward the trees.

"Can we meet again tomorrow?" Gray Wing asked her when they reached the edge of the forest. "You could show me around the woods."

Storm's green eyes glittered. "From what I've heard, you and your friends have already been over every mouse-length!" Before Gray Wing had time to feel disappointed, her gaze softened. "Okay. I'll meet you by the four big oaks at sunhigh."

Brushing her tail against Gray Wing's cheek, she turned and trotted away. Gray Wing watched until she disappeared into a clump of fern.

As Gray Wing turned and began climbing the moorland slope again, he spotted Rainswept Flower sitting on a rock just above him.

"I saw you there," she mewed, a spark of mischief in her blue eyes. "Who would have thought it—Gray Wing falling for a rogue!"

"It's nothing like that," Gray Wing mumbled, tearing at the rough turf with his claws. But he couldn't stop a thought from creeping into his mind: *I wonder if Storm would ever consider moving to the moor?*

CHAPTER 20
♣

Back in the hollow, Gray Wing noticed that Jackdaw's Cry and Hawk Swoop had their heads together, laughter in their eyes as they mewed something in low voices. He realized that Jackdaw's Cry was a full-grown cat now, taller than Hawk Swoop, and the way they were standing so close together made him think they were more than just friends.

"It will be good for all of us to have some kits around."

Gray Wing jumped. He hadn't realized that Dappled Pelt had padded up behind him, and was also watching the two younger cats.

"More mouths to feed," Shattered Ice grunted, though there was a gleam of approval in his eyes.

Gray Wing felt his pelt prickle. *I wonder what Storm is doing now. . . .*

Thinking about the silver she-cat made Gray Wing feel that every muscle and sinew in his body was bursting with energy. Scrambling out of the hollow again, he raced across the moor, pumping his legs to go faster and faster for the sheer joy of speed. The cool touch of the wind blowing through his pelt made him feel that he could run forever.

But as he reached the top of a rise, Gray Wing was almost carried off his paws by a hare that crashed into him with a squeal of alarm. Instinctively he lashed out, tearing its throat with his claws; it dropped twitching at his paws and was still.

For a heartbeat Gray Wing was pleased at the easy catch. Then he looked up to see Gorse and Wind heading toward him at a run.

"Uh-oh," he muttered, instantly taking a pace back. "Sorry," he added as the two rogues came up to him. "It landed right on top of me. I didn't mean to steal your prey."

To his surprise, Wind gave him a friendly blink. "We saw what happened," she mewed. "And it's a big hare, anyway. You're welcome to share."

"Sure," Gorse agreed. "We all have to eat, and there's plenty for every cat."

Gray Wing dipped his head. "Thanks. It was good the other day, learning about how you hunt rabbits," he added. "Maybe we could give you some tips about hunting too."

Gorse and Wind glanced at each other; Gray Wing hoped he hadn't offended them.

Eventually Wind purred. "That could be a good idea."

"Sure, but can we just eat?" Gorse asked, swiping his tongue over his jaws as he gazed at their prey.

Wind sighed. "Yes, greedy-belly. And while we're eating," she suggested to Gray Wing, "you can tell us more about yourself, and your friends. I've heard you come from far away."

Gray Wing looked at them, pleased that they weren't hostile any longer. "All the way from the mountains," he replied.

Impulsively he added, "Why don't you come and meet my friends?"

Gorse and Wind glanced at each other. "Okay," Gorse mewed. "And we can all share the hare."

Gray Wing began to have misgivings as he led the way, Gorse and Wind behind him, dragging the hare between them. *No cats have visited the hollow before. Even Storm didn't go all the way in.*

As he padded down into the scoop, he saw the others emerge from their nests under the gorse bushes and stare curiously upward at the newcomers. Tall Shadow padded into the middle of the hollow and waited for Gray Wing to approach her.

"What's all this?" she meowed.

"Er . . . this is Gorse, and this is Wind," Gray Wing replied. "They live on the moor."

Tall Shadow narrowed her eyes. "These are the cats we had trouble with," she reminded Gray Wing. "They accused you of stealing prey."

Gray Wing saw Jackdaw's Cry slide out his claws.

"We're sorry. We know we got that wrong," Gorse mewed, dipping his head politely.

"We've brought this prey to share with you," Wind added, flicking her ears at the body of the hare.

Tall Shadow hesitated, then gave a curt nod. "Welcome," she mewed, though her voice was still cool.

Taking that as permission, Gray Wing's friends gathered around the hare with Gorse and Wind. Between eating and answering the questions that Gorse and Wind kept asking about their journey and the mountains where they used to live, the cats soon grew more friendly. Even Tall Shadow relaxed enough to take a few mouthfuls.

Later, when Gorse and Wind had left, Rainswept Flower padded over to Gray Wing. "Maybe not all the other cats around here are our enemies," she commented. "Wind and Gorse seem pretty decent."

Gray Wing nodded, though he heard a sniff from Tall Shadow. He realized it would take a lot to make her accept any other cats.

A couple of heartbeats later, Turtle Tail appeared at the top of the hollow with a bunch of leaves in her jaws. Gray Wing narrowed his eyes in suspicion, tasting the air to check if she was carrying the scent of the Twolegplace. "Where have you been?" he asked.

Before Turtle Tail could reply, Cloud Spots appeared behind her, also carrying a mouthful of herbs. "Thanks," he mewed. "There's so much stuff growing by the river, it was a real help to have you there."

Guilt prickled Gray Wing like a claw in his skin. *I shouldn't be so suspicious.*

He followed Turtle Tail as she set down the herbs she was carrying beside Cloud Spots's nest. "I'm sorry, Turtle Tail," he told her. "It's not up to me to say where you can go."

Turtle Tail blinked at him, seeming happy that he'd apologized. "It's okay," she purred.

* * *

The following morning Gray Wing felt as though ants were crawling through his pelt. He had meant to get more bedding for his nest, but the task seemed utterly boring and pointless. He thought about visiting Clear Sky, but his paws didn't want to carry him in that direction. The sun had never crept so slowly up the sky.

"Hey!" Turtle Tail bounced up to him and butted his shoulder with her head. "Do you want to come hunting with me?"

Gray Wing stared at her, for a moment hardly registering what she had said. "Oh . . . no, thanks," he meowed at last. "I'm meeting a cat."

She gave him a curious look. "Who?"

"Storm. The one you met yesterday."

Turtle Tail drew back her head suddenly, as if some cat had swiped at her. To Gray Wing's surprise there was a hurt look in her eyes. "Okay. You do that," she muttered, and stalked off.

Gray Wing forgot about her odd behavior almost at once. *I have to go meet Storm!* He raced across the moor; sunhigh was still some way off by the time he stood at the top of the hollow where the four oaks grew.

Cool fronds of fern brushed his pelt as he made his way down the slope toward the trees. He pounced on a flickering spot of golden sunlight, then twitched his whiskers in embarrassment at the thought that he had been behaving like a kit.

I'd like to climb one of the oak trees, he thought. *Then I could leap down on Storm and surprise her!*

Gray Wing bounded lightly across the hollow and hurled

himself up the trunk of the nearest tree, trying to remember how Clear Sky and Jagged Peak did it. *They make it look so easy!* He clambered up several tail-lengths by digging his claws into the bark, but as he reached the lowest branches he got his head stuck in a clump of twigs and leaves, and couldn't see where he was going anymore. A piece of bark peeled away from the tree and he found himself dangling by one forepaw.

"Having fun?"

His belly freezing at the sound of the amused voice below, Gray Wing grabbed for support on the tree again and managed to look down. Storm was standing on one of the tree roots, looking up at him, her eyes gleaming with laughter.

Haredung!

As quickly as he could, Gray Wing scrambled down again, jumping the last couple of tail-lengths. "Hello," he mewed, trying to sound nonchalant. "I just wanted to find out how much you can see from up there."

"And hedgehogs fly," Storm responded, flicking her tail-tip over his ear. "Well, are we going, or not?"

Without waiting for a reply she led the way out of the hollow and plunged into the forest. Before long they came to a stream that chattered over stones, its surface glittering in the sunlight. Storm padded alongside it until she reached a dead branch that spanned it side to side; she ran lightly across and waited for Gray Wing to follow.

"Is this the stream that joins the river near those big rocks?" he asked as he jumped off the end of the branch to join her.

"That's right," Storm replied. "You've been there, then."

Gray Wing nodded. "I explored them with my brother. Do you live around there?" he added as they bounded on through the trees.

"Oh, here and there," she replied airily with a wave of her tail. "There are good places all over the forest. But don't go in that direction," she continued, angling her ears toward a tumble of rocks half hidden in the trees. "There are snakes, and their bite could make you sick or even kill you."

Gray Wing suppressed a shudder. "Thanks for telling me."

They followed another trickle of water down through a ravine hedged with gorse, and across a sandy hollow, where Storm paused to lap from the stream.

"Prey's good around here," she told Gray Wing. "There are plenty of mice and voles."

"And squirrels," Gray Wing added, remembering his hunt with Clear Sky and Jagged Peak. "There are lots of them in the beech trees farther on."

Storm looked up, glittering drops of water spinning from her whiskers. "You do know your way around," she meowed in a surprised voice.

"Actually, my littermate lives down here," Gray Wing explained. "Why don't you come meet him?"

This time Gray Wing took the lead as he followed the path that led to Clear Sky's new home. Four days had passed since he had hunted the squirrel with Clear Sky and Jagged Peak, and he was looking forward to seeing his brothers again.

Gray Wing soon picked up Clear Sky's scent, and Jagged Peak's too, mingled with another, stronger scent of a cat he didn't recognize. Rounding a bramble thicket, he found himself facing a large brown tom with yellow eyes.

"Who are you?" Gray Wing asked, halting abruptly and bracing himself for an attack.

"Who are *you*?" the tom growled. "This is Clear Sky's place."

Gray Wing gaped with astonishment. He had assumed this was a rogue who lived in the forest. Hearing the tom mention Clear Sky had left him completely confused.

"Clear Sky is my brother," he responded. "We're on our way to visit him. Is that a problem?"

"Only if you make it one." The rogue's sharp yellow eyes narrowed. "Clear Sky doesn't like strange cats wandering around here, close to his camp."

His what? Gray Wing thought. *Is that what rogues call the place where they live?*

"I'm not a *strange* cat!" he snapped, growing exasperated. "I'm his *brother*!"

The brown tom narrowed his eyes. "Okay. But just in case you're not telling the truth, I'll take you to Clear Sky myself. Don't even *think* about trying anything."

Beckoning with his tail, he led the way down a narrow track between ferns. Gray Wing exchanged a glance with Storm.

"What's all that about?" she asked.

"I have no idea," Gray Wing replied.

He followed the brown tom, Storm hard on his paws, until they emerged from the ferns into the sheltered hollow where his littermate had made his home. Clear Sky was stretched out in the shade of some brambles, grooming himself, while

Falling Feather sat beside the pool with Quick Water and the small yellow tabby she-cat Gray Wing had seen before. Remembering how aggressive the tabby had been, it was a shock to see her sitting peacefully beside his friends.

The brown tom stalked across the clearing and stood in front of Clear Sky. "I found these two on their way here," he announced, flicking his tail at Gray Wing and Storm. "The tom *says* he's your brother."

Clear Sky leaped to his paws. "He is. Hello, Gray Wing."

The brown tom looked disconcerted as Gray Wing and Storm padded over to Clear Sky.

"This is Fox," Clear Sky announced as Gray Wing touched noses with him. "He decided to join us."

"And this is Fox's sister, Petal," Falling Feather called from where she sat by the pool. "She's come to stay with us as well." Her eyes shone as she gazed at Fox. "Isn't it great?"

Shock struck Gray Wing like a flash of lightning. "Really?" he demanded, facing Clear Sky in bewilderment. "Rogues living among you?"

Clear Sky let out a *mrrow* of amusement. "We're rogues too, don't forget," he meowed. "So why have you come to see me?"

"I brought Storm to meet you," Gray Wing responded, gesturing the silver she-cat forward with his tail. "She lives around here."

"Welcome . . ." Clear Sky's voice began by being cheerful, then trailed off as he fixed his gaze on Storm.

Storm seemed lost for words. Gray Wing hoped she hadn't been intimidated by Fox's hostility.

"So . . . where do you live?" Clear Sky asked, obviously forcing the words out.

"Nowhere special . . ." Storm blinked rapidly. "I . . . er . . ."

"She goes to the Twolegplace sometimes," Gray Wing put in, since Storm seemed to be having trouble explaining herself. "But she's not a kittypet."

Neither Storm nor Clear Sky seemed to hear him. Clear Sky's blue gaze met Storm's green; Gray Wing had never seen such intensity.

"It's . . . very nice here," Storm went on, waving her tail around the hollow. "Comfortable."

"Yes . . . we like it."

Are they both completely flea-brained? Gray Wing wondered.

For a moment longer Clear Sky and Storm gazed at each other. Both cats' neck fur was slightly fluffed up, and their tail-tips twitched from side to side. Gray Wing wouldn't have been surprised if they had sprung at each other.

"Hey, why don't we—" he began.

"I have to go," Storm interrupted brusquely.

Clear Sky looked dismayed. "Why?"

Storm shook her head in confusion. "I need to hunt," she mewed at last.

"Well, come back soon," Clear Sky invited her, though he was clearly disappointed.

"I will." Storm turned and headed out of the clearing. Gray Wing glanced at Clear Sky, then turned and followed her.

What just happened? he wondered, bounding forward to catch up to Storm. "Are you okay?"

"What?" Storm turned to look at him, her green gaze distracted. "Oh, yes, I'm fine."

She headed toward the river and padded alongside it, in the direction of the four great oaks. Gray Wing realized their playful friendliness had faded like morning mist.

"Should we meet again tomorrow?" he asked as they paused on the edge of the trees.

Storm sighed. "I don't know . . . I'll see you around, okay?" Without waiting for a reply, she turned and plunged into the depths of the forest, leaving Gray Wing to stare after her.

CHAPTER 21
❧

Gray Wing couldn't understand how one day could make such a difference. The four great oaks stood the same as they always had, but their leaves were limp and still; there was not a breath of wind. The forest was gloomy, with no sun breaking through the clouds. Worst of all, there was no sign of Storm.

Hope sprang up in Gray Wing as he heard a rustle and saw fronds of fern shaking as a cat approached the bottom of the hollow. But his tail drooped in disappointment as Turtle Tail emerged into the open.

"Hi," she meowed, bounding toward him. "I'm hunting. Do you want to join me?"

Gray Wing shook his head. "Sorry. I'm waiting for Storm."

"Again?"

"Yes, again," Gray Wing replied, slightly annoyed at the hint of disapproval in Turtle Tail's voice. Then as all his hopes and doubts surged through him, he knew that he had to confide in some cat. "I . . . I really like her," he confessed. "I want her to come and live in the hollow with us."

Turtle Tail's eyes widened; Gray Wing was surprised to see sadness in their green depths.

"Oh . . . I see," she mewed. "I'll be off, then." She spun around, racing away swiftly in the direction of the Twolegplace.

But she said she was hunting, Gray Wing thought, then began to search for Storm. At one point he picked up her scent, then realized it was stale, probably from when she had met him the day before.

"Gray Wing."

That wasn't the voice he longed to hear. He turned and spotted Tall Shadow beckoning to him from halfway up the slope.

"Walk with me," she invited as he came up to her. "I need to talk to you."

Tall Shadow led the way through the forest and along the edge of the moor. "Tell me more about the new cats who are living with Clear Sky and Moon Shadow."

Gray Wing shrugged, peering through the trees in case Storm appeared. "I told you all I know," he replied. "They seem to have settled in well, as far as I could see."

Tall Shadow nodded thoughtfully. "Do you think we should invite Gorse and Wind to move into the hollow with us?"

Gray Wing was startled. He thought that Tall Shadow was the last cat who would want to do that; she hadn't been particularly welcoming when he had brought the two rogues for a visit.

"It's not natural for us," he began hesitantly. "In the mountains, there were no other cats. So it's hard for us to invite strangers in."

"I know," Tall Shadow agreed. "But maybe we should

consider it. It would be helpful to hunt together, and we would be stronger if dogs or foxes attacked." Sighing, she added, "I wish Shaded Moss was still with us. He would know what to do."

"Don't be too sure," Gray Wing told her. "This would be just as strange to him." He thought for a few heartbeats and then continued, "Perhaps we should do what Stoneteller said, and trust our instincts above all else."

"Well," Tall Shadow meowed, her voice suddenly sharper, "my instinct says we shouldn't be too hasty about letting other cats live with us. Not yet, anyway."

"That's fine by me," Gray Wing responded, though he couldn't help asking himself, *Then what about Storm?*

For the next few days, Gray Wing forced himself not to spend all his time looking for Storm. Instead, he kept busy with hunting and helping to improve the nests in the hollow.

He had gone as far as the river searching for moss when he heard a friendly voice hailing him. "Gray Wing!"

It was Gorse, with Wind just behind him. They bounded to join Gray Wing at the water's edge, both of them touching noses with him.

"Good to see you," Gray Wing meowed. "How's the prey running?"

"Fine, thanks," Wind replied. "Though that hare was the best catch we've made in moons."

"It was fun visiting your camp," Wind told him with a friendly flick of her tail. "Can we come and see you again? We could show you some of the best places for prey."

"Maybe another time," Gray Wing responded awkwardly. "We're kind of busy just now."

Gorse gave a nod. "No problem."

Gray Wing was relieved that the two rogues hadn't taken offense. He liked Gorse and Wind, and would have invited them but for his recent conversation with Tall Shadow. He understood her wariness of getting too close to strangers.

Then what about Storm? he wondered once again. But Storm didn't feel like a stranger to him.

Anxiety struck him as the silver-furred she-cat came back into his mind. *Maybe I should be worried about not seeing Storm . . . she might be in trouble!*

Saying good-bye to Gorse and Wind, Gray Wing abandoned the moss he had been collecting and headed across the moor toward the forest. Quickening his pace, he resolved to go right into the heart of the Twolegplace if he had to. But before he reached the edge of the trees he halted in surprise as he saw the silver tabby emerge from the undergrowth.

"Storm!" he called out.

Storm jumped, startled, and for a heartbeat Gray Wing wondered if she even wanted to see him. But as he bounded up to her he saw that her green eyes were warm with welcome. "Hello," she mewed. "How are things with you?"

"I'm fine," Gray Wing replied. He wanted to ask Storm where she had been, but he was worried about offending her. *She's here now, and that's what matters.*

Side by side the two cats wandered down to the river and crouched on the edge, gazing down into the water. Tiny fish were slipping in and out of the stones, their skin glinting in the sunlight.

"One of my friends can catch fish," Gray Wing remarked.

Storm's eyes widened. "Really? Amazing!"

Silence fell again. Gray Wing felt slightly awkward; there were so many things he wanted to say to Storm, but somehow he couldn't find the words.

"I wish I could invite you to the hollow again," he meowed at last. "But Tall Shadow is being a bit edgy about strangers just now. We can meet somewhere else, can't we?"

"Sure," Storm responded, though she didn't make any suggestions.

Gray Wing leaned over to brush muzzles with her, but she turned her head away and rose to her paws. "Well, I'll see you soon," she mewed cheerfully, and bounded off toward the trees.

Looking after her, Gray Wing felt hot with embarrassment. *Somehow I said the wrong thing . . . I don't understand her at all.*

Gray Wing collected his moss and headed back to the hollow. When he reached it and dropped his bundle beside the new nests, where Hawk Swoop and Cloud Spots were working busily, he spotted Turtle Tail, coming back empty-pawed from the direction of the Twolegplace. The scent of Twolegs was all over her.

"You've been visiting Bumble again," he asserted. Still off balance from the odd encounter with Storm, he couldn't summon up much patience for Turtle Tail. "Do you really want to be with her more than with us?"

Turtle Tail's ears flicked up and she lashed her tail. "Well, *you* don't seem to have time for me anymore," she snapped. "Perhaps if I had silver fur you'd feel differently."

"Don't be ridiculous!" But inside, Gray Wing knew that his friend was speaking the truth. He did want to be with Storm, more than any other cat. "Don't let your fur get tangled," he added more gently. "Storm's such a terrific cat, and I hope that soon she'll come here to live with us."

Turtle Tail gave him a blank stare. "Great," she mewed in a flat voice. "I'm totally happy for you both." She turned and stalked off, her tail in the air.

Gray Wing gazed after her, totally bewildered. Shattered Ice, who was standing close by, let out an exaggerated sigh. "Gray Wing, you have the sense of a rabbit sometimes," he muttered.

"I don't know what you mean," Gray Wing told him.

Shattered Ice just rolled his eyes.

Gray Wing shook his head in confusion, and went to help Cloud Spots and Hawk Swoop with the new nests. They were finished by nightfall, and Gray Wing had his best sleep for a long time, waking vigorous and refreshed. As he stood beside the nest shaking scraps of moss from his pelt, Turtle Tail padded up to him.

"Gray Wing, will you come with me?" she asked. "Just the two of us?"

"Sure." Gray Wing decided not to say anything about her odd behavior the day before. "Do you want to hunt?"

Turtle Tail shook her head. "I want to talk, but not here."

She led the way over the moor to where the waterfall thundered down into the gorge. Crouching beside it, she didn't speak, just looked down at the rushing river as it surged between the rocks.

Gray Wing sat beside her, beginning to feel impatient. "Well?" he asked.

"We had such a long, hard journey to get here," Turtle Tail began softly, "and we wondered if we'd ever reach the end. Now we have . . . but our destinations seem to be very different."

"True," Gray Wing meowed. "Clear Sky and the others—"

"I'm not talking about *Clear Sky*," Turtle Tail interrupted. She swallowed and took a deep breath. "I'm going to live with Bumble."

Gray Wing sprang to his paws, dismay filling him from ears to tail-tip. "No!" he exclaimed. "You can't be a kittypet! You're wild."

Turtle Tail flicked her tail. "Then I'll be a wild kittypet. I don't think there's a place for me here anymore, Gray Wing. I'll be fine." She rose and touched her nose to his ear. "You make sure to go for what you want. Promise?"

Feeling utterly baffled, Gray Wing nodded. "I promise."

Still not understanding Turtle Tail's decision, Gray Wing padded by her side until they reached the edge of the Twolegplace. When they could see the huge red dens looming up through the trees, Turtle Tail halted and turned to him.

"Will you let the others know where I've gone?" she asked. "I'm too embarrassed to make a big scene."

"Of course I will," Gray Wing replied.

"And I'll visit!" Turtle Tail sounded as though she had to force herself to sound cheerful. "Don't worry!"

She brushed her tail down Gray Wing's side, then spun around and raced toward the Twoleg dens. Gray Wing watched her out of sight. He felt empty, as if something precious had gone out of his life.

Things are changing all the time, he thought as he trudged away from the Twolegplace. *Every cat needs to choose their own destiny—and mine is with Storm, the way Turtle Tail's is in the Twolegplace.* Determination swelled inside him. *I'll ask Storm to come and live in the hollow. Tall Shadow will understand if Storm's my mate.*

For a while he padded alongside the river, but when he came to the huge rocks he turned to follow the stream that flowed into the main current. Excitement tingled through his paws as he imagined what it would be like to have Storm beside him, hunting, exploring, resting together in the shelter of their nest. When the time was right, they would even have kits together.

A flash of silver in the undergrowth alerted him and he halted as Storm came into view, a beautiful sheen of sunlight on her silver tabby pelt.

"Gray Wing!" she called, quickening her pace. "I was looking for you."

Delight like warm sunshine spread through Gray Wing. "I was looking for you, too," he told her. "I have something I want to say."

Storm's green eyes were troubled. "There's something I

have to tell you too," she announced. She hesitated, then went on, "I'm going to live with Clear Sky."

Shock ripped through Gray Wing, as cruel as a fox's claws. "Why would you do that?"

Storm's whiskers twitched. "I've seen a lot of him since that first time," she explained. "We sort of . . ."

Gray Wing suddenly understood. "Oh, right," he meowed. "Well, that's great."

Storm drew closer, her sweet scent washing over him. "I'm so sorry, Gray Wing," she murmured. "I wish things were different, but . . ." Taking a pace back, she added, "We'll still see each other. The forest isn't that big!"

She turned and padded away, her tail waving gracefully. Gray Wing dug his claws into the ground and clamped his jaws shut so as not to utter a word. Storm had made her choice, and it wasn't him. Gray Wing had never felt so alone in his life.

Maybe I owe my brother this, he thought as he tried to make sense of what was happening. *It was because of me that Bright Stream died, and now I have a second chance to make Clear Sky happy.*

CHAPTER 22

Gray Wing loped across the moor toward the trees. Cold claws of wind penetrated his fur and the grass under his paws was stiff with frost. The cold season was coming again.

Ahead of him the green mass of the forest was blotched with brown and yellow and russet. As Gray Wing drew closer the wind whirled dead leaves into his face. Under the outlying branches he spotted Rainswept Flower, leaping and bounding to and fro, her paws outstretched as she tried to catch the leaves before they reached the ground.

Gray Wing halted to watch her. "Having fun?" he asked after a few moments.

Rainswept Flower spun around and stood blinking in embarrassment, her forepaws scuffling the ground. "Well . . . er . . . it's good exercise," she mewed.

Gray Wing let out a sympathetic purr. "The forest is changing so much. All these colors . . . and the leaves falling. It was never like this in the mountains."

"We didn't have trees like these," Rainswept Flower agreed.

She leaped into a drift of leaves in a hollow among the roots of a tree. Scrambling up with bits of leaf sticking to her pelt, she let out a yowl of delight. "I love the crunching sound they make!"

Gray Wing's paws itched to try, though he knew he needed to keep hunting. Just then, Jackdaw's Cry appeared through the trees, his tail twitching and his eyes sparking with anger.

"What's wrong?" Gray Wing asked, padding up to him.

"I just tried to visit Falling Feather," the black tom growled. "But some cat I've never set eyes on before turned me away. He said Clear Sky didn't want any cat in that part of the forest."

"That's flea-brained!" Rainswept Flower exclaimed. "Didn't you tell him Falling Feather is your sister?"

"Of course I did," Jackdaw's Cry replied. "It didn't do any good. He just showed me his claws . . . and he was a lot bigger than me."

"I'm sure it's just a misunderstanding," Gray Wing meowed, remembering how Fox had halted him on the way to his brother's new home. "Clear Sky would never stop any of us from visiting."

Jackdaw's Cry let out a grunt of annoyance. "Then he should make sure his cats know that."

Gray Wing thought for a moment. "I'll go and see what's happening down there," he decided. "I haven't been to Clear Sky's part of the forest for a long time." *And I haven't seen Storm in over two moons.*

He plunged into the trees until he met the stream, then followed it down toward the hollow where his brother lived. As he veered along the track that led to Clear Sky's home, he picked up a number of mingled cat scents, some of which were new to him.

Clear Sky must be gathering more rogues to live with him.

He was drawing close to the clearing when two cats stepped out of the undergrowth and blocked his way. One was Fox, the other a vaguely familiar white tom; Gray Wing realized he was one of the rogues who had attacked Storm. The yellow she-cat, Petal, was sitting on an old stump a couple of tail-lengths away.

"What are you doing here?" the white tom demanded roughly.

Gray Wing bit back an angry reply. "I've come to visit Clear Sky."

"He's Clear Sky's brother," Fox put in. "But that doesn't give him the right to hang around here anytime he feels like it."

"Well, that's a good excuse," the white tom sneered. "I think you've come to steal our prey," he added to Gray Wing.

"How is it 'your' prey?" Gray Wing's neck fur began to bristle up as anger started to build inside him like a gathering storm cloud. "It's not yours just because it's near where you live. Prey is for every cat."

"Well, Clear Sky doesn't see it that way," Fox snarled, sliding out his claws. "I think you'd better shove off, before we make you."

Gray Wing hesitated, wondering what to do. *I can't fight both of them!*

"Now," the white tom growled, taking a pace forward so

that he stood nose to nose with Gray Wing.

"What's going on?" The clear meow came from behind Gray Wing; he felt it like the touch of cool water on a hot day. He turned to see Storm. "Hello," she continued, with a friendly nod. "It's good to see you again."

Gray Wing dipped his head, hardly knowing what to say to her.

Before he could find words, the white tom turned to Storm. "This rogue was stealing our prey," he explained.

"Really?" Storm mewed cuttingly. "I don't see him *carrying* any prey, do you? I don't smell any prey-scent on him. Could it be that you're just a pair of crow-food-eating flea-brains?"

"We're only doing our job," Fox protested.

Storm rolled her eyes. "This is Clear Sky's brother, Gray Wing. You've met him before, Fox, and you, Petal," she added to the she-cat, who was trying to look as if she wasn't involved with any of this. "He can visit Clear Sky any time he likes. Come on, Gray Wing."

With a contemptuous flick of her tail, Storm pushed past the two toms and led the way down the track toward Clear Sky's clearing.

"Why are those cats so hostile?" Gray Wing asked, his confusion pushing aside the awkwardness he felt meeting Storm again.

Storm glanced at him over her shoulder. "Clear Sky thinks it's important to build a strong community, and he believes part of that is keeping other cats away from the prey that we hunt."

"I see," Gray Wing murmured, though he wasn't sure that was true. *Isn't there enough prey for every cat?* "How do you like it here in the forest?" he asked.

"It's a safe place where cats can look out for each other," said Storm, with another flashing glance back at him. "Clear Sky and I will be happy to have our kits grow up here."

Gray Wing felt that the words would choke him, but he forced them out. "Congratulations. I'm really happy for you."

As Gray Wing and Storm pushed their way through the barrier of ferns that surrounded Clear Sky's clearing, Clear Sky rushed over to them. Ignoring Gray Wing, he laid his tail across Storm's shoulders.

"Why did you leave the camp?" he demanded. "You should be resting! What about our kits?"

I guess losing Bright Stream has made Clear Sky extra protective, Gray Wing thought.

Storm didn't seem to appreciate Clear Sky's concern. "I'm not going to break apart because I go for a walk," she retorted.

"It's still a risk you don't need to take," Clear Sky asserted. "Now go to your nest and take a nap."

Storm's eyes blazed with fury, but she didn't protest, just stalked off and disappeared under an elder bush.

Gray Wing felt awkward that he'd witnessed their argument, but his embarrassment faded a moment later as Jagged Peak came bouncing up to him. "Gray Wing! It's so good to see you! I've got so much to tell you."

"It's good to see you, too," Gray Wing responded. Jagged Peak was almost fully grown now, his eyes bright and his pelt shining with health. "Are you—"

"I'm quite busy just now," Clear Sky interrupted. "What do you want, Gray Wing? And by the way, Jagged Peak, you're supposed to be hunting. Off you go."

Gray Wing blinked in surprise to hear Clear Sky giving orders, but Jagged Peak didn't seem to mind. Ducking his head to Gray Wing, he scampered off happily.

"Do you mind if I have a drink?" Gray Wing asked, flicking his tail toward the pool at the center of the camp. No cats were there, and he wanted to be sure he could tackle Clear Sky without any of the others butting in.

Clear Sky twitched his ears impatiently, then nodded. "Sure, help yourself."

Gray Wing padded to the water's edge and lapped a couple of mouthfuls he didn't really want. He took a moment to collect himself, then he turned back to his brother.

"Jackdaw's Cry told me that he wasn't allowed to come and see Falling Feather," he meowed, shaking water droplets from his whiskers. "I wanted to know what that's all about."

Clear Sky shrugged. "I know Fox and Frost can be a bit too keen on guarding the boundaries," he admitted, "but it's the only way to keep cats safe."

"What?" Gray Wing looked at his brother in confusion. "Boundaries?"

"I'm trying to protect our new home," Clear Sky explained, sounding a bit defensive.

"I can see that." Gray Wing chose his words carefully. "But it worries me that you're creating divisions between us—I mean between the cats who came from the mountains."

"That's not true!" Clear Sky insisted. "You're all welcome to visit at any time."

"Then maybe you should tell Fox and Frost that—" Gray Wing began.

A terrified screech interrupted him, and he spun around to see Falling Feather and Moon Shadow racing across the clearing.

"What happened?" Clear Sky demanded.

"It's Jagged Peak!" Falling Feather panted. "We were hunting a squirrel, and he fell from the tree."

"He can't get up," Moon Shadow added.

"Show me," Clear Sky snapped.

Gray Wing's belly lurched with anxiety as he followed his brother and the other cats out of the clearing. *Not Jagged Peak*, he thought, anguished, remembering the young cat's energy and courage. *He can't be dead!*

A few tail-lengths into the forest the cats halted at the foot of a tall beech tree. Jagged Peak lay in a clump of crushed fern; relief rushed through Gray Wing as he heard his little brother groan. *He's alive!*

But one of Jagged Peak's hind legs lay at an odd angle. Blood was trickling from a gash and clotting in his fur.

"What can we do?" Falling Feather asked worriedly.

"I'll get Dappled Pelt or Cloud Spots," Gray Wing meowed at once. "They'll know how to help him." He set off at once, only halting for a heartbeat to yowl back at Clear Sky, "Tell Fox and Frost to let us through!"

Gray Wing raced along the edge of the trees and back across the moor, forcing out every last scrap of speed. Wind blew through his fur and he felt the rough moorland grass scrape his belly.

When he reached the hollow, Cloud Spots was out hunting, but Dappled Pelt was there, stretched out in a patch of weak sunshine and talking quietly with Shattered Ice. She leaped to her paws at once when Gray Wing told her what had happened.

"Of course I'll come," she mewed. They set off.

Clear Sky and his cats hadn't dared to move Jagged Peak from where he lay among the ferns. Falling Feather was crouching beside him, licking him gently and murmuring encouragement. She rose and stepped back when she saw Dappled Pelt. "Can you do anything?" she asked.

"I'm sure I can," Dappled Pelt replied soothingly. "Jagged Peak, I'm going to take a look at your leg, and then decide what's best."

"Okay," the little cat rasped, his voice taut with pain. "I'm glad you're here, Dappled Pelt."

The slender tortoiseshell bent over Jagged Peak's leg, sniffing all down its length. "Do you have any marigold?" she asked Clear Sky.

"We can get some," Clear Sky replied. He flicked his ears toward Moon Shadow. "You know where it grows?"

Moon Shadow nodded and dashed off.

"Gray Wing, can you find me two long, straight sticks?" Dappled Pelt asked. "And a few lengths of bindweed."

"Right," Gray Wing responded.

He padded deeper into the wood, spotting bindweed twining around a fallen tree, and a tangled heap that he suspected was an old rook's nest. He chose two straight sticks, and tore off some bindweed, then made his way back to Jagged Peak.

"Thanks, Gray Wing," Dappled Pelt meowed. "Jagged Peak's leg is broken," she continued, "but if we bind it up with these sticks, the bones will join again. I've never done this before, but I watched Stoneteller once when Sharp Hail fell off a rock. He was fine. You will be too, Jagged Peak."

"I hope so," the little cat murmured.

"Now this is going to hurt a bit," Dappled Pelt warned him. "Some cat find him another stick to bite on."

After Clear Sky had shoved another stick between Jagged Peak's jaws, Dappled Pelt straightened his injured leg and fastened the two sticks on either side of it with the lengths of bindweed. Jagged Peak let out a shrill wail and bit down on the stick so hard that it splintered.

"Okay," Dappled Pelt mewed. "The worst is over. You were very brave, Jagged Peak."

Moon Shadow reappeared with a mouthful of marigold, which Dappled Pelt chewed up. She trickled the juice into the gash on Jagged Peak's leg.

"He needs more of that every day," she instructed Clear Sky. "And he could do with thyme for the shock, and poppy seed to help him sleep. Do you have any of that?"

"We can find some," Clear Sky replied. "But, will you stay and look after him? He needs you."

Dappled Pelt looked startled, exchanging a glance with Gray Wing. "I suppose so," she agreed after a moment's hesitation. "Gray Wing, help me carry Jagged Peak to his nest. Be careful not to jog that injured leg."

Jagged Peak was obviously in pain as they moved him back to his nest in the camp, and he was barely conscious by the time they settled him among the moss and fern.

"Clear Sky is right; I do need to stay," Dappled Pelt meowed, though she didn't look happy about it. "Gray Wing, will you let Tall Shadow know where I am?"

"Of course," said Gray Wing. Bidding good-bye to her and to Clear Sky, he left the camp, trying to glimpse Storm as he padded past the elder bush. But all he could see was a pale blur that might have been her silver fur, lost in the shadows of her den. She didn't call out to him.

CHAPTER 23

After Gray Wing left Clear Sky's territory, he couldn't stop worrying about Jagged Peak. There was no cat to tell him how his little brother was doing. Gray Wing wished he still had Turtle Tail to talk to.

I've been missing her ever since she left to live with Bumble, Gray Wing realized. She hadn't come to visit as she had promised, and though Gray Wing sometimes picked up her scent on the giant rock beneath the four oaks, he never saw her there.

Sometimes I feel as if I'd lost one of my own paws.

Dappled Pelt stayed with Clear Sky for the next half-moon. The sun was setting when she finally made it back to the hollow, shaking her pelt in annoyance as she padded down to join the others.

"Honestly!" she exclaimed. "Any cat would think Clear Sky wanted to keep me a prisoner. I've been stuck in his . . . his camp, he calls it, with hardly enough room to stretch my paws."

"How is Jagged Peak?" Gray Wing asked.

"He can use the leg again," Dappled Pelt replied. "He's still limping badly, but that should improve with time." She flopped down beside Shattered Ice. "Oh, it's good to be back!"

"I'm really glad to see you," Hawk Swoop mewed. "I'm expecting kits with Jackdaw's Cry, and I was worried you wouldn't be back in time to help me. Cloud Spots is great, but he's not the most sympathetic cat on the moor."

"That's great news!" Gray Wing purred, while Shattered Ice murmured congratulations.

"With the cold season coming, it's not the best time," Dappled Pelt meowed. "But don't worry, Hawk Swoop. Cloud Spots and I will make sure you're fine. We'd better start gathering herbs to store," she added. "Then we'll have everything you need if there's an emergency."

The day after Dappled Pelt's return, Gray Wing went out on the moor to hunt with Jackdaw's Cry, Rainswept Flower, and Shattered Ice.

The sun had just cleared the horizon. A cold breeze blew across the moor and the grass was furred white with frost. The moorland pools and streams were rimmed with ice. Every cat's breath puffed out in white clouds, and they fluffed up their fur against the chill.

"I wonder if it snows here," Rainswept Flower meowed. "It's getting cold enough."

Jackdaw's Cry nodded. "If it does, my kits will need better shelter. I wonder if we ought to move into the trees, just until the cold season is over."

"That might be asking for trouble from Clear Sky," Shattered Ice grunted.

Jackdaw's Cry's ears flicked up in protest. "Clear Sky doesn't own the forest!"

"Come on," Gray Wing interrupted, uncomfortable with

the hostility against his brother. "We're supposed to be hunting. Who can catch the first rabbit?"

To his relief, the two toms dropped the argument and all four cats spread out to cover a wide stretch of moorland, though they stayed within sight of each other. It was Rainswept Flower who spotted the first prey, breaking into a run to pursue a rabbit that pelted away from her toward a gorse-covered bank.

Gray Wing took off after her, hoping to intercept the rabbit before it could escape into its burrow. But while he was still several tail-lengths behind, Rainswept Flower reached the top of a ridge and vanished down the other side. A heartbeat later Gray Wing heard her voice raised in a screech of alarm.

"Rainswept Flower!" Gray Wing yowled.

His heart pounding, he raced toward the spot where he had last seen her. He found himself on the edge of a hollow in the moor, almost surrounded by gorse bushes. More gorse and rocks lined the slope down to hummocky ground at the bottom; the grass that grew there was sparse. At one side was a large boulder, and in the center a stretch of loose, bare soil.

"Rainswept Flower!" Gray Wing yowled again. "Where are you?"

Shattered Ice and Jackdaw's Cry panted up beside him. "What happened?" Jackdaw's Cry demanded.

"Rainswept Flower . . . just disappeared," Gray Wing replied, still stunned at the speed with which she had vanished. *Is there something down there that eats cats?*

"What's that?" Shattered Ice asked, pointing with his tail.

The loose soil in the middle of the dip was heaving. Suddenly Rainswept Flower's head popped up. She scrabbled at the earth with her forepaws, but the sandy soil at the hole's edge kept crumbling away. "Help me!" she yowled.

Jackdaw's Cry began to bound forward, but Gray Wing blocked him with his tail. "We have to be careful," he warned, "or we might all end up down there."

Gray Wing led the way more cautiously into the hollow. "Are you okay?" he asked Rainswept Flower as he drew closer.

"Fine," she replied. "I've swallowed some soil, but I'm not hurt. There are rabbit burrows under here, stretching in every direction."

"Really?" Shattered Ice's voice was sharp with interest. "Are there any rabbits?"

Rainswept Flower shook her head. "All the scents are stale."

The ground gave way a little under Gray Wing's paws as he reached Rainswept Flower's side, but it bore his weight. "Push with your paws when I say 'Now!'" he instructed her. Cautiously he leaned over and fastened his teeth in her scruff. "Now!"

Rainswept Flower pushed upward as Gray Wing heaved. For a few heartbeats he thought they would both end up down the hole, but then Shattered Ice reached to grab Rainswept Flower's shoulder on one side. Jackdaw's Cry grabbed the other, and soon all four cats tumbled backward, safe on solid ground again.

"Thanks!" Rainswept Flower gasped, spitting out soil and shaking loose earth from her pelt.

"We should get away from here," Jackdaw's Cry meowed.

"Wait a moment." Shattered Ice was peering down the hole where Rainswept Flower had fallen, scraping experimentally at the edge with his forepaws. "If we dig out this loose soil," he explained, "we could get into the tunnels."

"Why?" Jackdaw's Cry asked.

Without replying, Shattered Ice plopped into the hole. There was silence for a moment, and then his voice came from a little farther away. "Rainswept Flower was right! There are lots of tunnels here. And the soil is soft. We could easily widen them so that we could fit down them."

"Gorse and Wind often hunt rabbits into their burrows," Gray Wing meowed, beginning to see the possibilities.

A gleam woke in Jackdaw's Cry's eyes. "You mean we could chase the rabbits all the way to their nests?"

"Not only that." Shattered Ice reappeared, and after a moment scraping at the loose soil on the edge of the hole managed to scramble out unaided. "The tunnels stretch a long way. If there's a battle, we could travel in secret to other parts of the moor."

A shiver of horror traveled through Gray Wing as he fixed his gaze on Shattered Ice. "What are you meowing about— a battle? We're *friends* with the other cats around here. Who would we be fighting?"

Shattered Ice gave him a doubtful look, but Gray Wing turned away. "The tunnels will be useful, sure," he mewed. "For shelter, and for hiding from foxes and Twolegs."

Rainswept Flower nodded. "We need to tell Tall Shadow

about this. I'll go and get her."

While they waited, Gray Wing and Jackdaw's Cry went down the hole with Shattered Ice and began digging out some more of the tunnel system.

"You're right," Gray Wing murmured, gazing down one of the black passages. "They seem to stretch a long, long way."

He watched anxiously as Jackdaw's Cry plunged into the darkness, then reappeared backward, his paws scuffling the earth excitedly.

"It could be done," the black tom meowed. "We'll need to dig air holes that will let light in too. And we could bring moss down for nests. Hawk Swoop and our kits would be safe and warm here."

As he was speaking the light suddenly faded. Gray Wing turned and managed to make out Tall Shadow's head blocking the hole. A moment later she jumped down to join them.

"This is great!" she exclaimed. "It's just what we need. Have you scented any dogs or foxes down here?"

Shattered Ice shook his head. "Only stale rabbit scent. I think the rabbits must have left when the tunnels started falling in."

"Hmm . . . we'll have to be careful that they don't fall in on us," Tall Shadow mused. "All the same, I think we should move our whole camp down here. In the cold season we can make dens underground, and when the weather's warm we can sleep under the gorse bushes."

Jackdaw's Cry gave a little bounce of enthusiasm. "Great!"

* * *

Over the next few days the cats moved across the moor to the new camp, digging out spaces for dens and transporting the bedding for new nests. Cloud Spots and Dappled Pelt carefully carried their store of herbs and found a safe place to keep them in one of the tunnels.

Jackdaw's Cry was the most skillful at exploring the burrows, finding several that stretched for long distances beneath the moor, and others with exits nearby among the gorse bushes and rocks on the slope of the hollow.

Gray Wing still had mixed feelings about living underground, even for part of the time. He had to force himself into the enclosed, stifling spaces, but he could see the opportunities that the tunnels offered.

The hollow was too exposed. Down here, we have shelter and we'll be safe from foxes. A heartbeat later he added reluctantly to himself, *And . . . just maybe, from other cats.*

CHAPTER 24

Gray Wing was returning to the new camp, a rabbit dangling from his jaws, when he spotted two cats approaching from the forest. Dropping his prey, he waited for them.

As the cats drew closer, he recognized Jagged Peak and Frost, the big white tom who had joined Clear Sky. Jagged Peak was leaning heavily against Frost for support, and Gray Wing could see that he was hardly putting his injured leg to the ground.

It's been more than a moon since Jagged Peak fell from the tree, Gray Wing thought worriedly. *I'd have expected him to be able to walk properly by now.*

"Greetings," Gray Wing meowed, dipping his head as Jagged Peak and Frost came up to him. "Have you come to visit?"

Jagged Peak gave him a miserable look, while Frost didn't acknowledge his presence at all. Helping Jagged Peak to lie on the ground, the white tom turned away without speaking and bounded back across the moor.

Rude furball! Gray Wing thought. "What's happening?" he asked Jagged Peak.

At first Jagged Peak didn't reply, glaring at Frost as he

vanished into the distance. Then he glanced back at Gray Wing, giving his chest fur a couple of embarrassed licks.

"Come on," Gray Wing encouraged him gently. "You can tell me."

The young cat hesitated a moment longer. "It's my leg," he confessed eventually. "It isn't healing well enough, and it looks like I'll probably always limp."

He paused again; Gray Wing gave his ear a sympathetic lick.

"Clear Sky says . . ." The words seemed to struggle out of Jagged Peak, ". . . that . . . because I can't hunt anymore, I'm not contributing to the group. He says I have to leave his territory. I . . . I don't think I can survive on my own, especially with the cold season coming. Gray Wing, can I come back to live with you?"

"Of course you can!" Slow anger was beginning to burn in Gray Wing's belly, but he hid it from Jagged Peak. "You're welcome . . . and we've got a new camp now. Come and see."

Picking up his rabbit again, Gray Wing let Jagged Peak lean on his shoulder until they reached the hollow.

Tall Shadow was there, investigating one of the burrow entrances with Jackdaw's Cry. She turned and bounded up to Gray Wing as he and Jagged Peak staggered down the slope. "What's all this?" she asked.

Gray Wing explained, while Jagged Peak hung his head, looking desperately unsure of himself.

"That's terrible!" Tall Shadow let out a snort. "His own brother! Jagged Peak, of course you're welcome here. And I'm sure we can do something to help that leg. Dappled Pelt and Cloud Spots are out right now hunting for herbs, but they'll take a look at you as soon as they get back."

"Thanks, Tall Shadow," Jagged Peak mewed, blinking gratefully.

"Come sit under this gorse bush." Gray Wing helped his brother to a sheltered spot and dropped the rabbit in front of him. "Help yourself, while I see about a nest for you."

There was a good pile of moss and bracken just inside the main tunnel entrance; Gray Wing dragged some of it into an unused side burrow, digging out some of the soil to make the space wider. Then he went outside again to get Jagged Peak.

The young cat had finished eating, and looked up drowsily at Gray Wing. "It's good of you to let me stay," he murmured.

Once Gray Wing had settled him into his new nest, Jagged Peak drifted off to sleep; the struggle across the moor had clearly exhausted him.

Gray Wing waited until he was sure his brother was okay, then climbed out of the burrow again. "I'm going to talk to Clear Sky," he told Tall Shadow, before leaving the hollow and bounding off across the moor.

The path that led to Clear Sky's camp was guarded by Fox, who drew back as Gray Wing appeared. Gray Wing was slightly disappointed; for once he was itching to sink his claws into some cat's fur.

When he reached the clearing, he found Clear Sky lapping from the pool at the center of the hollow.

"I've just been talking to Jagged Peak," he announced as

he stalked up to his brother.

Clear Sky raised his head and shook water droplets from his whiskers. "I thought you might want to talk about that," he admitted.

"Have you completely lost your mind?" Gray Wing asked. "Jagged Peak is your brother, and he's always been loyal to you!"

Clear Sky nodded, but he didn't look guilty at all. "I'm sorry Jagged Peak is hurt," he began, "but the good of the group is what's important. Every cat has to contribute, or none of us will survive. I gave Jagged Peak time to recover, but it doesn't look like he'll ever be able to hunt again."

"But he's family!" Gray Wing protested, hardly able to believe he was hearing these words from his own brother.

"That's exactly why I had to be tough with him," Clear Sky meowed. "The other cats won't trust me if they think I'll make exceptions to the rules for my own kin."

Horror and disgust overwhelmed Gray Wing. *This isn't Clear Sky! Not the brother I love so much!*

Hardly knowing what he was doing, Gray Wing leaped on top of Clear Sky, lashing out with his claws. Clear Sky bared his teeth in a snarl and clamped his forepaws around Gray Wing's neck, lunging for his throat. Gray Wing fought him off with thrashing hind paws, but Clear Sky was too strong for him. Within a few heartbeats he lay on the ground, Clear Sky pinning him with one paw on his neck and another on his belly.

Clear Sky gazed down at him, hostility flaring in his blue

eyes, his chest heaving. "Get out of here," he growled, stepping away from Gray Wing. "And don't come back."

Gray Wing scrambled to his paws and headed out of the clearing. Grief and anger surged over him so that he brushed blindly through the undergrowth. When a cat appeared on the track in front of him, he almost launched himself into another attack, before he realized that it was Storm.

"Gray Wing—what's the matter?" she asked.

Gray Wing gazed at her, forcing himself to calm down. Her belly was heavy with her kits, but her silver fur was as soft and shining as ever.

"It's Jagged Peak," he explained. "I can't believe Clear Sky would do that to him."

Storm nodded, her green eyes troubled. "I understand how you feel," she mewed. "But Clear Sky would never have asked Jagged Peak to leave if he hadn't known he could come to you. I know he seems cold, but he's really not."

"Then why do it?" Gray Wing growled.

"He's worried by all his responsibility," Storm explained. "He really does think he's acting for the best."

Gray Wing shook his head sadly. "That still doesn't make it right. And you know that."

Storm didn't reply, but she looked worried as she dipped her head to him and continued along the track.

His heart surging with grief, Gray Wing returned to the hollow. Tall Shadow was waiting for him. "What did Clear Sky have to say for himself?" she asked.

Gray Wing gave an angry shrug. "Nothing new. Jagged

Peak can't hunt anymore, so he has to go 'for the good of the group.' I can't believe it was Clear Sky saying those things!"

"Neither can I," Tall Shadow agreed, her tail-tip flicking to and fro. "You should always put your own family and friends first—every cat knows that! It's far more important than the good of the larger group."

"Clear Sky doesn't see it that way," Gray Wing muttered.

He padded across the hollow to look in on Jagged Peak, and found him awake again and talking to Cloud Spots.

"I'm pretty sure we can improve your movement," the black-and-white tom was meowing. "If your injured leg won't bear your weight, you have to strengthen the other three."

"How can I do that?" Jagged Peak asked doubtfully.

"I'll figure out exercises for you," Cloud Spots promised. "Even here in your nest you could bend and stretch your legs to make the muscles strong."

Jagged Peak tried, pushing with his forelegs and his uninjured hind leg, then went limp again, puffing out his breath in a sigh. "It feels weird," he complained.

"You just have to get used to it," Cloud Spots pointed out. "Don't forget you've been lying in your nest in Clear Sky's camp for more than a moon. No wonder your legs are weak."

"Cloud Spots is right," Gray Wing agreed. *And Clear Sky must have destroyed Jagged Peak's confidence, throwing him out like that and calling him useless.* "I'll help you, and you'll feel better soon."

"Dappled Pelt and I will work on some more ideas," Cloud Spots meowed. "You wait, you'll be hunting prey again soon."

Jagged Peak blinked sorrowfully. "I don't think I'll ever catch prey again."

* * *

As the days grew colder and the last of the leaves fell from the trees, prey became scarcer. Rabbits were staying in the warmth of their burrows, only venturing out to feed quickly in the early morning and at twilight, so that the cats had to range further in search of something to eat.

Gray Wing had ventured into the forest and picked up the scent of a squirrel. Stealthily he crept through the under-growth, trying not to set his paws down on crunchy dead leaves. Slipping silently around a bramble thicket, he spotted the squirrel nibbling a nut in the middle of a clearing.

I can catch that, he thought, pressing himself to the ground as he prowled forward. *It's well away from the nearest tree*.

Each paw step brought him closer to his quarry. Gray Wing was readying himself for a pounce when he heard an outraged yowl and something heavy landed on him from above, knock-ing the breath out of him. The squirrel leaped up and fled for a nearby ash tree, scurrying up the trunk and disappearing into a hole.

Gray Wing squirmed out from under the weight and scrambled to his paws. Fox was facing him, his neck fur bris-tling and his tail bushed out to twice its size.

"Prey-stealer!" he snarled.

"The prey isn't yours!" Gray Wing retorted, lashing his tail. "It belongs to the cat who catches it."

"This is Clear Sky's territory." Fox took a threatening pace forward. "So the prey belongs to him and his cats."

Movement at the corner of his eye alerted Gray Wing; he turned his head to see his littermate emerge from a clump of bracken at the edge of the clearing, followed by Storm. Gray Wing took a pace toward his brother. "Clear Sky—" he began.

Fox leaped at him, bowling him over and cutting off his words. He pushed his face close to Gray Wing's, his yellow eyes glazed with fury and his teeth a paw-length from Gray Wing's throat. Forced to defend himself, Gray Wing thrust at him with his hind paws. But Fox was a big, muscular cat, and Gray Wing couldn't free himself. He felt Fox's claws dig into his head and slash across his forehead. Blood trickled into his eyes, half blinding him.

Pure panic throbbed through Gray Wing. This was no light skirmish; Fox really meant to hurt him. *What is Clear Sky doing? Does he want Fox to tear me apart?*

Summoning all his strength, Gray Wing lashed out with his forepaws. Unable to see more than a blur of brown pelt, he couldn't aim his strikes; he just knew that he had to get this cat off him.

Gathering all his strength, Gray Wing struck hard with one forepaw. There was a choking cry from Fox. Something warm gushed over Gray Wing's paws. The weight that was pinning him down suddenly vanished. Gray Wing staggered to his paws and swiped blood out of his eyes to see Fox lying on his side among the debris of the forest floor. Blood was pouring from his throat over the dead leaves; Gray Wing's pelt was sticky with it and it clogged his claws where he had dealt the blow. Fox gave one last powerful kick with his hind legs, and was still.

Clear Sky bounded forward to stand over the brown tom's

body, then turned a look of horror and accusation on Gray Wing. "You killed him!"

Gray Wing felt as if his whole body had turned to stone. "I didn't mean . . ." he stammered.

Clear Sky glared at him, his narrowed blue eyes like chips of ice. "That's it," he snarled. "We're finished. You killed Fox, when he was only doing his job."

"But he—" Gray Wing began.

"I said, we're finished," Clear Sky interrupted, his voice cold. "I have no brother. Get out of here."

"You can't mean that!" Gray Wing protested. "After all we've been through together?"

But there was no regret in Clear Sky's cold eyes. He said nothing, only sliding out his claws. Gray Wing realized that unless he left now, he would end up fighting his brother.

Gray Wing met Clear Sky's cold gaze, trying to accept that it was the last time. *Killing Fox was an accident, but Clear Sky will never believe that. What can I do but go and never come back?*

But before Gray Wing could turn away, Storm stepped forward. Her belly was swollen and her movements slow; Gray Wing could see that she was near to kitting. She gave Fox's body a regretful glance, then padded past him to confront Clear Sky.

"I've had enough," she mewed. "I'm going back to live in the Twolegplace. There'll be better shelter there for my kits when they're born."

Clear Sky's eyes widened in shock. "Don't be ridiculous. You need me to look after you."

"That's just what I don't need," Storm retorted. "You treat me like a helpless kit, and I'm sick of it. And I can't bear the way you treat cats when they step over your so-called boundaries. You don't have the right to tell cats where they can and can't hunt. Fox would be alive now if it wasn't for you throwing your weight around."

For a moment Clear Sky was utterly dumbfounded.

In the silence, Storm turned to Gray Wing. "I'm sorry," she meowed. "I should have understood all this when I saw how Clear Sky treated Jagged Peak."

Dipping her head to Gray Wing, she gave Clear Sky a long, sorrowful look, then turned and padded off through the bracken.

CHAPTER 25

❧

Gray Wing swung around urgently to face Clear Sky. "Go after her!" he pleaded. "Bring her back and help her raise your kits. She needs you!"

Clear Sky didn't move, though there was sadness in his eyes as he watched Storm leave. "It's no use," he mewed. "I must put my community of cats first. If Storm can't accept my decisions, then we can't be together."

"But don't you love her?" Gray Wing protested.

"Of course I do. But she made her choice, and my future lies here."

The anger in Clear Sky's voice and expression had faded, replaced by an icy determination. Gray Wing realized that nothing was going to make him change his mind.

"I'm sorry it has to be this way," Gray Wing meowed. "And I'm sorry about Fox. I didn't mean to . . . but he attacked me first."

"He was doing his duty." Clear Sky turned to go, then glanced back. "How is Jagged Peak?"

Gray Wing felt a tiny spark of hope. "He is doing fine," he replied. "Cloud Spots has worked out some exercises to strengthen his good legs. Jagged Peak complains all the time, but he does them." Feeling slightly daring, he added, "Why don't you come and visit him?"

For a heartbeat Clear Sky hesitated. Then he shook his head. "What's past is past," he mewed. "I can't look back. I have responsibilities now, cats to protect, and that means I have to let Storm and Jagged Peak go."

Gray Wing was disturbed by the intensity in Clear Sky's blue eyes as he spoke. He sighed, accepting that Clear Sky had set his paws on this path, and nothing would make him turn back. "If you change your mind, you're always welcome," he told Clear Sky.

Though I wonder if that's true, he added silently to himself. *Would Tall Shadow welcome him into our camp? Would Jagged Peak?*

Dipping his head to Clear Sky, he turned and headed back toward the moor.

The cold season clamped its claws onto the moor, freezing the streams and pools and turning the grass to thorns of ice. Hawk Swoop was huge with kits, and Gray Wing spent a morning helping Jackdaw's Cry dig out a new, bigger den in the tunnels so that she would be sheltered from the cold winds when she gave birth.

"This is wonderful!" she sighed as she flopped down in the nest of moss and bracken the toms had prepared for her. "Now I can't wait for the kits to be here."

Gray Wing left her with Jackdaw's Cry and went out into the open, feeling a cold breeze ruffle his fur. Seeing Hawk

Swoop so close to kitting reminded him of Storm. *She must have had her kits by now*, he thought. *It's been a moon since she went back to the Twolegplace. I hope she's okay.* As soon as he had formed the words, he knew what he had to do.

He had to go and look for Storm.

The race across the moor warmed Gray Wing and left his heart pounding. When he reached the forest he chose a path that took him around Clear Sky's camp in a wide circle. *I've got to avoid trouble today. I've more important things to do than arguing with Clear Sky and his cats.*

Gray Wing's paws slowed as he reached the outskirts of the Twolegplace, but he made himself carry on. As he moved cautiously along the hard stone paths, he looked for landmarks that would take him to the den where Turtle Tail and Bumble lived.

They might know where Storm is staying now. And it will be good to see Turtle Tail again.

At first Gray Wing made good progress. He remembered a big den with a strong reek of monsters and rows of thick, weirdly colored tree trunks standing outside, and an open space with a stretch of grass and bushes and Twoleg kits running here and there and yowling.

But as Gray Wing turned the corner beside the open space, he heard a sudden flurry of barking. Whipping around, he saw a small black dog hurtling toward him.

Fear slammed into Gray Wing. He raced down the path with the dog hard on his paws. At the next corner, he knew he should cross the Thunderpath, but monsters were growling past in both directions, and if he stopped to wait for them the dog would catch him. Gray Wing rounded the corner and pelted on.

Moments later he knew that he was lost. Twoleg fences and dens passed him in a blur as he fled from the dog. Though he didn't dare to pause and look back, he could hear its barking close behind him, and smell its rank scent.

Then Gray Wing darted around another corner and halted in dismay. The end of the path was closed off by a huge Twoleg den. There was no way out; it was as though he was trapped in a tunnel, with the dog at its mouth. With nothing else to do, he turned, bracing himself to fight.

The dog was bounding down the path toward him, its jaws gaping. But before it reached him, Gray Wing heard a voice above his head.

"Gray Wing! Up here!"

Gray Wing's eyes widened in shock as he looked up and saw Turtle Tail, balancing on a ledge beneath a hole in the side of the Twoleg den. He bunched his muscles, and as the dog bore down on him he leaped. Turtle Tail leaned over, grabbing his scruff to help him scramble onto the ledge beside her.

"Thanks!" Gray Wing gasped.

The dog stood just underneath, yapping in annoyance.

"Shove off, flea-pelt," Turtle Tail meowed, then added to Gray Wing, "This way."

Jumping from the ledge to the top of a wall, Turtle Tail led the way past several Twoleg dens until the wall came to an end and she had to leap down onto a stretch of smooth grass.

"It's such a surprise to see you!" she exclaimed, her eyes shining as Gray Wing jumped down beside her. "It's so great that you came to visit me and Bumble."

Gray Wing gave his shoulder an embarrassed lick. "Actually, I'm looking for Storm," he admitted.

Though Turtle Tail didn't move, the light died from her eyes. "Oh," she mewed flatly.

"I know she came back to the Twolegplace," Gray Wing continued, aware that somehow he was saying the wrong thing, but needing to discover anything Turtle Tail could tell him. "Have you seen her? Do you know where she's living now?"

Turtle Tail seemed reluctant to answer, scuffling the grass with her paws. "I'm not sure—"

"Of course we know!" A new voice joined in, and Gray Wing looked up to see Bumble sitting on the fence at the opposite side of the stretch of grass. The plump tortoiseshell plopped down and padded over to join them. "Don't you remember, Turtle Tail? Storm went to live in that old monster den."

"Oh . . . yes," Turtle Tail muttered.

Gray Wing was pretty sure she had known all the time. "Thanks, Bumble," he meowed. "Can you show me the way?"

Bumble hesitated for a moment. "I won't go *in* with you. That place gives me the creeps."

Gray Wing glanced at Turtle Tail, wondering if she would come too. But she simply mewed, "I'll see you later," and streaked across the grass to the fence, leaping over it and vanishing.

Sad and confused, Gray Wing followed Bumble back along the wall, then down beside a Thunderpath with monsters passing by so close together that he almost despaired of getting across. The noise beat at his ears and he felt the stink soaking into his fur.

Finally a gap opened up; Bumble yowled, "Now!" and they darted across side by side. Another monster roared by as they reached the other side; the wind of its passing ruffled their fur.

"That only missed us by a paw-length!" Gray Wing exclaimed.

Bumble led him past Twoleg dens with huge holes in their sides, covered by shiny transparent stuff that showed glaring lights and bright colors within. Crowds of Twolegs were walking to and fro; Bumble and Gray Wing had to slip along close to the wall to avoid their clumping paws.

"I don't know how you can stand living here!" Gray Wing exclaimed.

Bumble glanced back at him. "Well, I don't know how you can stand living out in the open, getting cold and wet the whole time. We both get used to it, I guess."

Eventually Bumble led Gray Wing around another corner. A vast red stone den stood in front of them. Empty holes gaped in its side, and a huge entrance yawned like an open mouth.

Bumble flicked her tail. "There you go. I'll wait for you and show you the way back."

Gray Wing's eyes widened in shock. "Storm lives in *there*?"

Bumble nodded. "There aren't many places to stay around here, if you don't live with a Twoleg."

Horrified, forcing back panic, Gray Wing padded up to the entrance and went inside. The only light came from the holes in the walls. A vast stretch of stone lay in front of him, broken at intervals by stone trees that held up the roof. A foul reek washed over him from Twoleg debris scattered here and there, and beneath it he picked up the stale scent of monsters.

"Storm! Storm!" he yowled.

There was no reply. Gray Wing padded forward, glancing from side to side; there was nowhere here where Storm could be hiding.

A few tail-lengths away, a stone slope led upward. Gray Wing bounded to the top, then emerged more cautiously onto the next level. He saw the same thing: dark desolation, more rubbish, more stone trees, and no sign of Storm. A damp, chilly draft ruffled his fur, and he could hear the distant drip of water.

Up and up Gray Wing climbed, until he guessed he was almost at the top of the den. Still he couldn't find Storm, and she didn't reply when he called out to her. *Was Bumble wrong? Maybe Storm doesn't live here.*

Hesitantly approaching one of the gaps in the wall, Gray Wing saw how far he had climbed. He almost felt as if he was back in the mountains, looking out from a high peak. The Twolegplace was spread out below him, monsters creeping along like shiny beetles. Beyond the Twolegplace was the mass of the forest, mostly gray-brown now that the leaves had

fallen, with patches of dark green here and there where pines
grew. Beyond the forest Gray Wing could just make out the
swelling line of the moor, and he longed for the clean air and
the vast stretches of grass where he could run and run.

A faint paw step behind him made Gray Wing spin around.
"Storm!" he exclaimed.

The silver tabby she-cat stood a couple of tail-lengths away
from him. Gray Wing's heart swelled as he looked at her. She
had clearly given birth; she was thin, her sides sunken and her
fur filthy and matted. But her green eyes were still as brilliant
and beautiful as ever.

"Storm," Gray Wing repeated, taking a pace toward her.
"You've had your kits—are they okay?"

Storm nodded. "Three of them . . . and yes, they're fine."

"Where are they?" Gray Wing asked, glancing around.
"May I see them?"

The silver-gray tabby hesitated for a moment, then shook
her head. "Better not."

Disappointment gathered over Gray Wing like a dark
cloud. "But they're my family too. Please, Storm. You know I
would never hurt them."

Storm shook her head again, more decisively this time.
"These are *my* kits," she meowed.

Frustrated, Gray Wing wondered what he could do to
change her mind. Clearly she had decided to cut him and
Clear Sky—and all that she had experienced with them—out
of her life.

*But is that the best choice? Why doesn't she want help from any cat to
look after them?*

Gray Wing wanted to ask those questions, but in the face of Storm's proud, challenging gaze, the words wouldn't come. Dipping his head in acceptance, he murmured, "Good-bye, Storm. If you change your mind, you know where to find me."

Then he turned away and padded down, down through the bleak levels of the monster den, until he was out in the open, where Bumble was waiting.

CHAPTER 26

With every paw step he took away from the Twolegplace, Gray Wing became more and more convinced that he was doing the wrong thing. That night, he slept only fitfully. His cozy nest in the new camp seemed full of thorns and pebbles. And when he closed his eyes, all he could see was Storm, so thin and desperate, and yet full of courage.

As dawn light began to trickle over the moor, Gray Wing came to a decision. *I won't give up on Storm. She and her kits are part of my family now. Family should look after one another.*

On his way across the moor, Gray Wing kept a lookout for prey, and pounced on a rabbit as it popped its head out of its hole. *I'll carry it to Storm's empty den, to help her feed her kits.*

Gray Wing saw no sign of Clear Sky or his cats as he padded through the forest, but as he approached the Twolegplace he spotted Turtle Tail racing away from the red stone dens. Her ears were flattened and her fur fluffed up in panic.

Gray Wing bounded across her path to intercept her. "What's the matter?" he asked.

Turtle Tail's eyes were stretched wide as she fixed a wild gaze on Gray Wing. "You've got to come!" she panted. "Storm's den is under attack!"

Without waiting for a reply, she spun around and raced back toward the Twolegplace. Gray Wing dropped his prey and took off after her. An image of the desolate den came into his mind and he wondered what could possibly attack something so huge.

Turtle Tail must be wrong! But if Storm is in danger, I have to help!

Before the den came into sight, Gray Wing could hear a low rumbling sound, which grew and grew until it filled the whole world, as if thunder was breaking right overhead. The air was thick with the scent of stone and dust and the reek of monsters.

Gray Wing's whole body shuddered with apprehension. *Something terrible is happening!*

As he skidded around a corner, shoulder to shoulder with Turtle Tail, Gray Wing got his first sight of the den. He halted as sharply as if he had slammed into a wall. The huge den was half hidden in a cloud of dust. Behind the billowing screen Gray Wing spotted a vast monster. Its paws were bigger than he had ever seen before; its sides were a glaring yellow, and it had shiny silver jaws that were steadily chomping into the red stone walls of the den.

"Storm! Storm!" he yowled, but the roaring of the monster was so loud that his voice was drowned.

He turned to Turtle Tail. "I'm going in."

"You can't!" His friend's eyes were wide with terror. "The monster will eat you too!"

Ignoring her, Gray Wing took a pace forward, but at that moment, with an even louder thunderclap, one side of the den collapsed in on itself. Broken stone flowed onto the path like water. More dust billowed out, choking Gray Wing and making his eyes sting.

For a moment Gray Wing felt that he had been turned to stone, his paws frozen to the ground. *Surely Storm would have heard the noise of the monster before now? She must have brought her kits to safety!*

But as the dust began to clear, Gray Wing spotted Storm's panicked face staring out of a gap in the wall of the den, high up near the top. Her jaws gaped wide in a silent plea for help.

"I'm coming, Storm!" Gray Wing yowled.

For a moment his gaze met Storm's. Then the yellow monster took another bite out of the wall. The whole den tilted sideways, beginning to collapse, and the silver she-cat vanished from sight.

Gray Wing and Turtle Tail crouched close to the ground as the stone crashed down. The roaring was so loud that pain clawed at Gray Wing's ears. Surging clouds of dust blotted out the den and the monster.

Gradually the sound died away. Gray Wing looked up, realizing the monster had stopped its terrible feeding. Staggering to his paws, he raced forward into the debris. Through the dreadful dust and rumble of settling stones, he heard a feeble cry.

"Storm!" he called. "I'm coming!"

Frantically he dug into the rubble. Scraping away shards of stone, he touched silver fur, and cleared away the debris with desperate paws until Storm's body lay exposed. Her legs were stretched out stiffly and her eyes were closed. Dust clotted in her fur. Beside her, half buried in the wreckage, were the three limp bodies of the kits she had tried to protect.

Oh, Storm . . .

Gray Wing bent his head to lick her fur, and at that moment Storm's green eyes flickered open. She blinked, focusing on Gray Wing, then raised her head a little to see the three bodies of her kits.

"My kits . . ." she whispered brokenly. "I just wanted to keep them safe!"

"You did all you could." Gray Wing comforted her.

"Tell Clear Sky . . . I'm sorry . . ." Storm's faint whisper died away. Her head flopped back and her eyes closed.

Gray Wing rested a paw on her chest and bent his head toward her muzzle, but she wasn't breathing. *Good-bye, Storm . . .* he thought, numb with grief. Feeling his heart breaking, he collected loose stones to pile gently on her body.

A tiny movement in the dust alerted him. He turned his head in disbelief to see that one of the kits—a sturdy ginger tom—was stirring a little.

He's not dead!

A renewed rumbling told Gray Wing that the remaining walls of the den were shaking around him. He dug away the rubble that partly covered the kit's body and grabbed him by the scruff. As the walls collapsed, he dragged him clear, stumbling out onto the path in a chaos of rolling dust and flying splinters of stone.

"This way!" Darting forward, Turtle Tail shoved Gray Wing around the corner and out of the worst of the dust. "Where's Storm?" she asked.

Gray Wing set the kit down gently. "Dead," he choked out.

"And the other two kits. But this one's alive . . . just."

Crouching side by side, Gray Wing and Turtle Tail licked vigorously at the little ginger tom until he began to squirm feebly and let out a tiny wail.

"He's going to live," Turtle Tail meowed. "Come on, I'll help you carry him back to the forest."

Ignoring Gray Wing's protests that he could manage, Turtle Tail lifted the kit gently by his scruff and set off down the path, Gray Wing limping alongside her. They didn't stop until they left the Twolegplace behind and reached the outlying trees.

"Let's catch our breath," Turtle Tail suggested, puffing out a sigh as she set the kit down.

Gray Wing sank to the ground. His pelt was matted and filthy, and his pads stung from walking over the splintered stone. He couldn't forget the look in Storm's eyes as she gazed at him with the den falling around her.

If only I'd gotten there sooner, I might have saved her!

"I know you're blaming yourself," Turtle Tail murmured, her sympathetic gaze resting on him. "It wasn't your fault." She hesitated, then added, "You're thinking of Bright Stream, aren't you? But this time is different: there's a survivor. Clear Sky has a son." She bent her head to lick the tiny kit's ear. "You must take him to his father."

Instinctively Gray Wing reached out a paw to scoop the kit toward himself. He didn't want to lose this last connection to Storm. "I loved Storm too," he whispered.

"I know." Turtle Tail's voice was gentle. "But this kit is not your son."

Gray Wing let out a sigh; in the midst of his grief, he knew that Turtle Tail was right. "I don't even know what to call him!" he mewed.

Turtle Tail bent her face close to the kit's and brushed her muzzle against his. "What's your name, little one?" she asked.

The kit looked up at her, bewildered. "I don't know," he squeaked.

"Maybe Storm hadn't decided on names yet," Gray Wing meowed.

Turtle Tail glanced back at the Twolegplace, as if she was picturing the collapsed den. "What about Thunder?" she suggested. "He was born of Storm, in the *midst* of a storm of stones and dust, yet he has survived."

The ginger kit let out a high-pitched mew.

"I think he agrees!" Turtle Tail exclaimed, her gaze warm.

Taking a deep breath, Gray Wing rose to his paws. "Come on, little Thunder," he meowed. "It's time to meet your father."

Turtle Tail bade Gray Wing farewell and headed back into the Twolegplace. Picking up Thunder by his scruff, Gray Wing plunged deeper into the woods, staggering from exhaustion as he found the track that would lead him to Clear Sky's camp.

Before he reached it, there was a rustle in the undergrowth and three cats stepped in front of him: Frost, Petal, and a black-and-white tom Gray Wing didn't recognize.

"You're not welcome here," Frost growled, his neck fur bristling.

Petal fixed him with a hostile gaze. "You killed Fox."

"It was an accident," Gray Wing replied, speaking with difficulty around the kit he was carrying. He remembered that

Petal was Fox's sister, and couldn't blame her for her anger. "Clear Sky knows that."

"And who is this kit?" The black-and-white tom pushed up close to Thunder, who whimpered and tried to shrink away from him.

"I'll tell Clear Sky, not you."

For a heartbeat the three cats glared at Gray Wing. *I can't fight all of them*, he thought despairingly. *And I'm so tired of all this hostility.* "Just take me to my brother," he asked.

At first the three cats didn't move. Then Petal stepped back, beckoning him with her tail.."Okay," she mewed. "But don't even think about putting a paw wrong, or you'll wish you'd never been kitted."

The black-and-white tom stayed on guard, while Frost and Petal escorted Gray Wing along the track, one on each side.

It's like they think we're spies, or we're their prisoners.

Clear Sky leaped down from a tree as Gray Wing and the others entered the camp. He bounded across the clearing and faced Gray Wing. "What do you want?" he demanded.

Gray Wing glanced at the other cats, and Clear Sky waved them back with his tail. When they had retreated to the edge of the clearing, Gray Wing set Thunder down at Clear Sky's paws. "This kit is your son."

Thunder dipped his head and blinked shyly up at his father.

Clear Sky's shocked blue gaze was fixed on Gray Wing. "Where's Storm?" he asked hoarsely.

Gray Wing bowed his head. "Storm is dead." While Clear Sky stared at him, stunned, he told of how Turtle Tail had warned him, and how they had reached the collapsing den in time to witness the death of Storm and the other kits. "She spoke to me before she died," he finished. "She asked me to tell you she was sorry."

Clear Sky shook his head, bewildered, his blue eyes filled with pain. "I can't believe this . . ." he breathed out. "Not Storm . . . not such a dreadful death." He paced away for a few paw steps, then turned back toward Gray Wing and his son.

"Take him away," he meowed. "There's no place for him here."

"What?" Gray Wing couldn't believe what he was hearing. "He's your *son*!"

"I can't raise him." Clear Sky's voice was bleak. "It's my fault his mother died. If I'd stopped Storm from leaving, she would still be alive. What kind of life can I give her kit?"

Gray Wing began to understand. If Thunder stayed in the camp, he would be a constant reminder to Clear Sky of what he had lost.

"How can I raise a kit?" Clear Sky demanded. "I have too much to do here, protecting these cats."

"You have cats who will help you!" Gray Wing retorted. "Thunder needs you."

Clear Sky shook his head decisively. "No. What he needs is a father who can take care of him—who doesn't bring bad luck to every cat he cares about." His voice was hard, filled with anger and self-loathing.

Gray Wing knew there was no point in trying to persuade him. Shocked to the depths of his fur, he meowed: "This truly is the end of our brotherhood. I can't recognize you anymore as the beloved littermate I grew up with and traveled here with."

Sadly Clear Sky nodded. "If you can't accept me as leader of these cats, or understand what I'm trying to do for the good of every one of them, then there's no relationship left between us."

He turned and walked away, leaving Gray Wing and Thunder alone except for the watchful guards. They moved forward, flanking Gray Wing to escort him out of the territory.

Gray Wing's patience snapped. "We can see ourselves out, furballs!" He curled his tail around Thunder to guide him, letting him walk on tottery legs out of the clearing and down the track that would lead to the moor.

"What happened?" Thunder asked, sounding utterly confused. "Was that . . . my father?"

"Yes." *And I wish he wasn't.*

"Are you sure?" Thunder persisted. "Why didn't he like me?"

Gray Wing heaved a deep sigh. "It's complicated. But it's not your fault."

By the time they reached the camp on the moor, Thunder was exhausted and Gray Wing had to carry him again. The other cats rose to their paws as Gray Wing pushed his way through the gorse bushes that lined the rim of the hollow and padded down the slope.

Tall Shadow came to meet him. "Who's this?" she asked, flicking her tail at Thunder. "Where did he come from?"

Gray Wing set the kit down; Thunder looked half asleep, not really aware of where he was. "His name is Thunder," he told Tall Shadow. "He is Clear Sky's son."

Hawk Swoop, her belly heavy with kits, took a pace forward. "Are you flea-brained?" she demanded. "Why did you bring him here? Clear Sky will use him as an excuse to attack us."

"He won't," Gray Wing mewed quietly. "He didn't want Thunder anywhere near him."

As briefly as he could, he told them of Storm's death and his meeting with Clear Sky. While he spoke, Hawk Swoop's gaze softened as she looked down at the tiny kit. When Gray Wing had finished speaking, she nudged Thunder to his paws and curled her tail around him, pressing him close to her swollen belly. "Come, little one," she murmured as she headed toward her tunnel-nursery. Glancing over her shoulder at Gray Wing, she added, "I'll look after him."

Tall Shadow gathered the other cats together with a sweep of her tail, then leaped onto the top of the tall rock at the far end of the camp.

"You all heard Gray Wing's story," she began. "Now we have to decide what to do with this kit. Can we keep him here?"

"I don't think it's a good idea," Shattered Ice replied. "He's a stranger. We're not his kin—"

"*I'm* his kin," Gray Wing pointed out. "So is Jagged Peak."

"Yeah." Jagged Peak spoke up from where he sat at the entrance to his den. "He has a right to be here."

"But his closest kin is Clear Sky," Shattered Ice retorted. "And how do we know that Clear Sky won't change his mind and demand him back?"

"Then we send him back." Rainswept Flower spoke impatiently. "If his father wants the poor little scrap, then that's a good thing. But meanwhile, how is he supposed to survive if we don't keep him?"

"It will be difficult to care for him," Cloud Spots mewed thoughtfully. "He needs milk . . ."

"Hawk Swoop is near enough to kitting," Dappled Pelt responded immediately. "She already said she would look after him. How can you—"

"I said it will be difficult." Cloud Spots flicked his ears. "I never said we shouldn't try."

"But is any cat thinking of Hawk Swoop?" Jackdaw's Cry sounded argumentative. "She'll have her own kits to care for— my kits. It's not fair to expect her to manage another one."

Dappled Pelt glared at him. "She's made her decision."

"I have a right to—" Jackdaw's Cry began.

Tired of the debate, Gray Wing padded to the front of the group of cats, just below the rock where Tall Shadow was standing. "If Thunder is Clear Sky's son, then he is my kin," he meowed determinedly. "This will be his home from now on. Drive him out, and you'll lose me too."

"Gray Wing!" Tall Shadow sounded shocked. "There's no need for that."

"Then let Thunder stay."

Tall Shadow's gaze swept across the cats below her. "Does any cat object to that?"

The cats glanced at each other. Rainswept Flower gave a decisive nod. "What sort of cats would we be if we refused to help him?"

No cat argued with her. Jackdaw's Cry muttered something under his breath, but he didn't speak his objection aloud.

"Then it's agreed," Tall Shadow announced. "Thunder is one of us." She leaped down from the rock into the midst of her cats.

Gray Wing dipped his head to her in gratitude, then turned away and spotted Thunder sitting at the mouth of Hawk Swoop's burrow. Clearly he had heard every word of the debate that had raged over his head, and he looked horrified, his eyes wide and scared.

Padding over to him, Gray Wing rested his muzzle on the little cat's head. "You're safe now," he murmured reassuringly. "From now on, I will be your father."

DAWN OF THE CLANS
WARRIORS
THE SUN TRAIL

BONUS SCENE!

Read on to see how the forest rogues reacted when their
territory was invaded by the mountain cats. . . .

CHAPTER 1

❧

The badger drew back, its jaws stained with blood, and let out a snarl at the two kits cowering in front of it. Scraps of fur were still snagged in its blunt claws. After a heartbeat that seemed to last for seasons, it turned and lumbered into the undergrowth. With a final flash of black-and-white fur it vanished, leaving only its overwhelming stench.

Petal threw back her head and lifted her voice in a wordless yowl. She tried to sound threatening, but all she could feel was grief and anguish for the cat who lay sprawled at her paws, her tabby fur torn away and her blood soaking the dead leaves underneath her mangled body.

"Stay away, filthy badger!" Petal's brother, Fox, stood at her side, his brown fur bristling. "Don't come back!" Petal could hear the tremor in Fox's voice and knew that his whole body was shaking as violently as hers.

Like the badger will listen to a couple of kits, she thought. *It could have snapped us up in a mouthful.*

A chilly breeze blew through the forest, rattling the branches and sending a few more dead leaves to whirl through the air. Petal's shivers increased as she felt claws of cold sinking through her pelt.

"What are we going to do now?" she asked.

Fox turned to her and touched her ear with his nose. "We'll have to look after ourselves now," he replied. "We'll be fine. We have to be." He turned his face away from the sight of their mother sprawled on the ground before them.

No, we won't, Petal thought. She could tell that Fox was trying to sound braver than he felt. *We don't really know how to hunt. Mother never had the chance to finish teaching us.*

Looking at Fox—he was strong and compact but still smaller than some of the prey they would need to hunt—she saw how unprepared they both were. *What chance do we have, alone in the forest?*

She began to claw at the dead leaves, showering them over her mother's body. After a heartbeat Fox joined her, and the two kits scratched at the debris on the forest floor until their mother was completely covered.

Who will look after us now? Petal wondered as she sat with her brother. Then another thought tore through her. *Who will look after our mother?* She raised her face to the sky and closed her eyes. It was as though she were drowning; it was hard to breathe. Something that felt as heavy as a stone sat in her chest, where her heart had once been. *Will I ever know happiness again?*

She opened her eyes, and looked again at the outline of her mother's dead body beneath the leaves. "Stay safe," she murmured. "Wherever you are now."

"Come on," Fox meowed, cleaning his claws. "We'll go and hunt."

He wouldn't look Petal in the face, and his voice sounded matter-of-fact, but she knew he was only trying to help. *We have to survive now, on our own,* she thought. *He's doing his best.*

Side by side, Petal and Fox padded through the forest. Petal started at every unexpected sound from the undergrowth. She knew that Fox was just as scared, however much he tried to hide it. There was no knowing if that badger would attack again—it knew they were without protection now.

Petal's belly growled hungrily. She tried to taste the air for signs of prey as their mother had taught them, but she couldn't pick up any scents. *Am I even tasting the air in the right way?* she wondered, trying to remember her mother's lessons.

Fox sniffed around the roots of an oak tree, a spot where their mother had often snapped up a mouse or two, but he found nothing.

"All the prey is snug down their holes," he grumbled. "How are we expected to catch anything when it's as cold as this?"

As the sun moved down the sky, Petal began to be afraid that her brother was right. Now and again she spotted a bird perched on a branch above their heads, and once a squirrel whisked up a tree trunk in front of them and vanished into a hole. None of the creatures seemed to be scared of them.

And why should they be? she asked herself. *We're only kits.*

A familiar scent drifted past her. She halted, her nose twitching and her whiskers quivering. "Do you smell that?" she breathed out.

Fox sniffed the air. "Cats!" he exclaimed, his yellow eyes gleaming with excitement. "We're saved! They'll share their prey with us!"

He took off, scampering through the undergrowth in the direction of the scent. Petal scurried along behind him. A few heartbeats later they broke out into a clearing. Twilight was gathering, but they could still make out three cats curled up together in the shelter of a mossy boulder.

"Hi!" Fox meowed, skidding to a stop in front of them.

Petal halted at Fox's shoulder, her excitement fading as one of the three—a skinny gray-and-white she-cat—sprang to her paws and faced them with fierce green eyes.

"What are you doing here?" she demanded, her lips drawn back in the beginnings of a snarl.

Petal took a deep breath. She had never seen such a hostile cat. The only cat they had really known was their mother. *And she was so kind and gentle, not like this cat at all!* "We . . . we're on our own," she stammered. "We were hoping for . . . looking for food." She hoped they wouldn't be forced to retell the story of their mother's death—not so soon after . . . She shook herself.

Glancing at Fox, she saw that his fur had started to stand on end, reacting to the other cat's hostility. *Calm yourself!* she willed him. They'd come here for help, not a fight.

The she-cat's green gaze raked over them like a bunch of thorns. "Then you should look elsewhere," she hissed. She slid out her claws, leaving Petal in no doubt about what would happen to the kits if they disobeyed.

The other two cats said nothing, but their eyes were hard and unsympathetic.

Petal and Fox backed away. "What's the matter with her?" Fox muttered. "Why doesn't she want us to stay?"

Petal shook her head. "I don't know." The world had become a colder place, even in the few moments since covering their mother's body with dead leaves.

Petal and Fox turned away from the other cats. Petal tried not to hear the snarls behind them, warning them never to bother these cats again. Her drooping tail brushed the ground as she and her brother trudged on through the forest. The last of the light was fading fast; Petal shivered afresh at the thought of spending the night without their mother's warm body curled around them.

Then there was a rustling in the undergrowth. "Look!" Fox whispered, pointing with his tail.

Petal gazed in that direction and spotted a squirrel nibbling on a nut at the foot of a nearby beech tree. At once both kits flattened themselves to the ground and began to creep up on it the way that their mother had taught them. Petal's jaws began to water at the thought of sinking her teeth into the prey.

"Just *what* do you think you're doing?" a voice growled behind them.

A lightning bolt of shock passed through Petal, and she sat up to see the gray-and-white she-cat standing over her. *How did she get here so quickly and silently?*

Fox crept on for another paw step, and let out a squeal as

the gray-and-white cat cuffed him around the ear.

At the same moment a big tabby tom flashed past them and flung himself on top of the squirrel as it tried to leap to safety up the tree.

"Hey!" Fox protested. "That was our prey!" But all he got was another cuff to the ears.

The gray-and-white she-cat pushed her face close to Fox's. "All prey around here is *ours*," she snarled. "Learn that now, before you get really hurt."

Petal bristled in anger at the threat. *It's not fair*, she thought, as the tabby tom padded past her, the body of the squirrel dangling limply from his jaws. *We saw it first!* But she was too scared to make her objection aloud.

The two cats melted back into the trees, happy to leave Fox and Petal with nothing to eat. *They don't care that we're just kits. They're leaving us to die*, Petal thought as she watched them go. *We're truly on our own.*

"Come on," she mewed to Fox, feeling her spine stiffen. "Let's find somewhere else to hunt. I'm not going to let us starve to death!"

"Why were they so mean?" Fox pleaded, bringing up the rear. All his bravery had melted away.

"It doesn't matter," Petal snapped. "We learned a lesson today. From now on it's just us. Just the two of us . . ."

They walked farther into the forest, as if they could leave all their pain and grief behind them. Petal didn't care if she never saw another cat again.

CHAPTER 2

Petal and Fox slid through the undergrowth, their senses alert for the smell of prey. Even now, so many moons after the death of their mother, they spent most of their days alone.

Petal stiffened at the scent of squirrel, but a heartbeat later she realized the scent was stale; the squirrel must have passed that way the day before. Then a faint sound just ahead warned her of the approach of prey. Two mice appeared, scuffling along the edge of a bramble thicket.

Petal glanced at Fox, who was padding along at her shoulder, and signaled with her tail for him to stay where he was. With breathless caution, she started to work her way around the two mice, making sure that every paw step was silent and that she didn't let her shadow fall across the two tiny creatures.

It's been so long since we ate. . . . We need this prey!

They'd come a long way since their early days as orphaned kits, and had managed to survive alone. Occasionally they joined in a hunt with other cats, but that was rare. Mostly they hunted alone. Petal never let them forget that they had only themselves to rely on.

At last Petal dropped into a crouch beyond the mice and leaped toward them, letting out a snarl, trying to sound as menacing as she could. *That gray-and-white she-cat taught me something; I can make myself really scary now!*

The mice, panicking, scuttled straight at Fox. He slammed down a paw on one of them, and grabbed the other by the neck with his teeth in one smooth movement.

"Great catch!" Petal exclaimed as she bounded back to his side.

"You sent them straight at me," Fox meowed, dropping the mouse. "Besides, you could have caught them yourself, you know."

Petal preferred to hunt like this: setting up the catch but letting her brother make the final kill. Ever since their mother died and the gray-and-white she-cat refused to help them, she had realized they needed to work as a team. *I'd be lost without Fox*, she thought. Yes, she could have killed the mice on her own—but she preferred working with her brother, and knew that was better for him, too. She remembered how forlorn he'd looked when they'd padded away as hungry kits. *It's important that we work side by side*, she thought. *It's all we have.*

Aloud she mewed, "We've got the mice, so who cares?"

Fox blinked at her affectionately and didn't push the matter. They settled down and ate their prey in quick, hungry bites.

Petal was swiping her tongue around her jaws, wishing for something a bit more substantial than a mouse, when she heard a loud birdsong. Looking up, she spotted a robin singing on a branch a few tail-lengths away. It puffed out its fat red belly and scanned the area with bright beady eyes.

Typical robin bully, she thought. *Making that racket to claim his territory . . .*

As she watched, a chaffinch landed on the same tree branch. At once the robin broke off his song and flapped his wings fiercely until the chaffinch hopped backward and took off again.

Petal set her teeth and let out a hissing breath. *I hate bullies! And I hate robins! It's time to show that bird who's boss. . . .*

"You stay here," she muttered to Fox. "I'll enjoy killing this one on my own." Yes, they normally hunted as a team, but this was about more than hunting.

Flattening herself to the ground, Petal sneaked forward until she reached the bottom of the tree. The robin hadn't noticed her. Petal slipped around to the other side of the trunk and clawed her way upward paw step by paw step.

But as Petal slid onto the robin's branch her tail brushed against a spray of leaves, making them rustle. The robin let out a loud alarm call and darted away, vanishing among the trees.

"Mouse dung!" Petal exclaimed.

Scrambling down the tree, she headed into the forest after the robin.

"What are you doing?" Fox hissed after her. She shook her head at him quickly, telling him to be quiet.

Soon she reached a hollow and slipped into hiding behind a bush, where she waited for her breathing to calm. Her ears were pricked as she listened carefully.

Just as she had hoped, not many heartbeats passed before she heard the robin's strident song again. *Stupid creature! Now I know exactly where you are!* Petal crept toward it, clinging to the shadows to hide her movements. It was perched on another tree branch; luckily, this bark was soft, making it easier for Petal to sink her claws in silently and climb up until she was only a tail-length from the robin.

This time, little bird . . .

Petal was stretching out her claws when a cat's yowl sounded from somewhere in the forest. The robin launched itself into the air and vanished into a thick stretch of shrubs.

Letting out a snarl of annoyance, Petal let herself drop to the ground. Fox came running up to her as she landed. "Did you hear that?" he asked.

More cat yowls and meows reached their ears as he spoke. Petal signaled with her tail for Fox to follow her as she crept toward the noises. "I don't recognize those voices. . . ." she murmured. Even though she and Fox kept themselves separate from the rest of the cats in the forest, they knew most of the others by sight and sound.

Using every scrap of undergrowth for cover, Petal and Fox slipped forward until they reached the edge of a wide, shallow dip in the forest floor, and crouched together in the shelter of a holly bush. Gazing into the hollow, they saw several cats, some sitting, others pacing around and examining their surroundings.

"Hey, we *do* know them!" Fox meowed. "They're the cats who've settled in the clearing with the pool. Don't you remember?"

A hazy memory took form in Petal's mind. "That's right," she murmured. "They chased us off when we tried to find out what they were doing there."

Petal's paws tingled with apprehension. She realized she had seen a few of the cats even before that. "I met some of them another time, too, when I was hunting with Nightheart and Leaf," she meowed. "That black tom was stalking a squirrel in the forest. I would have left him alone, but Nightheart and Leaf jumped on him. Then his friends came to help him, so I had to get involved, too. That gray tom was there, and the white she-cat."

"We'd better stay away from them," Fox grunted. "They're trouble, sure enough. I hope they're not thinking of moving in here for good."

As he was speaking, the gray tom suddenly froze, then swiveled around, staring straight at the holly bush where Fox and Petal were hiding.

"He's seen us!" Petal meowed. "Run!"

CHAPTER 3

❧

"*We have to get away!*" *Petal* panted as she raced along beside her brother. "I've been in one fight with those cats. I don't want another!"

She and Fox pelted as fast as they could through clumps of fern and around bramble thickets. Low branches swiped across their faces.

Petal couldn't hear any sound of pursuit from the strangers. *Maybe they're not following us . . . but I'm not sticking around to find out!*

The two cats were running so hard that neither of them took much notice of where they were going. Then without warning the undergrowth thinned, and they burst out of the trees to find themselves on the bank of the river.

"Mouse dung!" Fox gasped, scrambling to a halt at the very edge of the water. "Another paw step and I'd have fallen in!" Petal knew how much her brother hated water, so she was surprised when he added, "We'll have to cross. That'll stop those other cats from chasing us."

This must be bad, Petal thought, *if Fox is willing to cross the water!*

Even so, Petal was warmed by her brother's courage. *We*

can do this together! Glancing around, she spotted a series of stepping-stones leading across to the other bank. Water was washing their surface, but even if they were slippery, they were a better option than swimming.

"Over here!" she mewed, darting toward them.

Fox followed her, with a glance toward the edge of the trees. None of the strange cats had appeared yet, but Petal could hear yowls of pursuit and knew they had only heartbeats to make their escape.

She leaped onto the first stone, flinching at the chill of river water on her paws. *I might not be the best hunter, but I can do this.* . . .

Petal could hear splashing that told her Fox was following her. She leaped from rock to rock until she reached the middle of the river, the strong current surging all around her. *We're going to make it*, she thought, pushing off in a powerful leap to the next stone.

But as Petal's paws landed, the rock lurched under her and she felt herself sliding into the river. Water slopped onto her belly fur. With a screech of alarm she clawed frantically at the slippery surface, and managed to stop herself a mouse-length before the river engulfed her.

She could hear Fox yowling in distress behind her.

"I'm okay!" she gasped out. *I didn't survive that badger to drown now!*

Another cat voice rose over Fox's, calling out a greeting. Petal let out a hiss of fear and anger as she turned awkwardly on the sloping surface of the rock so that she could look back at the bank.

The gray tom and the white she-cat stood watching at the

water's edge. "Come back!" the gray tom called. "We won't harm you."

Like I believe that! Petal thought. But she knew that she and Fox had no real choice. Trying to cross the river was becoming too dangerous.

"It's no good!" she yowled to Fox. "We'll have to go back."

Carefully they began to make their way to the bank. Petal found that her legs were shaking with tension; with every jump her mind revisited the dreadful moment when the rock had tipped under her paws.

Fox had reached the bank and was standing quietly beside the two newcomers. *They haven't attacked him . . . yet.*

Petal braced herself for the leap onto the last rock. But she was so tense and tired that she misjudged the distance. Her forepaws hit the stone but her back legs landed in the river, and before she could scramble to safety the river swirled her away.

"Help me!" she shrieked, flailing her legs helplessly in the cold, angry water. "Fox! Help me!" There was nothing for her claws to grip, no way of keeping herself afloat as her pelt grew sodden and heavy.

Fox leaned dangerously far from the bank and stretched out a paw. His claws brushed through Petal's pelt before the strong, rapid current snatched her out of reach. Petal's screech of terror was cut off with a gurgle as her head went under. Water filled her mouth and nostrils. *I'm going to drown!*

She resurfaced to find herself a tail-length from the bank. Desperately she tried to push through the water but couldn't make any headway. River water choked her; she couldn't cry out anymore.

There was a yowl of despair from Fox. Then Petal caught a glimpse of the gray tom racing along the riverbank, outstripping her until she lost sight of him.

A moment later, still struggling to stay afloat, Petal spotted him again. He had halted beside a large rock on the riverbank, and as Petal was carried down toward it she heard his yowl of effort over the roar of the water as he pushed the rock into the river.

The surge from the splash swamped Petal. Her head went under again, but a heartbeat later the current threw her up against something hard. Scrabbling frantically, she realized it was the rock. She could get her head out again and she clambered painfully upward, away from the smothering water. Fox leaped from the bank to the top of the rock and helped her by leaning over and fastening his claws into her scruff.

Coughing and choking, Petal managed to scramble to the safety of the bank. Both the gray tom and the white she-cat were standing there, looking at her with concern in their eyes.

"Are you okay?" the white she-cat asked.

"Fine," Petal gasped, and added to the gray tom, "You saved my life!"

The gray tom shrugged. "It was nothing. I'm Clear Sky, by the way, and this is Falling Feather."

Petal sank shivering to the ground.

"I'm Fox," her brother mewed, his voice shaky with relief. "And my sister is Petal."

"Hey!" Falling Feather meowed, with a sudden startled

look. "We know you, don't we? You were in that fight when
that idiot Moon Shadow was hunting a squirrel. And later on
we chased you out of our clearing."

"That's right." Clear Sky nodded. "And Falling Feather,
you thought they might be cats we could invite to live with us
one day." He blinked thoughtfully. "Interesting . . ."

Petal was feeling too cold and exhausted to pay much attention. Feebly she started to groom herself, thinking she would
never get the taste of river water out of her fur.

"Lie on either side of her," Clear Sky instructed the other
two cats. "That way she'll get warm quickly."

Fox and Falling Feather instantly settled themselves beside
Petal, who let out a grateful sigh as the warmth of their bodies
began to drive away the chill of the river. She was surprised
at how easily Fox had obeyed Clear Sky's command, but she
wasn't blind to the gray tom's authority. *He's clever, too. He knew
what to do to save me.*

Clear Sky's blue gaze ranged over her body, and Petal
became painfully aware of how skinny she must look with her
fur plastered to her ribs.

"When did you last eat?" he asked.

"We had a mouse apiece earlier on," Fox replied, not pointing out that the mice had been the only prey they had managed
to catch for days.

Suddenly Petal's stomach gave a massive rumble. Clear Sky
and Falling Feather both let out snorts of amusement.

"Okay," Clear Sky meowed. "You need food. I'll go and hunt."

"If you go straight into the trees," Fox told the gray tom

as he turned away, "you'll come to a heap of boulders with a spring trickling out. That's a really good place for shrews."

Clear Sky flicked his tail in acknowledgment, looking impressed. "You know the forest very well," he commented.

"Not bad," Fox responded, sounding encouraged. "And Petal is really good at climbing trees and coaxing out prey."

"No, I—" Petal began to protest, embarrassment almost making her forget her shock and exhaustion.

"It's true!" Fox interrupted. "You have more skills than you give yourself credit for. You just don't use them as much as you could, because you're so keen that we hunt together."

Petal was aware of Clear Sky examining her with interest before heading off into the trees. Her pelt prickled uncomfortably, and she wished she knew what he was thinking.

When he had gone, the cats fell silent. Petal relaxed as Fox and Falling Feather leaned in to her.

"Lick her fur the wrong way," Falling Feather instructed. "That's the best way to get her warm quickly."

Petal remembered being licked like that by her mother, when she was a tiny kit. Soon she began to feel warm and rested again. *I was afraid of these cats, but they're really kind.* . . .

"Have you lived in the forest long?" Falling Feather asked eventually.

"We were born here," Fox replied. "But our mother was killed by a badger when we were kits."

"That's terrible!" Falling Feather exclaimed. "What did you do?"

"It was tough," Petal began. "We couldn't hunt properly,

and we thought we would starve. Then we smelled some other cats. . . ." The terrible memory of that rejection surged over her, as powerful as the river water, and she couldn't go on.

"They didn't want anything to do with us," Fox finished for her. "Since that happened, we mostly just stay with each other."

"I'm so sorry," Falling Feather murmured. Petal felt the white she-cat's tongue rasping around her ears. "I know what it's like to lose a cat you care for." She hesitated and then went on, "We traveled here from the mountains, a long way away. The cold season is harsh up there, and there wasn't enough prey for all of us." Her voice quivered as she added, "Clear Sky's sister, Fluttering Bird, died because she didn't have enough to eat. She was only a kit."

Petal pressed her muzzle against Falling Feather's shoulder, pain clawing at her for the kit she had never met. "That's hard," she whispered.

"Her death gave us the determination to come here and find a better life," Falling Feather continued. "We didn't want any cat to suffer like that again."

Warmth crept through Petal from ears to tail-tip as she listened to Falling Feather. *That's exactly how I feel!*

"Some of our friends have stayed on the moor," the white she-cat meowed. "But we like it best here in the forest, so we're settling in that clearing with the pool. The one we chased you away from." She gave Fox a long, sparkling look from blue eyes. "I've always thought that was a mistake. It would be good if both of you could join us."

Fox was gazing at Falling Feather with the same intensity,

as if he couldn't tear his glance away. Before Fox or Petal could reply to Falling Feather's offer, the ferns at the edge of the forest parted and Clear Sky reappeared. Two shrews and a vole dangled from his jaws. "You were right about the shrews," he commented, dropping his prey in front of the others.

Clear Sky and Falling Feather each took a bite from a shrew and then exchanged the rest before finally digging in.

"Why do you do that?" Petal asked, her pads pricking with curiosity.

"This is how we eat in the mountains," Falling Feather explained between mouthfuls. "It reminds us that we always need to share."

"We don't exchange like that," Fox responded, as he and Petal tackled the plump vole. "But we do share. Petal and I share everything."

Petal felt her strength returning as she gulped down the succulent prey. *Living with these cats could be good*, she thought. *I'm not scared of them anymore.*

"Clear Sky, I asked Petal and Fox if they want to join us," Falling Feather meowed when she had finished eating. "You know what we were saying, about being stronger if our group was bigger."

"I don't know . . ." Fox began.

Petal wasn't sure why he sounded reluctant. He seemed smitten with Falling Feather. *Maybe he's worried that we won't be able to contribute*, she told herself. *But he's a good hunter, and so am I. . . .*

"You already said how tough you've found it, living alone," Falling Feather reminded Fox.

"And now that more cats are moving into the forest, you'll need the protection of a group," Clear Sky agreed. "You'll be able to protect the other cats in your turn."

Fox nodded slowly. "That seems good. . . . What do you think, Petal?"

"I think it sounds great," Petal replied, warmed by the strange cats' kindness. "Can we come and meet the others?"

Falling Feather let out a yowl of pleasure, while Clear Sky gave Fox and Petal an approving glance. "Right away," he agreed. "Are you feeling strong enough to walk back into the forest?" he asked Petal.

Petal sprang to her paws, shaking the last drops of water from her glistening pelt. "I feel strong enough for anything!"

As the other cats rose and headed back into the shadows of the trees, Petal heard the robin singing once again. Somehow the thought of the little bully bird didn't bother her anymore. She was sure that everything in the forest was about to change.

I'll work hard and improve my hunting skills. And I'm pretty sure that in the future no cat will be able to push me around. . . .

The mountain cats have begun to settle in their new home,
but tensions are rising between Clear Sky and Gray Wing—
and Thunder is caught in the middle.

CHAPTER 1
❧

The new growth of moorland grass rippled under a warm breeze that ruffled Gray Wing's fur, telling him that the cold season was coming to an end. Green shoots were springing from the ground in all directions, and bright yellow flowers had appeared on the gorse bushes that dotted the landscape. The distant sound of birdsong promised abundant prey in the moons to come.

A few tail-lengths away, Thunder was letting out excited squeals as he wrestled happily with Hawk Swoop's kits, Lightning Tail and Acorn Fur. Gray Wing blinked affectionately as he watched them rolling around on the soft grass, batting at each other with flailing paws, their claws sheathed. He had asked Hawk Swoop for permission to take them out for a hunting lesson.

"Okay," the tabby she-cat had agreed. "But mind you don't let them go too far from the camp." Now Gray Wing was content to let the kits play for a few moments, enjoying their carefree antics.

Farther across the moor, he could see Cloud Spots and Dappled Pelt returning from the direction of the river, bunches of fresh herbs clamped in their jaws. Rainswept Flower emerged from a clump of gorse carrying the limp body of a rabbit. She dragged the prey into the hollow where Jackdaw's Cry and Shattered Ice were digging out more earth to open up a new sleeping tunnel. Hawk Swoop and Tall Shadow sat close together, grooming themselves while they talked.

This feels like home now, Gray Wing thought, remembering their long journey from the mountains and their struggles to establish themselves on the moor. It had been hard to accept Stoneteller's vision of a better home to be found if they followed the sun trail. The journey had been full of danger, and yet they had made it through. *Life's good here*.

"Lightning Tail, you be a hare." Thunder's voice brought Gray Wing's attention back to the kits. "I'll show you how to catch one."

"Okay." Lightning Tail began hopping from side to side, imitating the irregular movement of a hare.

Thunder glanced at Acorn Fur and meowed, "Watch this!" Flattening himself to the ground he crept toward Lightning Tail, who kept glancing over his shoulder to see whether the older kit was catching up to him.

Thunder waggled his haunches and shot forward in an enormous leap. When he landed on top of Lightning Tail the black kit let out a squeal and rolled over on his back, wrapping his paws around Thunder's neck, so that the two toms collapsed to the ground in a bundle of wriggling fur.

Clear Sky and I were just like that once, Gray Wing thought with a prickle of sadness. *How did we ever come to quarrel so badly?*

"You're dead!" Thunder yowled. "I killed you!"

"I want to do it for real!" Acorn Fur announced, bouncing up to them. "I'm going to be the best hunter ever."

"That's good," Gray Wing mewed, padding up to the kits. "But you've got a lot to learn before then."

"I can creep like Thunder." Lightning Tail pressed himself down and squirmed along with his paws scrabbling in the grass. "See?"

"Great," Gray Wing responded, ignoring the kitten's tail, which was waving around in the air. "But there's more to that than catching prey. Out here on the moor, prey can see you from a long way off, so what do you have to do?"

"Leap on them . . . like this!" Acorn Fur screeched, jumping on top of her brother and knocking him off his paws.

Thunder dived in to join them. They would never catch anything if they couldn't pay attention, but Gray Wing held back from reprimanding them. It felt good to watch the happy, healthy kits.

They're so big and strong . . . twice the size of poor Fluttering Bird.

A twinge of grief passed through him as he remembered his sister, who had died in the mountains because there hadn't been enough food for her during the cold season. He felt a rush of protective love for Thunder and the others; he was determined that they would grow into strong, healthy cats.

The cold season wasn't so hard. There was always enough prey. Gray Wing still found it difficult to accept that the snow here wasn't as thick as the snowfall in the mountains, and it didn't stay around for so long. The frosts burned off much earlier in the mornings. There had been few days when they couldn't hunt or find water to drink, especially in the forest, where the trees provided shelter from the worst of the cold weather. He suppressed a sigh. There were still times when he missed his home and his mother, Quiet Rain, but the easier life on the moor meant the kits had survived, and would soon see the warm season return.

Thunder and Lightning Tail kept wrestling, yowling loud enough to scare off all the prey on the moor. Acorn Fur broke away from them with a sudden shriek. "Watch me!"

She raced into the hollow and vanished down the tunnel opening where Gray Wing had seen Jackdaw's Cry and Shattered Ice working earlier. He headed after her, his heart beginning to pound. There was a whole network of tunnels underneath the moor, mostly burrows dug by rabbits. The cats had begun to enlarge them to make dens, but some places weren't yet safe. And being in the burrows never felt natural to Gray Wing. It was so dark and confining, he found it hard to breathe. *Besides, if she goes too deep into the tunnels we might not be able to get her out.*

To Gray Wing's relief, Acorn Fur reappeared almost at once, thrust into the open again by another cat close behind her. As the cat emerged, Gray Wing saw it was her father, Jackdaw's Cry. Shattered Ice stuck his head out behind the other two, an annoyed look on his face.

"Stay away from here," Jackdaw's Cry scolded Acorn Fur. "This tunnel isn't safe yet. Shattered Ice and I are still digging it out." He gave his daughter a sharp tap on the nose, his claws sheathed. "Aren't you supposed to be having a hunting lesson with Gray Wing?"

"She is," Gray Wing called down to him. "Thanks, Jackdaw's Cry."

The black tom gave Gray Wing a nod of acknowledgment before vanishing into the tunnel again with Shattered Ice.

Acorn Fur turned away, her tail drooping, and trudged back up the slope to the top of the hollow.

"Wow!" Lightning Tail exclaimed as she joined the others. "That was awesome! Now we know how to get our noses whacked."

Acorn Fur glared at him, but didn't reply.

"I think you should show us again," her brother teased her. "I'm not sure I could get it right."

"Really? Then *this* is how you get your nose whacked, fleabrain!" Acorn Fur hissed, swiping her paw across her brother's nose.

Lightning Tail leaped back. "Hey, that hurt!"

"That's enough," Gray Wing meowed, getting between the littermates before a fight could develop. "We're supposed to be hunting, remember?"

To his relief the kits began to settle down, scuffling about until they found comfortable spots to sit. They looked up at him with wide eyes.

Gray Wing glanced around for something to help the young kits learn. He noticed movement underneath a gorse bush; a rabbit moved a little way into the open, nibbling at the grass.

"Look over there," he told the kits, pointing with his tail, "but *don't* move. See the rabbit? I'm going to catch it."

The kits nodded, with sparkling eyes and impatiently twitching tail-tips.

"First," Gray Wing went on, "I'm going to let it come away from the bush a bit. It's likely that the entrance to its burrow is hidden there somewhere. And when I'm chasing it, I'm going to keep a careful eye on it so I can guess which way it's going to run."

While he had been speaking, the rabbit had moved even farther into the open. Gray Wing watched carefully, waiting for just the right moment. Then, in a spurt of energy, he took off after it, reveling in the sensation of his muscles stretching and the breeze streaming through his pelt.

He was within a few tail-lengths of it before the rabbit realized he was there. It fled with a squeal of alarm, its white tail bobbing up and down. Gray Wing kept his gaze fixed on it, racing across to intercept the creature as it tried to double back toward the safety of the bush.

The rabbit's paws skidded as it veered away again. But within a few strides Gray Wing had caught it, slamming his paws on its shoulders to thrust it to the ground, where he killed it with a bite to the throat. Satisfaction flooded through him.

Picking up the still warm body of his prey, Gray Wing trotted back to the kits, who were watching admiringly.

"Great catch, Gray Wing!" Thunder exclaimed.

"I want to do that," Acorn Fur meowed.

"You will, soon," Gray Wing promised, pushing the rabbit underneath the branches of a nearby gorse bush. *I'll come back to retrieve it when we've finished.* "In fact, you may have a try now. Who can find some prey?"

The kits sprang to their paws, gazing around and sniffing vigorously at the air. "All I can smell is that rabbit," Lightning Tail complained.

"Then let's move," Gray Wing meowed, leading them a few tail-lengths away from the hollow. "Thunder, can you see anything?"

Gray Wing had already spotted a mouse nibbling on some seeds in a clump of longer grass. As it slipped between the grass stems, the tops began to wave about, and Thunder spotted the movement.

"There!" he whispered, angling his ears toward the mouse.

"Okay, go for it," Gray Wing told him.

Immediately Thunder pressed himself to the ground and began to creep forward.

Gray Wing shook his head, still keeping his voice low so as not to alarm the mouse. "No. I already told you, that way of hunting might work in the forest, where there are plenty of places to hide, and sounds in the trees that would cover your approach. But it's no good out here, because your prey can see you from a distance. You've got to rely on speed."

"Oh . . . okay." Thunder rose to his paws again, the tip of his tail twitching in frustration, then hurled himself across the moor toward the grassy tussock where the mouse was hiding.

"Faster!" Acorn Fur shrieked.

"Stupid furball!" Lightning Tail slapped his tail across his sister's mouth. "Now look what you've done!"

The mouse froze, as if it had heard Acorn Fur and realized there was danger near. Then it shot out of the long grass, scurrying toward an outcrop of rock a few tail-lengths away. Thunder tried to put on an extra burst of speed, but somehow he managed to get tangled up in his own paws and lost his balance, landing on the ground with a thump. The mouse dived into a gap between two rocks and vanished.

Thunder scrambled upright, gave his pelt a shake, and plodded back to the others with his head down. "Sorry," he mumbled.

"It's okay," Gray Wing responded, resting the tip of his tail on Thunder's shoulder. "You'll do better next time."

Glancing at Thunder's huge white paws, he could understand why the kit was so clumsy. He was obviously going to grow into a big, powerful cat, but he was at the gangly awkward stage now, not in full control of his movements. *His time will come*, Gray Wing thought. *He just needs to be patient.*

"I want to try now," Acorn Fur meowed. "If you haven't scared all the prey away."

"What?" Thunder's eyes widened indignantly. "If you hadn't—"

Gray Wing raised a paw to stop the bickering. "We'll look for more prey," he began. "There's bound to be something."

"There!" Lightning Tail pointed with his tail.

Gray Wing turned to see a small flock of birds pecking at the grass near the rocky outcrop where the mouse had vanished. He nodded. "Go for it."

Lightning Tail at once dropped into a crouch like Thunder,

as if Gray Wing's instructions had passed right over his head.

"Run, flea-brain!" Acorn Fur squealed at her brother. She took off, racing across the grass with her tail streaming out behind her.

Watching, Gray Wing admired her speed, but she was letting out excited little squeaks as she ran. A few birds had already flown off at the sound of her first squeal, and the rest of the flock rose into the air long before she got anywhere near them.

Lightning Tail, who had followed her as soon as he realized his mistake in trying to stalk, halted and turned back with a disgusted expression. "Now who's a flea-brain?" he asked.

Gray Wing shook his head, trying to hide his amusement. "You all still have a lot to learn," he murmured.

He was waiting for the two kits to come back when he was distracted by Thunder thrusting himself into a tremendous leap. Gray Wing saw that one of the birds had alighted a short distance away. Thunder's front paws reached out and batted the bird to the ground as it fluttered up in a vain attempt to escape.

The young cat straightened up with the limp body of the bird in his jaws. His eyes were shining. "I got one!" he announced, his voice muffled by his mouthful of feathers.

For a moment Gray Wing couldn't give him the praise he deserved. That massive leap had reminded him too much of Clear Sky, Thunder's father. *Like when he killed that hawk, not long before we left the mountains.*

The pain of remembering the days when he and his brother

were so close washed over Gray Wing again. He hadn't ventured into the forest or tried to see his brother since Clear Sky had refused to acknowledge Thunder as his son, and that had been before the cold season started. At their last meeting, Gray Wing had even declared that Clear Sky was no longer his brother. The loss of his closest family member felt like a thorn in Gray Wing's heart, but he couldn't forgive him for the harsh rejection of Thunder.

Gray Wing sighed. *I've been trying to raise Thunder to show kindness and compassion—but is Clear Sky's character going to come out in him, no matter what I do?*

THE TIME HAS COME
FOR DOGS TO RULE THE WILD

SURVIVORS

BOOK ONE:
THE EMPTY CITY

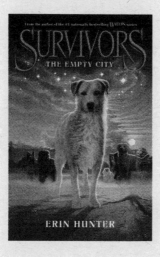

Lucky is a golden-haired mutt with a nose for survival. Other dogs have Packs, but Lucky stands on his own . . . until the Big Growl strikes. Suddenly the ground splits wide open. The longpaws disappear. And enemies threaten Lucky at every turn. For the first time in his life, Lucky needs to rely on other dogs to survive. But can he ever be a true Pack dog?

Warriors: The New Prophecy
Follow the next generation of heroic cats as they set off
on a quest to save the Clans from destruction.

Warriors: Power of Three
Firestar's grandchildren begin their training as warrior cats.
Prophecy foretells that they will hold more power than any cats before them.

Warriors: Omen of the Stars
Which ThunderClan apprentice will complete the prophecy that
foretells that three Clanmates hold the future of the Clans in their paws?

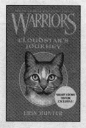

Warrior Cats Come to Life in Manga!

HARPER

An Imprint of HarperCollinsPublishers